Passion
& Revenge
Across the
Centuries

Shades
of Red

Nina
Green

Shades of Red

'Red is for you – the colour of Mars,
Blood and Berries'

Nina Green

Publishing Details and Acknowledgements
All characters and incidents in *Shades of Red*
are fictional and any resemblance to persons
living or dead is purely coincidental.

Shades of Red
Copyright © 2018 Nina Green
Published in 2018 by
Pendragon Press Ltd.

The right of Nina Green to be identified as the Author of the
Work has been asserted by her in accordance with the
Copyright, Designs and Patents Act 1988.

Cover image: top right: watercolour; © Nina Green
Cover image: bottom left: by Carlos Caetano; Landscapes in my dreams

CONTENTS

⁓

William Wordsworth:
Lines on Hardknott Roman Fort

A dark plume fetch me from yon blasted yew,
Perched on whose top the Danish Raven croaks;
Aloft, the imperial Bird of Rome invokes
Departed ages, shedding where he flew
Loose fragments of wild wailing, that bestrew
The clouds and thrill the chambers of the rocks;
And into silence hush the timorous flocks,
That, calmly crouching while the nightly dew
Moistened each fleece, beneath the twinkling stars
Slept amid that lone Camp on Hardknot's height,
Or, near the mystic Round of Druid fame
Tardily sinking by its proper weight
Deep into patient Earth, from whose smooth breast it came!

*Remains of the granaries within the walls
of Hardknott Roman Fort*
*Original image by: Mick Knapton at English Wikipedia

ONE

~

There is nothing like an investigation into murder to create an adrenalin rush. The red four-by-four wagged its tail, hugged the single car-width road and growled responsively to the increased pressure of Darcy West's foot on the accelerator. Brant may turn up his nose and snort derisively at 'flash townie Dinkies' but the 2-door sporty model was nippy enough for city driving to and from the office, yet robust enough to deal with the rigours of out-of-town reporting, plus home-life in an isolated farm house, and a couple of boisterous and often muddy dogs. Hedgerows and boulders blurred the windows as another switchback bend was left behind and the car hurtled toward the next.

It feels strange to be working on home ground, she thought, slowing slightly to admire the kaleidoscope of sun-dappled fields mottled with native woods of birch, rowan and oak already aglow with autumnal red and gold, the richness of colour accentuated by the grey backdrop of bare fells that jutted against the horizon. Her patch in theory, she supposed, but not in practice. Even though the farmhouse she shared with Brant on the cliffs above St. Gildas Bay was only twenty miles or so distant, this western wilderness of the Lake District National Park was rarely part of her remit. Commuting to and from the offices of the *Manchester News* left little time for walking or sightseeing, in fact for anything these days, least of all shared leisure activities, she thought, recalling Brant's words of accusation during their latest spat on the subject. Her face clouded at the memory of the recent tension that at times stretched the fabric of their relationship though thankfully not to breaking point. Brant was the love of her life, but her work as a reporter with a vibrant city newspaper was akin to breathing and there could be no question of giving it up.

Deliberating abandoning the uncomfortable topic of her marriage, her mind turned to the second reason for a lack of familiarity with this area. Nothing much that was newsworthy occurred to disturb the peace and tranquillity of its fells and valleys. Not since the devastating year of the foot and mouth outbreak – and not, that is, until today. Her assignment was to investigate a shotgun attack that from press releases issued by the hospital increasingly looked like becoming a murder inquiry. The sign at the left of the road proclaimed 'Barrenber Ground'. She braked and turned in at the entrance. The familiar buzz along the spine told her a story lurked within the grey walls of this isolated farmhouse.

Jane Tulley stood with arms folded, her formidable bulk filling the doorway.

"Reporter you say?" It was uttered with barely disguised contempt and the dark-circled eyes narrowed with suspicion as they flickered first over Darcy then the car parked by the gate. "Bide Bob – you too Fly," she shouted to the two collies that were flinging themselves against the yard fence in a flurry of gravel, dried sheep droppings and red tinged earth. The bleating of ewes disturbed in their cropping came from the adjacent field as they jostled hedges and crowded the gate. Dogs and barking temporarily subsided, and two pairs of eyes watched Darcy with vulpine glare and something like glee as she stepped back in alarm. The command from their mistress did nothing to subdue the muted threats that rumbled from
within the shaggy throats, nor did she make any effort to reinforce it. "And from Manchester." There was no attempt this time to hide the scorn.

"That's right," Darcy confirmed, and a prickle of annoyance overlaid her alarm. "And that's a fair distance I've come to see you, Mrs Tulley," she added, pushing a cluster of dark curls off her face with an habitual gesture.

"Didn't ask for you to." The tone was sulky now but Darcy's trained ear detected distress behind the resentment.

"I came because I want to help."

"Now and why should the likes of you want to do that?"

"Because I think there's more to this business with your husband."

"Like what?"

"You tell me. It was a routine visit wasn't it?"

The woman's face darkened, and the well-defined brows knit over her broad nose. "There's nowt untoward on this farm, miss. We're clean – and I defy Government or anyone else to find disease in our stock."

"I believe you," Darcy said evenly, taking in the shiny paint of the tractor parked by a bank of well-kept outbuildings, and the clean-cut treads of massive tyres as yet unblocked by years of mud. At least this hill farm was no victim of hopelessness and poverty-induced neglect. Yet a sense of unease, of something not right with this place, persisted. "That's why I want to know what pushed your husband into shooting the guy from Defra."

The older woman shrugged shoulders muscled and toned from years of lifting fodder and pitching hay into feeders on walls of bier and stable.

"Well you've a wasted journey. It's all been said." As if sensing their mistress's imminent retreat indoors and therefore a second agreeable opportunity to launch an assault on the fence and the visitor's nerve, the dogs set up their barking again.

"I said bide," she snapped, and Darcy was heartened by this indication that the Tulley woman was not about to disappear and slam the door.

"It may be your only chance to help your husband," she tempted, raising her voice over the cacophony, and recalling that whilst not exactly reserving his right to silence, Ted Tulley had given away little since his arrest. In his statement he had claimed the Defra official 'had attitude' and was 'looking for summat that wasn't there', and that was about it. Which, Darcy reflected, did little to explain why a man with no previous for violence – or any form for lawbreaking come to that – should be goaded into taking a pot shot at a government officer. Jane Tulley hesitated and pushed a lock of dark hair sprinkled with grey back from her face in a gesture of weariness.

"And what can you do?," Her sigh conveyed a depth of despair. Noting the lined forehead and thread-veined skin coarsened by working outside in all weathers, Darcy felt a stirring of compassion.

"I'll give you a fair hearing and report," she promised, lowering her voice as the barking of the dogs subsided again into a low grumble. Jane Tulley stared into her face as though searching for evidence of trickery or deceit. Then with a sigh and minute shake of the head she looked at the ground and gnawed her bottom lip in an agony of indecision. Darcy fought the temptation to pursue her case, sensing that any pressure could tip the scales the opposite way.

"You'd best step inside then," Jane Tulley said at last, opening the door wider.

Darcy stifled a sigh of satisfaction and followed her indoors.

About an hour later, Darcy blinked on stepping out from the dim farmhouse into the autumn sunlight.

"I'm not sure, I'll have to clear it with my editor," she replied to the woman's query as to when the feature would appear in the *Manchester News*. "I'll send you a copy when in it's in though," she promised on impulse.

"Thank you," Jane Tulley replied with a dignity that moved the younger woman. "That's good of you."

"Try not to worry." The words sounded trite even in Darcy's ears, leaving her feeling helpless and inadequate. Then the professional came to the fore. She had done her job, and would see the case got a fair report. More than that she could not do; Jane Tulley had made no surprise revelations to account for and excuse her husband's aberrant behaviour. Whatever secret Darcy's hunch had primed her to expect, it had not been forthcoming.

4

However, the woman had warmed to a sympathetic ear, and opened up to provide a full profile of an honest and previously upright man struggling to earn a living in harsh and often cruel conditions. Her frank talk about his disgust at the way the foot and mouth epidemic had been handled by the government, inadequate compensation, and the distressing number of farmers forced to sell up, and his own subsequent bitterness at the near-loss of their own livelihood was another matter.

Good column material – but hardly conducive to helping his case; on the contrary, it would appear to give him a motive. Darcy shrugged almost imperceptibly; maybe that was all there was to it, and this time her intuition had been wrong. Yet the feeling of something not right, of a certain *strangeness*, persisted. On instinct Darcy turned and glanced over her shoulder. The bare fells strode the horizon: a marauding band of dinosaurs, grey and ominous in their remoteness and bulk . A shiver ran through her; it would be good to leave this place.

"Thanks for the tea and your time, Mrs Tulley. I'll be in touch," she said with a sympathetic nod, raising her voice as the dogs set up their customary racket and were promptly silenced this time by their mistress.

"He's a good man, my Ted. Normally he wouldn't hurt anyone."

That word 'normally' tugged at the remnants of Darcy's hunch and made her pause on her way to the car. That and the despair in the other woman's voice, hinting perhaps at awareness that her last chance was walking away and therefore the barriers had to come down at last.

"So what went wrong for him, Jane?" Darcy moved closer, her tone caressing, reassuring and intimate, designed to encourage confidences. Jane Tulley gnawed at her bottom lip as she struggled between the need to confide and the desire to keep her secrets.

"Summat got to him."

Darcy reached out to touch the other woman's hand, but something in her bearing, the arms crossed over the heavy breasts and the aura of reticence mixed with indefinable fear, made her arm drop to her side again.

"What do you mean, Mrs Tulley?"

"I dunno." Emotion had thickened her voice, stressing the local accent and rounded vowels. "There's summat bad up the'er." Jane Tulley looked over towards the west, to fells blued by distance and purpled by remnants of mist. Her features hardened and fear stared out from her eyes.

Darcy moved in closer again.

"Like what?"

"I don't rightly know, but it's bad."

"Up where? And what makes you say so?" Darcy pressed, but Jane Tulley's lips compressed as though she was afraid of having said too much already. Without another word she retreated and closed the door.

Darcy walked to the car then tutted with annoyance and paused before getting in. Her new ankle boots were caked in red mud. It must be due, she thought scraping it off on the edge of a sharp stone by the gate, to some sort of mineral content. Even more annoying was the knowledge that the Tulley woman would be watching and grinning behind the lace curtains. Irritation evaporated as that improbable thought was dismissed. Stephen Pettigrew, the man shot by her husband, was in a critical condition. Jane Tulley had little to smile about.

TWO

~

The rural vista of lane, woodland and fell had changed to one of a ring road crawling with traffic, a forest of road signs designed to confuse, and high rise offices, those urban mountains of concrete and metal with glass glaring redly at the sinking sun. Not as pretty, Darcy acknowledged as she parked up, but there came that undeniable buzz of pride as she walked towards the towering glazed façade of the *Manchester News*. Instinctively she glanced up at the fourth floor to her office window as it winked in the last rays seeming to flash a Morse code welcome. Pushing through the swivel doors and the knots of people coming or going depending upon their particular shift, she crossed the lobby and signed in at the imposing reception desk.

"Hi there," she called to several acquaintances, then "catch you later," to a couple of workmates from 'Editorial' as she made her way to the lifts.

Yes, Fortune had smiled on her, she acknowledged five minutes later, gazing out of that same window at the streams of ants and dinky cars caught in the rush hour mêlée below. If it were not for the lucky breaks she would have been one of them, instead of enjoying the perks that came from being a favoured member of staff on a prestigious newspaper. And she added with a flash of unaccustomed humility, getting paid for what she most wanted to do.

"Okay, Frank, I'm on my way," she said with a grin as the console on her desk buzzed and a red light flashed its impatience. And if she was honest, she thought shutting the office door behind her, luck had played a part in creating the perfect lifestyle to go with it. The nature of Brant's work – and her own – dictated independence during a working week spent at her town flat, coupled with 'honeymoon' weekends together at the isolated farmhouse on the remote west coast of Cumbria. Or it had, she reflected whilst walking along the corridor to Frank Kelly's office, until Brant got broody and started pushing for more togetherness and less independence – at least in her case. And there lay the rub as they say. Or was she being selfish? Her brows knit in a frown that darkened the grey of her eyes and hardened her features so that briefly her face reflected her true status: a 'thirty-something' like so many others, trapped in a career versus bio-clock conflict. But this was work, so she would worry about all that later. Replacing the frown with a smile that restored the inherent youthfulness to her face, she tapped on the door and entered.

Frank Kelly glanced up and growled "What took you so long?"

Darcy smiled in response to this unpromising greeting.

"I believe in keeping my men waiting," she dared, suppressing a grin.

The bull head with shock of dark wavy hair now greying at the temples shot up and the shrewd eyes narrowed as he studied her face. A minute passed whilst the fat Havana moved from one side of his mouth to the other via skilful contortions of lips and tongue, a trick that over the years had become his trademark.

"Cheeky bitch," he said mildly at last.

Darcy breathed easily again; the outcome of their games was always unpredictable, that was what made them addictive. That and the fact that they were exclusive to her, an indulgence to mark her privileged position and their special working relationship. Oh yes, it was professional, yet Frank at times had indicated he would not be averse to something different, but such complications were definitely not on her agenda.

"Anyway, got no home to go to?" He glanced at the battered little clock that sat on his leather-topped executive desk, a leaving present from the boss at his very first job as junior reporter on a rival paper another life-time ago.

"Just off."

"You've only been here five minutes," he grumbled contrarily.

Darcy hid a smile behind a forced cough as an image came to mind. She had often visualised him as a reincarnated Henry Tudor, though as yet he had only made number two of the prescribed six wives.

"I drove up north to interview the Tulley woman, you know, the wife of the guy that took a pot shot at Simon Pettigrew and put him in intensive. He's the man from Defra," she added, talking too fast in her eagerness, and knowing it.

"Yeah, yeah." Frank chewed on his cigar and made an 'okay let's have it' gesture with one large hand as though in anticipation of what was to come.

"Just thought I'd report back before signing off."

"Good of you," but the side of his mouth devoid of cigar turned upwards to soften the irony. "But you never 'just' do anything!" The North Country voice became richer as he relaxed. "So?"

Darcy shrugged. "Disappointing. In terms of what she's telling anyway," she added before he could order her to ditch the project .

"But?"

"It felt wrong."

A long sigh escaped Frank's lips. "Not the famous Darcy West hunch again!"

"Oh, very amusing. " The frown returned to Darcy's brow as she struggled to match words to an intangible feeling then abandoned the attempt. "Anyway, there was something she said as I was leaving so I'd like to try her again."

Her editor surveyed her through narrowed eyes, the cigar momentarily still as he weighed the odds.

"Nah," he said at last with a shake of his bear-like head. "Forget it. Do a reader-interest on her and leave it at that."

Darcy's lips tightened and she stared at the ceiling, struggling for control before turning her attention back to her boss. As usual, the desire to do something proved to be inversely proportionate to the resistance met.

9

"She's hiding something Frank."

"You want to believe it."

"And you're not being fair."

"But I'm the boss," he said brutally. The cigar was manipulated to the other side of his mouth and his hand went to the computer mouse, signalling an end to the discussion.

"Have I ever let you down Frank?"

"Plenty."

"Not so – I come through in the end."

"After giving me serial heart attacks! Anyway, there's still your piece on the Underground Suicide Bombers to finish. For Chris'sakes Darcy, London is under siege and you're chasing bloody farmers!"

"One more visit – please?"

"Save the wheedling for that poor guy who married you," he growled, but a grin appeared at the corner of his mouth as he closed the last of his programmes and shut down the computer.

"I'll go on my own time," she offered, tilting her head to one side in the way he found hard to resist.

"Damn bloody right you will."

"But you'll print my story?"

"What story? You ain't come up with anything yet"

"The one you're going to let me write!"

"We'll see. Now out!"

Darcy gave him a radiant smile. "Thanks, Frank."

"Wait a minute – I've not-,"

Darcy left in a hurry and snapped the door shut before he could call her back.

Right now the farmhouse on the cliffs seemed a long way away. Listlessly she moved around the smart and spacious flat, her pad during the working week that tonight seemed too small to contain her restlessness. Brant, when she 'phoned to let him know she was safely back in Manchester, picked up on it.

"You're missing home," he stated when she admitted to feeling unsettled and fidgety.

"I'm used to working away." Her lips tightened at the familiar theme.

"But not to coming back here mid-week," he persisted. "Maybe you should do it on a regular basis – then you would be used to coming home too." The teasing tone failed to mask the seriousness behind the suggestion.

"It's not about that," she denied quickly, There was something about that place I went to, and Ted Tulley's wife. She has a secret; I want to know what it is."

"The famous Darcy West nose twitching again?"

"You're beginning to sound like Frank."

"Home from home then."

Darcy sighed and ran her fingers through the loose curls that sprang back again as she released them; again that teasing tone that of late Brant had adopted to disguise hurtful insinuations. A no-win situation. If she challenged him he denied it and accused her of reading things into innocent words. The familiar surge of anger rose from her solar plexus. Set up yet again. It was so unfair and dishonourable to conceal barbs in the guise of being concerned, and so uncharacteristic of Brant: his honour and integrity had attracted her from the day they met. Basically that was unchanged, she admitted fairly, it was this baby thing and his fear that time might be running out.

"You still there sweetheart?"

"Yes, I'm just rather tired." Which is true, she thought sighing.

"You don't have to travel. You could stay home and work freelance from here." The tone was low and persuasive, the seductive Brant that had attracted her even more. But the touch paper was already ignited. *Please Brant, not tonight.* Navigating the minefield was such hard work; evasion was the better tactic.

"I want a career Brant, not a cosy job. Anyway, I'll go get my bath now and have an early night."

"Okay, you do that."

The stiffness was there in his voice, the tension palpable. A sudden familiar cacophony in the background offered a diversion.

"That's Mab and Brock! They've heard a badger or something," she said lightly to defuse the tension. "So what have they been up this week then?"

The two Springer spaniels were around five years old now, but still a lively handful. Brant's silence told her the cue to recount some amusing anecdote had failed.

"Okay love, I'll say goodnight and let you go. Give them a hug for me, and tell them I'll bring a treat if they're good," she added, determined to avoid an argument. The clipped 'goodnight then' response and the click of the receiver being replaced made her wince. It was unsettling at night, that dash of cold water and subsequent sense of alienation that inevitably followed. Come weekend they would have to sit down and talk it through but it was time to switch off for tonight. Rising from the settee she poured herself a glass of wine, went into the bathroom and turned on the taps. After a lengthy soak in perfumed water and the mellowing effect of Pinot Noir she felt relaxed and ready for bed.

An hour or so into her sleep the moaning grew louder and her head turned restlessly on the pillow. Then a sharp cry caused the waters of sleep to surge and propel her to the surface. A half-minute or so passed before her mind registered that the sound had come from her own lips. She lay immobile, in a state of confusion, staring at the chink of light at the top of the lined curtains, then at the same reflected in the wardrobe mirror. She struggled to make sense of her surroundings. This looked nothing like her bedroom at the farmhouse. Her pad in Manchester, that was it. Gradually awareness returned and with it curiosity as to why she should think herself back up north amongst the fells of Cumbria. Also, the room was undeniably familiar, so why did it feel unaccountably strange?

Sliding herself up into a sitting position she leaned across and grabbed the satin day cushions from the other side of the divan and stuffed them at her back. Since her marriage the single bed had been replaced by a double so that during one of Brant's rare trips to Manchester they could spend the night together in comfort. If only his warmth and strength were next to her now to dispel this sense of unreality. But it could be six months before he came to town again. Not that he spent overlong at the farmhouse or the observatory on the cliffs. His work as an astro-physicist regularly took him away from home.

Her thoughts slid away from home and Brant as the vague unease that clouded her mind thickened into anxiety. A shudder shook her shoulders; the room felt icy. Why had she been crying? The dream eluded her waking mind but the sense of fear persisted; a familiar feeling, one that tugged at the strings of memory but refused to unravel its secret. Her head lolled against the pillows but she forced her eyelids open again, unwilling to risk sleep and its shadows. Suddenly her eyes widened and electric buzzed in her solar plexus as something flickered in her field of vision and sleepiness fled. There it was again. The light – or was it movement? – in the mirror opposite that tugged at her attention. Alarm flared deep in her stomach as the red firefly flickered at the mirror's centre. Was it reflected glow from a neglected aromatherapy candle that was burning low in its holder? Normally she took great care to extinguish them before falling asleep.

Deciding it needed checking out, she flung back the duvet and prepared to swing her legs over the edge of the bed. Only nothing happened. Her struggles ceased and she fell back against the pillows, gripped by panic as the inability to move registered. The paralysis that immobilised her legs was creeping up her body, into her arms, then shoulders and neck in a chill tide. At the same time she felt a buzzing along her nerve paths as though an electrical charge was passing through them. Her eyes widened in fear and her mouth opened to cry out but no sound came. Yet her mind was lucid. This, she thought petrified, was what it must feel like to be in a catatonic state, to be living in a coma devoid of life to all observers but with consciousness painfully focused. Perhaps it was some peculiarly potent dream that had her in its grasp. I am awake, she told herself fiercely. As though to prove the point, though in what manner was not exactly clear, her glance slid sideways to the alarm clock on the bedside table. The fingers registered 12.20a.m.

THREE

~

The glow in the mirror intensified, drawing her attention. The red was shifting, a crimson mist that thinned here and thickened there, revealing disturbing glimpses of shape and shadow lurking beneath. She shivered as the cold intensified along with the light. Helplessly she watched the red mist swirl and shift revealing a scene that was drawing her in: stark walls silhouetted against cruel crags and a livid sky, and a strange circular structure in the foreground. A dark mass at the mirror's centre writhed and metamorphosed, an amoeba-like blob of protoplasm elongating and semi-dividing into a shadow-being. A dull gleam at the figure's breast was repeated at the plumed helmet on the arrogantly held head. Mesmerised now she watched the scene being played out, felt herself watched in turn and became aware of a throbbing at the centre of her forehead as she was drawn into the mirror like some modern-day Lady of Shallot. Only this was no Lancelet but an unknown warrior from an earlier age and there was little of the Romance about him but rather a force to be feared.

He too seemed charged with that same energy that coursed through her body but many times stronger. It drew her to him: something within flowed from her body towards the man in the mirror. An unbearable sadness and urgency struck her between the eyes as though an electrode was inserted and planted there and a current sent buzzing through. She lay there for some time whilst silent tears slid down her face. Vaguely she realised the angst was not her own, that she was picking up the painful emotions that swirled around the figure in the mirror. At last the image began to dim. The glow faded first into twilight then darkness relieved only by the reflection of the strip above the curtains. The sense of a presence, of not being alone persisted along with the accompanying fear. Then that too subsided, and there was a sense of an unseen force retreating, diminishing and finally letting go.

Gingerly she tried to move her legs. At first the leaden limbs resisted her efforts as though they belonged to somebody else, but then inch by inch the paralysis gave way. A great shudder of a sigh escaped her as she pushed with her feet against the mattress until upright against the pillows. Experimentally she flexed the muscles of her arm then reached out to the switch of the bedside lamp. The warm amber light that flooded the room made a mockery of both paralysis and vision. Yet the former had happened and the latter remained vivid in her mind. She was shaken by the experience, and even more disturbing was the realisation that a craving had her in its grip: a yearning to know the location of that place in the mirror, and the identity of the man within it.

Neither of them is real, she fiercely reminded herself; neither had existence beyond this room, outside of her imagination. Yet the emotion persisted, refused to be lulled by logic. Foolishly, tears threatened again. The desire to speak to Brant, or rather the reassurance of hearing his voice, was immediate and instinctively she reached for the telephone. Half way through dialling the number of his mobile the thought struck that perhaps it was too late to be calling, and he was staying in a London hotel. Pausing in her dialling she glanced at the alarm clock and gasped.

It appeared that during that strange interlude time had stood still. The hands still showed 12.20a.m. precisely.

The following morning she listened with one ear to the end of the News bulletin whilst nibbling at a piece of toast but actually eating little. Now and then she glanced at the T.V. but saw nothing except that vision in the mirror. Again and again her mind ranged over the

15

possibilities. She dropped the toast onto the plate and nursed a cup of coffee instead. There had to be a rational explanation. Both for the vision and accompanying pseudo-paralysis (because of course it could not be real), and for the lingering sadness and need that haunted her even now. A few minutes later her face brightened and she replaced the mug of coffee on its saucer with a decided snap and a tap on the remote cut off the BBC newsreader. *The half awake, half asleep phenomenon.* That was the answer. The memory of psychology lectures at Hilldean University rose to offer hope and comfort. Now what was it called? Her mind sought refuge in the everyday activity of problem solving, anything to detract attention from the fact that she had been unable to move a limb or utter a word.

Suddenly she clicked her fingers. Got it! *Hypnogogic imagery* that was it. A borderline state in which the mind functions between fantasy and reality, a demi-world where the sleeper feels fully awake yet is nonetheless akin to dreaming. And a state, Darcy recalled, that is often induced by stress. She gave a nod of satisfaction: it fit. As for the lingering feelings, often vivid dreams produced them too so the same effect was only to be expected following a psychological aberration such as this. That left just one piece missing from the jigsaw: the fact that during the episode time appeared to have stood still. She had purposely looked at the alarm clock to check the time at the onset of the experience and it had registered 12.20a.m. At a guess, ten or more minutes must have passed during which she lay immobile on the bed, actually it had felt like longer. Yet on coming out of it, when she had checked again, the hands of the clock had not moved on. However as she watched before settling down again, the clock behaved normally and on checking the hands against her wrist watch, they corresponded. It had to be something to do with the waking/dreaming state. Maybe it was similar to drowning, when victims were supposed to 'see' their whole life pass before them in a matter of seconds.

As an analogy it sucks, she admitted rising from the table, but it had come close and there would be other models that fit. At least the hypnogogic theory held, and solved the whole jigsaw bar that one piece. Shrugging herself into the jacket of her trouser suit she went to collect her bag from the bedroom. Picking it up from the chair next to the dressing table, she paused and looked thoughtfully into the now innocent face of the mirror. With a little shake of the head she turned and was about to head for the door when something on the carpet caught her eye. Frowning she dropped to her haunches and on picking up the object felt a tingle of shock run along her spine. The small clod of earth rested in the palm of her hand. Reddish earth that brought to mind dried blood – and a particular location. On leaving Jane Tulley at Barrenber Ground, the mud on her boots was also red.

OUT OF TIME I:
Mediobogdum c. AD 124

~

The mountains of this remote place shuddered beneath the shouting of orders, the chink of metal, the thunder of many horses' hooves and the rumble of wheels on stone. The leader of this noisy but undeniably awesome cavalcade sat his horse with dignity and ease, the two moving as one. The mare pulled back in response to the pressure of his knees and the gentlest of tension on the reins as the road once again skewed sharply round an outcrop of rock and at the same time dropped at a vertiginous angle. He turned his head slightly to reassure himself that the cavalcade of troops and supply wagons were coping with the rigours of this unbelievably steep, narrow and winding road that traversed the mountains with unforgiving wildness. He saw they were holding the road like good men and steeds, the iron-shod hooves of the latter sparking against the granite surface; and the supply wagons, albeit creaking and swaying alarmingly, were still upright and progressing as the mule masters held them in check.

Satisfied, he turned back from the imposing view of red-cloaked legionaries with sunlight sparking off helmets and armour and nodded slightly before turning his attention back to their destination. The stone-built fort of Mediobogdum sprawled below them, crouched on a plateau on the mountainside, and roughly half-way down this damnable road that dropped to the steep-sided valley, stretching within a few miles of the western coast and the fort of Glannaventa that guarded against invasion from the island of Hibernia.

I'll wager, he thought with a malicious smile, that Mediobogdum's prefect would right now be fighting off an almost uncontrollable urge to run in the direction of the latrines! A movement caught his eye above and to his right, and the glint of sun on metal abruptly terminated pleasurable contemplation of how he would deal with Marcellus. Instinctively his hand went to the gladius at his belt but hovered there without drawing the short-sword as he realised the possible assassin was a woman. She was posing – and that was the only word for it – on a natural platform of rock above the approach road to watch their arrival. A pair of ravens sailed and dived about her head, uttering guttural cries and seeming to be a part of the scene she had obviously staged for his edification.

He reined-in Gaudita and motioned caution to Justinus, the youngest and most favoured amongst his six tribunes who, gladius already in hand, had nudged his horse forward to protect him whilst holding back the troops. She was not, he mused, as he had imagined the local women would be all coarse wool, knotted locks and a bone structure more suited to horses than humans, but had a sleekness and poise to match that of any Roman lady though beyond that detail the comparison plummeted into jest.

She was a slight figure clad in a skirt of leather with silver bosses, her fragility belied by the tautness of toned muscle visible above the lacings of hide boots and leather wrist bands. He had to acknowledge she initiated respect as well as lust. A blue cloak of finest wool rippled and lifted in the wind revealing the provocative cones of the tooled metal breast plate that, given the reddish lustre had to be struck from copper at least, and might even be fashioned from the uniquely-coloured gold of Cambria, that country to the south west with which they traded and colluded. Her armour, like the rest of her apparel, was chosen for effect rather than protection, denoting a sense of drama and occasion of which in line with the Roman ideal he begrudgingly approved. Her dark hair streamed out in the wind from beneath a silver band worn low on the forehead, and a silver torque around her throat caught the rays of the sun and flashed defiance. Her eyes sought his and boldly held his gaze, her expression conveying

19

a fearlessness and scorn that as yet he had failed to witness in any man let alone a woman.

Her appearance was fleeting but unforgettable. He held up a peremptory hand to order the lowering of raised spears, the short pilum designed for ease of use by the cavalry. Justinus barked sharp orders for the woman to be pursued and apprehended. Even as he was about to forbid this action she flung up her head, stared straight at him and turning on her heel disappeared over the crest of the outcrop. Ignoring Justinus' warnings about spies and the possibility of her being a decoy for a band of Brigante warriors waiting to ambush them from the cover of the boulders, Antonius halted him and waved the cavalcade onward down the precarious incline.

"So what could the natives do against a large detachment of Roman cavalry and infantrymen?" he lightly reproved Justinus.

"Have you forgotten the massacre of our own legion at the hands of Boudicca a couple of decades ago, legatus," Justinus said stiffly, nonetheless signalling for the retinue to move slowly forward. "Over two thirds of the men of the Ninth wiped out and it took years to get the legion back to strength again. But they say it has never been the same."

"Yes, yes," his commander said tetchily, "but I'll wager you that girl up there was the daughter of a local chieftain stamping her foot from a safe distance! These Northerners won't readily bend the knee to Rome like the client kingdoms further south. Now, let's get this outfit down safely and put the fear of the gods into that dog Marcellus!"

With one last glance at the now deserted outcrop, he forced the provocative image from his mind and focusing on the business in hand, urged Gaudita cautiously forward.

FOUR

~

It was good to be home, at the farmhouse eyrie that nestled atop the sandstone cliffs of St. Gildas Bay. The familiar warmth lay between them like the fleece of a Herdwick, that most hardy and ancient of Lakeland breeds that grazed the sparse and windswept pastures of the cliff top. Our only neighbours – and that's the way we like it, Darcy thought smiling as she snuggled in closer to Brant's naked body, the curve of her back slotting into the hollow between his abdomen and drawn up knees; Apart from the mysterious dome of the observatory rising behind Sheep Howe, the closest building to the farmhouse was the Priory Inn a couple of miles away beneath the cliffs that guarded the village of St. Gildas. Brant murmured and an arm snaked around her breasts as the globe of her buttocks warmed his groin. A passing gull keened and *yuk-yuk-yukked* as it glided over the yard and paddock and was closely followed by its even more raucous companion. The sound penetrated the open window so that Brant stirred and sleepily opened his eyes.

"About time you awoke, lazybones," Darcy teased, turning to tweak the hairs on his chest. "A disgraceful way to spend a Saturday afternoon!"

"Well, if you will insist on keeping me here as your sex-slave."

"Brant Kennedy – it was you who picked me up and dropped me onto the bed!" she protested with a laugh.

"And a good idea it was too! Now go mash your man a pot o' tea woman!" The cultured voice fostered by Oxford was dropped in favour of his native Cumbrian lilt with its broad vowels, at present grossly exaggerated. "And scut off fast mind – no firtlan' around in the kitchen. A'hm waitin'!" he added, leaning over to slap her rump as she rolled out of bed.

"Very good sir!" She laughed and picking up a cushion from the chair by the door hurled it with devastating accuracy at his head.

It was even better to have the spark and then the peace back between them, she thought later as they sipped their tea in bed whilst gazing out at a blue sky shadowed only by flocks of noisy seabirds. The journey up north to St. Gildas Bay had been something of a trial, the prospect of a joyful reunion being tainted firstly with unease generated by that weird mirror-vision and clod of red earth, and secondly, anxiety about her possible reception. However the first had diminished with the passage of daylight hours, and the second proved to be unfounded. Brant had folded her in his arms and greeted her with such obvious delight on his return from London that it was easy to forget past tensions and relax into their relationship again.

She cast him a sidelong glance now from beneath her lashes, and felt the familiar buzz of love and desire as she scanned the dark hair and tanned face with its full lips, and eyes that could change in seconds from the bluey-grey of the distant fells to the greeny-blue of a slate-bottomed pool. As they had done so now due to the sun streaming in at the window, dappling the quilt and speckling the iris with flecks of amber and gold. A sudden rogue image of an infant with those same wide set eyes and rosebud version of the full mouth brought an unprecedented rush of desire to her already warm and love-soaked loins. Her face blenched with the shock of it as the void in her womb ached and melted in the heat of unexpected yearning. Shocked by her reaction she swiftly recanted. The truth of it was babies constantly cried, dribbled and messed their nappies and worse still, put an end to budding careers. She raised a hand slightly as though to ward off the offending notion and Brant, becoming aware of the movement, turned his head.

"What is it love?"

"Just thinking what a handsome guy I married," she responded lightly, and with a swiftness born of preservation. The last thing they needed this weekend was to get back on the baby tack. She breathed easily again as he looked pleased and his hand casually brushed her bare breast. Then his fingers teased her nipple and it perked instantly to his touch.

"I might let you have me again – providing you play your cards right."

"But my ace seems to have gone missing; I'll just have to find it." She smiled provocatively then ducked beneath the duvet to conduct the most intimate of searches that Brant bore with commendable fortitude.

"So what's troubling you Darcy?"

She turned and gave him a speculative look as they strolled along the cliff path that evening. In order to deflect his unexpected question, she paused and picked up a stick to throw for Mab and Brock. She straightened up and shrugged.

"Nothing."

"Come on, tell me," Brant cajoled as she threw the twig and watched the two Springer spaniels scamper to retrieve it in a flurry of fur, dried leaves and long grass. He tucked her hand into the crook of his arm in a confidential sort of way. How perceptive of him, she thought bending to pick up the stick again as Mab dropped it at her feet. In truth, with the onset of twilight her thoughts had returned to the strange events of the previous night; obviously he had sensed her retreat and picked up on her anxiety.

"It's just the time of year. Autumn is always a time of nostalgia and well, a certain sadness in the air don't you think?" She tossed the stick and Brock, determined not to be outdone this time, pushed Mab out of the way. "Especially here," she added, gesturing at the smoky sky and dreaming fells, "and at twilight." The sense of solitude was heightened by the *slap-suck-slap* of waves against the base of the sandstone cliffs and now, as they moved further along the path, the swirl and skirmish of water rising and retreating over the shingle of the cove. The squawk and chatter of thousands of gulls nesting on the striated cliffs, deafening at the onset of their walk, had become subdued with the fading light and now subsided into eerie silence. A white shape, ghostlike in the loaming, glided through the dusk, a straggler belatedly heading for the collective roost.

"Enough for now Brock," she said absently, as the dog nudged her leg with the stick for her to throw yet again, then retreated, tail momentarily drooping, at her words before finding a substitute interest in a rock bearing an interesting scent, perhaps of fox or badger.

As the September twilight deepened, so did her anxiety and the poignancy that pulled at her soul. Unbidden the fragmented image of an unknown warrior came to mind, and the desolate walls he inhabited.

"It's not just the twilight, is it?"

There it was again: that uncanny ability to latch into her thoughts. She paused to glance up at Brant and was momentarily stunned by a similarity of stance and arrogant tilt of head; an effect of the twilight obviously, and as fleeting as the sea mist that sent tentative tendrils snaking shoreward. Even now, as she anxiously scanned his face, it was gone.

"No." She collected her thoughts whilst he waited patiently for her to continue. "An odd experience, and it's still haunting me."

"Tell me."

So as they walked back to the farmhouse through the deepening dusk Darcy recounted the incident.

FIVE

~

"You were dreaming," was Brant's immediate and predictable response.

Darcy paused and turned to face him, shaking her head so that droplets of fine mist sprayed from her dark curls in an iridescent halo.

"I was awake."

"You only think you were. Sometimes it feels that way."

Again she shook her head in a negative gesture.

"I checked the time – twice." Haltingly she confided the details. As she finished her breath rose in tiny clouds to stain the night air white, and she gave an involuntary shiver.

"You were caught for a moment in that half-way state between sleeping and waking, and it felt like much longer," Brant stated, adding before she could protest "As for not being able to move – during sleep our bodies actually do go into a state of temporary 'paralysis' to prevent us harming them whilst threshing about in our dreams. By the time we wake nerves and muscles are back to normal," he continued, now very much the physicist, "but sometimes we're caught in that limbo stage and the 'paralysis' persists so we panic, which causes mild hysteria – a sort of reaction – that prolongs the feeling of not being able to move." Taking her arm he drew her to him and with a swift gesture tugged up the collar of her fleece. "So you see, no worries! Now come on, it's getting cold," he added, kissing the tip of her nose before pushing her gently on.

"I came to pretty much the same conclusion, but didn't know about that 'paralysis' stuff; it all fits except for one thing," Darcy said frowning as she pushed back a lock of hair that had strayed across her eye.

"And that is?"

"I found a clump of compacted red earth on the carpet; you know, as though it had been left there by a shoe or boot."

By now they had reached the farmhouse. She saw by the mist-frazzled halo of light shed by the back porch lamp that Brant was frowning as he opened the door.

"You checked the doors and windows I take it Darcy?" he demanded, pausing on the threshold to anxiously scan her face.

"Of course. Nobody had broken in, it was nothing like that."

He ushered her indoors, followed her inside and bolted the door.

"Okay, take your coat off and sit by the Aga whilst I pour us a drink," he ordered as she shivered again. "Autumn's arrived all right; tonight could see first frost." He moved over to the dresser and brandished a bottle of single malt. "To warm you up?"

"Wine for me please."

Anything stronger might lower her resistance to the strangeness that still lingered.

Darcy sat on a huge old poufé that trailed a wisp of stuffing, the result of the dogs' claws and one of their officially prohibited but nonetheless regular mad indoor chases. They lay now with their backs against the Aga, coats steaming as moisture from the mist and heavy autumnal dew evaporated in the heat. The odour of damp pelts and the rhythm of heavy breathing were strangely evocative. A yearning that stirred deep within turned quickly into an ache of sadness and need to know. It's nothing, she told herself fiercely, just the Spirit of Autumn getting to me as it always does: the poignancy of vibrant colours contrasting with ephemeral mists, the last minute scurryings and Earth's palpable preparations for the Big Sleep. Hell girl, you must be hormonal, she told herself with a dismissive shake of the head.

"Here we are."

She blinked and focused on her surroundings then took the glass from Brant's hand. The warmth and subdued golden light that bathed the kitchen soothed her and put fear to flight. A few sips of her favourite Pinotage later and her tense muscles began to relax.

"You are absolutely sure there was no evidence of a break-in?" Brant watched her face as he twirled whisky round his glass. Momentarily transfixed, Darcy watched the golden lights swimming in its depths as they caught the glow from the lantern suspended by a chain above the Aga.

"Absolutely."

"No workmen?"

She shook her head and made a dismissive gesture with her hand.

"Then you must have trodden it in yourself. Did you check your shoes?"

"I didn't think. But you're probably right. I got red mud on them back at the Tulley place."

Given his anxiety for her safety, better not to mention that she had taken them off in the vestibule.

Brant nursed his drink and stared into its depths, then looked up and held her gaze. "You know I worry about you staying there alone."

"I've been okay for over five years now," she said reasonably, but her stomach began to churn in anticipation of what was inevitably coming.

He sighed and flicked his glass with a sudden movement of his middle finger so that his nail hit the glass. The 'ping!' it made echoed around the space that was opening up between them before dying away.

"Manchester has changed!"

"No Brant, *life* has changed," she countered evenly, but holding onto patience with growing difficulty. "It changed with the World Trade Towers. Then Al Qaeda and I.S. Suicide bombers and all that shit isn't about to go away. Terrorism is here with us and know what – we have to learn to deal with it! Do you think I don't worry about *you* when you go off to the City? But I can't throw one and try to make a prisoner of you every time you use the underground or enter a government building. As for who is in danger, let's face it, the Department is more concerned with success than your safety!"

His lips tightened at this euphemistic reference to MI5. She could not help that; it was the truth. Though not directly employed by the division, his services as an M.O.D. astro-physicist were frequently sought in matters of space security and infringements and at times it got pretty hairy. For instance that pre-war assignment involving a meteorite and a rogue scientist's attempts to sell to Bin Laden the lethal particles contained within it could easily have been his last. Although she had to admit that her determined chase for a story had resulted in her playing an even riskier part in that particular caper, but guilt was an unaffordable luxury she told herself.

"It's my job Darcy, and you knew that when you married me."

"Reporting is mine – and you knew *that*," Darcy retorted, her patience snapping despite an earlier resolve to avoid confrontation. Recalling it now she instantly regretted her outburst and putting down her glass, crossed to his chair and perched on his knee.

"Come on sweetheart, don't growl at me," she cajoled, twining her arms around his neck.

"I was concerned," he said, arms still crossed over his chest in a gesture of defence.

"I know." It was the truth, and time to end this before it spiralled out of control. "And to make amends, you can cook dinner this evening!" she added with an innocent smile. "And for starters – you can pour me a refill," she said rising to pick up the empty glass and wave it in his face before he worked out who was to be the penitent.

"You are incorrigible."

"But you love me."

"For my sins!" He grinned and rose to his feet. Taking the glass he kissed her on the forehead then poured her a generous measure of wine.

"It will cost you later," he warned.

"No doubt." And well worth it, Darcy thought as the threat to the evening's pleasure subsided.

She moaned and her head moved to and fro on the pillow. There it was again, the grey walls silhouetted darkly against a livid crimson sky. And again that strange circular structure in the foreground. The shadows at the centre were beginning to whorl and coalesce and give definition to his form, but something was tugging her away from the scene. Her mind resisted but the pull to the surface was inexorable. Her eyes opened as a voice penetrated sleep.

"Brant?" She stared vacantly into his face, unable to focus thoughts and powers of recognition.

"Wake up sweetheart." He shook her gently by the shoulder, bringing her fully awake. "What was it, a nightmare?"

"It's okay," she murmured, reluctant to talk about it without knowing why. Settling down again with Brant's arm about her for reassurance, she made up her mind to do some research. If such a place existed she would damned well find it.

OUT OF TIME II:
Arrival – Mediobogdum

~

Autumn, just over two decades into Hadrian's reign and a day when the mist was slow to dissolve as the sun slid over the ridge of the pass. Human voices barking orders rose from within the walls of the fort, along with the clash of many boots caused by studs sparking off stone as men scurried to carry them out. Yet, thought the sentry at the south east tower as he watched this buzz of activity, it was too damned quiet. A sort of 'hushed expectancy' Remus would call it. Clever with the words was Remus. His cleverness had not done him much good that morning though, had it? The sentry's lips turned down in a grimace. Six lashes and all for spitting in the courtyard. All of a sudden spitting was a flogging offence. And all because some top brass was coming. Spit and bloody polish. Sticks and whips and officers with lips tight as a frozen sheep's arse.

It had been that way ever since the messenger arrived from Eboracum. Stuck up bastard. He might as well have had 'Northern Headquarters' stamped across his forehead. Thought he was a cut above them all, he did. A meal, a mug of ale, a fresh horse and at dawn he had been on his way again. Arrogant bastard – but that was the legions for you: full of their own importance and efficiency. Odds on they daren't even piss without first measuring out the distance. The sentry sniffed his disdain. Well he would be a Roman Citizen one day, when he had twenty five years service under his belt. A long way off yet, still it was not a bad life. At least food, ale and even wine were plentiful here, providing a soldier knew the ropes.

The sentry longed to run a finger beneath the helmet strap to ease the chafing, but knew the price of doing so and therefore resisted. It was getting to him, the lack of chatter and half-hearted grumbling that normally was so much a part of fatigues. Unnatural he called it. But then the bulk of the garrison was already assembled on the parade ground. His body palpably stiffened and his neck craned as he listened. No, he was not mistaken. There it was again: the ring of iron-shod hooves on paved road and the steady rhythm of marching feet. And now he could make out the rumble of supply wagons, and the gods knew what else.

A sidelong glance revealed the first of the riders silhouetted against a bloody sky at the crest of the pass.

Shoulders back, head up and stand at attention – or pay later. They came swarming down now, in and out, up and down, now visible now hidden by outcrops of rock. My but they look good. Plumes nodding, boar's hair bristling, a scarlet plume of smoke wending its way down the mountain flank. The silence was broken by the creak of leather and chink of metal combined with drumming of feet and hooves. The sentry craned his neck as far as possible without risking detection. At a rough count some eighty legionaries, a full century of infantry and the whole led by a company of mounted officers at least a dozen strong. At the rear a team of mules and pack horses strained, eyes rolling and showing the whites, muzzles flecked with foam. Not a fresh team either; they had the look of beasts that had travelled far, probably from Galava on the lake. Leather sheets and hawsers were stretched to the limit to cover each load. This Big Hat didn't travel light; he must be a showy bastard.

There they go, past the parade ground and no need for apologies there, the sentry thought with a certain smugness. The finest in the province and our lot look good at attention. Out front Lucius our signifer looks the business with his uniform and helmet covered in wolf skins as he proudly holds our vexillum aloft. The polished bronze staff glints in the rays of the sun, and the banner billows slightly in the breeze so that the words COH 1V that tell the world who we are and that we are part of the might of Rome appear to ripple and move, and the tassels hanging from the cross bar rise and sink with heart-catching grace. It's enough to bring a lump to a man's throat.

Now on to the approach road flanked by centurions, beneath the archway formed by their vine sticks (which is better than using them on a man's back) as the blare of trumpets is thrown back by the mountains. They clatter now beneath the porta praetoris to the arched gateway of the principia. And now they dismount, all that is except one: their commander. A proud bastard by the looks of him, sitting that showy chestnut as though he rules the world and with the purple edge to his cloak to back him up.

And there is our prefect Marcellus, fawning all over the newcomer. He will have no need for the senna pods tonight. No soldier here would be in his boots right now. This legatus looks a real tough bastard, the type that would have a soldier's balls on a platter if he flouted the rules. Shame about Marcellus really; he wasn't bad as prefects go. He could have kept it all to himself but give the man his due, he always saw his men right too: a side of salt beef here, a goat cheese there, and – always welcome – an amphora of wine for the barracks. Rome must have got wind of the scam. That's it then, an end to the easy life.

Sextus Tacitus Antonius, commanding officer of Legio IX has arrived

SIX

~

The steep and winding way over Wrynose Pass had seemed daunting but turned out to be a doddle compared to the drive over Hardknott Pass to her destination. It *does* exist – and there it is, Darcy thought triumphantly as she stood beside the car that she had inched into a passing place at the summit of Hardknott to survey the ruins below. She was still shaken by an ascent via three-in-one gradients and hairpin bends on a scary narrow road flanked by a chasm: a silver snake of water writhing across its floor way below and warning her not to get it wrong. A few deep breaths of mountain air steadied body and nerves and the view now inspired exhilaration rather than terror. The square of the ruined fort squatting on its plateau mid way down a rugged mountain devoid of trees or habitation, and the strangely shaped ruin a few metres to the south of it, still inspired awe and respect. The walls were bounded by bracken and grasses, the latter close-cropped by the unconcerned Herdwick ewes that were dotted about, nibbling and chewing and, unlike herself, apparently unimpressed by the antiquity and spectacular location.

It had not taken much research; the circular structure and dramatic location amidst barren fells were unique and distinctive. An aerial photograph featured on the ancient history web site had made these Roman remains instantly identifiable. Furthermore it was the only one to be found with that visible and peculiar round hypocaust at the entrance to the bath house as she now knew it to be: she could hardly have imagined that feature and had never visited this place before. That meant the fort in the mirror was real, and could only be Mediobogdum, named apparently for its situation in the middle of the bend, and just as nerve-jolting was the discovery that it was situated a mere mile or so from the Tulley place.

Her initial thought had been to contact Caro Stevens at Hilldean University. She and Caro went back a long way, to their days as freshers at Hilldean. Following graduation Caro had obtained a lecturing post in the Archaeology Department and her extensive knowledge of the subject had proved invaluable on many an investigation. But the desire to see the place first and establish it really did exist had been overwhelming. The web site had furnished basic information: the fort was of local granite faced with sandstone from nearby Gosforth and covered circa three acres, and deemed to have been built in the reign of the emperor Hadrian. A fragment of masonry had been found bearing his name, as the information plaque at the beginning of the approach road attested, though she supposed this could have been added later when Hadrian succeeded Trajan. That it could be attributed to one or the other seemed to be beyond dispute. Looking down on the ruins from her standpoint at the summit, the 'playing card' shape was plain to see, that and the remains of the towers at each corner. Each of the four walls midway along had its own entrance, and the remains of the approach road apparently took the visitor directly up to the *porta praetoris* or main gateway.

'Which is where we shall soon be so stay with it,' she said with a laugh, responding to the grunts and whines of impatience issuing from the car's partially open windows.

The decision to bring Mab and Brock along had been made at the last minute from the need of company on this bizarre trip, though she shied from admitting it. That it was a shame for them to be indoors on this sunny October morning was the preferred version. Normally when Brant was called away and she left for the *Manchester News* or to go on location, they lodged with a retired farmer's wife now living in St. Gildas village who was glad of Brant's generous payment for the service. Brant had left for London that morning, but

Darcy had decided to book a couple of days leave from the Paper in order to pursue the mystery of her 'vision', and at the same time investigate the case of the Defra shooting. The plan was to call on Jane Tulley after visiting the fort.

The descent was no less nerve shattering than the ascent. Her white-knuckle grip on the steering wheel tightened as the car hurtled down the switchback that passed for a road.

"Bastard!" she ground out from between clenched teeth as the bumper bounced off a boulder on one particularly nasty bend and the tyres squealed their protest as she hit the brake. One last bend followed by a heart-stopping nosedive and at last the plateau of rock was reached. She nosed into a roughly formed parking space and heaving a sigh of relief, switched off the engine.

Getting out of the car she looped stray strands of hair behind her ears to stop the wind from whipping them across her face. A harsh croaking overhead brought her head up. A pair of ravens. She stood and watched for a moment as they wheeled and rode the air currents. She had read somewhere that they bonded for life. Just as well out here in this lonely place she could not help thinking. They were also acknowledged flying aces and more sinister, Masters of the Scavengers Guild. Well, no self-respecting ruin would be without them, she thought smiling. The smile froze as suddenly she became aware of the towering heights that surrounded the fort. They seemed to loom even higher than before and herself to dwindle by comparison. Much like Alice, she thought, except this is no Wonderland. Forget white rabbits and mad hatters, but it was easy enough to imagine pterodactyls gliding overhead, or the roar of Tyrannosaurus Rex bouncing off the rocks as he flung back his head and celebrated the kill. To the right the pass crawled up to the skyline and everywhere reared walls of raw and barren rock. Her flesh crawled as realisation struck, of how cut off she was from the rest of the world and civilisation.

Shaking her head to dispel any fantasies she opened the car door, allowing Mab and Brock to leap out and prance about with excitement. "Calm down idiots," she said mildly, but allowing them to psyche up to their walk before calling them to heel. Less trouble than babies, she thought with a grin, looping the strap of the camera case over her head, though Brant of course would not agree. But this was not the time to be thinking of that; today was time-out, an exciting diversion from Frank's moans and Brant's baby-making campaign. A glance at her watch told her it was just gone nine which gave her a couple of hours to explore the site before finding a pub for a spot of lunch. Calling the dogs to heel she made her way to the approach road then paused to tug off her sweater and tie the sleeves around her hips. Although it was still early the sun warmed her back through the cotton shirt as she made her way over the rutted track that trailed up the fellside. A dull ache low in her back caused her to pause and stretch her spine before moving on. It was not perhaps the best time of the month for this excursion. She had not said anything to Brant before he left for London; there had been enough discord over this subject. Her lips compressed at the memory: to him every period underlined her lack of maternal instinct, and the fact that her body-clock was inexorably ticking away.

Shrugging off the unpleasantness of these thoughts she paused to shoot some pictures, marvelling again at the fort's amazing setting. Ignited by sunlight, dying bracken blazed spectacularly. From all around came the grumble and splash of water as it jostled through channels etched in peat or foamed down rock faces. Loose stones rolled beneath her feet like marbles as she approached the remains of that odd circular-shaped building bearing a bronze plaque inscribed with the legend 'BATH HOUSE'.

"Okay guys, let's take a look," she called, stepping over the crumbling walls, but Mab and Brock hung back, heads and tails lowered. Darcy frowned then ignored them, her attention claimed by a feeling of someone close as she walked around the interior. She whipped round, but the space was empty. Yet there remained a faint sense of outrage, as though someone watched and resented her intrusion.

She glanced at the dogs. Mab was crouching low to the ground, showing the whites of her eyes. Brock was standing with hind feet splayed but head hanging, a confusion of aggression and fear that was a sure sign of insecurity. The ears of both dogs were cocked and their heads tilted as they listened intently. Stepping back onto the path she called them and continued on her way. It was only the wind soughing through dry grasses she told herself, resisting the urge to shiver as the day suddenly felt less warm.

On reaching the main gateway she found that the stone archways had disappeared and a few blocks of sandstone were all that remained of the central pier. Nonetheless it was still impressive: grey walls snaked to left and right, straddling the flank of the fell and following its undulations. It was not difficult to imagine this place in its heyday. *What is today's password? Will I be allowed to enter, or more to the point, leave at will?* She entered into the spirit of the thing, pretending the centuries had rolled away and that she was an unauthorised visitor preparing to answer the sentry's demand as to her identity. Suddenly she shivered as the sunlight was dimmed and the amusing mind-game flashed into scary reality. She could only describe it as a blurring of the edges as the translucent blue light that bathed the fells intensified and streaked around and above the walls, tracing the original height and arches. She blinked; the image disappeared. The pall of cloud lifted, the sun's rays streamed down and everything seemed as before.

She suddenly became aware of Mab and Brock, or rather of their whimpering as they cowered, bellies to ground.

"Oh hey, come on you guys," she said calling them to her, but they backed away in tandem. "Come on now, let's not be silly about this," she coaxed, reaching for their collars but both dogs shrank from her hand.

"Okay, we'll do it the hard way," she bantered, taking two leashes from the pockets of her combats and clipping them onto their collars. She tugged them, panting and hind feet dragging up dust, over the threshold and into the fort. A shudder ran along her spine and she tried to ignore the sensation of having brushed against somebody as they passed. She watched disconcerted as Mab vomited on the ground and Brock's hackles rose like a porcupine's spikes. They had never behaved this way before. Taking care to hide her apprehension, her voice as she spoke to them was calm and low. They seemed reassured, but remained subdued and looked at her with eyes that seemed to say *why must we do this?* They followed as she moved on but uncharacteristically stayed close, making no attempt to surge and strain at their leashes as they normally would when excited by fresh sights and smells, but instead walked quietly by her side.

The grounds of the fort were covered by what once must have been a criss-cross of neatly paved and cobbled roads, but these were now hidden by turf and loose stones chequered only by sunlight and cloud-shadow. The foundations of the original buildings still remained though, and she approached the one situated at the centre of the square. *HEADQUARTERS* the plaque informed her. She stepped into what once must have been a courtyard but here too the cobbles were overgrown with turf cropped short by invading sheep. Mab and Brock skulked at the entrance and steadfastly refused to enter. Shrugging off the feeling of unease that still clung to her like a cobweb, she ignored them and ran off more shots. It was all too easy in this place to be intimidated by glowering fells and an oppressive sense of desolation; to feel alone but not alone.

On to the Commandant's House. She stared at the plaque and wondered what sort of a man he had been. A right bastard no doubt, seething with arrogance and his own importance: sexy though, given all that leather and metal. She grinned at the image thus conjured. What a turn-on for the local talent! Amusement and idle speculation ceased abruptly and she spun on her heel. The sense of not being alone was stronger in here. An image flashed to mind, fragmented and veiled by time: an impression of weathered skin and hard green eyes tempered by a sensual mouth. A couple of seconds later it vanished. Leaving in a hurry she made her way to the rear entrance or *porta decumana* which, the web site blurb exhorted, must be passed through in order to enjoy the magnificent panorama. So she made her way to the edge of the precipice and stood on an outcrop of rock.

The web site blurb was not exaggerated: the view was breathtaking. She tried hard to simply enjoy it, despite the oddest sensation that somebody shared her space. She took several shots of the rear of the fort then focused on the panorama that formed the backdrop to the precipice. On the eastern horizon Crinkle Crags raised giant blisters of rock to the sky, and the triangle summit of nearby Bowfell poked its head through the clouds. To the west the Scafell range brooded in majesty and an atmospheric blue haze. Ten miles or so to the west the sea shimmered like a mirage, and between her and the coast stretched the flat greenness of a deep valley scoured by ice when ancient glaciers melted.

Below at the bottom of the ravine the silver snake of the river writhed its way to the sea.

She leaned forward, unable to drag her gaze away. Her awareness of being observed sharpened almost but not quite into focus. The feeling was rather like that of being introduced to someone for the very first time yet feeling it wasn't, because on both sides there is instant rapport, a sense of familiarity that stops short of recognition. As she stood gazing down into the precipice, a mist began to rise from the valley floor below. She watched mesmerised: the vapour was tinged with the rose of a belated autumnal sunrise. It began to spin, became a vortex rushing up to meet her, a kaleidoscopic whirl of colour and madness that was echoed inside her head as vertigo struck. It rose to obscure the view, billowing and growing both in density and colour. She swayed on her feet, fighting a rising tide of nausea and fear.

The colour deepened to crimson, a stain that spread until all was obliterated from her sight. All, that is, bar a shapeless shadow a metre or so ahead, no more than a darkening and thickening of the vapour at the edge of the precipice. A spiral of dried leaves spinning and shifting shape. As she strained to see it elongated, expanded and contracted, angles and proportions becoming sculpted and refined into a semblance of human form. Filled with terror she opened her mouth to cry out, but the crimson mist seeped into her throat and muffled all sound.

OUT OF TIME III

~

A shrivelled leaf skittered across the fellside, ducking and swerving, a wild thing seeking to escape the chill breath of the wind gusting down from the summit. Inexorably, despite the mouse-like scuttle for safety, it was driven on to the north-facing precipice where it hovered, seemingly suspended on air, before whirling over the brink. Sextus Tacitus Antonius stood on the overhang of granite and stared glumly down at the floor of the chasm. Though not above average height, he was an imposing figure due to the fact that he held himself erect and had an unmistakeable aura of authority. At least today the autumnal sun had brought a little cheer to this godforsaken land. Succumbing to an impulse to feel the last of the day's warmth on his skin, he removed his helmet revealing dark hair cropped in the military fashion. It was lighter at front and temples and here mirrored the bronze of the dying bracken around him; the forerunner to grey, he supposed, though prematurely in his view. He consoled himself with the knowledge that others, especially women, saw it as an attractive feature. Tucking the helmet beneath one arm he turned to survey the sea to the west.

As he peered into the westering sun it could be seen that his face was weathered but lacked the swarthiness of the Mediterranean people. The flesh was lean and firm despite the cobweb of fine lines at the corners of mouth and eyes, the latter being a clear and luminous green. Raising a slender hand to his face he absently traced with one finger the deeper line that ran from the nostrils to a mouth that displayed sensitivity when it was not compressed in displeasure as it all too often could be. The nose was often remarked upon, not so much in terms of shape or size but for his habit of looking down it at soldiers who had the misfortune to fall beneath his inspection, or dignitaries stupid enough to incur his contempt.

A sense of something or someone brushing against him made him scowl, dip and turn on his heel, gladius already in hand. Nothing: this place was making him jumpy as a cat in a houseful of dogs. The fort behind him hummed with muted life as the garrison went about its daily business, but none were closer than the sentries patrolling the rampart that ran the length of the rear wall. As he sheathed the short-sword his shoulders rose in a spontaneous shudder. The feeling of someone close persisted, of someone sharing his space. A *female* feeling. What had given him that idea? Something intangible: the softness of touch maybe, or perhaps a whiff of perfume; or maybe it was that faint warm-blood type smell that as a boy he had been aware of at certain times in his mother and sisters, and that had vaguely excited him and caused his manhood to stir without him knowing why, except that it was to do with the secret and forbidden things of women. This intimate memory and present possibility brought a flush to his cheeks and the knowledge gave rise to an uncomfortable sense of vulnerability.

But then his expression hardened. Not *her* surely, with her devastating combination of witchery and innocence; the one he had forced from his thoughts and the crannies she inhabited in his heart from the day he arrived at this hell-hole. That first image was etched on his soul. A half-smile softened his mouth. She was as he had often imagined Boudicca to be, that legendary queen of the Iceni and scourge of Rome prior to her overwhelming defeat. He had always felt a secret and guilty regret about her humiliation and rape of her daughters, perhaps on account of her undisputed single-mindedness and courage – good Roman values – or maybe because something about her reminded him of his adored mother and her barbarian spirit. The daughter of a noble and from a Romanised family, Calpurnia had been an acceptable and even desirable bride for his father but allegiance to Rome had stopped short of her soul. Antonius' eyes filled with pain and tenderness. Upon her untimely death from summer-fever this had been her legacy to him: a life-long conflict of allegiance.

His thoughts shied away from the pain of that memory and returned to the enigma of the native woman who had captured his imagination and whom he had encountered again on firstly a routine visit to the local settlement, then on any occasion he could contrive. Thanks to his mother and her non-Roman origin he had grown up bilingual, though under strict orders from her never to divulge their secret by speaking her native tongue in front of his father. Now he had reason to be grateful for those secret conversations that allowed her to keep alive her roots. Due to his mother he could converse with the woman from the settlement who both fascinated and infuriated him in something close to her regional dialect, close enough at least for mutual understanding. Conversely the elder who seemed to be in the role of her guardian spoke in the native tongue to his people but with startling fluency in Latin to his Roman visitor. On being asked where he had learned the language, he had evaded giving an answer in his usual maddening manner by answering with yet another question: *in the same place perhaps you learned to speak ours?'* and one which he declined to answer. His mind slid away from the mystery of the old man back to his delectable ward.

Even as her image returned to mind he felt his loins tighten and chest constrict so that he breathed with difficulty. No, he must forget her: no more seeking her out as he took his customary morning ride on Gaudita hoping for a glimpse of her by the well, but coming upon her instead deep in some forest glade, or within the palisade of her settlement (and how many times could he return on the pretext of an inventory?). Despite the feisty banter – she was apparently not intimidated by his rank and power – her ice was beginning to melt.

But that was all he needed, a feud with the local Brigante because he was philandering with their leader's woman, for although not actually stated, at a guess there was an understanding between her and the chieftain. He was yet to encounter him, but by all accounts he was nobody's fool and would stand no messing. His pride would never let fear of offending Rome stand in the way of avenging a challenge to his manhood. It was difficult to understand, he mused, why Rowana should appear to prefer flirting with a – shall we say *mature?* – Roman officer when her handsome and youthful intended was so obviously enslaved by her beauty and feisty spirit. As leader of the clan he could offer her wealth and status, whereas fraternisation with himself and what these ungoverned northern tribes still saw as 'the Enemy' could bring her ruin and disgrace if not an early death. But a girl such as she, he reassured himself, would value the refinement, worldly experience and power embodied in an officer of Rome. More than this, she would be unable to resist such a challenge.

Antonius thoughtfully stroked a chin shaved that morning but now, like the fells and valley around him, darkening with an evening shadow. He must remember his brief to keep a low profile and suss out the mood of the locals. On the strength of his report Rome would decide future policy in respect of this far-flung province of Britannia. Under cover of course of sorting this pilfering dog Marcellus. He spat into the chasm at his feet and dwelt briefly and with pleasure on ways of dealing with the prefect. No, an outbreak of hostilities now would scupper that mission along with any future chance of promotion. Not that his present position of command in the famous IXth was to be sniffed at: no other legion shone with the same lustre. All the same, a cosy governorship would be appreciated after so many years at the sharp end.

Yes, the sharp end: where his senses were trained to detect any change of odour, sound or movement even before the footfall registered. He whirled round, knees slightly bent body at an angle rather than full on to reduce the target area.

"Justinus." He sheathed his sword and felt the tingle at the nape of the neck begin to subside and the thump-thud-thump of his heartbeat slow to its normal rhythm. His features relaxed as his favourite tribune approached and saluted.

"The men are assembling for the review sir."

Antonius sighed and rubbed a finger mark from his helmet with the edge of his cloak.

"Very well; but I know exactly what to expect."

The younger man jerked his head in the direction of the fort.

"Doesn't do much for Rome's image does it. How are you finding your quarters?"

"Not bad. At least the place has heating and a private latrine."

"I bet Marcellus was cursing at having to turn his quarters over to his 'illustrious visitor' as he called you!" Justinus laughed at Antonius' expression of distaste. "I know, he's a right arse-toad. I heard he turfed out the chief centurion from his end-suite and moved in there."

Antonius shivered, though whether from the harshness of the elements or that earlier sense of presence it was hard to say.

"This damned wind hasn't stopped blowing since we arrived," he complained, folding his arms across his chest whilst turning his face from the bite. "And worse to come. I can think of better ways of spending winter than being holed up here with ice, snow and a pack of morons."

"As the rest of us commonly do!" Justinus challenged with a grin.

"Balls Justinus! The modern army doesn't know the meaning of hardship. Now in my early days as an officer..."

He paused as Justinus sighed, looked up at the sky and laughed, suddenly looking less than his twenty-five years.

"Insolent pup!" But Antonius' tone and expression were indulgent. "Hold hard," he added, "or I'll recommend you to Hadrian for a permanent posting at Mediobogdum!"

The look of amusement on Antonius' face swiftly changed to one of irritation.

"Damn Hadrian for sending me on such an mission at this time of year. He chose a better time and destination for his visit to Britannia a couple of years back! You wouldn't catch him in this god-forsaken place. Oh no, it was the comfort an comparative civilisation of Eboracum for him!"

Justinus fingered the hilt of his sword.

"Does Marcellus know the reason for this mission?"

"The overt one yes. Lack of correct reports and returns, and the complaints we've had from merchants when they've had their carts and mule trains checked. It seems Marcellus's men have quite a reputation for brutality and helping themselves! A general scruffiness and lack of order – and of course, the question mark over the amount of provisions regularly ordered and delivered."

Justinus chewed his lower lip before venturing a further question.

"The overt reason you said – there is another?"

Antonius looked thoughtful and did not immediately respond but searched his tribune's face. As though satisfied with what he saw he nodded and explained:

"To gather information about the temper and politics of the locals. Though to do so without raising suspicion is not an easy task. How much to believe of what we are told is another."

"Why does Hadrian need it?" Justinus dared.

"To decide their future."

"He may attack?"

"Or attempt to pacify and go for at least partial integration." Antonius shrugged before continuing, "It depends on my report. Either way, he intends to end the problem of these northern tribes for ever. But not a word of this Justinus."

"I can keep my secrets sir," Justinus said stiffly.

Antonius nodded and touched him lightly on the shoulder to show no offence was intended.

"Right, the parade ground rostrum it is then." he took the helmet from beneath his arm and rammed it onto his head, turned his back on the precipice and marched to the via decumana. As he passed through the rear gate ahead of Justinus a surge of longing stopped him dead. Then he shrugged and continued on his way. Tenderness was a stranger who entered unbidden, bribed judgement and stole a man's pride. There was no room for such things in the life of a military commander. Pushing aside such thoughts he called over his shoulder to Justinus,

"I promise you, someone will pay if this winter I have to suffer chilblains, piles and frost-bitten chestnuts!"

Banter and man-things fit him with the comfort of personal armour.

SEVEN

~

The red mist was clearing rather more quickly than the numbness and fear that gripped Darcy's mind and deadened her limbs. Outwardly she made no movement despite the inner struggle that waged. All attempts to move back from the precipice failed due to a numbness that held her rooted to the overhang. The valley floor spun at the far end of a rose coloured vortex and appeared to rush upwards and draw her in so that her rigid body swayed in an effort to meet it. An intense desire gripped her: to let go and allow herself to be consumed. Her head whined and buzzed deepening the sense of unreality. By contrast a soft breeze caressed her face and arms, the gentle touch of invisible fingers that filled her with longing so that she whispered:

"Who are you?"

Tears coursed down her cheeks and perspiration beaded her forehead as nausea rose from her stomach and gagged her throat. *I am going to die.* That was the only certainty, the sole thought that penetrated the lingering tendrils of mist.

Gradually the fog lifted from her mind and her thoughts became lucid, which made fear all the more acute. It was a delusion, she told herself fiercely, feeling as though she was fighting for her sanity. There was nothing physically amiss therefore there could be no paralysis, she could move at will. Only it was not happening. Abandoning all attempts at movement she closed her eyes and concentrated with all remaining strength on quelling panic and restoring a sense of normality. When she opened them again the pall of crimson had completely disappeared. Valley and fells were bathed in the unique luminosity that Turner had called Venetian in character and sought to capture on canvas. The recollection of this irrelevant piece of information did much to restore a sense of reality. The heaviness ebbed from her limbs and she knew with absolute clarity that it was possible to move again, and to prove it stepped back several paces from the brink of the precipice.

She blinked rapidly several times, unsure now as to whether that blood-stained atmosphere had existed only in her imagination, an illusion triggered by the rays of a peachy sun diffusing through perfectly normal autumnal vapours rising from the valley bottom. As for the shadowy figure of a man at its centre, the flicker of cloak and flash of burnished metal, they all had to be figments of her imagination, a fantasy fired by that image in the mirror and invoked by the atmospheric location. That, and the desire for a story. But even if this was the case, she argued with herself, it could not explain the pain and force of those emotions, the yearning that still enmeshed her soul with threads of silk, nor the sense of a brooding presence that still lingered. *Who are you?* she found herself repeating against all the laws of logic. Becoming aware once more of her surroundings and situation she turned and scanned the area for Mab and Brock. Her stomach lurched uncomfortably; the two dogs were nowhere to be seen. She called their names in a voice edged with anxiety and suppressed panic. If anything happened to them she would never forgive herself, but more to the point neither would Brant, she told herself making for the *porta decumana* at a run.

The atmosphere within the walls of the fort was oppressive and purple cumulus rolled across a previously empty sky. The raven pair soared and dropped, then soared again, wing feathers splayed like black rags tattered and tossed by a capricious wind. A quick and frantic search of the remains told her Mab and Brock were not within the fort. Running down to the main gate in what now amounted to semi darkness, her foot turned on one of the many loose stones and a cry of pain was wrenched from her as fire seared her ankle. The sob of fear and frustration died in her throat at the sound of barking coming from directly in front. She limped forward calling the dogs by name and almost weeping with relief as the prospect of facing Brant with the news that she had lost his beloved spaniels began to fade. The pain of her ankle was nothing by comparison.

Their crouched shapes were just visible through the gloom of gathering storm clouds. They were waiting beyond the gateway, faces anxious, heads lowered and bellies close to the ground. At her reappearance they leapt to their feet, rumps wriggling and paws pounding the spot with excitement, yet steadfastly refusing to cross the threshold and rush to her side when she called their names, an unprecedented event that was alien to their nature. A distant growl of thunder reverberating around the fells brought her head up sharply and the dogs whined and stared around them, eyes wide with fear. Yet they had never previously been frightened of storms, she recalled. A glance at her watch told her it had stopped at just gone 9a.m. – the time of her arrival at this place. A shudder ran through her as the memory arose of a similar phenomenon the night of the vision in the mirror. Tension coiled in her stomach as in the second after a cup is dropped and before the smash of impact.

Lightning streaked across the sky and a minute or so later a crash of thunder made her automatically duck her head. A fresh wave of nausea and weakness assailed her, as though someone had turned on a tap and drained off her energy. The whining turned to low growls in the throats of Mab and Brock. Almost immediately this appeared to be echoed as thunder rumbled in the distance. Time to make for the safety of the car. The first fifty-pence sized raindrops slapped her arms and face as she moved towards the dogs as quickly as her injured ankle would allow. Only someone, she realised with a shock of despair, didn't want her to leave. Waves of anger rather than yearning battered her mind into submission and closed the gap in the walls. An invisible barrier of emotion held her prisoner as effectively as any portcullis.

No matter how she pushed against it and told herself nothing could prevent her from leaving, the barricade held. Her feet were rooted in the ground. Pain streaked down her spine causing her mouth to gape but no scream came out. There came a great temptation to drop to her knees and plead for release. *Who are you?* her mind screamed, *why are you keeping me here?* The growling had turned to a frantic barking and the forefeet of the dogs left the ground with the force of each bark as they witnessed her distress. Streaks of blue light shot around and above the walls followed by a cannonade of thunder such that it set the dogs racing in circles whilst emitting high pitched yelps of terror. Eyes starting from head, they cowered beneath a boulder as the boom ricocheted between mountain and rock.

Gobbets of rain fell faster and with a force that stung her exposed skin; in less than a minute her clothes were soaked and her hair plastered to her skull. The rivulets running down her face blurred her vision and she squeezed her eyes tight against the sting. She stood rooted, a craven, pitiable thing, shoulders drooping in despair and muscles twitching with each fresh assault on her senses. Lightning flashed, thunder boomed and the air stank of sulphur as the growling, prowling storm dogs abandoned low grumblings for full-throated attack. Fuelled by self-disgust a surge of anger made her shout:

"Let me go, you bastard!" and the force of that cry propelled her through the gateway. She ushered the dripping dogs from under their rock and oblivious now to the pain of her ankle, hurried down the track to the car and all but threw them into the back where they huddled together without protest. Never again, she vowed, turning the key in the ignition and holding her breath until the engine kicked into life. Even with the wipers turned on full the road was barely visible through the curtain of rain. It snaked up to the crest of a pass shrouded by black cloud – a daunting sight to behold under any conditions but terrifying in this storm. Nevertheless, it was the only way back to normality. Taking a deep breath she aimed for the first of the gradients and tensed herself for the bite.

EIGHT

~

Her neck snapped forward then back again as the nose of the car hit a rock, shuddered to a halt and stalled. Oblivious to pain she released the seat belt and swivelled round in response to the commotion at her back. The rear door had come open; she must have failed to shut it properly in the panic of leaving the fort. It now gaped, admitting the howling wind and a wash of driving rain. The two spaniels were struggling up from the floor where they had been flung in the headlong flight; there had been no time to fasten them into their safety harnesses. Brock was halfway through the door and Mab was attempting to jump back onto the seat to climb out over his back but suddenly yelped and dragged her leg.

'No! Stay!' Darcy cried, mindful that she had no idea where the car had come to rest and that any sudden movement may send it plummeting into the abyss. Even as she shouted both dogs disappeared through the aperture into the gloom.

Momentarily immobilised by shock she stared after them then realising there was only one thing to be done because leaving without them was not an option. She turned and opening the nearside door with care, gingerly climbed out, gasped at the onslaught of wind and rain and inched forward in full expectation of feeling the ground suddenly give way beneath her feet. But the car was not teetering on the brink she realised as her eyes became more accustomed to the murk and wind-shredded ragged clouds. Instead it had at first run roughly parallel with the road then obliquely at an angle of some forty five degrees or so and had finally come to rest against a boulder, stopping well short of the precipitous edge. At worst she had pranged the nearside bonnet and smashed the headlamp. Having ascertained that the car in all probability was drivable and therefore their means of escape still viable, with head lowered and shoulders hunched against the assault she turned her attention to finding the dogs.

"Mab! Brock!" Her words were torn from her lips only to be borne away on the howl of the wind and lost. It's hopeless, she thought, tears streaming down her face along with the rain as she stumbled around shouting their names. Even if she could restart the car and manoeuvre it back onto the road, how could she leave them here in this wilderness? It was unthinkable – and how much more so to explain such an action to Brant? He would see the whole ill-fated venture as heedless and irresponsible. Even if she were to try and explain what drove her there, he would not understand. That thought pushed her on with renewed vigour until her throat was sore from shouting. It was no use; she would have to summon help. Digging deep into a pocket she pulled out her mobile 'phone, released the key lock and with fingers that shook from cold and distress, pressed the speed dial for Brant's number. He would know who to call locally for assistance. It was with a mingled sense of despair and relief that she realised there was no signal, a fact that should have been obvious given the surrounding mountains. At least the ordeal of confession was delayed.

She was about to give up and make her way back to the car with the idea of driving to someone – anyone – for assistance when a sound, heard in the brief hiatus between gusts of wind, caught her attention. She took a step forward, decided it was probably wishful thinking, then heard it again.

"Mab! Mab! Come Mab!" she called, recalling that the bitch had cried and limped when escaping the car. Maybe her injury would prove a blessing in disguise if it meant an inability to run very far. The rain had abated slightly and the lapse between wind-gusts had lengthened. Darcy stood very still, listening. It was louder this time, a high-pitched whine interspersed with the yapping of a frightened dog. She moved in the direction of the sound, straining ears and eyes, facing into the rain and hail that stung her forehead and cheeks. It could turn out to be a double blessing; if Mab was hurt her brother would not stray far. In fact if she was not mistaken that was his bark she could hear. Sure enough Brock came dashing towards her out of the storm, eyes wild, coat dripping and feet flying. He jumped up once in ecstatic welcome then turned and rushed back the way he had come, pausing to look back and bark, making it plain that he wished her to follow.

Mab was lying in a hollow, and after a brief examination it was clear she was more frightened and exhausted than hurt. Both dogs were overjoyed at the reunion and the sight gave Darcy fresh heart.

'Come on girl, let's see if we can't start that stupid car,' she said softly, using the belt from her jacket as a lead by slipping it through Mab's collar in case a clap of thunder or flash of lightning startled her into renewed flight. Not that she would get very far, given that limp and the shivers of shock that rippled along her back. Both dogs had been traumatised by the incident Darcy realised, filled with remorse at her stupidity. The drag on the improvised lead was more pronounced with every step. Stooping she hauled up the mud-caked and exhausted Mab and carried her the rest of the way, staggering beneath the considerable weight. Just as she felt unable to go a step further and was fearing herself lost, the silhouette of the car loomed into view through a fresh deluge of rain and hail.

The engine started without fuss and she manoeuvred the stick to engage four wheel drive and then the gear lever into reverse position. The wheels spun and whined and kicked up a shower of turf and mud but she persevered and eventually inched the vehicle backwards away from the boulder. The dogs, sensing her renewed tension and disliking the noise, whined in the back and scrabbled at the door. 'No worries gang, we're still alive!' Darcy called over her shoulder, not quite managing to suppress the tremor in her voice as she sought to reassure the trembling dogs.

"Lie down – and *stay*," she added, reinforcing the command with a gesture of her hand as she sought to see through the steamed-up rear window and persistent downpour as the car inched backwards. All they needed now was to run too far to the right and off that edge. Then into first gear and more sliding and whining and a heart-stopping bump over a larger than average stone or clump of heather and subsequent stalling of the engine. But then they were back on road with solid tarmac beneath the wheels. "We did it!" Resisting a foolish urge to turn and make a rude sign in the direction of the fort, Darcy turned the vehicle's nose to home and with infinite care this time, continued the drive over the pass.

The pass was behind her and the tension eased enough for her to slacken the white-knuckle hold on the steering wheel and sit back on the seat. More from the need to hear a human voice than any desire to actually listen to what was being said, she switched on the radio. The volume was turned low so as not to interfere with the maelstrom of thoughts whirling around in her mind. That creepy feeling of being watched or followed lingered, making her glance in the mirror but there was nothing reflected in it to cause alarm. However a sense of dread lingered, generated by that line of elephantine fells bulked against the sky and scarred by the zigzagging of the pass; the kind of unease that comes from being enmeshed in a disturbing dream or a situation that defies all logical explanation.

I can't think about it now, she told herself firmly, as a wash of emotion arose. Later, when she was safely home being soothed by a hot bath would be the time to take off the wraps and see what lurked beneath. Instantly an image of the circular bath house arose, not as a skeletal shell but a building filled with red-tinged steam and male bodies, naked, lean and muscular some dripping still from the plunge, others gleaming from the application of fragrant oils. For a moment her nostrils were filled with the faint scents of thyme and lavender spiked with cloves. Her ears picked up echoes of strident laughter and muted hum of conversation of men seated in a row at the latrines, holding what looked like washing up sponges, or bending forward to dip them in a channel of running water at their feet. The splash of water, the hiss of steam, the human sounds: an unlikely cacophony merging with an impossible scene. The car swerved and almost nose-dived into the hedgerow that flanked the road. A jerk of the wheel and a mini-skid coupled with some deep breaths and a few crude curses dispelled the images and brought the car back under control. Darcy forced her mind back to the present and concentrated on driving home.

Her gaze and attention remained firmly fixed on the narrow road flanked by hedges and dry stone walls. At least the storm dogs had given up prowling the sky and retreated to their cosmic kennel. Tree and shrub still dripped from the deluge and bowed to the westerly wind, but despite the lowering sky the rain had stopped. Absently she watched the tumult of withered leaves escaping from the hedgerow . It was almost hypnotic, the way they swirled and scuttled across the road, little brown mice scurrying and colliding in their haste to flee the metal predator. That's right, think about anything but those men of ancient Rome. Especially do not dwell on the one that haunts both precipice and mind. Or was it heart? Whatever, refuse to let him in – ever again.

As though to endorse this resolve she turned up the volume of the radio and became absorbed in a discussion about global warming. The news followed and her attention was suddenly sharpened by hearing a familiar name. So absorbed in the item was she that it was necessary to swerve on rounding a bend to avoid hitting an oncoming Land Rover. It concerned the case of Ted Tulley and the shooting of Simon Pettigrew from Defra. It seemed the latter was still in intensive care but his condition had deteriorated. She heard with a sense of shock that the vehicle manned by employees of a private 'rentaguard' contract company to transport Ted Tulley to court from the secure mental unit where he was being held on remand, had been parked in the wrong area. As a consequence they had picked up another prisoner by mistake and Ted Tulley had been left temporarily unguarded. He had taken his chance. Darcy chewed her bottom lip and tried to concentrate on the road ahead. If Simon Pettigrew died, Ted Tulley would be a desperate man. And he was on the run.

NINE

~

Her hair was a damp and tangled mess, her clothes and shoes mud-spattered and soaking wet and her mind in turmoil, but the chance to stop off at Barrenber Ground to see Jane Tulley was too good to miss. Her proverbial nose for a story was already on the twitch; chances were that Ted Tulley would make for home and his wife would take him in. Granted there could be danger here, but leads like this were hard come by.

Ted's weeks of enforced absence were already having an effect: the entrance to the farm could easily be missed due to an overgrown hedgerow and several overhanging goat willow stragglers, limbs drooping beneath the weight of the earlier torrential rain. The farm dogs set up their usual cacophony and hurled themselves against the mesh in a frenzy of dripping coats, snapping mouths and bared teeth as she parked the car and approached the house. She looked nervously at the pen and back again to the car but there was not so much as a growl issuing from it; obviously Mab and Brock – given the trauma of the day's events – had decided that discretion was definitely the better part of valour. Surreptitiously her gaze ranged over barn and outbuildings but there was no visible sign of Ted Tulley's presence.

Her third and loudest knock at the door brought some success. It opened a crack and Jane Tulley's head appeared. The normally ruddy face was pale and the strain of events apparent in the drawn features and dark circles beneath eyes that surveyed Darcy with hostility and suspicion. Darcy adopted a matter of fact manner.

"Hello Mrs Tulley, remember me?"

"Aye."

"I was passing, thought I'd stop by and see how things were."

The door remained almost shut.

"I'm busy."

"I won't keep you a moment."

"No time, have to do everything me'sel' these days."

"Of course. It must be hard."

"What would you know about that?" The lines gouged into her face by toil and weather deepened into bitterness. It was difficult to distinguish the words given the continual barking and growling of the dogs that on this occasion she made no effort to silence. It was vital to get her talking if that door was not to shut completely.

"Did you approve of my initial article Mrs Tulley?"

"It was fair," she admitted begrudgingly.

"I drafted a follow-on."

"Oh aye."

"Yes, but things have changed now haven't they? We need to talk."

Immediately Jane Tulley shut down communications. There was almost something vulpine about the pinched face and half-closed eyes. Darcy was irresistibly reminded of a vixen guarding her cubs – or in this case was it mate?

"Mebbe, but he's not here." This Tulley woman had sussed her thoughts.

"Surely this is where he would make for? I mean, his home and woman. And Jane," Darcy's use of the woman's forename was deliberate, as was the intimate tone, "I wouldn't blame you for taking him in – I would do the same for my husband. But the best way of helping him now is to persuade him to give himself up. If that man dies, Ted is going to need all the help he can get."

The door began to close; Darcy placed the palm of her hand against it and pushed.

"Maybe I can help. Write a supportive and understanding piece. But you have to trust me Jane." She had to raise her voice to be heard over the renewed baying of the dogs as though they sensed their mistress's hostility and imminent retreat.

"Wouldn't do any good."

"It might. But you have to confide in me."

"He could be anywhere."

"But you know him better than anyone. You must have an idea?"

"He tells me nowt these days." Her voice faltered and her eyes looked past Darcy into the distance as she retreated into a private past. "Bottom meadow it was, aye and he's not bin the same since he found…" and as though suddenly becoming aware again of Darcy's presence she blinked and abruptly stopped.

"What Jane? What did he find?"

But the foxy eyes narrowed still further. "I've told you: I know nothing."

The door was slammed shut with such force that it jarred Darcy's wrist and forced back her arm.

Walking back to the car she constantly looked over her shoulder as the snarling and barking reached a crescendo. But it was not simply fear of the dogs breaking loose that made her do it. It was a sense of being stalked as she walked to the gate with determined steps that hid her inner anxiety. The crack of a dry twig snapping caused her to look up sharply from securing the gate catch. A buzz of electricity stabbed her solar plexus; she was just in time to see the overhanging branches, undergrowth and bronzed bracken swish back into place as something, or someone, disturbed them. She almost called out, shouted Ted by name but decided against it and hurried to the car. If it was Ted Tulley out there, he was a desperate and potentially dangerous man.

On arriving at the farmhouse on the cliffs her nerves were further frayed by the sight of a light spilling out from a ground floor window into the autumnal dusk. Had she forgotten to switch off the study light? Fear gripped her stomach region and tightened her chest because this was not an option. She never entered Brant's study when he was not there; much of his work was classified and she respected his space. "Stay! she commanded in an undervoice as the dogs leapt up in response to the car door opening. She got out to investigate. A brief examination revealed no other vehicle and she stood immobile, staring at that oblong of light as though in doing so for long enough her gaze might penetrate the window and reveal the room's secret. Emotional and physical exhaustion coupled with the penetrating chill from wet clothing robbed her of the power to make decisions. She hovered indecisively, almost weeping at the prospect of having to drive away from the hard-won warmth and haven of her home, if haven it was no more.

Ted Tulley's name flashed into her mind and she spun round intending to run back to the car. Even as she moved common sense mocked this fear: he had no idea where she lived and in the unlikelihood of his following her from the farm, on the deserted coastal road she would have been sure to spot his headlamps reflected in the mirror. At the same instant the front door of the house opened. Darcy felt her legs giving way beneath her and ran for the car whilst she was able. Light spilled out onto the cobbles of the forecourt and from the rear of the car burst the sound of frenzied barking. This was followed by her scream as footsteps sounded and her arm was grabbed from behind.

TEN

~

The grip tightened as she screamed again and struggled frantically to escape.

"Darcy! It's okay, it's me."

It took a moment or two for the familiarity of the voice to penetrate her panic. "Brant?" She sagged against him, weak with relief, then as often happens in such situations, relief was vented in a volley of anger. "Shit! What the hell are you playing at? You scared me half to death!" she shot at him, stepping back to stare at his face through the gathering gloom.

"I thought you would realise-,"

She gestured with her hand as though to physically brush aside his words.

"I thought you were in London!"

"I'll explain later love, go indoors now and get warm."

She was shivering with cold and shock but had been unaware of it until now. The sound of Brant's voice had triggered a fresh burst of barking from Mab and Brock; she hesitated and turned to look at the car.

"Go on." Brant gave her a gentle shove adding, "I'll bring them in."

Suddenly drained Darcy made her way towards the house.

Brant rubbed the worst of the mud off Mab and Brock before settling them in their basket by the Aga then poured a couple of drinks. Whilst doing so he explained that his car had broken down on the M6 and had been towed to a garage in Kendal for repairs, forcing him to abandon his trip to London, book a taxi to the Old Priory Arms and from there beg a lift in a farmer's Land Rover for the final leg of the journey along the cliff top road. "But given the state of you," he commented, handing her a glass of whisky, "I'd say my day must count as pretty bloody tame. Darcy, what the devil have you been up to?" He gestured at her mud-spattered jacket, ripped trousers and sodden feet. "And what happened to Mab?" Hearing her name Mab limped over to him and he ran his hands over her hind leg. "Nothing broken, thank goodness, but a nasty sprain." Somehow his words implied neglect on her part.

"I'll give her some arnica in a moment, that will fix it. What was wrong with your car?" Darcy parried, feeling the liquid fire of the whisky beginning to warm the inner chill, enabling her to blink back the threat of tears.

"An oil leak actually, but you haven't answered my question."

She bent her head, loosening with her fingers the tangle of corkscrew curls created by her drenching on the fell, but also to avoid looking at Brant.

"Okay, remember that weird sort of dream-that-wasn't, the one in the mirror at the flat," she glanced up at him briefly then continued as he nodded, "Well I did some research and identified the place by the remains of that circular building. It's Mediobogdum, a Roman fort over near the Tulley place – the farmer who shot the Defra guy?" she prompted as he looked puzzled, then sighed and added, "Brant this is going to take a while and I'm-,"

"Sorry babe, of course." Brant had the grace to look contrite. "You go get out of those damp clothes and into a hot bath. I'll finish drying the dogs, feed them and give Mab her arnica, then we'll catch up later. Here, take your glass with you."

He topped up her drink. After stroking Mab's head and murmuring soft words, she took it from him, pressing a brief kiss on his lips out of gratitude at being given space and time alone to come to terms with the day's crazy events.

Some time later as she finished relating the most credible ones amongst those events, Brant's expression conveyed not only scepticism but also something that she could not quite define but which came close to exasperation. She confined her story to the strangeness of the fort itself, the suddenness of the storm and the inexplicable behaviour of Mab and Brock whilst suppressing any mention of a personality and that sense of formidable presence.

"Okay, so now you've identified and sussed out the place you can forget it sweetheart."

She was curled up next to him on the settee in the sitting room, warmed and comforted by the blaze of a log fire, the softness of candlelight and a pasta and wine meal prepared by Brant whilst she was soaking in the bath and which she had eaten with relish despite protestations of not being hungry . He turned and gave her a hard look when she failed to respond to his words.

"Okay?"

"M'mm."

"You don't sound sure."

How could she explain that already an inexplicable yearning to return was eating away at her earlier resolve. Here, cocooned in the warmth and security of their home, listening to the crackling of the fire and the snoring of the dogs and surrounded by all the other trappings of normality it was hard even for her to believe what had occurred. To Brant it must seem she had lost the plot; yet the longing remained. Flashbacks of a mist-filled precipice and a fort trailing red vapour from roofs and towers that by logic could not be there filled her with confusion, but none so much as the image of a shadowy figure standing astride a rock, cloak edged with the purple and stirred by the salt-wind that gusted in from the coast. The image disturbed, yes but more so the accompanying emotions. "Who are you?" she whispered, staring into the blackened timbers jutting from the central glow of the fire.

"Excuse me?"

She blinked and turned to Brant in confusion.

"Oh, nothing."

"You're planning to go back there aren't you?" This time the irritation was plain to both see and hear by the frown etched on his forehead, and the clipped tones of his voice.

"Maybe."

The hint of defiance meant to discourage more questions only provoked further resistance.

"Darcy – you were soaked, filthy and stressed out, the dogs likewise and the car pranged into the bargain. Thank God Mab was the only one to get hurt!"

"I'll pay for the car – and take Mab to the vet's to be checked out, okay!" Darcy set her glass down on the table with a snap and rose to her feet. Brant's face flushed with anger.

"Don't be childish! It's not about that and you damned well know it."

"Okay, so you were concerned," she conceded, but then added: " Do you think I don't worry when you go out on assignments? Afghanistan and Iraq were bad enough, but the London underground is more of a danger now than any centuries-out-of-commission Roman fort!"

His eyebrows went up and he gave her a long speculative look so that taking the point, she had to grin.

"Okay, so I looked like I'd returned from combat." Strangely, that remark with its military connotations seemed to bring *him* closer, render events more real because that was exactly how it had felt.

Brant rose and pulling her to him kissed her full on the mouth.

"Pax?" he whispered in her ear.

Pax, Latin for peace and oh God, she had to stop this. To save replying she nibbled his lower lip and gave him a lingering kiss. By way of response Brant pulled her down into the embrace of the massive and ancient sofa.

As his hands wandered over her body caressing and testing her nipples for arousal, against her will her consciousness returned to the remains of the fort on its wild and forlorn fellside. All it required was a sort of opening up, a looking with an inner eye, a scanning of what appeared to be a blank screen at the back of her mind but one that would suddenly burst into brilliant colour and intimate detail so that every blade of grass on the hillside stood out with startling clarity. More real than real, that was the only way to describe it. The images floated in and out of perception and were difficult to hold on to but this became easier once the knack was acquired. This she discovered entailed a sort of looking through rather than focusing on the image.

Yes, there he was, a figure standing on the wall, watching and waiting. *For what? For whom?* Red mist, Red cloak and copper breastplate but he was not standing close enough for her to distinguish his features. A similar build to Brant. Yes, *Brant*. She blinked hard, aware that her attention had wandered and started to caress him again until he groaned with pleasure. She paused as the image on the outcrop exerted a stronger pull. The aura of power combined with loneliness fired her with a potent mix of emotions.

"Let me in," Brant whispered, his hand questing as he became more insistent.

She stared at the face above her, shrouded by shadows as the flames of the candles flickered and leapt, and for an instant wondered who had spoken. Then he slipped inside and her body responded of its own volition; her mind however remained elsewhere.

"Is that good?"

Brant sounded unsure of himself, as though aware of her essential absence. She fought to quell the sense of irritation as his voice intruded and broke her concentration, then immediately flooded by guilt murmured something appropriate and focused on his rhythm. But resistance to Mediobogdum and its guardian was token. Inexorably the shadowy figure drew closer. A fantasy with a difference and nothing more, she told herself relaxing into Brant's stride. The enigmatic personality conjured by the loneliness and power of the place had fired her imagination. Yes, just a fantasy, and fantasy never hurt anyone.

Almost she could believe it.

Brant increased the pace. Darcy worked hard: climbed, climbed and climbed again but each time slid down from the peak by inches of frustration and strangeness. Brant's penetration failed to reach her essence. He stopped, propped himself up on one elbow and she saw the beads of perspiration glistening on his brow.

"What's wrong babe?"

She shook her head and whispered:

"Just can't make it."

He grunted and renewed his efforts whilst she did her best to respond.

What would it be like with *him?* That thought and the clarity of detail shocked as much as it aroused. Slim hands, yet strong and bearing a seal ring of gold with a huge emerald eye. The papered walls of the farmhouse disappeared to be replaced by the granite and sandstone blocks of a building within the fort. He was standing in the corner, shadows falling across his face. He beckoned and the seal ring winked in the light shed by the little boat-shaped lamp. Her nostrils caught the smell of the oil-soaked wick as it burned and shed its subdued light.

This could not be for real. Doubt, like rain coursing down a window, distorted her vision. Disjointed images moved across that inner screen: red pottery, a gilded stool with scrolled ends, and a helmet, the plume of boars hair bristling Rome's defiance set aside. Weathered calves thonged with leather, a cropped head and the gleam of polished armour. Stone, timber and tack; a low bed beneath the window and a beckoning hand. She reached out to the figure waiting in the corner; fear made her withdraw.

"Relax and let go Darcy."

She tried to obey the whispered command but her stomach knotted with tension. There was something odd about Brant. He felt different, not like the man she knew. Shadows crowded the room. Back in a flash to that fort on the fell where the figure still waits in the corner, then back again in an instant and his features are illuminated by the flickering light of the candles. The bulk of the shoulders look the same, and the dark hair with a strand loosely curled around one ear. Darcy frowned and struggled to pinpoint the change. A sort of Jeckyll and Hyde feeling that grew stronger by the minute. *Like making love with a stranger.*

She stared at the face that hovered mask-like above her and saw something she did not like staring out from behind the eyes. From the kitchen came the rumble of Mab and Brock's disquiet.

"Brant?" Panting now from panic as much as exertion she placed her hands on his chest and heaved.

"What is it? What's wrong?" Brant froze in mid-thrust. He sounded bewildered, then irritation took over as the dogs continued to growl, the sound now issuing from behind the closed door as they abandoned their basket by the Aga .

"Quiet!" he snapped and they lapsed into subdued silence.

"Sorry. I thought the dogs had heard someone." Half afraid he would guess her guilty secret Darcy ran fingers that trembled slightly through his hair and thrust her body towards his urging him on. Unable to resist, Brant resumed thrusting and increased his rhythm. The figure still waited in the shadows. She reached out with her mind but was ready to recoil upon impact.

"Come on, Darcy, come on!" Brant urged in her ear. He sounded normal, yet it was still there, the strangeness that clung like a spider's web. She shivered. The room seemed darker, the shadows deeper and a glance at the fireplace showed her the flames from the smouldering logs were sickly and blue tinged. Excitement was spiced by fear. Go with it, she told herself; see if it is real. Brant. *Brant?* Confused now by mounting pleasure and a sense of change she struggled with her emotions then finally gave herself up to the pull. The warmth and softness of skin slid beneath her hand. He grunted with pleasure as her fingers ran over his shoulders and back to the base of the spine.

"Oh God!"

There was an explosion of sound and movement as she heaved him aside and the dogs scrabbled at the door with their claws and set up a frenzied barking.

ELEVEN

~

There was a blink as shadows leapt for cover then steadiness as the room recovered from shock. Darcy stumbled from the settee and hit the light switch.

"Shit! Darcy, you sure know how to time it!" Brant's voice rasped with frustration.

Ignoring his words she stood still and silent wondering how it could happen; how, even for a millisecond, the warmth and softness of skin beneath her hand could change to the coolness and hardness of metal. But it had. And there had been a faint smell of hide mingled with some pungent herbal scent she recognised but in her present state was struggling to name. Rosemary, that was it. *Rosemary for remembrance.* Isn't that what they say? Something of her fear and confusion must have shown in her face. Brant was staring at her in silence, hair damp with sweat and plastered to his forehead. She noted the flush of desire fading from chest and face, the affronted expression.

"For Chris' sakes Darcy – what the devil got into you?"

She shook her head, stunned by the uncanny aptness of this apparently innocent remark. Resisting the temptation to say *I wish I knew* she answered lamely

"The dogs – I thought they must have heard a prowler." She wanted to break the awkward silence but could think of nothing to say.

"Come here love." Brant's expression softened and he patted the vacant cushion. Clutching her disordered clothing she went and sat next to him. He placed an arm about her shoulders and drew her close. "Is it something I did – or didn't do?" he asked quietly.

On hearing the self doubt and insecurity in his voice Darcy knew she must put his mind at ease.

"Of course not."

"You would tell me?"

"Absolutely."

"So what then?"

"You'll think I've lost the plot."

"Try me."

"Okay, it's not just that place that is scary, there's something," she coloured, took a deep breath and blurted "It's more personal than that. Like –, well it keeps intruding, pulling me back, wanting something from me but I don't know what," she finished in a rush.

Brant turned to face her and took hold of her hand.

"Sorry Darcy, I just don't buy that crap about hauntings and unquiet spirits."

"Oh? So who was it taught me that bridges, stepping stones and twilight are crossing places between realities and time zones? And that the Spirit of the Land inhabits every rock, river and mountain?" she protested, pulling herself upright to give him an indignant look. "You are steeped in your Celtic past!"

He coloured slightly, coughed and smoothed down his hair.

"Whatever, as a scientist I have no doubt that the mystery of Time one day will be explained – but by people like Stephen Hawkin, Darcy – not mystics and peddlers of the paranormal."

She inched her body away from his.

"I know what I saw and felt."

"Look, you panicked, okay – convinced yourself that the mountains and isolation were something else. Most of us get a buzz from such places. Throw in a romantic ruin and the stage is set for a full-blown Heathcliff and Cathy routine!"

"Don't patronise me! It's not like that." She blinked back tears of anger and frustration.

"And I didn't really say that!" he said immediately with the rueful schoolboy smile of a man who knows he has blown it. "Hear me out, yes?" he pleaded, placing a finger over her lips, "You're due on any day now so you're also a tad hormonal."

"That's right, blame it on 'time of the month'. How typical a man-thing is that?" she blazed, in reality more incensed by this evidence that due to his baby obsession he was obviously monitoring her menstrual cycle. It felt like an intrusion into her privacy, a clinical claiming of that which rightfully belonged to her and nobody else.

"I simply mean you are more sensitive at this time, more easily upset and your judgement may be coloured by your emotions."

"There is nothing wrong with my judgement," she stated, then added "and I started this morning so that blows your theory out of the water!"

The sadness and disappointment were plain to see in his expression. The baby thing again. Don't be drawn in, she told herself, move on to something else. Fortunately it seemed Brant was of the same mind; before she could divert his attention by asking when the car would be ready he pulled her towards him again.

"I don't want you to go there again love." The quietness with which he uttered the words conveyed the depth of his concern. "Whatever the explanation, something about the place is obviously giving you grief," he continued when she failed to respond, "After all, it's not as though it's a formal assignment from Frank and you have no choice. So come on," he smiled and wound one of her curls around his finger, "forget Russell Crowe darling, real gladiators were just sad bastards intent on staying alive by butchering their mates!"

"And you're a patronising one!" she snapped, getting up from the sofa and walking to the door, as she did so pulling her robe closer to protect her nakedness. "And for the record he wasn't a gladiator, he was an officer of the legionary high command."

She stood with her hand on the door knob as a stunned silence expanded to fill the room. Noting Brant's expression of bafflement mixed with something difficult to name, she abandoned the search for a suitable excuse for her words. Further digging would only entrench her deeper into this hole. She settled on a light note saying with a forced smile:

"If I didn't know you better I might suspect you of being jealous!"

But Brant was not smiling. He made a gesture with his hand as though to push back something he could not understand.

"Sweetheart, I don't think this is funny any more."

Rather than stand and argue Darcy made a tactical retreat.

Two thoughts devastated her as she entered the kitchen to attend to Mab and Brock. Firstly how could she have known his rank with such certainty? (and devastatingly, when did 'it' become 'he'?); and secondly why had she reacted to Brant's disparaging remark with such vehemence? At a loss to answer she anchored her bathrobe in place with the tie belt and let out the dogs prior to settling them for the night. She stood for a moment listening to the muted roar of the surf beyond the cliffs whilst marvelling at a midnight sky studded with stars and hosting a hunter's moon. The sharp *ke-wick, ke-wick, ke-wick* autumnal call of the tawny owl as opposed to the more usual hooting caught her attention. Like most townies she had always assumed they made the traditional *tu-whit, tu-whoo* but Brant had taught her that the two calls were rarely heard together. He had an enviable natural wisdom, she acknowledged, the kind that ran through bone and blood, had its roots in this land and could not be learned from books. Maybe he did sense something bad about that place and she was not hearing him properly. That would explain his uncharacteristic behaviour . Suddenly she shivered as though, as her grandmother used to say, someone had walked over her grave. There would be a frost tonight. An image crept into her mind of white crested fells, walls silvered by moonlight and the slink of a wolf hunting amid the ruins for human carrion. She shivered again and calling to the dogs retreated indoors.

Her thoughts returned to those two crucial questions. It was not, she decided whilst giving Mab and Brock their supper treat of buttered rolls and dish of warm milk, simply that she had 'seen' with an inner vision a man wearing a cloak edged with the purple that denoted senatorial status. Not that she was knowledgeable about matters Roman, but that much at least was remembered from school history lessons. No, it was more than that. The presence felt during that nightmare return journey over the pass, and during their lovemaking tonight exuded the unmistakable aura of authority, the confidence and assurance of a man used to being in charge. Also the smooth metal armour suggested the body-mould type usually reserved for high ranking officers.

The second question about the force of her reaction to Brant's remark was more difficult to answer. Not from lack of an obvious reason, but more a reluctance to confront and accept her own feelings. In the end she settled or compromise. She had simply been infuriated by Brant's refusal to accept the validity of her experiences. Yes, that was it. The strength of her reaction was nothing personal, had nothing to do with loyalty or anything like it. He – 'it' she silently amended – intrigued the journalist in her, presented a mystery that cried out to be solved. Was that place still hosting his presence and if so *why*? And more to the point why was she the target? There was also an apparent connection with the Tulley case.

So where to from here? Hilldean University and her friend Caro seemed like a good place to start; they went back a long way to the time they were both freshers at Hilldean. But first of all her quarrel with Brant had to be resolved. Closing the door on the now sleeping dogs she returned to the sitting room where he was seated before the fire finishing a crossword she had started earlier.

"Nightcap?" he asked as though nothing had happened.

She decided to follow his lead and sat down next to him on the settee.

"Just a small one," she said with her head resting lightly against his shoulder.

They spoke little, neither of them referring to the incident, but the tension was palpable.

"Guess I'll make it an early night," she said eventually, finishing her drink.

Brant kissed the top of her head and murmured something about her having had quite a day but she chose to ignore this provocative comment and instead made her way upstairs.

Later, lying next to him in bed listening to his deep and regular breathing she decided upon a plan of action. Tomorrow she would have to return to Manchester and the office or Frank would be on the warpath. It was a pain, but at least it offered the opportunity to put recent events to the test. Research need not be confined to Cumbria; there were Roman remains in Lancashire. She would go on-line, choose a site to visit and judge her reactions. If they were similar, then it would prove she was somehow sensitive to Roman sites in general and there was nothing special about Mediobogdum. Of course that would also prove that dominant male presence to be a figment of her imagination. She shook her head to clear it of unwise thoughts. It would not do to dwell upon the possibility of a battle between relief and disappointment. However if she felt nothing, then it would indicate something special about Mediobogdum and her experiences there.

That would be the time to visit Caro at Hilldean University. In fact she would call the Archaeology Department the following morning and make a date; Regardless of the outcome of any fort visit, it would simply be good to see her old friend again. If anyone would know about Mediobogdum and its history it would be Caro; plus she would listen to her experiences with an open mind. Caro knew her friend and the workings of her mind well enough to accept there had to be more than mere imagination at work here. But should that not also hold true of Brant? She looked down at the shadowy form beside her, listening to the steady rhythm of his breathing and for a moment was consumed by doubt. Her feelings throughout their lovemaking and the apparent ghostly intrusion now seemed preposterous.

Then the vividness of that memory, plus the sure knowledge that she only had to mentally let go for the shadows in the corner to take on a sinister life of their own, banished doubt. How or why, she had no idea – but it had happened. But it was unfair to compare Brant's mind-set to Caro's. Due to the baby issue Brant was biased against her work in general seeing it as an obstacle to starting a family, so how much more so against a project that had become something of an obsession. Her mind balked at the word, but if her investigation was to yield anything worthwhile then honesty had to be the buzzword. So why had their intimacy apparently provoked the phenomenon?

She lay in the dark thinking the whole thing through, trying to make sense of an impossible situation. What if this entity or whatever it was had taken to coming through Brant because he was perceived as a threat? After all, Brant was trying to persuade her to stay away from Mediobogdum and this obviously did not suit. And come to think of it, what better time to intervene than when Brant was emotionally 'open' during their lovemaking, a time when his resistance was at lowest ebb? That had to be it. Either that or there was nothing there, no substance and like some pathetic romantic female with a ticking bio clock she had imagined the whole damned thing. If so that just left the other business. Well any connection with the Tulley guy would have to sit on the back burner until she returned to Cumbria. Exhausted but well satisfied with her plan Darcy drifted into sleep.

OUT OF TIME IV

~

Had it merely been a dream, a wish-fulfilment fantasy or had she really come to him in the night? Real or unreal, the memory of her warm flesh and enfolding welcome haunted him still. Inside the stables after a morning ride with Justinus during which they had passed close by the Britons' settlement, Antonius' head was filled with thoughts of an enigmatic old man and his beautiful but exasperating ward. Perhaps, he mused, patting Gaudita's neck prior to the groom rubbing her down, she was even more enigmatic than Myrddin. At times she was the feisty high-ranking female he knew who captivated and infuriated him in turn, and at others a largely invisible but strongly-felt presence that had about it an aura of strangeness. A presence not in the physical sense but an insubstantial figure tantalisingly glimpsed on occasion from the corner of his eye before it disappeared and, apart from the physical sensation of someone sharing his space, left him wondering if it had merely been a shadow. Was she using her hunting skills to soundlessly dog him? Or was it something darker and more sinister, an ancient and forbidden craft – if indeed it had anything to do with her at all? However no matter how intriguing those thoughts may be, more pressing matters awaited his attention. Leaving Justinus in charge, he left the stables and walked over to the praetorium.

And a poky hole it was too. He must think of getting a new wing built he mused as he stripped, poured hot water from the ewer into the bowl laid ready for him, and changed into formal uniform. Essential if he was to be confined to quarters for weeks on end during a winter when the fort would doubtless be snow and ice blocked for much of the time. Piles and frostbite remember! He smiled wryly; he had sworn to be away before first snow, but now the urgency seemed to have gone out of it, which of course had nothing to do with Myrddin's ward. It would give the men something constructive to do, provide a change from routine fatigues, repairs and maintenance – a monotony only relieved by a sprinkling of civic duties at Glannaventa some eight miles distant on the west coast. He would have to put in a courtesy appearance there soon, he thought reluctantly. Soon, as ice and snow choked valley and gully, even the flow of merchants and baggage that had to be checked would come to a halt. Boredom was bad for soldiers. There was nothing like action for honing the edge of a garrison, and if he was any kind of a judge, they would be seeing some before the year was out. But now to roast that pig Marcellus. he thought, leaving for the Principia.

He was seated at the table in his reception room and did not have long to wait before the knock at the door.
"Enter."
The guard pushed open the door then stood back at attention as Marcellus entered before closing the door behind the prefect. Antonius carried on writing and imagined he could hear the *thud-thud-thud* of the prefect's heartbeats. At length he set down his stylus, pushed aside the wax tablet and folding his arms, sat back on his seat.
"I've finished my inspection Marcellus. I imagine you know why I have sent for you."
Marcellus assumed an expression of surprised innocence.
"No legatus, I'm sorry."
"You will be."
"I beg your pardon sir?" Marcellus managed to look puzzled and affronted at the same time.
"The contents of the granaries do not tally with the adjutant's records." Antonius smiled unpleasantly as he picked up a knife, a

manicurist's tool shorter than a stylus with a handle inlaid with mother-of-pearl and a blade forged from silver. "I am sure you can explain why that is." He carefully pared the nail of his forefinger whilst speaking.

Marcellus ran his tongue over lips that were dry. "Ah yes, the clerical errors. I've had two clerks placed on the punishment roster."

"Good, a flogging should make them more careful – may even loosen their tongues. If not I can always have them staked out over the precipice. I hear ravens make short work of a man's eyeballs."

He looked slyly up at Marcellus, noting the sudden pallor of his cheeks and the beads of sweat breaking out along his lower lip. "But what about you, Marcellus? Spare me that trouble and I may be persuaded to deal more leniently with you."

"Me sir? Surely you don't blame me for their carelessness?"

"Enough of games!" he tossed aside the knife. "Confess or take their place."

Picking up a small wooden mallet he reached up to strike the copper gong that hung on the wall at his elbow.

"No wait!" Marcellus' hand as he reached out was trembling and his complexion turned a jaundiced yellow. "It's not easy keeping men happy in this gods-forsaken hole. I well, I pretended not to see," he finished on a scarcely audible rush.

"And to what exactly, were you blind?"

"Oh, an amphora here, a side of boar or salt beef there." Marcellus shrugged in a vain attempt at indifference.

"Two amphorae, 3 goats cheeses, a side of beef and one of boar – and that last month alone. I know exactly what you stole from Rome!" Antonius snapped.

Marcellus now looked as though he might faint with fear.

"I never saw it as cheating Rome!"

"You see yourself above Rome's jurisdiction then?"

"Of course not – but things are different out here. I swear I took nothing for myself, sir. Some of these men have been out here for years and feel forgotten by Rome. I suppose they saw it as their due – a small bonus."

"Hardly small! It sounds as though they had your sympathy, prefect."

Marcellus, though sweating profusely and obviously afraid, looked him in the eye.

"To a degree sir, yes." he said courageously, nodding curtly

"I see."

And now to the issue proper.

"And the weapon stores, Marcellus – what of those?" he prompted with deceptive mildness.

"With respect sir, I don't know what you are talking about."

The sound of Antonius' chair scraping the tiled floor as he rose sounded very loud in the sudden and ominous silence.

"I am talking of stolen weapons – and *treason.*"

He moved out from behind the table whilst drawing his sword. "To whom were they sold? The Brigantes? Who are your contacts?" he snapped, the tip of his sword dimpling Marcellus' throat.

Marcellus swallowed with difficulty.

"I know nothing of stolen weapons."

"Names – and quick!"

"I am innocent!"

"And ready to have it tortured out of you, then die?"

Marcellus drew himself upright and the movement, though slight, brought a pinprick of blood welling to the surface.

"No man would wish that, but I cannot tell you what I don't know," He said with difficulty as Antonius pressed a little harder and the red beads dripped from the tip of the sword.

Antonius stared him in the eye for a long moment. Marcellus met his gaze without flinching.

"I believe you," Antonius said at last, lowering the sword.

Marcellus closed his eyes and leaned against the wall, his breath escaping on a long sigh. Antonius returned to his seat behind the table and studied Marcellus' record in silence.

"You've been a bloody fool Marcellus," he said at last.

"I know sir." He stood with his hand to his throat, blood trickling through his fingers.

"You may not be a traitor, but there is still the matter of the missing provisions. What am I to do with you on that score?"

Marcellus grimaced and shook his head.

"I don't much fancy being fodder for ravens sir!"

"I'm sure you don't." Antonius turned his head and coughed to hide a flicker of amusement.

"I suppose I'll be kicked out of the army."

"Your offence certainly warrants it." He laid his hands on the table and looked thoughtfully at the distraught prefect. "Can you give any good reason why you should not be?"

"No, sir." Marcellus shook his head then stared at the floor. "Only that I would give my life for the chance to serve you and prove my loyalty – but it's too late now."

Antonius spread his fingers and appeared to contemplate them, then spoke quietly as though to himself. "Good record. First offence. A motive of loyalty to the men over personal gain. Obvious remorse. I suppose there is room for lenience."

"Sir?" Marcellus' head shot up as he dared hope.

"Right. I have reached my decision." After letting the prefect sweat for a few minutes longer, Antonius pushed aside the military record. "I am making you personally responsible for the granary and all provisions. Any more illegal bonuses and you take the rap regardless of the culprit, understand?"

"Yes legatus, fully." Marcellus looked as though he could scarce believe what he heard.

"As for the weapons business, you're to keep eyes and ears open and mouth shut. The culprits must think their activities still go undetected. Report anything suspicious directly to me. If there are traitors at Mediobogdum, I want to know who they are and who they are dealing with on the outside. A chance to prove your loyalty and serve me, Marcellus, but know this – foul up, and there won't be another."

Marcellus looked dazed. "I'm to keep my command?"

"That's up to you. Let me down and I'll have your balls on a platter."

"If I let you down sir, there will be no need. I'll hug my sword."

"Quite right – no point in castrating a corpse," Antonius said dryly. "Now get out of here, and set your men to rights."

"Thank you, sir." Marcellus gave a nervous smile and saluted with fervour before backing respectfully to the door.

He was taking a risk, Antonius acknowledged, but better to have this wily man under obligation and working for him under cover. As the door closed behind the prefect, Antonius reflected on what a good feeling it was to watch a man step back from ruin and smile.

Later, alone in the praetorium having dined and been waited on by the elderly veteran Gaeus he rose from his couch and stood by the window gazing up at scudding clouds, a myriad stars and a sickle moon that was sometimes hidden and sometimes shedding its light over buildings, roads and ramparts. The wind whipped the praetorium, howling at the windows and shrieking around the eaves. The flame of the lamp dipped and flared alternately in the draught from door and window. For a second it seemed he fancied he could hear the plaintive strains of a long-ago song sung to him by his mother, but perhaps it was just the wind sighing at the windows.

TWELVE

~

Darcy sang along softly to herself then switched off the radio as the car slid into the parking space, then turned off the ignition. Given the restrictions of an extended lunch hour begged from Frank, Ribchester was close enough to Manchester to fit Darcy's available window and therefore chosen for this reason rather than for the quality of its Roman remains. According to the on-line information excavation had revealed the base of a granary, but apart from this the remains were now under turf and only the contours and undulations of the land within a curve of the River Ribble gave any clue to their presence. In contrast to the austere splendour and remoteness of Mediobogdum, the narrow streets hosted a plethora of tea and gift shops all displaying 'Roman' themed souvenirs thus lending a certain atmosphere to the place. So, would she react to it at all? Darcy breathed deeply and emptied her mind of preconceptions as she strolled around the site prior to entering the museum.

That evening she stayed late at the office to make up the extra time. So engrossed was she in checking off the copy of an interview with a survivor of the underground terrorist blast that she jumped as the door was suddenly pushed open.

"Got no home to go to?"

"Nearly through Frank. Scary stuff, suicide bombers – makes you wonder where it will all end. How did it get like this?"

"Religious fanatics have always been with us; technology just makes them more visible and spectacular."

"And deadly," Darcy commented dryly. "But I wonder, is it down to religion, or political culture or simple lust for power?"

"You can't separate them out – and there's no such thing as a simple anything! There are always contributing factors and often one is used as justification for the other." Frank crossed to her desk and picked up the first couple of sheets of copy and began to scan the lines of script.

"You think religion is a cover for self-seeking?" Darcy asked frowing.

"Only by some of it's extremists." He took a chair from by the wall, swung it round and sat astride it cowboy style then finished reading the first sheet before continuing "And even then it's not that clear-cut, it gets mixed up with appeasement of prejudice and hanging on to power. Take Catholic Mary – responsible for crisping protestants, or the Jesuits responsible for the tortures of the Inquisition, or the persecution of the Cathars etc, etc, – need I go on? But in my opinion that's not what we are dealing with today," he went on without waiting for her reply.

Frank's cigar bobbed up and down as he got into his stride. "Your Romans now, they were pretty tolerant of another man's religion. Know that?" he asked removing the stub from his mouth and pointing it at Darcy.

"Er, no." Taken by surprise Darcy stared at him, taken aback by the aptness of the comment given her earlier trip to the Roman site at Ribchester, albeit one which had left her emotionally intact.

"Oh aye. They were pretty damn savvy; knew with the right kind of inducement you could change a man's loyalty and eating habits but belief in his gods ran in his veins and that was best left alone."

"That right?" Darcy played it cautious; Frank never brought up a subject without good reason.

"Suppose you heard the Tulley guy escaped."

And here it comes. Darcy nodded, deciding to keep quiet about her most recent and abortive visit to Barrenber Ground.

80

"Okay." Frank rose, cocked his leg back over the seat and pushed the chair away then dropped the sheets of copy onto her desk. "That's good stuff. Go interview the girlfriend tomorrow and write it up – then I suppose you could do a couple of days on the Tulley case."

She knew where he was coming from. The 'girlfriend' referred not to the survivor but the partner of one of the suicide bombers whose identity had just come to light. Frank was after an insight piece into how friends and family saw the bomber; the intimate profile that often seemed at odds with the stereotype portrayed by headlines that by their nature focused on actions rather than personalities. The Tulley case was to be her reward. "Thanks, Frank."

"Just come up with the goods Darcy."

"Do my best!" she quipped.

"You better – or it gets ditched. Now get off home before I offer to take you for a drink," he said gruffly, not looking at her as he made for the door.

Back at her pad she put aside the worries about Frank and how best to handle the problem of his intentions that had occupied her on the drive from the city centre, and made a mug of coffee intending to enjoy ten minutes chill time before rustling up a quick meal. The shrilling of the telephone came over as an unwarranted interruption, even more so when she answered the summons to discover that Brant was on his way to the flat. She had managed to keep the irritation from her voice when he explained the car had not been ready until around four that afternoon, so rather than drive overnight he was breaking the journey to London as it was an opportunity to spend another night together. Which was great, she told herself whilst rummaging through fridge and cupboards to see what could be rustled up. It was just that she needed a little space to clear her mind and get it back into working gear for the following day and her interview with the bomber's partner, which after all was serious stuff. Also it would prevent her brooding over the fact that Ribchester had invoked an absolutely nil emotional response which left the ball squarely in the courtyard of Mediobogdum. Now that did provoke response but one she would rather not confront at present.

She whisked up a soufflé then made a start on mushrooms stuffed with chopped almonds, red pepper and onion sautéed in garlic butter. Glancing at the clock she decided there was time to whip up a dessert of crêpes with crème de Grand Marnier. The sophistication of the proposed dinner had nothing to do with a guilt trip about her initial reaction to Brant's call, she told herself whilst sifting flour and chopping vegetables, and everything to do with making his sleep-over a bit special. He would be expecting either to dine out or be given a freezer dinner. Besides all this culinary activity left no time for brooding on the scary fact that today's non event at Ribchester seemed to support the possibility of a green-eyed commander from ancient Rome being able in some inexplicable way to impact upon her life.

Despite this frenzy of culinary activity images of Ribchester arose as she chopped onions and wiped tears from her eyes: the replica of the silver parade helmet found in a mud bank of the Ribble being the most memorable. The emptiness of the holes where eyes had once looked out had been slightly disturbing but that was all. Stones, inscriptions and fragments of everyday life – all very interesting of course, but well, *dead,* and even more so when compared with the palpable buzz in the air at Mediobogdum where energy still lurked within its ancient walls. Except for the dicing game, she conceded briskly stuffing mushrooms and glancing at the clock. That at least had evoked real men, patrolling ramparts in all weathers, sustained by thoughts of a mug of ale and a gambling session with their mates. But that was about it. Ribchester lay beneath a shroud of turf and rural serenity and did not, she reflected ruefully as she licked her fingers and reached for a cloth, raise so much as a solitary goose bump. In fact the interview with Jamila had disturbed her more.

The fact that the girlfriend of the suicide bomber now had a name, and therefore a personality like herself or any other had given her a whole new take on the situation. This was not now some anonymous, evil woman who in line with public perception 'must have known what he was up to' and therefore knowingly harboured a mass murderer, but probably a woman devastated both by losing the man she so obviously loved and the awareness that he had a secret life apart from herself that had resulted in many innocent and horrific deaths. I know what that feels like, Darcy thought soberly, recalling her devastation during the St. Gildas Man project when it seemed Brant must be in with an elite enclave of powerful conspirators and assassins. Sadly though, Jamila would never know the relief and joy of discovering her partner was not a traitor but an undercover agent. From information just received, Darcy didn't mind betting that the woman knew nothing of his deadly activities and intent.

If she still felt the same after interviewing her, it meant a controversial piece had to be written and gotten past Frank. Not that he wouldn't agree with her view, but he was not into losing readers or the paper being identified with radicalism and sympathy with a terrorist's girlfriend would inevitably be interpreted by many as sympathy with the terrorist. However pack mentality had not so far dictated her ethics and it was not going to do so now. The story would have to be told as it was, but not tonight. Years of practice had enabled her to flick the emotional switch to the 'off' position on returning home, if not with ease and not completely, then at least with partial success, otherwise all too often impartiality would fall victim to personal involvement.

One thing at Ribchester had made an impact, Darcy recalled, whipping up the soufflé mixture. She smiled to herself now as she stacked used crockery in the dish washer and recalled the mural that stretched the length of one wall at the military museum. It showed soldiers seated in the latrine having a sociable chat and holding their little sponges on sticks in lieu of toilet paper. How civilised: central heating, loos and heated baths. She had imagined those remote soldiers of the Empire disappearing into the woods armed with a shovel. Suddenly the thought occurred as she placed the mushrooms in the skillet that these were not shadows lost in time but real people and individuals in their own right. She thought then of the presence that haunted her: would knowing his name have the same potent effect? The sudden flashback of the red mist experienced in the car on the return journey from Mediobogdum and first witnessed in the circular bathhouse outside the main fort, took her by surprise.

She frowned and blinked hard then looked again at the cooker. There was no mistake: the steam arising from the pans on the hob had taken on a reddish tinge. Tilting and raising her head she sniffed the air as Mab and Brock might do on catching the scent of a rabbit. Her frown deepened; added to the pungency of basil and garlic from the dishes being cooked were the scents of thyme and lavender spiked with clove. Her ears resounded with strident laughter and the hum of conversation, the sounds muted and distorted as though they reached her through a long tunnel. Instinctively she stepped back and shook her head. At the heart of the red steam that was slowly spreading to fill the kitchen she caught glimpses of naked male bodies some dripping water, others glistening with oil.

Suddenly the bath house scene dissolved and reformed before her eyes into a terrifying inferno. Flames licked at blackened timbers causing them to come crashing down so that she instinctively ducked to avoid being crushed. Her body began to tremble and nausea gagged her throat as tendrils of smoke crept across the room and invaded her body through mouth and nostril. Wracked by coughing she moved further back towards the door but then a familiar paralysis struck. Impotently she strained every muscle in order to flee but was unable to move or call out for help. A chill entered her body as a dreaded presence pressed against it and invaded her mind and spirit.

Anger. Anger that beat against her in waves of frustration. The hissing of steam grew louder in her ears, the sound of a pressure valve about to blow beneath unbearable pressure.

Existo it hissed, and again *existo!*

A scream was wrenched from her throat as flames rose at the window, blackening and melting the Venetian blind before licking their way up the adjacent wall.

Existo! Existo!

Despite her meagre knowledge of Latin, the meaning of that malevolent hiss was unmistakably clear. Eyes wide with terror she watched as the flames rose higher and threatened to engulf the kitchen.

84

"No! No You do *not* exist!"

The energy of that illogical cry carried her forward and out of the grip of whatever held her in thrall. She blinked hard several times to dispel the image and made a dive for the hob intending to turn off the gas. A second scream ripped through the kitchen as a flame made contact and seared the tender under-surface of her forearm. Tears of pain and fear blurred her vision as she lunged for the heat control and snapped it to the 'off' position. With amazing rapidity the flames at window and cooker disappeared. The remaining cloud of smoke lost its reddish tinge and turned a menacing black. With the danger of fire extinguished the relatively minor threat of culinary disaster acted as an antidote to shock and prodded her into action. Grabbing a tea cloth from the table she threw it over the pan of mushrooms, whipped it off the hob and dropped it onto the drainer. Close to tears she surveyed the blackened contents of the pan then stared in disbelief as the plume of smoke snaked through the open window and realisation struck. Where there had previously been a blackened and twisted blind with melting slats there was a perfectly normal one displaying no evidence of fire. She gazed around in disbelief: instead of a scorched and smoke-grimed wall at the side of the window and behind the cooker there were only perfectly clean tiles. She shook her head in disbelief and suddenly weak, sank to her knees on the floor.

How long had she knelt there? It seemed like seconds but must be longer. Fears about delusions and mental breakdown kept her there, until the trivial concerns of normality once again came to the rescue. The soufflé! She rushed to the oven and whipped out the dish in the nick of time and placed it on the surface as gently as her shaking hands would allow. The ominous bubble and sizzle of sauce sticking to pan sent her rushing back to the hob armed with a wooden spoon. Comfort came from knowing she was functioning normally and obviously was not after all on the brink of a breakdown. Nevertheless, coming as it did in the midst of this rescue operation, the sound of the front door opening and closing, then Brant's voice calling her name brought her once more to the brink of tears. She had planned to have a delicious meal ready and waiting before showering and slipping into something slinky, and now the evening was ruined.

Happily it turned out not to be so. With one glance Brant took in the scene, gave her a massive hug, pushed a glass of wine into her hand and ordered her to drink it whilst he attended the burn on her arm with an aloe vera dressing which he then protected by means of a plastic food bag secured in place with freezer tape. This done he sent her off to the bathroom with instructions to relax in a soothing tub whilst he removed the debris and dished up the surviving food.

They ended up laughing over the mushrooms, with Brant gallantly vowing he really wasn't that keen on them anyway, was partial to deflated soufflé and that the rest of the meal was a triumph. Darcy allowed him to think that the burn on her arm was due to carelessness, and he was obviously assuming her shaken and subdued demeanour was due to the kitchen drama. With instinctive wisdom Darcy decided not to disillusion him. More stress would inevitably arise from relating her experience of fires that left no visible trace, steamy ancient baths, and the oiled and naked bodies of long-dead Roman soldiers.

THIRTEEN

~

Later, seated in the lounge with what was left of the wine, they swapped updates on their day.

"So how did it go?" Brant asked, his expression unfathomable as she disclosed her trip to Ribchester and hinted at the reason behind it.

"Nothing to report really." She did relate the details of the latrine mural and amused him with her witty comments, but sensed the disapproval behind the apparently benign interest.

"So, a waste of time then?"

"Not really." She sipped her wine, taking her time and deliberating over how much to disclose.

"Oh?"

"Well," she said carefully as Brant raised his eyebrows and waited in silence for her explanation, "It made Mediobogdum seem more real, as an active fort I mean, manned by real people. And in an odd way what happened to me there seems less crazy and more acceptable."

Brant's expression was now definitely closed, his voice cool.

"How come?"

"Not sure, a knock-on effect I guess. I got to thinking about the many accounts of sightings – some of them accepted by respected historians – of so-called phantom armies, or individual soldiers who had died a violent death, for example in both World Wars. See where

I'm coming from now? Then there's the famous story about the house haunted by one of Cromwell's men; the phantom army of Souter Fell near Keswick; and much more interesting to me, the legionaries visible from the knee up as they march along the ancient floor level at York on the site of the Roman fortress. The present floor is several feet higher than the original of course."

"You are obviously still into your research," he observed after a moment of silence during which the ticking of the grandfather clock and the crackling of the logs in the grate sounded louder than normal.

"Meaning?" Darcy frowned despite efforts to hide her irritation.

"I hoped tonight's dinner was by way of celebrating the end of that assignment."

"It's just nice to go special now and then," she said shrugging non-commitedly.

Suddenly leaning forward he pulled her to him and held her close.

"I worry about this one Darcy; I don't like the idea of you wandering around that place on your own. You are putting yourself at risk, especially with that deranged Tulley guy loose in the area."

"But he's a solid problem, so one you can handle," she quipped in his ear.

"Don't be flippant please Darcy," he said stiffly, leaning forward to pick up the late edition of the *Manchester News* from the coffee table where Darcy had dropped it on her return from the office.

"Lighten up sweetheart; besides, I haven't said I'll go back."

"But you will."

There was a finality and grimness about his words that stirred the hairs at the nape of her neck.

"Okay look, it's obvious to me you are not going to drop this thing whether I like it or not." He folded the newspaper again without reading it and dropped it back onto the table before swivelling round to face her and continued before she could protest: "so if I offer to help – or at worst suspend disbelief and support your efforts instead of giving you earache about that place – will you agree to at least consider starting a family in say a year's time?"

Darcy scanned his face in silence before replying. Was Brant's suggestion emotional blackmail – or simply a practical solution to an issue that threatened the stability of their marriage? Ruling out the former suspicion as unworthy, she nodded her head in agreement.

"We have a deal?"

She nodded again.

"Promise?"

"I promise to seriously consider it," she said cautiously.

"That's all I ask."

"Okay, we have a deal." Darcy smiled and returned his kiss to seal the bargain. "So how can you help?"

"I only said I would try."

"You must have something in mind."

Brant settled back against the cushions of the settee and looked thoughtful.

"Okay," he said at last, "is there any sort of pattern emerging? Say, time of day, location or any conditions that seem to trigger the phenomena you described?"

Darcy frowned as she recalled the various incidents. They had occurred both during the day and night; at their farmhouse on the cliffs and at Mediobogdum itself of course, but also here at the flat, and she gave an involuntary shudder on recollecting the initial episode with the mirror and tonight's horrific scene in the kitchen so that Brant leaned forward to squeeze her hand. The flashbacks and accompanying paralysis had at times occurred whilst she was consciously trying to make sense of the mystery, but had also arisen spontaneously, like when they were making love.

"Not really," she said slowly, then added, "Oh, except for one."

"And that is?"

"Red. The colour red." She gave his a hand a squeeze to demonstrate her appreciation of his efforts to understand and reassure.

Hesitantly Darcy recounted the various manifestations, from that first deposit of red earth on the carpet the night of the mirror image, through to the drama in the kitchen that very evening but confining her account to the images in the billows of scarlet steam, thus omitting the more scary and incredible details for fear of Brant retracting his promise to help out of concern for her safety.

"Okay," he said slowly, watching her face intently as though picking up on her attempts to play the whole thing down. "So first window we both get, we go to the observatory, right?"

"To do what?"

"Look at a few things."

"Like what?" she persisted, intensely curious now and aware of a burgeoning sense of excitement.

"Not sure yet." Not to be moved, he shook his head.

Sensing Brant's misgivings about the wisdom of making this offer, Darcy refrained from pressing him further for fear he might retract.

"Time for bed, I think," he said getting up abruptly and leaving the room. Realising she was exhausted from her ordeal, Darcy followed him to the bedroom.

Despite exhaustion sleep kept slipping from her grasp like a bar of soap in a bath tub. She lay in the darkness listening to the steady rise and fall of Brant's breathing that told her he was already asleep. Why is it, she thought half irritated, half amused, that we women lie awake fretting and gnawing over emotional problems whilst men flick some magic switch and promptly fall asleep? She shivered and pulled the duvet up around her chin. The temperature in the room had dropped. A glance at the illuminated digital display on the clock told her the heating was not set to go off for another hour. It wasn't just cold; the room had an unpleasantness about it. The atmosphere felt charged.

Don't move, she told herself biting her lower lip, just lie still and listen. There was nothing to hear but Brant's breathing, and now her own, loud and irregular in her ears. Her eyes ached from straining to peer into the shadows cast by wardrobe and dressing table due to the orangey glow from the streetlamps beyond the window. Involuntarily her stomach contracted and her face and hands turned clammy. Something was crawling over her skin with a touch as light as the wind up there in the mountains. She could not breathe, felt about to suffocate. It was no use struggling; despite straining her limbs would not move in response to her will. Then conscious thought ceased. Throw the mind out of gear and let it run free – you know you can, she told herself.

A shutter clicked open. Only long enough to allow her to 'feel' hair of bronze, the sharp angles of nose and jaw, the hardness of metal and softness of fine cloth and leather. Her mind traced the line of a smile that chilled. Fear switched her back again and the shutter closed. He is here, was her only thought. The darkness opened up revealing the brink of a vortex, a whirlwind of ice and fire that was sucking her down to its centre. The humming inside her head sharpened to a whine. Her forehead hurt, seemed about to burst. *Punishment by sound.* That was how it felt. The penalty for staying away, for failing to comply with the dictates of this terrible will.

Scream for Brant.

Non licet

She gasped, sensing without fully understanding the words that her intention had somehow been picked up and forbidden. Needlessly, because when she opened her mouth to disobey no sound emerged. A lump of ice lodged in her solar plexus, emitting ripples of fear and chilling the whole of her body. Brant was only inches away yet might as well not be there, powerless as she was to alert him to her plight. Her heart hammered in her chest and her scalp crawled. Then the whispering began. Just odd words, disjointed and garbled as though reaching her through some distant scrambler but not totally devoid of sense. Contrary to all logic she knew what was being said. One word she did know and it was reapeated:

Veni, veni!

As before, up there at Mediobogdum, she was being called back and frustration at her rejection, and failure to return, was all too clear. Yet from what – or whom – was she retreating?

Momentarily curiosity overcame fear. Inexplicable though it was she knew the words inside her mind were uttered in Latin, but not the language of the classroom. She had retained enough from far-off school days to establish that fact despite her abysmal performance in

91

that department. It was a sophisticated and probably ancient form with a curious intonation that must be regional. Regardless of her inability to translate more than the odd intermittent word, understanding was instant as meaning transcended words. It was as though, by some mysterious meeting of minds, that she shared access to a universal language. A moment's silence then more disjointed phrases, spoken too fast and furiously for her to distinguish anything other than the emotional content of frustration. Terrified for both her sanity and safety nonetheless she tried to communicate, focusing on feelings instead of words, conveying a sense of outrage at being violated and held captive, and a fierce desire to be released.

It seemed the entity that gripped her had other ideas. Down, down she sank, into the eye of the hurricane where the cacophony of anger ceased. She was an island floating on a sensuous sea of womb-like warmth and silence. Her limbs, though still incapable of movement, felt heavy and sank into the mattress. The tactics changed. There was a nucleus of heat glowing deep in her belly, a familiar warmth so that her eyes flew open in shock. Not for long: her eyelids were weighted with sensuality. Spasms of emotion shuddered through her as the warmth intensified. Her womb began to melt and heat spread outward in ripples that ran the length of her body, reaching her extremities so that even her fingers tingled with desire. Every sense seemed heightened and supernormal. Waves of pleasure engulfed her, washing away resistance with an intensity that bordered on pain.

And there was the knowing, the sense of a love that was overpowering because sweetness and joy were spiked with poignancy. It was all there: the sorrow of parting; the scent of earth and the waxed lilies of death. Insights fluttered like bats against window panes before veering off again into the dark. Jumbled and out of sequence as though Time itself had no sensible meaning. Hair the colour of bracken darkly bronzed by the frosts of autumn; an unaccustomed smile; a ringed hand; the red of berries; the blue of forget-me-nots. She moaned softly as her heart felt about to burst. Silent tears of emotion ran down her cheeks as invisible fingers reached inside to touch her at the centre.

This was intimacy as never before. A steady climb, as when Brant was taking her up to climax only multiplied a thousand times. Impossible to cope with; impossible to resist. *But there is nobody here!* That was just it, no *body.* No hands cupping her breasts, no legs entwining hers, no phallus with which to thrust yet the effect was the same. The spiral screwed tighter and she was drawn up and out of her body in the way of a cork from a bottle of wine. This was like nothing in this world: no touch, no metal, no leather, no skin or bone and *no stranger.* Not any more since this touching of essence. She could almost reach out and touch the hands, the hair and a face from which the lines of severity had temporarily been erased. Silent tears coursed down her cheeks. She was floating away from her self, from Brant and the mediocrity of life. Up and up towards implosion as volts of power screamed electric blue along her nerves. *One could die of a love like this.*

OUT OF TIME V

~

The fragrance of the steam infused with frankincense, rosemary and cedarwood was having its soporific effect. It swirled around the caldarium and also inside his head. As the heat of the hot room opened his pores allowing the day's grime and dross to escape in runnels of sweat, so the herbs opened his heart and mind, releasing bitterness at this uncivilised posting and the brutal role he may be forced to play, and momentarily filling his being with grace. Justinus and the bath house were receding. Closing his eyes he was back in the glade: she is seated upon a rock singing. A breeze stirs the leaves and sunlight dapples the forest floor. He holds out his hand. *Cara, Cara,* he murmurs and moans softly. But she freezes like a startled doe then leaps from the rock, her eyes blazing hate before she turns and melts into the green-shaded gloom. His muscles tense with frustration and anger at her refusal to accept his advances and pay due respect.

"Are you all right sir?"

He blinked and looked around him in an attempt to clear his mind, then at Justinus who was watching him with concern.

"I must have drifted off – it's been a tedious day."

"So you've given Marcellus a second chance?"

Antonius wiped the sweat from his face with a white linen towel.

"He's learned his lesson, realises how much he almost lost. Punishment for the sake of it is sterile."

"But can you be sure…?"

"Marcellus is a misguided fool not a traitor," Antonius interrupted. "There is something in what he says about Rome's neglect of the men who keep her furthest outposts safe."

"That does not excuse stealing." Justinus was frowning and obviously not in sympathy with his superior's lenient attitude.

"No, but the powers that be are not blameless in forcing him to that action. What other recourse did they have? Rome can be a remarkably deaf old lady when she chooses! And he found the courage to speak up for his men." Antonius replied in a tone designed to discourage further questioning of his decision. "Besides the pilfering was always secondary. There is much more at stake here – I sense the stink of treason! Marcellus is now under obligation to me; that makes him useful."

"As a spy?"

"Precisely. Now, enough – last one in the cold plunge sits with Rufinus and hears his endless duty list and report!"

Later he lay on his bed in the praetorium and smiled in his sleep. She was giving in; the fight was going out of her and he could feel her limbs relaxing, her body responding to his lips, his hands – and any moment now she would yield her secret warmth to his manhood. *Wolf-spit!* He cursed and his body jerked in shock as a wild screech interrupted the delicious dream; a vision so real that at first he could not make sense of his surroundings. Why had she screamed? He pulled himself up against the cushions and tried to focus on the moonbeam that striped the winter-covering of animal skins. Did she not realise who he was and the honour of being chosen? He started as a second shriek ripped through the silence and a white shape, wings outspread, glided past the window. Only the ghost owl. *Besotted fool!* He shook his head to clear it of fantasy. He needed a breath of air and in any case, sleep for the time being had fled.

"Easy soldier!" He spoke quietly on approaching the sentry standing guard on the rampart.

"Maximus," he gave the password of the day when courteously challenged by the man who had obviously recognised him as he mounted the wooden steps.

"All's well?" he routinely inquired.

"Aye, legatus."

"Good. I need some air and space to think."

"Very good, sir."

The sentry saluted and obviously taking the hint, moved along the rampart to his counterpart at the western tower leaving his commander alone. Antonius stood for while contemplating the moon-swilled wilderness of harsh beauty. The moon was almost at the full and the night was clear but for a few drifting clouds, affording a breathtaking view of fells and valley. Beneath the chill of bleached moonlight the mountains retreated into paleness and mystery. They seemed to him now as he wrapped his cloak closer around him against the cold remote and aloof in age and wisdom, shoulders hunched as they bore the weight of the midnight sky. The sprawl of Mediobogdum seemed to him an intrusion, an affront to their dignity.

She also intrudes – and often affronts – he thought, returning to the reason for his nocturnal wandering. In the principia, his own quarters, the bath house even, and yes, in his bed. Everywhere a sense of her presence. And often a breath of perfume or snatch of song teased his senses to drive him insane. She walked through his dreams without so much as a nod or 'a by-your-leave, sir'. He smiled at the thought. In fact he was growing so used to her presence that only her absence was remarkable. Then he would feel empty, wonder what was missing and there would be no rest until she returned. Madness to feel so, but true. Yet always she ignored or at best resisted him.

A distant chilling yet somehow incredibly poignant howl broke his reverie. A wolf calling to its pack, the sound echoing mournfully through the forest down in the valley and hanging on the night air before trailing away like the smoke from a spent lamp. Something within stirred uneasily: the intuition born of a long military career and an intuitive mother. The leader of the local tribe was behind his sense of unease. According to his spies, the Brigante warrior was a powerful presence in the area. Any uprising and he would have a hand in it for sure. Even more worrying were rumours of his betrothal to Rowana. Personal feelings aside, this could make her vulnerable should Rome order a campaign of subjugation. He scrutinised ravine and valley but nothing stirred in the ghostly light. No threat of danger tonight, he guessed. Turning he signalled to the sentry that he was departing. After a brief exchange and assurances from the sentry that all was well he left the ramparts.

He strode back to his quarters and entered in the hope that sleep would now find and claim him. Picking up the little oval lamp, his head turned warily; shadows leapt about the walls as he walked back to his bed. No doubt Marcellus had provided his men with an amphora of olive oil for their winter lamps! he thought ironically, setting it down on the small table by his bed. But who was she, this woman who haunted his dreams? It must be Rowana, but why did she appear to change and be surrounded by strangeness? If it was just a dream then surely he would see her as he expected, as her normal self. He leaned forward to extinguish the flame then in view of his dark thoughts, left it burning. Was she playing with his mind, using perhaps druidical arts to influence his thoughts from a distance? She would have to learn the folly of playing games at his expense. Soon he would let her know who he was in no uncertain terms, and compel an acknowledgement from her, if only in the world of dreams.

FOURTEEN

~

One could die of a love like this... even if it was only in dreams.

That thought and the accompanying jolt of fear intruded. She hovered, faltered in flight and began to plummet. Waves of shock, anguish and finally his anger hit and sent her hurtling down in search of safety. Down, down, down and then a shudder as on impact. As he receded her voice returned.

"Brant! Brant!"

"What is it? What's the matter sweetheart?" Brant grunted and half-turned.

Suddenly she knew she could not tell him.

"Nothing. I'm okay, just a dream," she said softly, holding her breath whilst willing him not to fully awake. The strangeness had passed, she was grounded again by the sound of his voice, and in any case how could she hope to explain? She released her breath on a long sigh of relief as he grunted reassurance and lapsed back into sleep. There came an overwhelming desire to be alone, to think things through in solitude. Taking care not to disturb Brant she slipped out of bed and crept to the small dressing room that doubled as her study.

She sat at the desk, head in hands and thought of Brant. The sense of guilt made no sense; it was crazy to feel little better than a whore. How could she be unfaithful with someone who did not exist? But if that was true it left only insanity. A classic "Catch 22" situation if ever there was one. From force of habit she picked up a pen and began to doodle on the empty page of her notepad. Aimless doodles on paper and endless circles inside her head. Weariness flooded her body. Glancing at the clock she saw it was almost 2a.m. The effort to move was too great. Easier by far to slump in the chair and close her eyes. The mystery of who was haunting her and what it was they wanted went round and round her brain. *Who are you? Who are you?* The question slipped into the circuit, a repetitive loop lulling her almost but not quite to sleep. Somewhere in the night a cat yowled and seconds later a dog barked in response and a milk bottle rolled and chinked against stone. Startled she sat upright, the pen dropping from her grasp to roll across the floor. She stared in disbelief at the sheet of paper illuminated by a circle of light from the angled desk lamp.

S. TACITUS ANTONIUS

The letters sprawled boldly across the otherwise empty page.

FIFTEEN

~

Students of every imaginable age, colour and creed thronged the tree-lined walks of Hilldean University campus as they jostled their way to lecture or seminar, hurrying down walkways lined with poplars, the leaves whispering and flirting their silver undersides in the breeze. Others conspired to block their passage by chattering in groups, their laughter staining white the crisp autumnal air as jokes were told, missed lectures confessed, or bouts of binge drinking bragged. Others squatted on the flight of wide steps that ran arena fashion above and around The Square. Here they chatted and drank coffee or coke from cardboard cups, then dropped them into a waste bin before sauntering off down one of the four avenues that led from The Square. A few youthful rebels brooded there in solitary anguish, reflecting perhaps upon the iniquities of tutor or system, and would crush their cup in impotent fist before dropping it onto the ground in a gesture of minor revolt.

Against this backdrop of normality beyond the windows of the study on the second floor of the Archaeology Department, the story just related to Caro Stevens, Senior Lecturer, by Darcy West investigative reporter, seemed even more preposterous. Darcy watched her old friend with anxiety, noting the puckering of the usually smooth white forehead beneath an abundance of dark hair cut short on the crown and worn in spikes streaked with purple and copper highlights. The slight flush of colour to the plump cheeks might be an indicator of adrenalin rush or equally of embarrassment on behalf of her friend. Darcy gave a nervous little laugh.

"So do you believe me – or think I've finally lost the plot?"

Caro ruffled the multicoloured spikes of hair with a hand that despite a large jade ring and beaded bracelets seemed at odds with the elegance of her vintage style velvet skirt and jacket: the nails were short and cut straight across giving a clue to her profession. Long tapering nails had no place at the bottom of a trench on a field dig. "I think," she said slowly at last, "that you truly believe these things happened."

"Not quite the same," Darcy said with a dryness and sharpness that hid her own embarrassment and disappointment.

"Hey, we've been through some weird times together, but even for you this one is a bit off the wall. And you expect instant answers? I need time to take it in and think it through – at least five minutes!"

Her final words robbed the rest of the sentence of any sting and made Darcy smile.

"Of course. Sorry. But *are* there any answers?"

"Well up to now it's leaning in your favour. More coffee?" Caro paused and indicated the cafetière on the table. Reluctant to stem Caro's flow, Darcy made a negative gesture with her hand.

"Okay so let's see what we've got. What you describe seeing would be accurate in terms of height and design of original walls and buildings and style of armour etc. But then," Caro paused and began tapping her front teeth with the nail of her thumb as she lapsed into a process of silent analysis that Darcy both recognised and understood well enough not to interrupt, despite the irritation to her nerves caused by the constant clicking sound of nail on enamel. "It's possible," Caro continued as though the silence had not occurred, "that you have come across computer reconstructions of the fort and other details whilst doing your research, so we have to discount them."

"I can't recall it but the images could be stored in my subconscious," Darcy agreed nodding.

"But that leaves all the spooky stuff and sense of a personality,"

Caro continued. "And frankly I don't have you down as a romantic novelist's heroine fantasising about knights in armour!"

"It's that old thing about the sum of the parts," she continued, leaning back on her chair so that the front legs cleared the carpet, an operation that momentarily distracted Darcy by its precarious nature given Caro's ample weight. But Caro was speaking again. "Just because one of them has to be discounted we cannot dismiss the whole experience. Maybe we should focus our search on whether this person actually existed or is a thought form conjured by your imagination."

"Excuse me?" Darcy said dryly.

"Make no mistake," Caro warned, "such entities can be potent and devastatingly real."

"There is something else." Darcy was delving into a pocket of her jacket. "I have a name," she said quietly at last, holding out a folded sheet of paper.

"Now you tell me!"

"I was embarrassed."

Caro unfolded and scrutinised the sheet in silence for a moment. "Do you know how Roman names work?"

Darcy shook her head.

"Okay, in the days of Early Empire it was usual for a male Roman citizen to have three names to distinguish him from non-citizens. The *praenomen* or familiar name – women were not often given this – followed by the *nomen,* or surname if you like, to indicate his family and finally the *cognomen*, his individual and distinguishing name. The common praenomens like Marcus, Gaius etc would be abbreviated. So Sextus, which meant 'sixth son', would be written as simply 'S' for short, as here." At this point she tapped the sheet of paper bearing the name then continued: "Your Roman probably would be referred to in formal documents by his family name combined with his *cognomen* i.e. Tacitus Antonius, but for everyday use by his cognomen 'Antonius'."

"I see. That's fascinating."

Darcy sat in silence for a while, a thoughtful look on her face as she digested this information and mentally tried out the names.

"So what does Tacitus mean?"

"The silent one."

"Nah! A bit of a *misnomer* if you ask me!" Darcy quipped, making Caro grin so that the tension broke.

"You still haven't told me how you came to discover his names." Caro raised an inquiring eyebrow. "I take it from research on the internet? "

"No, not exactly," Darcy was now totally embarrassed. Her account of events leading up to the appearance on the page of that sprawling signature were necessarily brief as all mention of the erotic content was suppressed. Instead she spoke only of a 'strong sense of presence' in the bedroom immediately beforehand and of being unable to sleep and therefore retreating to her study in the early hours of the morning. When she had finished she scanned Caro's face anxiously.

"So what do you think?" she ventured when Caro did not speak, However given the frown that creased Caro's forehead she was obviously deep in thought. Caro pursed her lips, blinked and focused on her friend.

"Well, given we still don't know whether this person historically existed or not – one of two things."

"Which are?

"The first explanation to come to mind – and this is probably the most likely one – as you drifted into a pre-sleep stage and were only semi-awake, your subconscious supplied the name-,"

"You mean I made it up?" Darcy interrupted, feeling defensive but also discomfiture at being protective of something that in logical terms did not exist.

"A lot of inexplicable things have been happening to you lately Darcy. I mean your subconscious mind is maybe trying to make sense of them by supplying a name for this entity – real or imagined – that seems to be invading your space." Caro paused and gave Darcy a thoughtful look. "And maybe *you*, the conscious you I mean, needs to believe this enigmatic man exists."

Darcy snorted derisively. "Why the hell should I want that? Have you any idea what it has been like living through this?"

"Are you and Brant okay?"

"Of course we are!"

Ignoring Darcy's indignant outburst Caro pushed back on her tilted chair in her usual laid back manner. "It's just that when we last talked, I got the impression there was some conflict going on over whether or not to start a family."

Darcy felt the colour warm her cheeks.

"Okay, but that issue apart we're fine together."

"Rather a big issue to discount," Caro ventured.

"Well yes. But we've got it sorted. Brant proposed supporting me in this, well, this 'investigation' if I agreed to consider starting a family in about a year's time. I agreed so now we are fine," Darcy explained.

"And how is he helping?"

"He isn't yet. We are meeting at his observatory when we are both next at home in Cumbria."

"Ah, so just when was this agreed?" Caro said, leaning forward so that the legs of the chair hit the carpet with a dull thud. She had the look of a cat tracking down a mouse.

"Okay, you needn't look so smug. Yes, it was last night."

"Sorry sweetie. I wasn't crowing, it's just that I'm getting more of a picture which is always satisfying," Caro said with a sympathetic smile so that Darcy's annoyance evaporated like a puddle on a hot day. "In a way the fact that your conflict with Brant was resolved last night works in a positive way."

"Excuse me?"

"With that stressful situation resolved you should have slept like a babe."

"You mean I no longer had a reason to imagine haunting and seduction by a burly Roman!" Darcy said dryly.

"Not quite that sort of romantic fantasy stuff Darcy," Caro reproached, "but not a million miles off target. Our minds are wizards at creating alternative worlds that are preferable to our sometimes unbearably stressful realities. But I don't now think that is necessarily the case here."

Somewhat mollified by this last sentence, and pushing back a stray strand of hair as though to smooth her ruffled pride, Darcy prompted:

"You mentioned two possibilities."

"That's right. The other being of course that somehow in a way that at present we cannot explain, but that is no reason to discount it, this man did exist and you have picked up on say ancient energy trails or something of that nature and automatic writing was the result. It's out of my field so I cannot say more than that really."

"But why *me*?" Darcy appealed, placing a hand to her breast.

"That I don't know, but I suspect a combination of things."

"Such as?"

"Stress and emotional conflict that maybe made you more 'open' and receptive to whatever is there. And come on, we all know about the famous Darcy intuition."

"Hunches, that's all." Darcy muttered, squirming on one of the battered armchairs that formed a feature of Caro's study and seminar room. Right now she felt like one of Caro's students, she reflected, and folded her arms across her chest to form a barrier as discomfort set in.

Caro it seemed was not to be put off. "Call it what you will Darcy West, you are no stranger to paranormal phenomena!"

"Okay." Darcy held up a hand, "but for now can we focus on the practical issues, like the fort and its history?"

"Sure." Caro sat back further in her chair, physically retreating to take off the pressure. "This department undertook a dig atMediobogdum."

"Really? I had no idea."

"It was before my time, back in the eighties I believe. I'll put up the final report and email you with the salient points."

"That would be great."

"Look I know you are backing off the psychic stuff, but I guess that was why you came Darcy. You need to be able to talk about this, to someone who'll take you seriously and not think you've lost your marbles!"

"You're right of course, and thanks for that Caro," Darcy said, nonetheless picking up her bag from the floor beside the chair. "It's just a bit much to take on board. Sometimes even I believe I've lost 'em!"

"Don't worry, I'd be first to tell you!" Caro said laughing.

"I don't think it's dawned on you how fascinating all this is for me!" she continued. "I'm an archaeologist for god's sake. Come on, would I turn down the possibility, no matter how remote, of first-hand info about life two thousand years ago? So," she tilted her head and gave Darcy a speculative look "can we work together on this?"

"Thought you'd never ask!" Darcy grinned and her shoulders lowered slightly as tension left them

"Okay, deal done. We can't speculate *ad infinitum* about the reality or otherwise of all this, it makes it very difficult to talk-," Caro paused abruptly and stared at Darcy, "What's wrong?"

Darcy blinked and resolved to ignore the sudden stirring of atmosphere that followed Caro's purely academic use of Latin. I carry this thing around with me, she realised with a shock. That meant there could be no escaping it.

"Nothing, just thinking," she excused herself as Caro repeated her query.

She said nothing when Caro shivered slightly then leaned forward to turn the radiator thermostat to 'high' before continuing:

"Anyway, instead of endless speculation I move that for the time being and until proved otherwise, we take it this person was real, if only for ease of communication. And talking of proof," Caro continued sitting back again on her seat, "there's something I'd like to suggest."

"Oh yeah?" Recognising Caro's tone from past experience, Darcy looked cautious.

"Regression. With a registered therapist of course. We may find answers to the question 'why me?' and then-,"

"No way!" Darcy interrupted, rising abruptly from her chair.

"Okay, forget actual regression." Caro raised a hand to calm Darcy down and added "But at least consider hypnosis in general."

"What good would that do?"

"Process of elimination. We may be able to dismiss all this hocus pocus as something arising from your own subconscious."

"Or not!"

The room was growing colder; time to leave before Caro was forced to experience his reality for herself. Scare her too soon and there would be an end to expert advice, not to mention invaluable emotional support.

"I have to push, Frank will be after my a'ss!"

"Okay, no probs."

Caro rose to give her friend a bear hug.

"I have a lecture coming up anyway. It's been great seeing you again. But do think about what I said Darcy, it could give us the breakthrough we need. My gut feeling goes against the 'all in the subconscious' theory; I believe there is something very odd going on. Hypnosis might give us a clue to something you have consciously missed like…" she paused for effect before dangling the carrot "what it is this Antonius wants of you."

Darcy paused and pulled back in the act of returning the hug to look her in the eye.

"You think there is something specific?" she said in a low voice, her eyes unnaturally dark from the adrenalin rush that she was trying so hard to conceal.

"Don't you?" Caro quizzed holding her friend's gaze.

Declining to answer Darcy left on a promise to stay in touch.

That night, Brant having left earlier in the day for London, she lay in bed alone mulling over those last words from Caro when suddenly the temperature in the bedroom dropped. She lay very still, huddled beneath the duvet and afraid to breathe for fear of what might come next. The orangey glow from the streetlamps filtered through the curtains into the room and deepened into red. Everywhere red light, reflected in the oblong of the cheval mirror, intensified and flung back again by the dressing table oval. She was slipping down into a long tunnel into the light and Caro's words 'what is it he *wants, wants, wants?* echoed along its length as she spun towards the opening at the far end.

OUT OF TIME VI

~

He wanted her, and knew he would sacrifice anything to satisfy his desire. This despite the experience and professionalism gained from a decade and a half of campaigning, and the logic beaten into him by his tutor and by which he had been tooled and fashioned throughout his childhood and youth. She appeared even more beautiful than he recalled, standing there in the hollow below with the setting sun shafting through the trees, turning the rising mist to rose and igniting the dark forest of her hair and suffusing it with fire. Engrossed in gathering herbs and various types of fungi that she placed in an oval basket carried on one arm, she paused to listen to the outpourings of a blackbird's throat and seemed oblivious to his presence. Not for the first time he thought how vulnerable she looked when divested of parade dress and clad in a simple robe, her only ornaments being the large penna securing her cloak and the silver torque that encircled her throat.

Rowana. Named for the silver-barked tree that her people held sacred. His mother, barbarian by birth and still ingrained with the culture, had told him how sprigs of rowan were nailed to the doorpost of dwellings, and the scarlet berries dried and strung on a thread for wearing around the neck to ward off evil intent. She turned and appeared to be looking in his direction and intuitively he drew back and deeper into the shadows cast by the gnarled oak that hid him from view.

Turning he held up a hand to silence Gaudita as the mare snickered her impatience to be off. Rowana had managed to let him know where to find her today without actually spelling it out and presumably therefore was half expecting him, but for now he preferred to observe her unseen. He held his breath as she moved forward a couple of paces but then breathed again as she stooped to pick a scarlet and white-spotted toadstool that he could only surmise was wanted for medicinal purposes, given its poisonous looks and reputation. *Or for magical practices.* Fleetingly he allowed himself to picture her beside a midnight cauldron of simmering herbs and reptiles, features distorted by the rising steam and glow from the flames, hair a mass of serpents writhing Medusa fashion around her head. *Rowana Spellbinder.* A strange fantasy that made his manhood grow in passion then just as swiftly subside in something like fear, a legacy again from his barbarian mother; Calpurnia had imbued him with a healthy respect for that which could not be explained.

It would go a long way to explaining his unhealthy obsession with the girl. He was about to step out and reveal his presence when she began to sing. He halted, unable to draw himself away from the clear voice and lyrical sound. As he listened his brows knit in a frown: where had he heard that song before? The words lightly touched the strings of memory so that they resonated with a faint but as yet unrecognised echo.

> *Fly Boduewedd thro' lonely Night*
> *And weep as you flee the dawn*
> *Shunned at cockcrow by beast and man*
> *For the Day must you ever mourn.*

The words wafted clearly to him on the pine and moss-scented breeze and seeped into his mind finally bringing a chill of recognition. *Boduewedd.* The Flower Maid: Calpurnia's song composed for him as a boy so how could any other know it? The notion of Rowana as medicine woman gathered force. Maybe he was mistaken, seduced by the mood of the moment. He listened closely, straining to catch the words. No mistake: the legend told of the maiden conjured from flowers for Lleu Llaw Gyffes, her beauty and eventual betrayal. Then came ultimate sadness, a haunting quality as the melody changed to a repetitive chorus as the singer told of Boduewedd's fate: to be turned into an owl and thus be confined to the night and shunned for eternity by all other birds.

Petals to skin and skin to feathers
Glide through the night condemned forever
For your shadow is tied to the moon, to the moon,
Yes, your shadow is tied to the moon.

Unexpected tears pricked at his eyelids causing him to curse his own weakness. A shiver ran through his body as the last note died. Did this place hold Calpurnia's spirit? The glade vibrated with light of such an intensity that it melted all form. The incandescence dissolved the tree tops and leaves of copper and gold were smelt in a circle of fire. A thousand bees droned inside his skull, the sound growing louder and louder until he almost cried out with pain. His eyes were tightly squeezed to shut out the glare that nonetheless permeated his eyelids. One again he was suffering the scorched vision inflicted in the deserts of Aegyptus and the snow-blindness of the Alps. His fingernails dug into ridges of bark as he prayed for the thrumming inside his head to cease. Then blessed silence and softening of light that encouraged him to believe that Calpurnia had not really made up the song herself but had said it was so to make him feel special. Yet reason told him it would be completely out of character; would be considered by her as unworthy – a rider that destroyed any comfort brought by the belief so he immediately suppressed it. Time perhaps to make his presence known.

A doe startled whilst browsing, she threw up her head and froze as though catching his scent and prepared to run when leaves and twigs crackled beneath his feet but then, on realising who approached, settled and stood waiting with customary arrogance .

110

"You should not be here alone," he said halting before her.

"I no longer am."

The implied intrusion when he had merely been concerned for her safety nettled him so instead of asking her about the song he responded frostily

"In fact you should not be here at all."

Her head came up and the dark eyes sparked fire.

"My people have always owned these woods."

"No longer I'm afraid. They lie within the outer security zone of the fort. This land has been requisitioned by Rome."

"Stolen you mean. Nobody shall keep me out of our woods." It was uttered as a challenge.

"Then you will be breaking the law."

"Not our law, Roman law!"

"And I am Roman,"

"Yes, I know."

Their eyes met and the enmity that sparked between them subtly changed to an aura of intense awareness and something approaching despair. The moistness of her semi-parted lips and the slanted eyes belied her defiant stance so that he was emboldened to say softly:

"Nevertheless I want you." He dared to raise his hand to stroke her cheek with infinite gentleness as one might caress a child. He had expected her to recoil but she seemed rooted in the earth, a lithe sapling true to her name. She held his gaze without flinching and the fire of defiance in her eyes could not now conceal the fact that she wanted him too. She raised a hand and laid it briefly over his where it still rested against her cheek. Light as a summer breeze it whispered of things beyond his wildest hopes. He would have spoken then, but without another word she turned and fled the glade. He did not immediately follow. It would not do for anyone to see them leaving together. Her pesky old guardian seemed always to be watching whenever he approached the settlement or any place that he thought Rowana might be. The creepy one who spoke always in riddles and seemed to be able to read his mind. What was his name now?

He was still puzzling over this as he emerged from the woods and Gaudita stepped onto the road.

"Myrddin at your service."

He spun round in the saddle and felt the colour drain from his face with shock. He would swear to the fact that he had passed nobody, yet there at the edge of the wood the old man leant on his staff, silver hair briefly transmuted to copper by the light of the dying sun. And again that trick of appearing to read his mind. It was as though he had conjured up this enigmatic ancient by searching for his name. It was grossly unnerving.

"Do not creep up on me like that old man, it can be dangerous," he snapped, ramming his already half unsheathed sword back into its scabbard.

"Oh I am too old to creep. You were preoccupied."

Antonius threw him a swift look wondering if there was a hidden significance behind the words in respect of his ward but the old man simply smiled and looked innocent. Antonius was about to tell Gaudita to move on when he became aware that the old man was staring at the mare with disturbing result. He neither spoke nor moved, yet Gaudita flattened her ears and whinnied, then fidgeted and back-stepped as though confronted by snake or wolf. He was about to admonish Myrddin for spooking his horse when she reared and flayed the air with her hooves. Taken off guard Antonius almost lost his seat and struggled in vain to regain control. It was all the more disturbing given the old man's silence; he simply stood there emitting something, Antonius knew not what, that was sending his animal berserk.

With one hand he snatched for the reins that had been jerked from his grasp, and with the other held onto one of the frontal saddle horns whilst also gripping hard with his knees as he attempted to regain control. She neighed and reared again. Still in silence Myrddin raised an arm, palm outwards, and opened his fingers so that a split appeared between the first and second pair. As if by magic Gaudita stood still, snickered gently and bowed her head in submission.

"I have never known her act thus; she is usually a gentle creature,"

Antonius complained, his tone and scowl indicating that he held Myrddin responsible for this irregularity.

"Yes, a mature mare like this usually gives a steadier ride," the old man agreed, stroking Gaudita's velvet nose so that she dipped her head and snickered softly with pleasure. "A spirited filly is a temptation I grant you, but mounting her may result in a serious fall," he added.

Antonius paused in adjusting a dislodged saddle strap but at these words his head shot up and he stared at the old man with open suspicion. Myrddin however returned his glare with an innocent smile.

"Wouldn't you agree, legatus?"

For answer Antonius grunted, scowled and turned Gaudita in the direction of the fort.

It was far from the pleasant ride he had anticipated. That ancient trickster sent shivers down his spine. Had he somehow spooked Gaudita on purpose as a means of making a point; one presumably meant to warn him off Rowana? Damn the meddling old devil; it was all designed to mar the pleasure of their meeting. Well, he would not allow it. His expression softened as he recalled the tenderness of that look and parting gesture. Pausing on passing beneath a heavily-laden rowan he reached up, picked a sprig of scarlet berries and briefly pressed them to his lips.

SIXTEEN

~

Rowan trees were everywhere, heavy and bleeding with berries in the light from the dying sun as civilisation was left behind.

"I'll be out of signal any minute Frank. Yes I know, but you did promise once I'd done the girlfriend follow-up, didn't you?" Darcy grinned and dropped into second gear as the first steep hairpin bend loomed on the approach to the track that snaked over the fells. She had left the interminable coast road to cut across the high ground and rejoin it further north, closer to the minor road that would take her to St. Gildas Bay and the track that led to the farmhouse on the cliffs. "Stay cool Frank; a couple of days, that's all. You're getting fainter, I'm losing signal." Laughing aloud now she switched off her mobile phone and unplugged the hands-free system, stemming Frank's furious protest in mid-stream.

A couple of days free of mobile hassle, she thought, swinging up and round and round again to the top of the fell and solitude at last. The late autumn afternoon was drifting into a magical twilight of greenish mauve sky and low lying mist that shrouded the valley down below. It was too high and bleak here for most trees; nothing thrived here but the shrubby gorse and odd rowan, the latter adept at finding a foothold in the most inhospitable rock and clinging on for dear life. She pulled into a passing place and opened the window to breathe in the air of loneliness, nostalgia and pre-winter decay of loam and bracken. In spring the cry of the curlew would bubble up with unbearable sweetness and the skylark would sing out it's heart on high, but today the silence was broken only by the eternal gurgle and rumble of water over stones, the symphony of this part of the Lakes.

Brant would not be home until the following day, she recalled starting up the car again; which would give her precious me-time in which to switch off and relax into her homecoming with the minimum of fuss and cooking. Much as she loved Brant, it was pleasant sometimes to potter about in scruffy gear, eat or not as the mood took her and with no-one to consider but herself. She could stop off at the village of St. Gildas and pick up Mab and Brock or carry straight on and let Brant do it tomorrow. She decided on the latter course; Mrs Jenkins was a friendly soul who loved to gossip and 'catch up on the crack from the City' if Darcy called, but tonight getting home was top of the agenda.

Tomorrow would be soon enough. On impulse she had telephoned Jane Tulley before leaving her office and on getting no answer had left a message on the answering service to say she was on her way back to the Lakes and would like to drop in at the farm the following day for an informal chat. From there, no doubt, both road and inclination would take her to Mediobogdum. It seemed with each mile travelled the desire to return increased. However it also seemed that each mile brought a lessening of solitude. She frowned and slowed on spotting a police car in her mirror. For several miles it dogged her progress, then turned off down a minor track as though the driver was satisfied with her legitimacy and so had swerved off down a minor side road. She breathed more easily again and relaxed her grip on the steering wheel, only to spot another police car parked in a lay-by, and a third about a mile down the road lurking at a junction.

Of course, she realised tapping her forehead with the heel of her hand on realising her stupidity; Ted Tulley – he was the reason behind all this police activity in such a sleepy neck of the woods. So far he had not been recaptured and the search was still on. An unnerving thought, but she was safe enough in her car and her visit to Barrenber Ground would take place during the hours of daylight. Besides the vicinity would be crawling with police. Not that Ted Tulley would be easy to find; he had grown up in this countryside with fugitive-friendly fells, woods and gullies that offered many a place to hide.

On arriving at St. Gildas in the dark and starting the long lonely climb to the farmhouse, leaving the dogs seemed less of a good idea. In the beam of her headlights the pale snake of a track slithered away to wind its desolate way up the cliff. Gorse and scrub leaned into the twilight, spindly arms like Tolkien's Ents, and waiting to clutch any person reckless enough to pass by. In the failing light the stunted trunks appeared to twist and writhe, struggling to free themselves from the earth in which they were rooted. The companionship of Mab and Brock would have helped take the edge off the darkness and desolation. However given the narrowness of the trail the only way now was forward; apart from reversing the whole way in the darkness – a strategy that was not to be recommended and which she had no intention of attempting.

No, there was nothing for it but to go on alone. The radio helped. She switched it back on, having turned it off earlier after becoming bored by a clumsy drama that was striving to make a belated point about the war in the Middle East but succeeding only in portraying harsh tones of black and white whilst missing the subtle shades between. Now however, regardless of content, there was comfort to be had from the sound of another human voice. 'I wish you were coming home tonight Brant," she whispered aloud as the prospect of arriving alone in the dark at their isolated farmhouse also lost its appeal. She hunched over the wheel, peering through the windscreen at the path ahead as the headlamps sliced the darkness. Shadows leapt back at her approach, each one making her stomach flip with shock. Bushes and scrub now became human forms crouching in ambush and subtly moving in the half-light.

There is nobody here, she told herself fiercely, rounding a bend and still climbing. Normally it didn't bother her, being here alone, but tonight she had the jitters. A startled cry was wrung from her and the vehicle almost stalled as it rounded another bend and a pair of yellowish green eyes stared into the headlamps. A fox. Just a damn fox fixated by the beam for a full thirty seconds or so, staring at her as the car advanced until it seemed she must hit the target offered by that white chest-blaze or risk stalling the car – and a backward roll down the steep incline. Instinctively her foot moved to the brake but collecting its wits at the last, the fox darted to the verge and disappeared into the shadows. Damn fool, he was more scared than you were, she told herself with a forced laugh at her foolishness. *Oh Brant, Brant.* But he was hundreds of miles away in London and unaware of her need. On impulse she tried her mobile phone in the hope of getting a signal this close to the summit, but the illuminated screen failed to give any bars. It would have been reassuring to hear Brant's voice, but perhaps it was for the best: had there been a signal he would have picked up on her anxiety and been worried. Needlessly too; there was no real danger, just an irrational feeling of being spooked. She let the mobile drop into the well under the gear lever and concentrated instead on driving over the difficult terrain.

To make matters worse tendrils of mist were drifting inland from the sea reducing visibility and strengthening the sense of danger. Because despite telling herself there was nothing to be afraid of, the hairs at the nape of her neck were prickling and the nerves of her stomach buzzed at every shadow and rock. She started and one hand left the steering wheel and instinctively covered her mouth to stifle a scream as a white shape ghosted across the windscreen. Then another, and another just visible ahead in the thickening mist and she almost laughed aloud. Gulls: stragglers making a tardy way to the nest at nightfall. *Cool it Darcy-girl; it would be all too easy to lose the plot.* Her breath evened out, the blood stopped pounding in her ears and her heart was slowing again to its normal rhythm as the car rounded a bend in a particularly steep stretch of track. The form at the verge that she took to be a gorse bush suddenly moved. She screamed and slammed on the brakes. The engine stalled as a shadowy figure leapt into the road directly in her path.

SEVENTEEN

~

That scream seemed to echo around her ears then hang on the ensuing silence. Temporarily immobilised by fear and shock she stared at the shadowy figure looming in the mist and staring belligerently through the windscreen. Wild images of cloaks and legionary armour flashed before her eyes. Her skin crawled as she waited for the redness to descend and the paralysis to hold her victim. Up here alone there was no hope of help or escape; maybe this time she would die. Her mind was paralysed by fear. Before she knew what was happening the figure disappeared. Seconds later she screamed again as the door on the driver's side was yanked open.

Numbed by shock she stared at the intruder, unable at first to register what she saw. No red mist, no cloak or armour, no phantoms in the night. Instead the solid form of a man, and in the light shed by the interior lamp a face she recognised from the Paper.

"Ted Tulley!"

"Where've you bin eh?"

The voice was thick with a local accent, the breath heavy with stale alcohol and tobacco. Incongruously her brain registered the lilt at the end of the sentence that was reminiscent of the Welsh language. She stared at him, too shocked still to answer.

"I've bin waiting for you. Waiting a long time in the cold."

The words were uttered with a softness and complete lack of emotion that was more disturbing than any loud-voiced threat.

"You could have been injured, jumping out like that," she managed at last, fear turning to relief shot through with anger.

"Not right to keep a man waiting that way. Cold. Very cold."

"Move out of the way please."

"I've waited a very long time."

There was anger in the voice now but the eyes that regarded her in the fast fading light were wide, with an unnaturally fixed stare. He's lost his marbles, she thought, panic gnawing at her insides. Whatever happened, she must not let him see her fear. Somehow she had to start the car and pull away without causing serious injury. "Move please, I won't ask again," she said with firmness whilst striving not to inflame him further. The safest strategy was to treat him the same as an interviewee who has turned nasty. She comforted herself with the knowledge that she had encountered several over the years and survived the experience. With a deliberately unhurried movement she turned the ignition key to restart the engine. Before she could realise his intention he reached up and grabbed the steering wheel. Training technique gave way to panic as she grasped his arm to push it away but found It unyielding.

"Let go!" She attempted to prise his fingers off the wheel but he held it in a vice-like grip.

"My husband is waiting for me; he will come looking if I don't turn up and he has a gun."

Ted Tulley shook his head in a chilling gesture of denial.

"No car. No dogs neither – and no lights at the place. Nobody there eh?" He made another gesture with his head, indicating the track ahead.

He knows where I live, she thought, suppressing a shudder. She picked up her mobile phone intending to bluff her way out.

"That ain't no good here."

The quietness and confidence, sympathy almost, in his voice made her feel sick with fear, reminding her as it did of a torturer playing with his victim.

"What do you want?" she asked coldly, with a forced calm she was far from feeling.

"Don't upset poor Ted; bin waiting a long time," he whined, his eyes still glazed and vacant.

"Don't be ridiculous!" She had been about to add that he could not have known even that she was coming to Cumbria, but then paused, cursing herself for that voice mail message to Jane Tulley. "I have never spoken to you before tonight, let alone arranged to meet you," she finished instead.

"Don't get clarty wi' me, missy," he snarled, sticking his face closer so that the alcohol fumes and stale tobacco hit her full on. Suddenly his gaze sharpened and his eyes narrowed as they lost that vacant stare. Startled by this U-turn she pushed back on her seat so that the belt strained across her chest. At least it was an end to that cat-with-a-mouse stuff that bordered on playfulness yet was more sinister than any aggression.

"You bin moidering my missus."

"I wasn't hassling her Mr Tulley. I wanted to help, felt there must have been good reason for what they say you did." She forced herself to speak quietly and calmly, picking her words with care so as to avoid accusations and the possibility of inflaming him further.

"I ken why you came."

"To write a sympathetic report on you, that's why."

"Nah. You knew about it. Came lookin', just like 'e did."

"Who? I don't know what you're talking about."

"You know reet eno' – the coins. *My* find, *my* hoard! That bastard from the ministry didna get it though, did 'e? But he got something else, something 'e didna reckon on. But knowin' it won't get you anywhere, will it?" he sneered.

Too true: this was going nowhere very fast. Obviously his twisted mind had concocted a grievance against her that was connected to at a guess, a valuable hoard of coins buried in the lower pasture, and the idea that she was after finding and taking it. In all probability Stephen Pettigrew had also fallen foul of Tulley's paranoid delusions. A chilling thought that Ted Tulley was prepared to kill to protect his guilty secret.

"Look, we can't talk like this," she said trying a different tack "I'm tired and need to get home. My husband is due back shortly and will want his dinner," she added artfully, trusting he would believe the lie. Surreptitiously she applied slight pressure to the steering wheel with her left hand to see if there was any play, but his grip upon it had not relaxed any. "Why don't I come over to your place tomorrow and talk with you and your wife? We can meet in one of the outbuildings or wherever you wish – nobody will know and I may be able to help," she suggested, her left hand inching its way off the steering wheel to the well at the base of the gear stick as she talked.

"So's you can grass me up and they catch me like a hare in a trap you mean? D'you think me daft or summat!"

She recoiled from the violence of word and tone and stayed silent.

"I know what you're after," he repeated, reaching out to grab her arm with his left hand.

"I don't know what you're talking about Ted."

"It's Tulley to you, bitch."

"I'm sorry, Mr Tulley. Please let go, you are hurting my arm."

It took all the self control she could muster now to adhere to her training and refuse to be provoked into retaliation or panic.

"We'll talk right 'ere." He yanked on her arm and twisted at the same time so that she cried out with pain.

"Out you come. I know what you want, but you won't get it. You're going to get something you didn't bargain for tho', interfering bitch."

Still surreptitiously probing the well of the gear lever, her fingers found what they sought and fastened around it. With a lightning movement she raised the mini-screwdriver and plunged it into Ted Tulley's right arm. With a yell of pain and surprise he released his hold and removed his other hand from the steering wheel in order to clutch at the wound. Instinctively he stepped back as dark blood began to ooze through his fingers. "Bitch!"

She reached for the key and fumbled to turn it in the ignition. Suddenly she had ten thumbs instead of two. *Come on, come on!* Slipping the gear lever into first she hit the throttle hard.

The car shot forward, taking her by surprise. Her heart missed a beat as the engine faltered, threatened to stall, then coughed into life again in response to her juggling of clutch and accelerator. Ted Tulley let out a bellow of rage and was thrown off balance by the sudden movement but to her knowledge was not actually struck by the vehicle. She automatically glanced in the mirror but behind her all was darkness. Without daring to reduce speed she leaned forward and out, seized the door handle and pulled with all her might. It shut with a reassuring thud and resulting sense of safety.

She breathed freely for the first time since Ted Tulley had stepped into her path. Seconds later however she sucked air noisily as the vehicle tilted at a heart-stopping angle on a bend she was taking too fast. Her foot eased the pressure on the throttle and the car swayed and righted itself. Take it easy, she told herself, the last thing you need is to roll it on this desolate track in the dark. Gradually the trembling of her legs ceased and her heartbeat slowed to somewhere near normal. Thank God, she thought relaxing her white-knuckle grip on the wheel, for a faulty C.D. player. The screwdriver had been left there by Brant the week previous when a disc had become jammed in the mechanism. She had meant to return it to the house but kept forgetting to do so. Once again she fervently thanked whatever powers that be for that fortuitous fault and an equally faulty memory.

It was with a sigh of intense relief that she left behind the treacherous cliff road and negotiated the bumpy track to the farmhouse. However as she pulled up before the dark building there came new pangs of regret about leaving Mab and Brock with their minder in the village. Several minutes passed before she could bring herself to leave the safety and security of the vehicle. Telling herself not to be a wimp she got out, tugged at her bags and, resisting the urge to constantly look over her shoulder made her way to the front door.

A cold wind had got up, a north westerly gusting off the sea to claw at her hair and tug at her clothing. It's whistling passage through the shrubbery, and the resentful thrashing and roaring of boughs bent beneath its will unnerved her so that she fumbled in her hurry to be safely indoors. By the beam of the mini torch on her ring she found the keyhole and manipulated the key. Before her numbed fingers could turn it in the lock however the chill hand of premonition touched the length of her spine with ice. Her heart beat faster and the breath once more gagged in her throat as she whipped around to stare into the moonless night. The beam of the l.e.d. torch was powerful in relation to size. As she swept it around shrubbery and forecourt. shadows leapt out with heart-stopping suddenness and tendrils of mist shivered then hovered ghostlike in the beam before being torn away by the wind. Nothing more alarming than vapour and swirling columns of dried leaves were revealed. No Ted Tulley, deranged and dangerous, stood trapped by the shaft of bluish light. Dismissing these misgivings as a natural reaction to her ordeal on the cliff Darcy pushed open the door and stepped inside.

Immediately she did so the sense of foreboding returned a thousand-fold. Normally she was not afraid of the dark, indeed she had already slipped keys and mini torch into her pocket, so confident was she of her bearings. However the darkness that enfolded her now was suffocating. It filled her ears and nostrils, a tangible thing that clung like cobwebs, clogging lungs and airways and stifling each breath. Vivid memories of childhood arose: of a mercifully brief time when new-school trauma coincided with the loss of a friend to meningitis and brought on choking asthma attacks. Now, as then, her chest heaved and mouth gaped and she sucked greedily in a vain attempt to fill her lungs with air. That was not all: it was cold, icy cold. Not with the normal dampish unlived in feel of a house with the heating turned off during a temporary absence, but a chill that penetrated clothing and skin to attack her body's core heat. Four steps into the hall and her teeth were chattering. A few more and a numbness seeped into mind and spirit, sucking out optimism and courage to fill her with despondency and whispers of despair. This chill had no place in the world of the living: it belonged to the pitiless sweep of pewter skies, wind-driven sleet and the heartbreaking loneliness of a solitary grave. A grave that lies beneath snow as pale as worms and death-lilies.

Had this same malevolence infected Ted Tulley's mind and driven him to the edge of insanity? The hoard he found must also have come from Mediobogdum, The coins, for now she was sure that was what he had accidentally dug up, were obviously Roman in origin and he had told Jane Tulley, hence her remark that there was 'something evil up the'er' as she pointed up at the fell and Hardknott fort. The pieces all fitted to make a coherent picture of why he should suddenly act out of character. The hoard was tainted, probably blood-stained and taken in treachery. Whatever had been released by his digging was feeding on his inherent greed and hatred of the authorities. As she pondered all this, the wind howled and raced down the funnel of the hall and she turned then gasped as the blast of icy air made contact with her face. Her hand flew to her mouth with shock at the sound of the front door banging shut. It seemed she had hit on the truth.

The numbness destroyed her power to act decisively and with purpose. She took several unsteady steps in the direction of the light switch then froze and turned in readiness for flight only to freeze again, terrified by thoughts of what might lurk within the darkness that prowled between herself and the door. *Stupid!* She had the means! Her hand fumbled for her key ring and the mini torch, and her knees felt weak with relief as her fingers closed around it. But those fingers were numbed by cold and made clumsy by stress and the key ring with its precious torch slipped from her grasp and fell to the floor. Cursing beneath her breath she bent to pick it up. For the first time she became aware of the smell. An unwholesome odour reminiscent of rotting meat, it had been faint at first but was growing stronger. It caused her to gag and the hairs at the nape of her neck to prickle. Desperately fighting down panic she crouched and ran her hand first over the pine floorboards then along the carpet runner that covered the centre of the hall searching for those means of freedom, the key ring and torch. Her scream bounced off the walls as her fingers sank into something soft and moist. Something that moved beneath her palm and writhed between her fingers.

EIGHTEEN

~

Close to hysteria she instinctively recoiled and scrambled to her feet. She moved gingerly in the darkness, stepping aside from whatever it was that fouled the floor and clung to her fingers like clots of Polycell. An involuntary shudder wracked her body and she scrubbed her hands on the side of her jeans to rid them of slime. She cringed as her foot encountered another obstacle, then on cautiously moving to the left, cried out as her shoe slid on something soft and slippery and almost sent her sprawling on the floor.

She stood immobilised by fear, trapped in a minefield of the unknown and not daring to make a move. The front door. Get your bearings; turn and retrace your steps as closely as possible and get outside. *Into the clutches of Ted Tulley?* Shaking uncontrollably now she dismissed this as a minor risk compared with the horror within. Her normally agile brain sluggishly processed the available information. What then? What if she managed to reach the door? Without the car keys there could be no escape. She groaned and but for the slime and the threat awaiting would have sunk to the floor in defeat.

She dithered for some moments, partly from the unremitting cold and partly from fear, unable to make a decision until the penetration of chill combined with the stench in her nostrils forced the way for common sense. Okay, whatever lurked on the floor was unpleasant but so far had wreaked no harm. Those keys were the passport to both freedom and source of light and they could not be more than inches away. It took several minutes longer to psyche herself up to the point of being able to do what had to be done. It was either that or stand here for hours until daybreak. Slowly and scarcely daring to breathe she moved her foot, gagging at the stench and feeling the icy air chilling her lungs with each breath.

Desperately she thought back to the moment of the keys falling from her grasp. She grimaced and willed her mind to bypass the horror and state of numbness that had followed.

"Yes! That's right," she whispered aloud as memory returned.

They had landed with a dull thud and therefore must have fallen on carpet rather than stone. Slowly, slowly so as not to kick them further away, the sole of her foot skimmed the Axminster runner then recoiled with the speed of a rattlesnake strike as the toe sank into something soft. The swiftness of that reflex action almost threw her off balance. She flung out her arms, steadied herself and froze again, heart thumping and blood rushing in her ears until she felt steady enough to carry on with the terrifying search. Her heart missed a beat and she emitted an involuntary sob of relief at the sudden sound of metal hitting metal. Keeping her foot poised over them to mark the spot she bent her knees, crouched and whispered her thanks

to she knew not what or whom at feeling the coldness and hardness of metal against her hand. Slowly and with infinite care she straightened her knees until standing upright again. Taking a deep breath, her teeth unconsciously gritted and every muscle aching with tension, she sifted through the keys with numbed fingers, drawing her breath on a gasp as she almost dropped the precious find. She paused on gaining what she sought, stood for a moment trying to prepare herself for what horrors may be revealed. She took a deep breath then retched as the stench entered her nostrils and hit her stomach. Gathering all her courage she depressed the button on the tiny torch and aimed the beam at her feet.

The scream shuddered around the hall, up the stairs and bounced back to echo inside her head.

"Oh God! Oh my God!"

It was spoken in a hoarse whisper, as though spoken words on top of that scream would be more than she and this beleaguered house could bear. White coils glistened and heaved in the blueish circle of light inches from her feet. A sweep of the beam revealed several more heaving piles scattered along the hall. She turned and ran for the door, using the narrow path of light to dodge each godless mess in her path. The cold pressed at her back and the stench thickened in her nostrils as she struggled with the lock. It should have turned at a touch but held fast. The force of the wind slamming it shut, she told herself as the screams threatened to burst from her throat. By the light of the torch she selected the key and fumbled with hands that shook to get it in place. It would not turn. Despite the numbing cold beads of sweat stood on her brow and along her top lip. Abortively but in a rush of blind instinct she hammered at the door panels with her fists.

At first it sounded like the wind soughing through the letterbox. She whirled round, ears straining. No, there it was again.

Her head began to spin and the bitter taste of vomit rose into her throat.

Existo. Existo.

"No!" she screamed in denial, turning to face the dark space and sending the failing beam of the torch criss-crossing from wall to wall and sweeping up the wide old staircase. Nothing. Only those disgusting piles on the floor remained and the empty shadows that leapt to the macabre dance of the spotlight. It echoed along the hall and into her head: the distorted echo of a scrambled radio message:

Existo existo.

She covered her ears with her hands to shut out the impossible sound. It was no use, the words penetrated her mind, were repeated over and over, persistently and hoarse with anger.

"You only exist in my imagination!!" she cried in defiance, her voice rasping on a sob. The whispering stopped, but initial relief turned to even greater fear. A pressure was building up, pressing against eyes and ears, turning limbs to lead so that her arms dropped helpless to her side and her shoulders slumped beneath the awful burden. A sense of presence was building up, along the hall and coming closer. Her back was pressed against the door and her legs began to give way to an overwhelming sense of faintness.

"Please, don't do this. Please, please, leave me alone." The words came out as a soft moan, repeated over and over in her ears, yet she was by now incapable of knowing that the voice was her own. "Please, please…

The beam of the torch grew fainter and weaker and finally died. She sank to her knees, overwhelmed by the cold and utter darkness that was seeping from the depths of the hall into her mind filling it with hopelessness and despair.

It lifted suddenly, as though her plea had been heard and acted upon. Or maybe whatever had brought her to this point had retreated in satisfaction, feeling she had been punished sufficiently, brought to her knees and the proof of existence unequivocally made. It was still cold, but with an autumnal nip to the air rather than that paralysing chill of the grave and the stench seemed less foul in her nostrils. Cautiously she rose, stood for a moment testing both her strength and the atmosphere. The hall now felt empty, devoid of any menacing presence. She turned slowly to face the door, knowing before she touched it that it would open. She turned the handle then stepped back with a startled cry as the door swung wide and a gust of wind sent it banging back against the wall.

She stared out, gathering the strength to flee. The pall of cloud and mist had also lifted as though that too had been part of some unearthly manifestation. A melon-slice of moon hung in the sky and cast a glimmer of palest light along the hall and she could hear the rumble and roar of the waves pounding the face of the cliff. Her first instinct was to rush outside and run for the car, but she paused on the step instead and filled her lungs with clean air to rid them of pollution then stepped back inside the house. Driving away would solve nothing. By now it was clear that either she was totally mad, or whatever it was did exist in some unknown sense, either way this thing was with her wherever she went. Besides, Brant would soon be here and she couldn't let him walk in on that disgusting mess. Plus how could she run away without even knowing what those heaving piles contained? Whoever heard of a reporter running away from a mystery. At least not one worthy of the title.

But first there must be that gauntlet-run for the light switch. In the hope of a temporary recharge she switched on the torch and was rewarded with the faintest of glimmers. Armed with this she drew on the last reserves of courage and picked her way back along the first few yards of a hall that seemed twice as long as before and littered with more obnoxious piles than she remembered. Her hand went out to the light switch seconds before the torch battery died. What if the light failed to come on? Her hand wavered then made the decisive movement.

She blinked in the sudden onslaught of light, gasped and covered her mouth with her hand to stifle the rising tide of nausea and disgust. Unlike the flames of the pseudo kitchen fire at the flat and contrary to her hopes, this night's phenomena had failed to disappear. Despite having some idea of the horror in store the scene revealed triggered reverberations of shock. Mounds of earth littered the hall and the movement within them, previously seen by the meagre beam of the torch, was now clearly revealed as the writhing of countless fat, whitish worms, their pallor accentuated by the reddish hue of the soil. Apart from distaste at their presence in the house, their very paleness and glistening dampness spawned in Darcy a revulsion and deep primordial fear.

Numb with shock, her mind passed over practical issues such as how they had found their way into the farmhouse and instead revolved around the fear-fuelled question of what they might signify. Their appearance evoked the grave and the stench that still filled the air was redolent of death and decay. It was about *him* – as yet she was still not comfortable with referring to him by name – that entity from the remains of the desolate fortress that lay behind this onslaught. But what was he trying to say? And again that teased question: *what is he wanting of me?* She leaned against the wall, overwhelmed by the night's events and, drained of energy, remained like that for several minutes, cheek pressed against hunched shoulder in an attitude of denial. Eventually the practicalities of the situation caused her to pull herself together. Nobody else was going to clean up this mess, and she either stayed here and did it herself or decided here and now to abandon her home, get into her vehicle and drive away from the problem.

"You're made of tougher stuff than that Darcy West", she said aloud, and the sound of her voice introduced a note of much needed reality. Besides, how then could she ever return? This horrible image would be the one that went with her, and inevitably the one that remained. The place would be forever tainted in her memory and could never again be their home. That would seriously hurt Brant; he was as much a part of this place as the sea and skyscapes and the mournful cries of seabirds that haunted the cliff face. No option. Okay: coat off, sleeves up and get on with it straight away. The sooner tackled the quicker done, she told herself, dredging from childhood one of her Nan West's favourite sayings. Minutes later, armed with shovel, bucket, scrubbing brush and various cloths and potions she set to work.

Later, fortified by a hot bath and a stiff drink she felt able to look at the night's events without threat of panic returning. The hall was reassuringly clean and now smelled of rosemary and lavender oil. The choice of rosemary oil, its reputation to cleanse and purify over-riding the one for remembrance, was not coincidental. Denial had no place after tonight, she told herself grimly, bending to take another log from the basket and throw it upon the fire where it landed amid a shower of sparks. Not yet up to going to bed, she had prepared a mug of hot milk laced with honey and a shot of brandy and retired to the sitting room to drink it. The question now was how to deal with the situation. Start with the practicalities: there were a number of actions to be decided. First on the list, were the police to be informed about Ted Tulley and his threats? Undoubtedly they should be, but there was little now to gain. He would be well out of the area and holed up somewhere remote with blankets and parcels of food to sustain him provided by a loyal wife. They had failed to find him so far so why should they get lucky now? A farmer born and bred in the area, Ted Tulley would know every nook and cranny and the most sheltered and remote of hiding places. The nerves of her stomach fluttered again at the thought of the deranged farmer roaming the district. She took a sip of the hot milk and tried to ignore the fact of her shaking hand as she lifted the mug to her mouth.

But, she thought pragmatically, he had been prowling about the place for several weeks now so nothing there had changed. *Except that he has attacked you.* She put the disturbing thought aside and visualising the outcome of lodging information with the authorities, shook her head. Police officers would be crawling all over this place to no avail and there was Brant's top secret work as an astro-physicist to consider. In the absence so far of any positive lead, given this titbit the media would be in like a pack of wolves at the kill. The presence of the observatory would become common knowledge and undoubtedly Brant would be recalled and relocated. That thought was unbearable and settled the matter. No police. Which brought her to the second big issue of Brant. But her decision not to report the incident meant this one also was decided. Once Brant knew about Ted Tulley's threat and attempts to drag her from the car he would insist on calling the police – therefore he could not be told.

There was also a more selfish reason for glossing the incident, she admitted later on feeling settled enough to re-enter the hall, climb the stairs and get into bed. Brant would assuredly expect her to abandon the investigation and her solitary rambles over fort and fell. Albeit her first reaction once the shock had subsided was to vow to steer well clear of Mediobogdum and anything connected with it. Her soak in the bath however had given time to think this through and she had been forced to admit the obvious, that so far there had been little element of choice involved. She may well decide to back out, but would she be allowed to do so? No, the only way was to pursue it with even more determination and get to the bottom of the mystery.

"Okay Antony, whoever you are – I'm still in the game," she dared to say aloud adding grimly, "and if you do want my help in some way, you had better start treating me better!" The words and tone in which she uttered them gave her courage and a sense of being back in control.

Nevertheless she cast a nervous glance around the bedroom, wishing for the umpteenth time that night that Mab and Brock were back home. Her gazed flicked back again to the window, her attention arrested by a suspicion of movement. Heart thumping she stared at the red velvet drapes until her eyes ached. Again as she looked away they appeared to move. Shadows and exhaustion, she told herself brusquely. Everyone knows that exhaustion does funny things to perception. Nonetheless she glanced again, slyly this time from the corner of her eye. There was no mistake. There it was again: a wavelike motion passing from one curtain to the other. The creepiness of it, revealed by the light shed by the bedside lamp, raised goose bumps on her arms and her solar plexus was hit by a shot of adrenalin.

She turned full on to the window, watching with horror and unable to look away from the rippling material. It was windy outside, and the wind had been strong enough to slam the front door shut, she recalled with relief. The sensation was short lived. The window was closed. This she knew without a shadow of doubt because in view of what had happened earlier she had checked it on first going upstairs. She screamed as gentle billowing suddenly changed to a frantic and noisy flapping movement. *Red curtains; Red cloak.* The association was instant and automatic. Mesmerised but too terrified to get out of bed and run, she shrank back against the pillows.

"What do you want of me!" she shouted aloud, "What the hell do you want?"

Immediately the material ceased its rippling and hung in folds of normality at the window. She held her breath, waiting for the next move but nothing happened. Perhaps that involuntary cry had been taken as acknowledgement of his reality. Gradually each muscle, stiffened by prolonged tension, relaxed and she slumped against the pillows. She left on the lamp intending to keep watch throughout the remainder of the night but despite all the trauma, the lingering unease and fear of a recurrence a deep weariness set in.

But she was hungry, really hungry and the pangs were keeping her awake. There would be something in the fridge. Sure enough there was a dish of fresh pasta, a couple of tomatoes and salad leaves. It took no time at all to prepare. The plate of spaghetti glistening with pesto and sprinkled with strips of fresh basil leaves made the saliva run in her mouth. Carefully she wound several strands around the fork, using the spoon to prevent it unravelling and falling off the end. Then it was in her mouth and the aniseed flavour of basil hit her taste buds first. As she chewed she wound a second forkful ready for eating. The first one was washed down with a mouthful of Shiraz Cabernet found in a corked-up bottle left over from the previous night. The second mouthful wet and shiny with pesto sauce went in. It was good; but there was something wrong with the pasta. Once the spaghetti strands had lost most of their coating of pesto the taste was strange, in fact pretty foul. Her eyes widened and she suddenly gagged as the threads began to writhe in her mouth. She spat the foul-tasting mess into the heaving dish of white worms.

NINETEEN

~

Coughing and spitting Darcy sat up in bed. Retching uncontrollably she threw back the duvet and rushed for the bathroom where she was promptly and violently sick. For several minutes she rinsed and spat, rinsed and spat again unable to convince herself it was just a dream. She could still feel that writhing movement along her tongue, inside her cheeks and against the roof of her mouth, too distinct to be anything but real. Then as the fog of sleep began to clear certain facts surfaced in her consciousness. She had arrived here last night after an absence of several days, so there could be no half-consumed bottle of wine left over from the previous night. Neither would there be fresh pasta and salad stuff in the fridge; this was always emptied of perishables before they left. Heaving a sigh of relief she showered and dressed; if the events of the previous night were to be concealed from Brant she would have to look half decent.

Throughout the morning she attempted to work only to rise from her desk within minutes to mooch from room to room. She was unable to stop herself from periodically peering into the hall from the doorway of whichever room she was in, or finding an excuse to go upstairs, to get say a fresh towel from the airing cupboard or soiled clothes to throw into the washing machine. Yet all seemed normal. Except for an unusual quiet that had settled over the house; the result no doubt of the absence of Brant and the dogs. In the end she had abandoned the idea of work and closed the file 'Victim or Confederate?' a controversial follow-up piece on the families of terrorists that would either earn her a grunt of approval or a condemnatory scowl from Frank, and was about to shut down her lap top when she remembered that Caro had promised to email the results of her search on the Mediobogdum dig.

Clicking on the email short cut she murmured 'come on, come on', but reminded herself she was lucky to have internet access given the remoteness of the area. Brant had no problem at the observatory given the sophistication of the satellite equipment. Connection, and there it was in the In-box with the intriguing subject 'Trouble in Camp!'. Excited now she opened it up and read the message from Caro, skip-reading the usual stuff about how great it had been to see her again and asking if she was O.K. – and had she had any further thoughts on the idea of hypnotherapy? Caro ended by saying she hoped the attached info on the dig was of some interest.

The file, with its extracts from the report of the dig carried out by Hilldean University Archaeology Department in the eighties made interesting reading:

Mediobogdum is a typical fort of Hadrianic origin, Hadrian being an emperor of the Flavian gens and a military man intent on strengthening Rome's defences both close to home and in the remote provinces. Some well-preserved surface remains combined with the uniform lay-out enabled identification of the original buildings such as the Principia (Headquarters), corner turrets and granary. Various fragmented inscriptions and text etched into sections of wax-coated tablets preserved in the peaty soil – indeed the extremely acidic environment of the surrounding peat bog has resulted also in a wealth of preserved organic matter – indicated that the fort was occupied by the 4th Cohort of Dalmatians. Strangely, there is also evidence that a member of the Ninth Legion's high command. the Ninth being stationed at York, or Eboracum to give it its Roman name, along with a large detachment had visited Mediobogdum in c. AD 124–5. One such fragment, thought to be part of an order to resurface a section of the parade ground, bore a seal of office and partly decipherable word which undoubtedly once read 'Legio IX' when seen in its entirety.

Only an officer of the High Command could be responsible for that seal. That such an illustrious man was sent to an obscure and remote outpost like Mediobogdum, accompanied by a large detachment of legionaries, would indicate some kind of serious trouble' she read, 'either internally or with the natives – or perhaps both; maybe the first provided the perfect cover up to investigate the second.

Excavation of the barracks area appeared to support this theory. These were originally constructed of wood, and extensively spread fragments of charred timbers indicate destruction of all barrack blocks by fire. In the area of the stone built Principia and commander's quarters, charred roof and support timbers were exposed This widespread destruction could of course have been due to the routine Roman practice of firing the fort upon abandoning it to prevent its use by the native military. However the discovery of extensively spread fragments of bone and armour combined with the aforesaid evidence for the presence of a legionary commander in an obscure and particularly barren situation would be more indicative of enemy action or even massacre. Unlike the Romans, native warriors – whilst not being skilled in formal battleground manoeuvres which in any case were useless in that wild and wooded terrain – employed guerrilla tactics combined with the element of surprise with devastating effect.

The Ninth arrived in Britain in AD107/8 and built the fortress at York (Eboracum) which became the Roman Headquarters of the North and the legion remained for the longest posting in its history, at least a couple of years or so after being visited by Hadrian, accompanied by a detachment from the Sixth Victrix in AD 122. However it then mysteriously disappears from the Military Annals a fact that has made this legion the focus of much academic and general speculation. It is probable that the Sixth Victrix was then posted to Eboracum as a replacement. In conclusion, the legion was known to have suffered terrible losses at the hands of Boudicca and the Iceni in c.60–61 BC, and again via native rebels in the mists and swamps of Caledonia (modern day Scotland) some twenty years later. Given these catastrophic defeats the possible, or even probable, annihilation of a sizeable detachment at Mediobogdum, coupled with the destruction by fire of the original fortress of Eboracum, would seem to provide further justification for the practice of referring to this legion as the Unlucky Ninth.

Fingers fumbling the keys due to excitement, Darcy printed off the file before sending a holding message to Caro thanking her for the 'Wow-factor' info. and promising to catch up with her later. She then deleted Caro's email with its reference to hypnotherapy – it wouldn't do for Brant to find that – and closed down the lap top. So, she thought scanning the print-out, plenty to go on here. But how did it fit in with what had happened last night?

So far she had consciously tried to block events, to pretend they had not occurred with the result that they dogged her every step and skulked around every corner. Maybe that was the wrong approach. As the horror of the previous night's hours was diminished by daylight, better perhaps to sit down now and think it through to try and make some sort of sense of what had happened. Well, the presence of such a high-ranking man along with a large detachment of the renowned legion must be a unique and one-off occurrence. Given that inscription verified as 'Legio IX', and her visions of the standard bearing the same legend, it didn't take rocket science or Einsteinian intelligence to work out that the illustrious commander with the official seal must be the very same entity as the one haunting her days and nights. However, that brought her no nearer to knowing why she had been singled out and what was required of her, nor did it help to dispel the nagging anxiety about what might happen next. An hour or so later no logical explanation had presented itself. Following the attack by Jane Tulley's husband, she had abandoned the notion of calling at Barrenber Ground, so there was nothing for it but to go and collect Mab and Brock from Mrs Jenkins. Taking care to close all windows she grabbed jacket, bag and keys and locked the doors before leaving. Looking around nervously for any sign of Ted Tulley, she drove down the cliff road to the village.

Brant arrived home shortly after seven that evening. After a relaxed and informal dinner in the kitchen they sat with a bottle of South African Shiraz catching up on their doings since parting at the beginning of the week. Brant appeared to notice nothing amiss, or if he did he passed no comment. However at times, as when perking the coffee, Darcy would turn to find him watching her with an inscrutable expression. At others he would walk over to put his arms around her and ask if she was all right. If he thought she seemed extra pleased to have the dogs back and was keeping them unusually close by her, again he did not mention the fact. She was just beginning to relax and feel she had got away with it when he came up to her holding two glasses of wine and handing her one said:

"Now are you ready to tell me what is troubling you Darcy?"

"I don't know what you mean," she said guardedly, sipping her wine to hide her discomfort.

"Oh I think you do. This is Brant you are talking to, remember?"

She smiled, acknowledging that he above any could read her mood and pick up on negative vibes.

"Nothing, really. A rather nasty dream last night, that's all. You know how sometimes the feeling it leaves can colour your day."

"Sure. But it must have been pretty bad. What was it about?" He sat down on the sitting room settee, patting the space next to him so reluctantly, because this was getting a bit too close to the truth about what really happened last night, she obliged.

"Okay," he said some five minutes or so later, slowly nodding and with lips pursed, "so that is fairly disgusting," and in a droll sort of voice so that she had to smile despite the anxiety of relating that awful dream whilst concealing the Tulley trauma and the nightmare in the hall. She was grateful for the lightness of touch.

"Someone ate cheese for supper," he added, raising an eyebrow at her in a comical way, then turning to look at her in serious mode added "Or was pretty stressed out about something before going to bed." When she failed to respond he took her hand in his and looked deep into her eyes. "Well, Darcy? Has anything new occurred to upset you?"

"Only the dream itself," she lied, hating herself for the deception and resisting with difficulty the urge to confide the encounter with Tulley followed by that appalling homecoming. But she reminded herself of the consequences of doing so: almost certain relocation for Brant by order of the Department, and possible long separations if the new posting proved to be distant and inaccessible as was likely given the breach of security. No, it wasn't worth it.

He scanned her face for around a minute, his eyes narrowing in suspicion so that she felt forced to avert her gaze.

"Are you sure Darcy?"

"Positive."

"You would tell me?"

"What could possibly happen out here?" she evaded, pulling away from him to pick up the poker and prod the logs that blazed in the grate.

"Ted Tulley for a start."

Shocked by the on-target remark she almost dropped the poker then swiftly recovered.

"What about him? Has he been recaptured?" she asked with an innocent expression.

His lsigh smacked of exasperation and she wondered how much he knew, then told herself he could not possibly know anything and to keep her cool.

"No, that's just it. And the police think he is still in the area; apparently he was spotted a day or two back".

"He's probably miles away by now," she said dismissively, whilst at the same time careful not to overplay the nonchalance act.

"He's dangerous Darcy, deranged. You have to tell me if you see him, okay?"

139

She nodded miserably. Lying to Brant was shameful but it had gone too far for her to retract. Not for the first time she found herself wondering just how much he did know and whether he was involved in the case. His work was classified; he had signed the Official Secrets Act and would not divulge his involvement to her, she knew this from past experience. But no, this was ridiculous: a northern farmer attacking an official from Defra was not significant enough for Brant's Department to be assigned the case. Space-spies at Nasser, sabotage at the massive CERN reactor in France or matters of national security were more in its line. In fact it was a miracle Brant had been granted this few days of leave given the worries over terrorists in Britain, war-torn Syria and North Korea's nuclear programme.

His next sentence was strangely apt.

"Darcy there's been a change of plan; I have to return to London tomorrow," he announced, stroking her hair and looking apologetic.

As always she was struck by his perceptiveness – or was it their joint synchronicity? His words caused a stab of anxiety but she knew better than to ask if he was to be stationed at base or posted elsewhere. Keeping to this was far more scary these days in a world threatened by nuclear weapons and terrorists but that was the nature of his work.

"Oh Brant, that's a bummer."

"Sure is. I was so looking forward to these few days together."

"When will you be back do you think?"

"Sorry, no idea. Depends on how this next week pans out. I'll be in touch and update you as soon as I know anything."

"Okay."

"Sorry Babe," he repeated, kissing the top of her head, obviously interpreting her reticence as pure disappointment.

"Not your fault Brant. But it is one of the things that make me hesitate over the baby thing." Looking up into his face she noticed the clouding of expression and the slight tightening of the muscles around his mouth, but she had to make him understand that her reluctance to start a family wasn't entirely down to selfishness over her own career or mere caprice. "We have no settled home. Okay, say I agreed to be the conventional chief carer and become a stay-home mum for a spell, you would be called away at any time and I would never know where you were or when you might return," she said truthfully. "I would literally be left holding the baby, and strangely enough, that don't appeal overmuch!" she added on a lighter tone, sensing they were heading into a by now familiar minefield. "Plus," she continued when he failed to respond, "we are both in dangerous jobs. Not an ideal scenario for family life. Most people wouldn't think of taking on a dog in those circumstances!"

"So that rules out police officers, fire-fighters, miners, rescue workers and god knows how many others from ever having a family!" he countered, shifting his body slightly so that it no longer touched hers.

"That's stretching it a bit!" She swivelled round to face him and took hold of his hand. "Come on, darling. You have to leave tomorrow so don't lets spoil tonight with fighting. I'm not trying to renege on my promise to consider it, only this was an example of one of my chief worries about the idea and I want you to understand," she soothed. It was true, they were in dangerous jobs and each time he went away she could never be absolutely sure of him coming safely back and therefore tried to resolve any quarrel before they parted. She found herself wondering yet again why men seemed incapable of taking that one on board. Judging by the softening of expression at least he was following her lead.

"Fair enough." He smiled and squeezed her hand. "I know I tend to over-react on this one."

"No probs."

"Which reminds me of your side of that bargain," Darcy said suddenly sitting upright.

"I was going to suggest meeting at the observatory tomorrow, but now we'll have to put it off until I get back."

"So what's wrong with now?"

"You're stressed and tired."

"And feeling better by the second!" Put it off now and it may never happen.

Brant nodded. "I'll get my jacket."

The Land Rover lurched and bumped over the uneven ground beneath a velvet sky scattered with a million sequins. The roar of surf pounding the cliff face penetrated the slightly open window, punctuated from time to time by the hoot of a 'tawny' or screech of a barn owl Even now after countless visits to the observatory Darcy was still thrilled by the magic of this journey, especially the trundling ascent of Sheep Howe when the Land Rover keeled and listed and seemed about to turn over. However it never did so, and they were over the top and then that quick intake of breath as the silver dome of the observatory, incongruous in this spectacularly wild setting, came into view; a metallic monster straight out of Star Wars that never failed to give her a thrill. Her head almost bumped the roof as the vehicle trundled downhill to their destination.

Brant tapped in the code and used his electronic tag to unlock the gate of the perimeter fence and then the outer entrance. Watching, and noting the way their breath stained the autumnal air white and with the taste of salt spray on her lips Darcy was reminded of the first time she had come here with Brant, shortly after they met and immediately prior to the devastating events that threatened to end their relationship before it had chance to get started. But it had withstood the treachery and betrayal and also the test of time. I mustn't let us drift apart over this baby thing, she told herself, following him inside. On impulse she stood on her toes and planted a kiss full on his mouth.

"What was that for?"

"Memories."

"In that case remind me to bring you here more often."

"And for all the love."

"Plenty more where that came from," Brant said gruffly, fiddling with the lock as Cumbrian reticence about voicing emotions rose to the surface. "Right, let's get down to work."

She smiled and followed him through the sliding metal inner door into his dimly lit comfort zone.

A few expert clicks and taps from Brant's fingers on the server key pad and the observatory stirred from its dormant state and hummed into throbbing life. A row of red lights glowed around the interior of the dome and monitors flickered into working mode, displaying scenes of celestial pyrotechnics as data was transmitted and picked up from the heavens. Over the years she had learned to recognise many of the major constellations and still thrilled to the rainbow shimmer and fireburst of stars such as Pollux in Gemini. The spectacular spurts of red, blue, green and purple she now knew were due to electrical impulses used to give a visible record of the various intensities of light being transmitted.

"I still find it amazing."

"So you should!"

"Okay!"

"Well you are the only civvie to be allowed in here."

"I'm honoured."

"Of course."

She smiled to herself as he tapped away at various keyboards. This was Brant in his own domain, one he was sure of and where he was undeniable master. Gone was the diffidence, the reluctance to display emotion, this was his world and within it he exuded confidence and excitement. A tap of his fingers on the keys and the screen would display the universe as it was two thousand years ago or conversely, all things being equal, how it would look thousands of years hence.

"Can we put her up?" She said on impulse, nodding in the direction of the huge telescope.

"Don't see why not: it's a clear night and no turbulence."

Darcy recalled that atmospheric disturbances caused distortion of the images on the monitor; out there it would look like the twinkling traditionally associated with stars but in here, due to the immense degree of magnification, the images would explode and leap about the screens in a celestial firework display. No problem tonight though; out there it was still as the grave. An unfortunate thought: don't let it in, she silently exhorted herself as the tiniest tremor of recognition ruffled the atmosphere.

Brant's fingers moved deftly on the keys and she watched the crack appear in the dome above their heads. The gap widened, the sections of the ceiling sliding apart like the two halves of a giant walnut to reveal a growing sliver of sky dusted with Christmas card glitter. She watched entranced as they silently slid further and further back until finally only the heavens showed overhead. Darcy shivered slightly as moist night air redolent with salt-breeze, mosses and earthiness touched her face.

"Wonderful isn't it?" she whispered, awed by the vision.

"Sure is."

Brant was in his element.

Pegasus, Gemini, the Plough and many more, all the most well known and best loved constellations sprawled across the sky, Orion and the three stars that made up his belt being particularly bright on this night.

"Oh look, a shooting star!" she exclaimed, but still in a hushed tone; somehow loud voices had no place up here. She pointed to the arrow-trail of light fired from some Olympian bow but it faded and died even as she raised her arm. "That means good luck, doesn't it? Oh, and there's another Brant!" she whispered, grabbing his arm in her excitement.

"It's the best time of year for spotting them," Brant said, smiling at her enthusiasm.

"No, it means I'm double lucky to have you and be able to come to this magical place," she said squeezing his arm. He said nothing but squeezed her in return and kissed the top of her head. A few more taps of his fingers on the keys and a humming sound punctuated by several clicks brought her attention back to the interior. The monster of metal and cable standing on its reinforced platform at the centre was whirring into life. She watched it rear its head towards the apex; this part of the proceedings never failed to remind her of a Bond film set. Up and up the metal beast rose, coming to rest above the rim of the observatory from whence it could monitor the vast sweep of universe until ordered back to its lair. The images on the monitors below changed with lightning rapidity as Brant focused on each pre-

144

set quadrant of the heavens and targeted each constellation, zooming in on its stars and planets in response to Darcy's requests.

"Okay, the show's over," he said at last, reversing the opening sequence and watching as the telescope slowly lowered its massive head and settled down on its podium to sleep; a giant dinosaur subdued by the will of man. Almost immediately the two halves of the dome reappeared: steel jaws gradually nibbling away at the gap between until they finally met above their heads sealing Darcy and Brant inside and excluding the night sky and its stars.

"I've been giving some thought to these 'occurrences', for want of a better word," Brant began, wasting no time on preambles, "So just to recap: you say they are not specific to say any one time of day or night, weather conditions or particular location?"

"No. I've experienced them day and night, in storm conditions and sunlight, and both at the flat and the farmhouse – and of course at Mediobogdum." The name seemed to hang in the air then echo around the dome to return on a whisper. Darcy half turned and looked around her uneasily, noting how the ring of red lights seemed to be glowing more brightly, then turned back to Brant. "And the colour red is the one thing that stands out," he pressed, watching her face carefully as her mind replayed the events.

"I know it sounds crazy," she said in answer, "but red is the only common denominator that comes to mind – like red mist, red light and red earth: At the Tulley place, at my pad in Manchester the night I saw that weird stuff in the mirror and then last night-," she stopped, realising she had been about to divulge the nightmare in the hall the previous evening.

"What about last night?" he said giving her a sharp look.

"I was just about to say 'I had a nightmare', but I remembered I already told you about that," which was half-true she consoled herself, and thankful he seemed not to recall the dream's content.

"You are levelling with me aren't you Darcy?"

She looked away at a monitor, then at the metal ceiling dome, at anything other than those accusing eyes.

"Of course."

"Have you told me everything?"

"Would I lie to you?" she parried.

"Darcy, I've learnt that where a hot story is involved you feel justified, even obliged, to be economical with the truth!" he said with a half-smile that said it all. She hoped the dim lighting prevented him from seeing the rush of colour that burned her cheeks

"Maybe sometimes." Which again was true; she had no intention of saying more. Brant's reaction fully justified her decision not to tell. If he fussed like this over a few piles of soil, how would he deal with white worms, self-locking doors and obnoxious smells reminiscent of the grave?

"Okay," he said after an awkward moment of silence. "So we have the colour red."

Even in the dim light she could see that his stance had altered: hands across his chest and clasping each bicep he looked like a man holding in an exciting secret.

"You can explain it?"

"Not exactly. But a possibility did come to mind."

Darcy felt a stirring of foreboding.

"And that is?"

"Red shift."

The disturbing buzz in her solar plexus intensified, as though someone had prodded her with an electrified probe. Darcy tied to hold back the tide of ideas and questions seething around in her mind.

"Isn't that to do with distant light distorting Time?"

"Something of the sort."

I'm not sure I like the direction this is taking. Darcy nibbled her lip as her mind went into orbit. Red shift was not an entirely new concept to her, having run across it a couple of years back during that near-fatal encounter with a corrupt scientist and some lethal cosmic particles. But she had never really understood it. Besides this was different, not some obscure theory to explain things that may not even exist, but something that touched her everyday life and therefore made sense. Exciting, yes but also disturbing.

"Physics for Idiots please."

146

Brant nodded and thought for a moment with eyes half-shut.

"Okay, keeping it simple then, all objects and entities emit light. As events move away they are still emitting light unless they are sucked into a black hole and beyond the event horizon. Black holes are the result of large stars dying and collapsing in on themselves. The larger the star, the greater the gravitational pull. An event horizon, to give a simple analogy, is like a one-way membrane. Surrounding matter is sucked into it but can never return. But say some events escape that fate. In theory they can go on emitting light forever. So back to red shift. The further they are away the faster they move and the light they emit becomes red shifted."

"Which means exactly?"

"We're talking spectrum here. Rainbow, yes? Okay," he said as she nodded, "The colour of light emitted by things moving towards us and therefore closer is bluish; that of events moving away is reddish. So the further they travel away the more they shift into the red sector of the rainbow. As you may expect, the reddish portion is hotter than the cooler blue and most significantly for us, the light waves also become much longer. It's one of the Universe's great paradoxes: the further and faster events move away from us the greater the chance of their light waves reaching back to Earth."

"Which means?" Darcy said in little more than a whisper because she already had an inkling.

"We may experience those past events again, albeit a distorted and fragmented version. Look." He turned and swiftly tapped at a keyboard as though he thought she might protest if given the time. Her eyes were inexorably drawn to the monitor as it flashed from its dark and dormant state into vibrant life. Red. Swirling red. A whirlpool of crimson mist drawing her down to its centre.

"No, don't do this." It was whispered and Brant failed to hear, or at least to take note as he pressed more pads. She wanted to look away, to run from the dome back to the safety of the farmhouse but was unable to move or draw her gaze from the screen.

The red vortex began to fade until only a crimson haze remained. The whole screen seethed with movement and colour of varying

147

shades: crimson, scarlet and darkest red. Grey shadows then loomed at either side, shifted and began to take shape but the images were pixilated and indistinct. Then more separation and coalescence until the dark mass became recognisable as the mountains flanking Mediobogdum. Formations of cloud heaved and surged across summits, heavy-mob nimbus of an angry purple and bulging with dark intent. Racing as though on a speeded-up film they swiftly shrouded the heads of the giants: Bowfell, Crinkle Crags and distant, lofty Scafell. Then a rent appeared in the shroud allowing a single beam of brilliance to shaft a way through.

She gasped and put a hand over her mouth because there it was in the spotlight: the fort on a spur of the rock; not the crumbling remains she had visited but a fortress complete with earthworks, ramparts and stone towers, one at each corner and one either side of the imposing *porta praetoris* or main gate. Then came the sound, a rumble taken at first for thunder given the presence of nimbus cloud but proving too regular and consistent, so in vain did she wait for the storm. Closer and louder it came but accompanied by a different, more staccato sound and sending a chill through her body because now there could be no mistaking the source: the synchronised beating of purposeful drums and the clatter of many studded boots simultaneously striking stone.

Disbelieving of what she saw Darcy watched the plume of cavalry descend from the swirling clouds at the crest and wend its way down the pass: metal armour igniting as the wearers passed through that solitary beam; red cloaks stirring in the wind and with the motion of riding as they guided their mounts down the steepest gradients with the eagle standard held aloft and reflecting the fitful sunlight. They were followed by the marching ranks, the *pedes*. This she knew, but not where the word had come from. So real did all of it seem that she could hear the jingle of harness, the groan of straining hawsers stretched across supply wagons and sense in her nostrils the odour of oiled leather. She covered her ears with her hands to shut out the incessant and impossible sound but it thrummed inside her head.

She was there, standing on an outcrop of rock somewhere near the parade ground, watching the stream of military wend its way down from the crest of the past. The wind was blowing her hair and there was a sense of constriction low on her forehead as though it was encircled by a band to hold in check her unruly locks. As she watched there was something stirring deep inside, a hatred for the enemy and invaders of her people's land.

A hatred such as she had never felt before; one that burned with such ferocity that she could picture herself thrusting and hacking them into bits, taste the blood as it splashed her face and feel the warmth of it on her hands as she fought side by side with her father's warriors.

"Brant, stop it," Darcy managed to whisper, raising a leaden arm to tug at his sleeve. There was a whining sound in her head and like Alice she was growing smaller and smaller, was about to be sucked completely into the scene.

"Switch it off please!" But he had his back to her, did not hear nor witness her distress. The pixilation returned and the image of the legion disintegrated, became a shifting jigsaw with most of the vital pieces missing. She watched, sensing what was to come yet unable to look away as the red mist returned, swirled then parted again. At first she could scarcely distinguish the form amongst the dark shadows and dominant fells with their mantle of swirling cloud. Then there he was, standing with his back to her at the edge of the precipice. That air of authority again conveyed by the angle of the head, the set of shoulders and feet-apart stance, but there was about him too a terrible sense of isolation and loss.

The breath caught in her throat. Any moment now he would turn and look at her and she wanted and feared nothing more. Slowly, slowly in slow motion he began to turn. A quarter, then a half turn on his heel, head changing angle and profile beginning to appear. Within second, and for the very first time, his face would be revealed.

TWENTY

~

A couple of seconds more and his image would be full-face. She could not bear it, yet was unable to stop herself whispering his name. It left her lips and reverberated around the walls of the dome, bouncing off metal and plastic as though she had shouted with the full force of her lungs.

Antonius Antonius

She sank to her haunches in foetal position as though hugging and protecting her inner self. Brant was tugging at her arm, his voice distant and echoing as though reaching her from the end of a long tunnel and drowned by the beating of those eternal drums. Her head shot up in response to a sharp crackling noise. The monitor spluttered and threw a shower of blue sparks, belched black smoke and finally died.

"Are you all right? Darcy, answer me!" He released his hold on her to isolate the burnt-out monitor then turned back to her again. "Come on, let's get out of here," he said sharply, bending to place his hands beneath her armpits. Hauling her upright he half carried her to the exit.

"Stay there Darcy and do not move!" he ordered, opening the door on the passenger side of the Land Rover and ushering her inside. "I have to go back in there and do a safety and security check."

She did as instructed, limbs trembling and only dimly aware of her surroundings and the figure of Brant hurrying back to the dome.

It seemed like he had been gone hours. Glancing at her watch she saw by it's luminous dial and stationery second hand that it had stopped. That fits. Some ten minutes or so later a rush of relief left her feeling weak as she spotted the beam and circle of light from Brant's torch at the gate in the perimeter fence, then watched it draw closer.

"Sorry about that Darcy. Had to check and leave everything in good order," he said directing the beam onto her face so that she blinked and looked away. "Are you okay?" he asked, his voice disembodied behind the glare of the torch.

"What did you do – and why?" she demanded, ignoring the question.

"You look rough; I'll tell you on the way home," he said, slamming shut the passenger door. Taking her hand in his he turned on the engine and slipped into gear, then squeezed gently and let go to place both hands on the wheel as they began the bumpy ascent of Sheep Howe.

"What went on back there?" Darcy demanded as panic and trembling began to subside.

"I'm sorry Darcy I can see it was a disaster; I never imagined it would have such an effect".

"Not just on me apparently," she muttered beneath her breath.

"Y-e-e-s," he said thoughtfully, manoeuvring the vehicle through the narrow space between two overgrown tangles of gorse. "It did seem a bit odd, the way the machine blew like that – but these things happen," he added brusquely as though reluctant to admit any abnormality. "I really didn't mean to faze you my love," he said squeezing her hand gently then taking hold of the wheel again. "All I wanted was to surprise you-,"

"Well you managed that!"

"With a computer generated example," he continued ignoring the interruption. "I thought it easier to demonstrate rather than try and explain red shift. You see, the concept occurred to me some time ago as a possible explanation. I prepared the programme in advance but decided not to run it for you until I was sure you had picked up on this 'redness' thing yourself."

"You weren't to know what would happen," she said generously, touching his arm. "But it was bloody scary."

"Did you get the idea though? The red light, initially diffused then focused and images becoming first faintly discernible then clear and distinct, only to overlap one another, fragment again and finally fade altogether. Maybe that is how it is when we see light waves that are red shifted."

"Oh I got it all right."

"Sarcasm is the lowest form of grabbing a guy by the balls," he quipped, guiding the vehicle over the crest of Sheep Howe.

"But efficient," she said with a laugh, then instantly became serious again.

"This red shift thing – why has it never happened to me before?"

"I would guess at a freak change of circumstances that created favourable conditions for the phenomenon to occur."

"Like what?"

Brant shrugged expressively. "Climatic change maybe? Thinning of the ozone due to Global warming, a general atmospheric change that allows freak passage of red shifted light waves from time to time? I don't know Darcy, nobody does. Partical physics is sometimes like that: I can only make an educated guess."

"Well you're the guy best qualified to do so!"

Darcy's face had lost the pinched look and her eyes were shining with suppressed excitement.

"I still can't get my head around it Brant! Think of it – and where it may lead. As climatic changes intensify we may be able to view all sort of past events. Understanding of it may even lead to time travel at will!"

"Cool it Darcy," Brant cautioned holding up a cautionary hand. "We're talking theoretical possibilities here not physical actuality! It will probably never happen."

"Hawkin thinks it will!"

Brant sighed and tapped the steering wheel with the heel of his hand.

"Hardly. He has slightly modified his position that's all."

"From 'impossible' to 'possible' – that's quite a shift. In fact you might say a *red* shift!" she said stifling a bubble of spontaneous laughter at this display of professional preciousness.

"I think you should be prepared to do a runner when I get you home," he said amiably, and with a sideways look in her direction that made Darcy chuckle and think wistfully of less stressful times in their relationship.

But there were other things to think about at the moment. Like the question that had burned right from the outset. She waited until he had negotiated a tricky outcrop halfway down the steep descent of Sheep Howe before saying:

"Right, so for the time being let's take the theory as a possible explanation okay?" He nodded assent and she continued: "So why *me*? Why doesn't *everyone* experience these things?"

"Good question. I can't even manage an educated stab at that one! Thinking aloud though, maybe other things come into play: perhaps something unique in your perceptual apparatus, or rather something uncommon, which is much more likely. That is to say, others may share but not admit similar experiences due to fear of boss, partner, family or whoever accusing them of having lost their marbles! "Or," he paused and gave her a long look before continuing, "it may be down to something less tangible like heightened emotion and tuning in. Your 'hunches' and twitchy nose for a story are legendary Darcy, and whilst those labels are comfortable for you they are not very convincing to the rest of us. Being susceptible and receptive to the 'vibes' is what I suppose I am trying to say, though as a respected astro physicist I shall strenuously deny it if ever you quote me!"

"I wouldn't dare!" Knowing how much it must have cost him to make such a controversial suggestion, she smiled and touched his hand. "And the mini melt-down back there?"

"I wondered when you would get around to that one." Brant grimaced as the Land Rover drew up on the forecourt of the farmhouse and he switched off the engine.

He ran a hand through his hair and his expression, illuminated by the interior light as he opened the door, was one of acute discomfort. "I can't explain it," he admitted.

"Has anything like that ever happened before?"

"No." He answered reluctantly as though unwilling to feed the flames of her unease.

"So how about 'someone didn't like what you were doing'?" she said with a teasing half-smile, but the true nature of the question hung in the air between them.

"I'm not about to go there! That 'theory' lies beyond my scientific remit!" he said with an answering smile. "Now come on, let's get you inside and plant you by the fire with a large brandy," he added firmly.

"Sounds good. You know, it was the those drums as much as anything – I thought it was thunder at first. They did my head in," she confided as he grasped her hand and led her to the front door.

He paused and looked puzzled.

"Drums?"

"The ones on the sound track you made," she said impatiently.

"There wasn't one Darcy," he said gravely. " Leastways, not of my making; my programme was purely visual."

In silence because there was nothing left to say, Darcy followed him into the house.

TWENTY-ONE

~

Darcy drew back the curtains and looked out on a depressing vista of driving rain with trees threshing and ducking their heads to a westerly wind. Not a good day for the drive to Manchester but there could be no putting it off. Today was decision day in line with her self-imposed deadline following a sleepless few hours pondering the mystery of her Roman Invader as she referred to him in lighter moments. Questions had whirled around her head searching for answers but largely without success. For instance, taking the red shift theory as given and therefore accepting that something weird really was going on, then what was the nature of the apparent association? At best Red shift only explained the *appearance* of events or persons from long ago, not apparent on-going interaction. That apart, why did his presence take the form of intimacy one minute and displays of fury the next? Was love or hatred the motivating factor? And in either case, why had he chosen her? And most of all, what specifically did he want so desperately?

So was Caro's suggestion of hypnosis the only way forward? It was beginning to look that way. Yet it still scared her rigid, though if asked why it would be difficult to define. Was it fear of finding nothing but her own crazy delusions? Or maybe the opposite was true and it was fear of finding proof of his existence? Or maybe finding out they were in some way connected other than by a quirk of Time. It was impossible to tell. Out of all this mess, trauma and downright insanity one thing remained clear: until she uncovered his story and what it was that he wanted of her, there would be no peace of mind.

"I mean, what does a person do under these circumstances?" she muttered aloud, "where am I supposed to turn for help?" She could hardly go to the police and claim protection from a guy who lived some two thousand years back because he was somehow red shifting into her life, mucking up her hall and doing unspeakable things in the night! They would be after locking me up, she thought, and the image of their incredulous faces brought forth a smile despite her distress.

Whatever, Brant had gone back to London and she had to return to the Paper or risk Frank throwing one at her prolonged absence and inaccessibility. Do it, do it now she exhorted herself, wearied by indecision. Marching into her office before she had time to change her mind Darcy logged onto her computer and tapped out a message to Caro: 'Will give the hypno a go – be in touch later today when I get back to Manchester.' A quick click of the mouse and the cursor hit the 'send' button. Too late now to retract.

Darcy suppressed a grin as Frank Kelly swayed his bear-like head to and fro slowly as though irked by invisible chains. After greeting her entry into his office with "Good of you to come Darcy," uttered in tones of exaggerated politeness, he was now five minutes in and building mean steam. "I mean, it beggars belief! Best part of a week and not a bloody word! Okay, 'no signal for the moby'" he mimicked in a high tone so that she choked on laughter that bubbled partly from amusement but also nerves at this latest rollicking. She was back in church or assembly with her schoolmates whispering rude jokes or passing them along on a scrap of paper; she was always the one to collapse into helpless giggles and take the rap.

"Have you not heard of one of these?" he shouted, thumping the telephone so that the receiver leapt from its cradle to dangle and swing by the cord over the edge of his desk.

"Here we go Frank," she said cheerfully, retrieving it and replacing it on the console just as he leaned forward to do the same and she found herself inches from his temper-flushed face.

"Back off and shut up!" he muttered ungratefully.

"Sure." Darcy moved back from the desk and stood within easy reach of the door.

"And don't keep agreeing with everything I say – it doesn't suit you!"

"Okay Boss." She kept her face straight and felt the spurt of victory well up inside because she knew he was struggling to do likewise.

"What am I going to do with you!"

"Sorry, Frank. I didn't mean to wind you up."

"You never do!" He let out the heavy sigh of a man labouring beneath a great burden and she knew the storm had passed without casualties.

"So what *were* you up to? I do have to justify paying my staff you know."

"I'm on to something Frank, but can't tell you yet."

"No probs, that's fine. I'll just tell Max Dearden you were away for half the week but can't say where or why and he will be happy to pay you I'm sure," he sniped.

"I can tell you where – but you already know that," she dared, chancing her arm.

"Don't be smart miss!"

"As to why," she hurried on before he could kick off again, "I can tell you it is to do with Ted Tulley."

"Tell!" he demanded, taking a cigar from the cedarwood box, and allowing the lid to drop with a bang.

"I can't Frank. Something happened out there but I haven't told the police yet. I haven't even told Brant," she confided, watching him peel off the cellophane before ramming the cigar in his mouth.

Holding a lighter to it he puffed at the cigar until the end glowed red then did his famous hands-free manoeuvring trick to settle it into the right position.

"I'm onto something Frank, but if CID move in too soon they'll tramp all over with size thirteens and then hey, no story."

"Christ Darcy!" The cigar moved swiftly from one side of the mouth to the other, a barometer of rising agitation. "You know the script, you can't go withholding information during a murder hunt."

157

"Murder?"

"The Defra guy died night before last."

Guilt made her look away and fall silent. She had been so wrapped up in the personal trauma that she had failed to tune into the News – an unprecedented and inexcusable lapse for a reporter. That indeed altered things, she reflected.

"You have to report it if you know where he is Darcy."

"I don't though. Okay I saw him – but that was days ago and he won't be into hanging around."

"What do you mean '*saw* him?'" Frank asked, eyes narrowed beneath bushy brows.

"I didn't go to the police then," Darcy continued ignoring the question, "and now there is nothing to gain by doing so," she added, seeking to convince herself along with Frank.

"Except perhaps your life!"

"Don't go drama queen on me Frank!" she dared to say with a grin, but then at the memory of that cliff top encounter and Ted Tulley's threats the smile died and she averted her gaze. The cigar bobbed up and down and moved back to its original corner, seemingly of its own volition.

"He's wanted for murder for Chris'sakes! But if you don't buy that one, how about charges of story-chasing against public duty – blacklisting for you and serious loss of cred for the Paper?"

"It won't come to that and you know it. So why ditch a valuable lead? Let me go back when I've cleared my desk and I promise I'll get you a story," she wheedled.

"No deal."

"You have to give me time."

His teeth clamped securely on the cigar, "I don't have to give you anything."

"But you will, won't you?" she wheedled.

"Give me one good reason why I should."

She didn't hesitate.

"Because you're soft on me?"

He flushed and for a moment she feared having gone too far, but when he spoke his tone was subdued.

"That's unfair Darcy."

"You taught me Frank."

"To be cruel?"

"To use everything I have to get me that story."

"You're right, God help me." He cleared his throat and manoeuvred the cigar a couple of times. "But mess up on this Darcy and you're on your own, I ain't going to cover for you with the police."

"Thanks Boss."

"Just make it quick, stay safe and keep me in the frame."

"You'll be first to hear."

"That'll be the day. Go clear your desk!"

"I'm doing it."

She paused on stepping out into the corridor and poked her head round the door.

"Oh and Frank."

"What is it now," he growled, grinding his cigar butt in the ashtray.

"I have a soft spot for you too," she said softly.

"Be off with you child!"

The smile on his face as she closed the door told her she was forgiven for pushing the personal button.

Back in her office she set about clearing her desk as promised by finishing a follow-up piece on suicide bombers and preparing for her attendance at a press conference to be given that afternoon by Lancaster's Chief of Police in respect of the search for Ted Tulley, a prospect that brought on a rush of guilt as she recalled her recent encounter with the wanted man. However this swiftly subsided with the thought that she could not add anything relevant by informing the police, except perhaps that he was at that time still in the area; but if the hundreds of officers employed in the search had not already confirmed his presence in Cumbria or otherwise, then they were patently beyond help.

Finally before leaving her office she telephoned Caro and was lucky enough to catch her before she left to give her next lecture. Caro had found a therapist in Lancaster who could fit them in for Thursday afternoon if Darcy could make it. Suppressing a qualm of misgiving Darcy said she would be there and jotted down the address.

OUT OF TIME VII

~

As Rufinus' voice droned on through the interminable list of complaints, Antonius' eyes glazed and his mind slipped away into reverie about a possible meeting with Rowana in sun-dappled woods. Only to be jerked back again as Rufinus' words penetrated the pleasant fug.

"Serious breach, you say?" Antonius bluffed.

The chief centurion's iron-grey eyes reproved him for his lack of concentration.

"Young Longinus, sir," Rufinus audibly sighed, "You may recall I was reporting to you his insubordination. He was heard to curse the centurion who had just chastised him, remember?"

"Ah yes, of course." Antonius' lips twitched as. For a moment he had thought of the theft of weapons issue and imagined a far more serious offence. "Very well, stand him outside the praetorium until the end of the watch with the officer's staff in his outstretched hands," he decreed, but not without a twinge of sympathy for the young soldier who was obviously the victim of a tale-bearing toad amongst his fellow soldiers. But discipline and respect for rank must be observed and Rufinus was merely carrying out his orders to enforce strict obedience.

Rufinus nodded, satisfaction restored.

"Good. I can go now, can I?"

However the irony was lost on Rufinus.

"There's still the roster, sir."

Antonius groaned and with a sigh of resignation leaned back in his seat. Rufinus cleared his throat and continued his recitation.

"A-detachment – road repairs, there are some sets up at the western approach. B-detachment – Gallus is leading a fuel gathering exercise."

As the veteran's voice droned on Antonius mind returned to the possibility of an undercover rebellion and his report to Rome. There was certainly sufficient evidence for concern.

"…And E-division has gone to repair number four quay at Glannaventa. And that's the lot sir."

Antonius rallied his thoughts.

"And what would you like me to do Rufinus?"

"You sir?" Rufinus blinked, frowned and then beamed. "Ah, now you are pulling my leg, sir!"

"I suppose so – I wasn't quite sure!" Antonius murmured.

"I'll leave you to get on now, sir."

Rufinus saluted and took his leave. His smartness and straight back would put many a young soldier to shame, Antonius thought fondly.

He grinned: lessons were over for the day! And that mention of Glannaventa had brought to mind his intended visit to the fort on the estuary. Striking the copper gong he sent for Justinus and when he appeared, instructed him to prepare for the excursion.

The fort was situated at the mouth of the three rivers that converged at the busy harbour. The main gates were thrown back in welcome and a flourish of trumpets heralded their approach. Very edifying: a little ceremony never goes amiss, and all the more welcome after the austerity and wildness of Mediobogdum. Clattering through the gates now and the commander, a burly man with ruddy complexion and genial expression, steps forward in greeting.

"*Ave*, Legatus – and welcome to Glannaventa."

"Greetings Publius. A smart outfit, and I hear you run a tidy fort. And you boast the best bath house in the North!" Antonius had done his research: this man at least would not feel forgotten by Rome. Publius' ruddy complexion turned a shade redder with pleasure.

"Good of you to say so, sir. Our stables are at your disposal and a meal awaits your men in the Officers' Mess. Now, if you and the tribune will follow me, my wife Flavilla awaits us in the praetorium."

"A pleasant change that will be Publius. Justinus and myself have forgotten what it is to be entertained by a lady!"

They dismounted and left their mounts to be stabled. The praetorium, Antonius noted as they entered, was a large airy court house that put his own quarters to shame. Pink plaster and sandstone pillars were the order of the day, and the reception room boasted a mosaic floor of rich colours depicting Mithras, the soldiers' god, defeating the mythical white bull.

And what a charming lady she is too. Antonius smiled at Publius' young wife seated across from him at table. A little young and insipid for his taste, but her innocence and sincerity were refreshing.

"Little wonder you look so proud Publius," he said spearing a portion of beef running with juices and depositing it on his platter.

Publius looked mystified.

"Sir?"

"Your wife, Publius, your wife!" In a realm where jewels are rare, the richest man not the commander is king – and Glannaventa holds a pearl!"

This uncustomary gallantry brought raised eyebrows and a quizzical look from Justinus. Raising his goblet Antonius drank 'to the lovely lady Flavilla,' who smiled then, catching his eye looked demurely down at her dish.

"The food is excellent lady Flavilla," he continued, "I can see you run your household with a great deal of skill."

"You are too kind, legatus," Flavilla acknowledged, inclining her head.

"No, just too cautious," he responded promptly then added as she looked puzzled, "or instead I would say that I find your company a delight and your beauty a distraction from duty, but of course I am far too polite to tell you so," he added solemnly.

Flavilla smiled and coquettishness bubbled beneath the demureness.

"Your manners do you credit sir. You have saved me from having to confess that I am overwhelmed by your charm and sophistication."

"Flavilla!" Publius exclaimed looking scandalised.

Antonius ignored him and laughed with delight at this agreeable banter. Not such a milk-sop after all then.

"Then take care my lady, or you may tempt me into rudeness, and into providing Publius with a rival" he responded, aware that Justinus was regarding him with amazement.

That, he thought with satisfaction, would put Justinus off the trail and squash any ideas he may have of him being bewitched by Rowana. And it was a pleasurable exercise in its own right, he thought, smiling at the rosy cheeked and sparkling-eyed Flavilla.

Publius, obviously reassured that his guest had taken no offence at his young wife's daring and witty flirting, wiped his mouth, beamed and gestured to one of the servers to refill Antonius' goblet. Antonius placed his hand over it and smiling shook his head.

"No more, excellent though it is. Else when I make my inspection, for every soldier present I shall be seeing two!"

"Aye, well, they're a good set of lads, but one of each is enough to keep in line!"

Antonius put down his knife and server removed his platter.

"Any problems keeping them happy here?" he asked casually, but he caught Justinus' eye and knew he too was wondering if an organised network of pilfering and trading with the Brigantes extended this far.

"Not really. You haven't heard any rumours?" Publius replied anxiously.

"Not at all. I just know young soldiers!

"At any rate the answer is negative. Any real trouble must come from the native tribes. Do the Brigantes extend this far?"

"Aye. Though to be precise the tribe native to this area of north west Brittania is the Carvettii, but it has been absorbed into the Brigante kingdom."

"I see. One wonders how many tribes the Brigantes have annexed to themselves. Such growth of power must be a concern, and the motivation behind it."

"You think a possible revolt?"

"Who knows? But following an undercover mission to survey the tribes, our agents reported several large hill forts and all their communities are fortified by large walls, banks and ditches and they are proficient at working metal. They are a very large and advanced tribe."

"But the Votadini are up north from here surely?" Publius said frowning.

"They also report an extension of the Votadini territory into the southern and eastern areas almost reaching here. If they were to join forces with the Brigantes, we could be in a lot of trouble, Publius," Antonius explained grimly.

"Are they capable of that sort of complex co-ordination? These tribes are notorious for in-fighting and territorial issues?"

"Probably not," Antonius said replied dismissively, noting that Flavilla was looking anxious.

But a disgruntled Roman might be! he thought silently.

"So, you not only have the loveliest wife in the province but a well-behaved force as well!" Antonius said lightly, changing the subject for Flavilla's benefit.

"Oh, the younger ones whoop up the town now and then and cause a bit of a stir, but there's drink, girls and traffic enough through the port to keep them occupied most of their off-duty hours," Publius said nodding.

"What it is to be young!" Antonius commented with a smile.

"Aye, right enough. And some of them look as though they have only that morning stepped into their man-clothes," Publius replied adding with a grin, "but maybe that is just me getting older!"

"You and me both, my friend!" Antonius laughed. "Well, pleasant though this is, I think we must take the parade now."

"Of course." Publius rose to his feet. "Flavilla my dear, would you like to take a rest now and meet us on the officers' terrace later?" he tactfully suggested.

Flavilla rose and nodded then turned and said over her shoulder,

"I'm so glad you came – and you are not in the least proud and overbearing!" then flushed and bit her lip but he did not miss the twinkle in her eye.

"Flavilla, really!" exclaimed Publius .

Antonius threw back his head and laughed.

"I'm so glad to have disproved my reputation, mistress!" He turned then to Publius. "Your wife's a treasure, Publius, so don't dare scold her when I am gone or I'll have you banished to the wilds of Caledonia! Now to business. Until later my delightful lady Flavilla."

He saluted and Publius led the way from the Praetorium.

The troops had been reviewed, the fortress inspected and Flavilla had rejoined them. Military topics were now dropped as they strolled along the officers' terrace which afforded a view over the busy harbour. They paused to watch the scene below: shipping clerks and merchants dodged carts piled high with bolts of silk and linen, pottery, wine and other goods; and drovers prodded cattle and oxen ashore as barques were systematically unloaded Publius pointed to large baskets stacked on the quay side.

"Oranges from Hispania."

"In many ways Brittania is an amazing province," Antonius said, nodding. "So small, so far-flung yet her ports are an important link with the Great Trade Route," he observed, raising his voice to be heard above the cacophony that rose up from the melee below as cattle lowed in protest at being herded, winches groaned, dock-side traders cried their wares and people greeted one another, they too shouting above the noise. He watched as huge amphorae of olive oil and wine from Gaul were unloaded and taken on wooden carts to the huge warehouse for checking and distribution.

"There's a consignment of yours in that little load," Publius commented.

"Aye, and it had best remain intact!" Antonius said grimly.

"Oh I can assure you...."

"No Publius, I have no qualms about it leaving here in one piece," he quickly reassured the prefect. "I imagine your security arrangements are watertight."

"Absolutely. But you have problems within the cohort?"

"I was thinking more bands of thieving Brigantes on the way," Antonius covered smoothly, having no wish to divulge his suspicions of a conspiracy at this point in case he proved wrong. Appeased by this, Publius nodded.

A volley of military orders coming from an adjacent quay suddenly cut across the everyday clamour. Antonius' head swung round as he recognised the voice of Rufinus' optio who was in charge of E-division.

"A detachment of your men repairing number four quay," Publius supplied pointing. "Our men were employed elsewhere earlier."

Ha, yes, frantically preparing for my visit no doubt, Antonius thought, his lips twitching. His sudden decision had given little notice of his intending arrival; there would taken place a frenzy of tidying, cleaning and polishing of armour and weapons. The latter brought to mind the more worrying aspect of the Marcellus issue. Before he could diplomatically quiz Publius as to the state of his weapon store he became aware of somebody watching him via a seasoned commander's prickling at the nape of the neck and feeling of unease. He turned his head swiftly in the direction of the work party repairing the quay.

"Who is that soldier?" he demanded of Justinus as the man swiftly bent his head and carried on with his work.

"One Lupinus – a fairly recent newcomer to the unit. However he has already come to the notice of both Rufinus and Marcellus."

"Ah, a good man then," Antonius said artfully with a glance at Publius who was looking interested, and a warning look for Justinus.

"Could be," Justinus answered indifferently, catching on immediately.

Taking Flavilla's arm Antonius strolled on.

From the end of the terrace they could look down on the forum. The market place buzzed with noise and activity.

"Oh look, a fire-eater!" Flavilla exclaimed in delight as the half-naked man licked a flaming brand. Antonius took a deep breath of the bracing air to dispel the sudden spell of light-headedness and sense of having been here before which he knew to be impossible. The cries of market traders and sounds of craftsmen going about their business drifted up to them on the salt breeze, as did the aroma of food being cooked over red-hot braziers along with less appetising smells. Flavilla wrinkled her nose as fumes from the sulphur used for processing cloth, and the urine of the tanners' pools stung her nostrils.

"Time to make a tactical retreat, I think commander," she said playfully. "Do you not think so?" she prompted when he failed to answer.

"What was that?" Antonius started at the sound of her voice. "Oh, my apologies – I was watching that old man down there – the one juggling the coloured balls."

"Where? I do not see him," Flavilla said frowning.

"Over there-," he stopped and blinked. The dusty corner was empty. He shook his head slightly. "That's odd, I could have sworn he was there." For a moment he had been a boy again, back in the forum with his mother. The old man had given him a red ball. That was in memory of course, but the old man down there a moment ago had been real, of that he was certain. Insight struck like a bolt of lightning. *Myrddin.* The elderly man there had not only resembled the ancient of his youthful memory, but also Rowana's guardian. A shiver ran down his spine.

"Are you all right, sir?"

Flavilla was looking at him with open anxiety. He smiled and replaced the urbane mask.

"Too much wine after all perhaps! I fell into day-dreaming Flavilla. I may call you so, even though we have just met?"

"I should like that; I feel I've known you for ages," she responded ingenuously. I too, little lady, he thought, looking down into her face. He must take care here; it would be unforgivable of him to lead her into an impetuous affair that would bring her nothing but tears and disgrace and maybe result in the loss of her present status.

"And you must call me Antonius. And now I think we must return to the others or we will create a scandal!" he teased.

"How intriguing." She laughed then was suddenly solemn. "Antonius," she started, faltering slightly on daring to use his name.

"Yes?"

"I am so glad we met."

"So am I Flavilla. You have brightened an old war-horse's day," he said lightly.

"I do not think you old. In fact, if I was not already wed to dear Publius I should be sorely tempted to show you so" she said raising her head to look into his eyes. Raising her hand to his lips Antonius kissed it.

"And I to encourage you. But now we really must go before I forget myself and create that scandal," he said gently.

This is one innocent I shall not corrupt, he silently vowed as he led her back to Publius and Justinus who were deep in talk of military matters.

He glanced at the sky. The wintry sun now hung low over the heave and swell of the estuary. They really must leave if they were not to be riding in darkness. He turned to Publius and Flavilla.

"Thank you both for your hospitality – a most enjoyable day." His gaze lingered a fraction longer than was polite on the young woman's face, conveying what had been left unsaid. Faultlessly she looked him in the eye and he had no fears about her being indiscreet.

"It has been a great pleasure commander," she said formally, but her eyes told him she understood.

He was satisfied that she did not feel rejected, and could enjoy secret moments recalling their brief and harmless flirtation. Little enough, to leave her with; it could not be an easy life, surrounded daily by rough men and military talk and she probably put up with much. Turning from her he picked up his helmet from where he had left it on the terrace wall and concentrated on buckling his chin strap.

The detachment rode out to a blare of trumpets as they clattered beneath a guard of honour. As they progressed the last notes were drowned by the raucous laughter and snatches of lewd sailors' ditties that spilled from the mansio on the quayside. As they passed Justinus grinned and nodded slyly at the annex with its veiled windows and closed door.

"No Justinus, our tour of Glannaventa is not to include the brothel," Antonius commented dryly.

"Just an idea," Justinus shrugged his shoulders and laughed. "You must have been thinking bawdy thoughts – I was referring to the harmless hostelry rooms of course!"

"The hell you were! Impudent youth." Antonius chuckled, then paused to take a last look over the harbour, bringing the cavalcade at his rear to a halt.

He blinked as sunlight sparked fire off water: wavelets, broken rhythms of dancing light, golden and hypnotic. Then a lull with voices, colours and form all receding. The interlude with Flavilla had brought on a mood of nostalgia, releasing his well-battened down emotions. It was a short step from this delightful girl to a yearning for that other one, the one who devastated sleep. She was creeping into his mind and heart, constricting his chest until a man could weep with the pain.

"Sir?"

He blinked at the sound of Justinus' voice breaking into his reverie. He turned to him, carefully adjusting his expression.

"Just taking in the beauty of it, before heading back to those bleak mountains and cold austerity!"

Raising a hand, he waved the cavalcade on and with a slight pressure of his knees moved Gaudita forward.

"That soldier, Justinus, the one you called what was it – Lupinus?" he asked as they left fort and town behind.

"That's right – his nature suits his name I'd say!"

"Yes, there was something wolfish about him," Antonius agreed nodding as he recalled the narrow face and loose-limbed angular body of the man staring up at him from the quay. "So, what was the real reason he drew the attention of Rufinus and Marcellus?

"Nothing specific, but he is something of a loner and is gaining a reputation as a troublemaker."

"Oh, in what way exactly."

"Nothing directly chargeable. Grumbling, undermining morale and that sort of thing. But as I said, a loner so nobody pays much attention. That is, a loner within the company, but he has been seen off-duty around the settlement down-valley."

"Myrddin's village?" Antonius was immediately alert.

"Yes, but Marcellus thought it would be down to him fancying his chances with a local girl."

"H'mm. Keep him under discreet surveillance Justinus. There was something about his attitude back there that I didn't like."

"I'll set Marcellus to it in the morning."

"No, rather speak with Rufinus – until we are completely sure of Marcellus."

"You think there may be weapon-trafficking going on?"

"I think we should double the guard on the weapon store and be aware of any off-duty fraternising with the Brigantes."

"You think we could be harbouring a traitor? This man Lupinus perhaps and that he, or someone else, is supplying weapons for a revolt?" Justinus slowed the pace of his mount and stared at his commander.

All too likely – and what of Rowana then? We are on opposite sides of the Rubicon. Insane to carry on meeting. Even as he thought it, he knew he could not heed his own wisdom.

"Just keep an eye on him – and an open mind," Antonius repeated, nudging Gaudita forward so that Justinus could not see his expression or be privy to his secret thoughts.

TWENTY-TWO

~

Thursday afternoon came around all too quickly. I must be mad to do this, Darcy thought glancing at her watch. She was seated in the waiting room of a Dr Simon Reynolds with a determined Caro at her side who blocked any attempt to rise and bolt with a hand placed firmly on her arm. Darcy flicked through a glossy magazine without seeing anything on the pages, occasionally glancing at the soothing Monet 'water lily' prints on the walls whilst awaiting the summons to the inner sanctum. The door opened silently and closed again with an expensive *shu-sh-sh* behind the white-coated nurse who announced in an overly cheerful voice:

"Dr Reynolds is ready for you now," then added "You are the patient, aren't you Ms. West?" as both women rose to their feet.

"Caro stays with me," Darcy said hastily, pushing Caro forward before anyone could protest.

"As you wish; a trifle irregular but it can be arranged. I'll just have to confirm with Doctor. Please wait here a moment."

The nurse bustled away then returned a few minutes later.

"That will be fine. Come this way please," she said with a broad smile that was obviously meant to be reassuring but which Darcy found rather patronising; furthermore it did nothing to allay her fears.

"You okay?" Caro whispered, squeezing her arm as they followed the nurse to a dimly lit room to the muted strains of soft and relaxing music.

"I'll let you know afterwards," Darcy said, mustering a smile but inwardly fighting the urge to turn and walk out.

"Come in and make yourselves comfortable. If your friend will sit at the back here." Dr Reynolds, forty-something at a guess with a Scottish accent and smart casual in chinos and cord jacket, rose to greet them as they were ushered in. "I'll talk you both through before we commence, it's important you both understand and that you – Caro I think you said Denise?" he looked inquiringly at the nurse who smiled and nodded, "that you, Caro," he continued, "do not interrupt, whatever happens and despite anything you might hear. Any interruption or disruption of the procedure could be dangerous for Darcy here."

Caro indicated that she understood and was led by the nurse to a seat at the back of the room. At the end of the briefing Darcy lay down on the couch as instructed and tried to ignore the butterflies flitting around her solar plexus.

Relax, relax. Your limbs are growing heavy, your eyelids are so heavy they begin to close. Relax, relax...

There was no light, and she was still descending into darkness. The echo of the words grew fainter and ever more distant and sank into silence. Finally she came to rest at the bottom of the pit. This was not a good place to be: the darkness was all around her and suffocating, the silence deep and unnerving. She struggled frantically but abortively to rise to the surface. The blackness above was now relieved by a single muted red light at its centre; a malevolent eye that watched her every movement. *Mars... The red planet... war.* Words and whispers whirled around in her mind churning up feelings of hopelessness and despair. Her arms and legs threshed the blackness as it thickened and filled her mind. Then the heaviness and lethargy took over and she lay still and unresisting.

She lay inert for what seemed an age then a sense of threat caused her to stir and open her eyes. The red light was expanding to fill the void above. As it advanced she realised it was not a planet after all but a fireball, a sphere of licking, flickering flame devouring the darkness and filling the chasm with plumes and billows of smoke. She was choking and spluttering, trying to cry out for help but the smoke was filling her lungs. The heat of the flames seared her body, the crackling and snapping of their hunger smothering her cries. By the light of the inferno she saw what was blocking her way. The *porta praetoris,* the main entrance to the fortress. He was waiting beyond this barrier, this she somehow knew. He would save her, drag her inside and out from the furnace. She hammered against the massive oak doors that reared above her head, bruising and cutting her hands on the iron studs but making no impression. Veiled by smoke and flames, several helmeted figures patrolled the platforms high on the watchtowers that flanked the gates to either side. She cried out to the sentries for admittance, to be saved from the inferno. They shook their heads and raised their hands in slow motion, palms outward in a gesture of non-admittance. They were shouting something down to her, the words fragmented and distorted by the roaring of the flames. *Non licet, non licet, non licet.*

"*Darcy, come back. Wake up now, wake up, wake up....*"

The words were filtering through the fug, reaching her and pulling her back. She was floating up and up and up, rising above the flames and smoke into a bright white sky with several suns blazing in her eyes. Someone was screaming, the voice shrill and edged with terror. Who was it? Who was making that terrible noise? She was threshing around, trying to sit up in order to investigate but her body was weighted beneath huge studs and slabs of oak.

"Darcy, you are safe and can hear my voice. Wake up now."

Her struggles increased and like a tadpole newly hatched she swam for the surface but still couldn't burst through the surface skin.

"Darcy! You can hear my voice and you will obey the command. Now *wake up!*"

She opened her eyes in response to the urgency in the voice and stared in bewilderment at the white ceiling and its sunken down-lighters beneath which she was lying.

"Hush Darcy, hush. It's all right now."

Why was someone telling her to be quiet? She turned her head and stared without understanding at the troubled face of a man looming above her own. She stared in fascination as beads of sweat rolled slowly down his forehead.

"Darcy be silent!"

It was only then, as the sharpness of that command penetrated the red mist in her mind, that she realised she was the person doing the screaming.

"Where am I?" That whisper took all of her strength.

"I am Dr Reynolds. You are safe in my consulting room."

Darcy blinked several times then started to sit up but was gently pushed back again by the nurse in the white coat.

"Lie still for a while Darcy," she said, taking hold of her hand. The searing pain this caused brought forth a moan of distress. Raising the other one to a few inches before her face she saw it was reddened, bruised and bleeding.

"What happened to my hands?" She struggled again to rise but was pushed back against the pillows.

"It is a temporary thing Darcy. The marks will fade. in a moment Denise here will bathe them and apply a soothing cream," Dr Reynolds explained indicating the nurse with a gesture, "but first let's make you more comfortable."

"What happened to me?" Darcy whispered, overcome by exhaustion.

"You are safe now Darcy." Dr Reynolds repeated, wiping his brow with a white cloth handed to him by the nurse. She could still hear his voice; it was much calmer now but he was no longer speaking to her but reassuring somebody else. "Don't worry, she will be all right now."

Then Caro's voice, high and edged with anxiety asking him what had gone wrong.

"It happens sometimes; she went under very deeply. Normally she would have been able to hear my questions and answer them, thus giving some insight into her experiences. Unfortunately she sank beyond my reach. She is obviously a very good subject."

Then Caro's voice again saying something about cuts and burns and asking if there would be any lasting effect, and Dr Reynolds assuring her that there would not. The nurse was holding her arm and Caro was saying in an urgent voice

"Wait! What are you giving her?"

"Just a wee shot of Valium to calm her nerves. Please don't worry, I assure you this is routine where there is some distress."

Darcy turned her head on the pillow. There was a pricking sensation in her arm followed by a deep desire to drift and float above her worries and leave them all behind.

She opened her eyes again and immediately Caro's face loomed above.

"It's okay sweetie, you're all right now.

"How long have I been asleep?"

"Over half an hour."

Darcy lay for a moment digesting this information and testing her bodily sensations. No pain; the agony of her hands was now a mere discomfort. In fact she felt pretty good: relaxed and rested. She sat up, blinked and pushed back the white cellular blanket. "I'm out of here."

The nurse seated at the back of the room keeping watch on her patient rose at this and twitched the blanket back into place then plumped and arranged the pillows at Darcy's back.

"Dr Reynolds will need to examine you first, just to make sure you are okay."

"My hands are almost back to normal," Darcy insisted, holding them up to display the fading bruises and cuts. The reddening of the burns had also faded significantly.

"A general medical examination," the nurse amended, opening the blinds a little to allow the autumnal sunlight to enter. "Otherwise he can't discharge you."

"Best make sure," Caro soothed as Darcy's head began to rise from the pillow and she patently intended to ignore the nurse's advice. Giving in to her friend's anxious entreaties, Darcy sighed with impatience and lay still.

"Not a thing, I can't remember a thing," Darcy insisted moments later in response to Simon Reynolds' questions. A post mortem of events would only prolong this ordeal and all she could recall was darkness, flames and being refused admittance at Mediobogdum. That and the agony of her apparent injuries but this he knew about already.

"Okay, Darcy I'm going to leave it at that. Temperature, pulse, heart rhythm and blood pressure are all normal. I'm sorry to be unable to help you with your experiences, but I did point out to your friend here when she made the appointment that there are no guarantees."

"I understand."

"But should you get any problems be sure to contact me immediately."

"What sort of problems doctor?" Caro interrupted with a look of alarm.

"Sometimes, following deep-state hypnosis when the conscious mind blocks out the trauma, some people experience occasional flashback. Don't worry, it's pretty uncommon," he said as Caro looked anything but reassured.

"Can I go now?" Darcy demanded, hand grasping the blanket in readiness of throwing it off.

"Aye. But go home and be off to bed with a cup of tea. You need to take things easy for the rest of the day; you've had a traumatic experience remember."

"I feel fine." And she did, except for the burning question he must be asked by every single one of his patients. "Tell me though Doctor, did I say anything whilst under?"

"Only one thing," he said frowning, "You said *non licet, non licet*, over and over again."

"That's Latin, isn't it?"

He smiled. "It was when I was at school."

"What does it mean?"

Dr Reynolds cleared his throat.

"Actually it means *it is not allowed.*"

TWENTY-THREE

~

"You've had a traumatic experience," Caro protested half-heartedly as Darcy steered her towards a bistro close to the shopping centre. "You are supposed to go home and rest!"

"Nonsense. A coffee and Danish will do just as well." To be truthful Darcy's head was pounding and her stomach churning but she did not relish the thought of returning home alone; plus she could sense Caro's need to talk and guessed it was about guilt. "Don't use that as an excuse; it was the non-event of the year – and anyway, it's your turn and you'll do anything to get out of paying!" she teased.

"Well if you are sure."

For answer Darcy propelled her through the door.

As it happened the Danish was left half-eaten on Darcy's plate, but the cappuccino went down well and she ordered a second cup for them both.

"I should have known better. It's all my fault for pressing you into it," Caro was saying for the third time, licking her fingers as she finished her pastry. "that was good but under the circumstances I feel a right pig for being so hungry!"

"Put it down to nervous energy. Seriously Caro, don't be daft. Nobody twisted my arm. I do have a mind of my own you know."

"You could have been-,"

"But I wasn't!" Darcy interrupted. "Look, it was an experiment and now we have it out of the way and no harm done. Okay?"

Caro pressed her hand then apologised as Darcy winced.

"Okay. But your hands obviously still hurt."

"A bit, but they're getting there." Darcy held them out for inspection; the red weals looked less painful and the purple bruising had faded to brownish yellow.

"Are you sure you feel all right otherwise?"

"Fine. A bit sort of disoriented but as Dr Reynolds said, that will pass."

"So," Caro said eyeing Darcy through narrowed eyes and with a tilt of the head that said it all, "are you going to tell me what really happened?"

Darcy fiddled with her coffee spoon and drew it through the froth that topped her coffee. The doodle came out as a capital letter 'A' and she swiftly smoothed it out and replaced the spoon in the saucer.

"You know me pretty well don't you?"

"I guess."

"I was there. Outside the main gate at Mediobogdum. There were flames everywhere. I hammered and hammered but wasn't allowed in."

"Which accounts for the burns and bruises. Sounds horrific; no wonder you were screaming."

Darcy stared out of the window and tried to block the images that came whirling back.

"It really has got to you that place hasn't it?" Caro said watching her shrewdly.

"It's magic Caro. Scary but magic. The mountains dream; you can feel it. They brood too, and on a good day smile. Perhaps they even move."

"Excuse me?" Caro said wryly.

"The cosmic power within them is palpable. Oh, it may take a lifetime to move a couple of centimetres, a whole generation to weep one tear after we've raped and gouged and broken their bones. But yes, they move and mourn."

"Christ Darcy."

"I know. Devastating thought isn't it."

"I was rather thinking you scare me rotten. Take care Darcy. You're moving too far out, beyond where Brant or I can reach."

Darcy shrugged then smiled at her friend.

"Take no notice of me Caro; I flipped a bit back there that's all."

But I cannot wait to return, she silently added.

"So, what do you think it was all about then?" she said, sitting upright and forcing herself to sound normal.

"I may be wrong," Caro began shrugging her shoulders and pulling a face. "but my guess is whoever, or whatever is spooking you was giving the no-no. Maybe that approach is deemed as cheating."

"How do you mean?" Darcy said frowning as she put down her empty cup.

"Well, a bit like the spiritual quest of old. Maybe you just have to suffer the journey – in that context the words 'suffer' merely meant 'undergo', and similarly 'ordeal' meant 'quest' or something like – and without trying to take short cuts."

Darcy stared at her friend for a moment without speaking. It was a strange feeling, the way her words slotted into place like the final piece of a jigsaw.

"I guess you are right Caro," she said quietly. "Let's go."

They stepped outside into unexpected sunlight. Darcy closed her eyes as the brightness struck eyes that were still feeling sensitive, and for a second or so held her breath fearing a return to the crimson blaze. Nothing happened however and she opened them again and walked on, ignoring Caro's anxious glances. As they strolled through the shopping precinct on the way back to the car park Darcy nudged Caro and pointed.

"What has that dog got around its neck?"

Caro gave a perfunctory look and shrugged.

"No idea. Too far away."

They walked on and Darcy watched the Setter trotting towards them, all dancing feet and glossy-coated in the sunlight. That flash, the broad refraction caught her eye again as the animal sashayed along, feathered fringes swinging and swaying.

Caro suddenly stopped as they were passing a supermarket.

"Oh, I need to take home some coffee and milk."

"I'll sit on this bench in the sun and wait for you," Darcy suggested, feeling unequal to the noise and crowded aisles.

"Okay, won't be a sec." Caro disappeared through the door.

Darcy returned to watching the dog advance from the far end of the precinct.

A man was leading it by a length of frayed rope, and this along with his tatty raincoat and unkempt appearance seemed incongruous. The dog, given the domed head, fine bone structure and coat of silk, was obviously of good pedigree. Had he stolen it from a car? Or maybe, she thought feeling a rush of guilt at making such a judgement purely on the basis of his appearance, he had found it and was taking it to the police station. She watched the man shuffle along in shoes that were strangers to brush and polish and at least one size too large. In contrast the setter danced at his side in high-step. She shifted uneasily; they seemed to be homing in on her bench.

Suddenly he was before her, his smile revealing dingy teeth; one incisor bore a large chip.

"'Ere, take her a minute."

Darcy stared at him nonplussed.

"Go on," he urged shaking the end of the rope to emphasise the point, "take 'er." Eyes of rain-washed slate laughed at her stupidity. Instinctively she held out her hand for the leash. Next moment he had disappeared into the crowd.

"Oh God, this is all I need," Darcy muttered, convinced now that the stranger had dumped the dog and done a bunk. "Let's have a look girl," she soothed, and the dog sat patiently, a look of absolute trust in its eyes. Her fingers searched the long silky hair for a name tag. Her fingers encountered the coolness of metal. She drew out the chain from the apron of hair and stared at the oblong medallion. It was like nothing she had ever seen before: engraved with strange figures and symbols it had an air of antiquity. Two major figures guarded the large opalescent stone at the centre. The coolness and weight felt at home in her hand. The sensation grew along with a consuming desire to own the piece. This was for her, nobody else must have it. She was shocked by the ruthlessness and violence of her feelings.

"Take it."

She started guiltily. The man had returned without her noticing and was watching her with an odd expression as though he knew her thoughts.

"I couldn't possibly-," she started to say, sitting upright again on the bench, then faltered into silence, thrown by this man's oddness. Suddenly she was afraid. That aura of strangeness, suspected from the first but judiciously ignored, was now beyond question. Her head felt light, the shops, the people, the bustle all unreal. Only this man and the beautiful dog seemed real. And the medallion.

"Take it. It's for you," he urged, gently drawing the rope from her grasp; his fingernails were rimmed with black.

"But I can't possibly," she protested.

"Why not?" There was now a hint of belligerence in his tone.

"It's, well-, it's hers," she stammered, feeling foolish.

"Don't be daft, what would a dog want with a bloody necklace!"

A logic that unexpectedly made her want to laugh, partly from amusement but mostly embarrassment because the man's raised voice was attracting stares of curiosity from shoppers crowding the precinct.

"She's brought it for you," he said loudly, pronouncing each syllable with the slowness and deliberation one might use to a child that is slow to understand. The shoppers paused and gathered in groups to watch the entertainment. "Tek it, I tell yer. She's brought it all this way just for you."

"But *why?*" Darcy shook her head and looked at him in bewilderment.

" Because it's yours."

She shook her head. "No. No it's not."

"Are you sure?" he said quietly, his speech suddenly cultured.

A long moment of stillness and disquiet followed as Darcy looked into the slate-grey eyes and recognised wisdom and something else she could not define. He knew. He knew she was pretending not to know about the strangeness, that he had been sent for a purpose. Knew of her embarrassment and cowardice. Shame flooded her being. Oblivious now to on-lookers, she held out her hand. He moved his head slowly from side to side, beckoned and pointed to the ground at his feet. Obediently she moved forward, sank down on one knee and waited with bowed head. The chain felt cold against the nape of her neck as he slipped it over her head. As he released it, the weight of the pendant tugged at her heart.

The private ritual over she raised her head and smiled. "I don't know how to thank you – or her," she said stroking the dog's head. The pressure of the man's hands at her elbows brought her to her feet.

"Yes you do."

She understood yet didn't: yet knew it was something to do with all that had been happening, about seeing it through and doing whatever was required. "I'll keep it safe for ever," she vowed.

"Aye." He nodded solemnly. "Wear it from time to time, eh? And think of an old man and his dog."

"I will, I promise."

"I'll never forget you – or her," she called out as he led the dog away.

"What's going on here Darcy?"

Darcy became aware of Caro standing next to her, of the sharpness of voice and strained expression.

Darcy did not answer. She watched the old man shuffle away, the lace of one shoe trailing in the dust.

The precinct felt very empty.

OUT OF TIME VIII

~

Even from his position within the peat hut high on the moor above Rowana's settlement he could hear the beating of the drums that marked time for the unit of infantry marching over the pass. The sound reached him with a clarity made possible by the bare rocks of the surrounding mountains; the monotonous single beat richoted from each rock face giving the semblance of troops marching at triple time. On first hearing it Marcellus must have rushed to the latrine in similar time, a thought which made Antonius grin with amusement. The prefect's guilty conscience would cause him to relate this latest incursion by Rome to the fact of his fraudulent ordering of supplies! To be fair though that was now history and he was being the model prefect and doing his utmost to make up his lapse.

The smile died as swiftly as it had come. Little did the likeable rogue know of the real reason behind the sending of reinforcements. Despite his moderate preliminary report to the Emperor and senate, Hadrian had decided on a policy of subjugation rather than further attempts to integrate these fierce inhabitants of the North. Albeit unlike the southern tribes, the northern clans had resisted all attempts at Romanisation, had at best adopted a sullen pretence of no action and at worst were raiding and plotting insurrection at every opportunity. The very mountains and valleys hummed with hostility and conspiracy.

However his barbarian side inherited from Calpurnia sympathised with this reluctance to relinquish their culture and identity to an invader and even admired their courage and tenacity which after all, he excused himself, were good Roman values. A compromise of working for peaceful acceptance on a penalty/reward basis targeting the leaders with increased wealth and status for those who succeeded in getting their clan to toe the Roman line whilst largely allowing them their own culture, would in his view be more productive and humanitarian. But Hadrian harboured no such sympathies.

His expression hardened and his lips set in a line as he thought of the possible consequences, especially to Rowana and her people. In his opinion Hadrian was premature in his decision-making and a campaign of carnage would result in countless lives on both sides being lost. However given the Britons' guerrilla tactics in a nightmare terrain where they knew every tree, rock and gulley, the goddess Victoria could feasibly smile upon the Britons. Such a campaign could end in ignominious defeat for the legion. It had happened before and could happen again. The blame for a disaster arising from a wrong decision would be laid at his door, based purely on that preliminary and patently incomplete report which in any case favoured pacification and integration. The motive behind ordering a campaign of ethnic cleansing was Hadrian's quest for fame and glory. He had always admired the Emperor's military knowledge and prowess, but recently there was disturbing evidence of power-lust triumphing over compassion and common sense.

Antonius sighed and stared absently out of the doorway across a sepia sea of parched grasses undulating in the light breeze with the line of elephantine fells marching across the horizon. It was a day typical of this place and its inhabitants: a contradiction of dark clouds and fitful sunlight that suddenly blazed, firing grass and bracken with gold before subsiding again into mauve shadow. He was being set up and knew it but could do little about it; a prospect that made him itch with frustration. However if this was to be his fate then so be it; the gods and Hadrian would have their way, though these days Hadrian recognised little distinction between the two. There was still the question of Rowana and the dire implications for herself and her

185

clan, not to mention his own dilemma. Once a direct order cam through, allegiance to Rome would require him to order her death or at best enslavement along with the destruction of the settlement; his heart revolted at the prospect, as Calpurnia's barbarian spirit must surely do. That a son of hers could order the massacre of her people would, were she still alive, make her shrink from him in loathing and shame. It would destroy him too; not since the days of his youth when Ingenua – and how ironic a name for one who had proved more viper than innocent – had broken off their betrothal and married an ancient, fat but stinking-rich senator, had he felt this way about a woman.

He must induce Rowana to use her powers of persuasion on Myrddin. Maybe she could succeed where he would undoubtedly fail and convince him to move the clan on and save their lives if not their homestead. This possible solution lightened his mood to one of hope and optimism. Besides, he consoled himself, it was unlikely that Hadrian would make an immediate move, and autumn was inevitably sliding into winter. Snow-choked passes and stormy seas would delay the direct order from Rome, possibly until spring and by then the situation – or Emperor even, given Rome's transient loyalty! – may have changed. It was not unknown for these demi-gods to fall victim to their greed and lust for power and Hadrian was thought by some in the senate to be in danger of becoming self-seeking and over ambitious. Suddenly his eyes brightened as he saw a slight figure approaching through the tall grasses of the hanging moor. His heart leapt; she had kept their tryst. Time to *carpe diem* and put weighty matters aside.

Her hair was tousled by the wind and the hem of her cloak and blue robe bore a tide of red mud yet she entered the humble hut like a queen, bearing a tool with a sickle shaped blade as though it was a sceptre. His eyes had grown accustomed to the dimness, but she stood for a moment blinking and getting her bearings after the brightness of the day outside.

"You!" As always she affected surprise at seeing him. "Are you sheltering from the wind? Tired by your trek?" she taunted and moved from the doorway so that a shaft of sunlight slanted through and smote the rear wall, filling the air between with the dance of a million dust motes. Her eyes sought his and perceptibly darkened as the pupils enlarged and he felt an answering surge of desire. So regal was her bearing that secretly he felt an obligation to sink down on one knee; overtly he affected an air of authority deemed more suited to his position and heightened by a need to conceal his true feelings.

"Neither. A couple of days ago whilst out riding I spotted you in the woods again," he accused.

She placed the tool so that it leaned against the wall, then dusted off her hands.

"Is that why you asked me to meet you here today?" she taunted.

He suppressed a smile at her unintentional slip. She indulged in a method of arranging trysts without appearing to do so by a simple means of mentioning times and locations in response to his requests for a meeting, and all with apparent innocence. Such as today, and being 'unable to meet him having promised, since it had been sharpened, to return the peat cutter to the stone hut on the moor above the settlement'.

"Is that why you came?" he parried, then when she did not reply added: "Perhaps I intended to warn you that it is not safe to wander there alone." Banter aside this soon might be all too true, and his face clouded at the thought and he spoke more sharply than intended: "so stay out those woods."

Her head shot up and she brushed back strands of hair from her forehead with a gesture of impatience.

"Allow me to judge for myself."

"You are not qualified to do so."

"I have every right to be there, alone or not."

"Not by Roman law."

"Which has nothing to do with my people or this land," she flung back.

Suddenly her mood changed. The atmosphere in the hut still sparked fire but of a different kind. He became acutely aware of the earthy smell of the peat, that and the softness of its crumb mixed with shreds of desiccated grass, bracken and other wind-drifted leaves lying beneath his feet; of the ever-changing patterns made by splashes of sunlight on blackened wall as it filtered through the doorway; but most of all his senses sang with the heather and rosemary perfume that spiked the warm scent of her arousal. Her eyes were now heavy lidded and slanted, her lips slightly parted and swollen.

"And if I defy you?" She was teasing him, ignoring their quarrel and also the culture clash that forbad their liaison thus setting the lead for their usual game. It was of course the only possible way and he joined in the deception.

"I could have you up-ended and caned for the impudent child that you are," he said conversationally, removing his helmet and tucking it beneath his left armpit before stroking the cropped hair with his other hand. She put her head to one side, surveying him critically and with serious expression.

"I suppose you could. But I should have thought you would prefer to act for yourself."

Suddenly he felt even hotter than prior to removing his headgear. She was openly smiling at him now and he suppressed an answering smile.

"Infinitely. So take care I don't cut myself a switch!".

She did laugh then, and the sound sent a ripple of joy through his veins.

"You are too much of a gentleman sir."

"I begin to think maybe I am." he replied, but there was a strange look in his eyes and he was not laughing. She held his gaze and her eyes darkened with desire.

Simultaneously and in silence they moved forward and into each other's arms. Her lips and body responded to his ardour, but despite the force of his passion he hesitated. He held her a little way from him, searching her face, needing to know if she was aware that the kisses and caresses she was permitting were leading them to an act of the gravest significance. She held his gaze and for answer sank to the soft and fragrant floor, taking him down with her.

188

Later, when they moved apart, they surveyed one another without speaking, aware that the tide of their passion had swept them over the Rubicon: a state of intimacy from which there could be no return. Despite an overwhelming happiness he was overcome by guilt. Marriage was out of the question on both sides; anything less would be seen as a gross insult to herself and her people. It was totally irresponsible to continue their relationship knowing where it could lead. Yet he was powerless to resist, and he suspected it was the same for Rowana. From a small leather pouch attached to his belt he took a pendant of gold and silver set with turquoise and a large central moonstone.

"Come here," he commanded in tones designed to hide his awkwardness; gentleness did not come easy after a life spent watching his back in legion and senate. He held out his hands with the chain stretched between.

"Kneel, child," he said with a smile, expecting her to rebel as she usually did at this provocative term and even more so at the command. Instead she did as bidden, holding his gaze as she did so, a questioning look in her eyes.

"I had this made for my mother, but she died before I could give it to her. I should like you to have it," he finished in a low voice, flushed with embarrassment and annoyed with himself for having said so much. By revealing the preciousness of this token he had betrayed the depth of his tenderness and esteem.

"It is beautiful, but I cannot," she said, looking up at him still and shaking her head.

"Why not?" his voice had sharpened at this rejection of his gift.

"He would kill us both."

"He could try," Antonius said grimly in the manner of male lovers through Time immemorial when threatened with the revenge of a rival. "Who threatens you so? Not Myrddin, surely?" he demanded.

She shook her head in answer to his question.

"Who then? Tell me and I'll…"

"No, please! Leave it be, you can only make things worse."

He frowned and sighed with suppressed anger and frustration whilst considering her words. On the one hand he burned to ensure her safety and avenge her distress, but on the other sensed probing would confirm her betrothal, and better for his conscience and her honour that he could feign ignorance for as long as possible, thus delaying or even avoiding the necessity of confrontation.

"Very well, for your sake Rowana – and for now!" he agreed reluctantly. "Keep it hidden. Bury it in a box if you must but wear it sometimes in private and when you do so, think of me. But any further threats and I want to know."

She bowed her head and he took the gesture as a sign of assent and slipped the chain onto her shoulders.

She rose and cradled the pendant within her open palm. He said nothing, aware that due to the nature and sacredness of the carved figures on the piece he had also betrayed his mother's barbarian roots. He prepared for the inevitable questions and ensuing embarrassment, but she merely gave him a startled look and he was grateful for her sensitivity and discretion.

"You must have loved her very much. The moonstone is the magic eye. She stroked the large milky stone at the centre. "But what is this word?" she added pointing. He stood next to her, his head touching the dark sea of waves that was her hair, his nostrils filled with the scent of her, a heather, rosemary and new-cut hay smell that made his head swim. He touched the side of his nose in a gesture of embarrassment and failed to meet her gaze as he spoke.

"*Indomita*. It means 'She who is wild and untamed'."

He did not miss the startled look she threw him.

"Not my mother!" he said with a mischievous smile that made him look younger and served to lighten the tension of the moment. "I had a silversmith at Galava inscribe it only last week," he explained, referring to the fort and adjacent settlement at the eastern end of the pass. He had judged it distant enough for curiosity to prove insignificant. As it happened, whatever that man's thoughts on the matter he had not been foolish enough to ask questions nor would he be likely to gossip; his reputation had travelled swiftly it seemed. She repeated the word softly to herself.

"You chose the inscription for me then?"

"I should say so! Who else would merit it?"

She smiled broadly at this, then for a long moment held his gaze in silence. Taking hold of his hand she raised it to her lips and kissed the back of it.

"You have done me a great honour."

"You have done me a greater one, Rowana. Whatever happens, no-one can take today from us."

With great gentleness he took her in his arms and kissed her forehead, eyelids and lingeringly, her lips. They clung together like that for some minutes, each knowing the obdurate world waited beyond the haven of these humble walls.

"Go with care, my little love," he whispered as they finally broke apart.

"And you too, my Antonius," she replied.

His heart leapt with joy at the sound of his name on her lips. She turned and left him then, and his heart ached for what could not be as he watched her walk out of the hut and wade through the sea of grass.

He was waiting at the foot of the fell, much as Antonius had expected he would be. Would this meddlesome ancient never leave him in peace? And how much did he know of what had transpired between himself and Rowana? Or about the underground resistance he suspected was brewing?

"You had a pleasant walk sir?" Myrddin inquired pleasantly, as though nothing else was of serious import. But his eyes, usually misted by time and preoccupation, were now limpid as the pools scattered across the fells yet sharp as an axe blade caught by the sun. They bore into the heart and soul of the younger man and Antonius was afraid. A dreadful vision of death, fire and destruction filled his mind, making his mouth dry and his stomach churn. His sight became blurred and he blinked several times as Myrddin's staff appeared to move and change form. With horror he watched the transformation from wooden stave to writhing serpent complete with

191

flickering tongue and venomous fangs. Above it Myrddin's face loomed pale and pitiless as the grave.

Antonius felt his mind suddenly clear as though Myrddin had released it. It had to be a supernatural trick. He had to be one of the forbidden sect; it was the only logical explanation. Somehow Myrddin had sensed the turn events had taken and that he, Antonius, would be ordered to act out Rome's policy of repression. The Druidae, he knew, were not permitted to set down their arcane knowledge on parchment and, despite persecution by Rome, practised in secret. This man could easily be a Druid.

"No sir, I am merely old."

Antonius ran his tongue over lips that felt suddenly dry.

"The villagers come to you for counsel," he probed, recalling what Rowana had told him.

"I am accredited – quite erroneously – with a smattering of Raven Knowledge."

"And that means?"

"The raven sees and knows all. Roman hypocausts and heated floors are no match for ancient intellect."

"H'mm, maybe. And potions? No doubt they come for those too."

"At times, when they or their beasts are sick. Then there is the spate of fever that strikes each year."

"Fever?" Antonius repeated in sudden alarm.

"Aye." Myrddin pursed thin lips and stroked his cotton-grass beard. "When 'horn' means more than antlers and the tup clambers the ewe. Mind, those struck by Cupid's arrow don't seek to cure the poison but rather the power to infect!"

His bony shoulders shook with silent mirth.

Antonius did not join him in laughter. Cupid was a Roman god so what was this cunning old trickster implying? He must know about the trysts with his ward, his love for her and be warning him off. And were the words 'poison' and 'infect' referring to Roman seed and its implantation in a barbarian womb? If so, he was being a little too wise for his own good.

"My wisdom is merely illusion, seen by those with a simple need."

That mind reading trick again. Antonius threw him a startled look then swiftly covered his tracks by yawning and affecting polite boredom.

"And that is?"

"To hear their own wisdom from the mouth of somebody else! Only then will they accept it. I simply tell them what they already know."

Antonius shivered as Myrddin's eyes met his and the silence deafened in its intensity. Something was passing between them, a flow of energy that made his flesh crawl. Myrddin emanated power and his eyes burned with a light that commanded respect. Not for the first time this old man triggered a memory from the days of his youth. For an instant he was back in the thronged forum. The old man was sitting in a corner of the dusty market place juggling brightly coloured balls. They glistened and arced, weaving magical patterns in the air then lay still in his lap. The old man looked at him through eyes the blue of forget-me-knots as he held out the red ball.

"Take it boy," he said, "Red is for you. The colour of blood, Mars and berries." The boy hesitated. "Take it, and think sometimes of an old man," he said and the boy snatched the ball and ran away, but not before he had dropped one of his precious sesterci into the ancient's bowl. The vision faded and he was back at the foot of the fell feeling dazed and disoriented.

Myrddin's hair seemed to turn from grey to silver and an enigmatic smile softened the wizened features as though he had read the other's mind.

"Do I know you old man?" Antonius whispered.

"Far better to ask if you know yourself and what lies within your heart."

"Always these damned riddles!"

"Sometimes Truth is an unwanted gift that has to be enticingly wrapped."

"You are warning me old man?"

"Ah yes, about the coming storm." Myrddin nodded and looked to the west.

"Storm?" Antonius gave a snort of derisive laughter that was wholly relief and glanced at a tranquil blue sky overhead. Yet as he followed the direction of Myrddin's gaze he had to admit that the cloud was thickening; stratus giving way to bloated cumulus rolling in from the west, and the sun was turning pale and watery behind a murky veil.

"I knew you were out on foot and came to warn you," Myrddin said conversationally, "This storm when it comes may cause much damage," he added, his tone suddenly sombre so that Antonius' relief was short-lived and his suspicions newly aroused as to Myrddin's cryptic meaning: this was about Rome's change of policy or his relationship with Rowana rather than the weather.

"But this you already know and secretly dread." Myrddin intoned.

With gnarled hands he pulled the cloak tighter about his thin body as the wind freshened and suddenly turned chill.

The movement drew Antonius' attention to the large silver *penna* that secured the garment at the old man's throat. A ray of sunlight caught it, flashed, and was reflected and intensified so that momentarily he was blinded. He closed his eyes against the glare and when he opened them again, Myrddin had disappeared. Antonius looked up and shivered as the sunlight faded so suddenly it seemed someone had blown out the cosmic oil lamp. As he set off down the fellside thunder-dogs growled and raindrops the size of a silver denarius spattered his helmet.

TWENTY-FOUR

~

Darcy half-smiled at the medallion reflected in the dressing table mirror. *Wear it sometimes, and think of an old man and his dog.* She was doing so right now a couple of days after it had come into her possession. The large moonstone at the centre glowed blue then pearly white. Her mind went over the details again; the flash of sunlight on metal, the beautiful dog, the dishevelled man and herself kneeling as he placed the pendant around her neck. Incredible, yet it had happened. Upon closer inspection she had discovered a word engraved on the back but had no idea of its meaning. Oddly it looked to be Latin, yet the deities depicted on the front plus the symbols and scrolls had a distinctly Celtic feel. She must ask Caro. The light in her eyes dimmed; Caro had been distinctly cool on the journey out of Lancaster. She had backed off, had blocked any attempt by Darcy to talk of what had occurred by constantly changing the subject with comments ranging from what to prepare for dinner to what video she was planning to watch that night. Yet she must have seen most of what had happened and therefore understood her friend's need to confide and talk the thing through.

The sound of a vehicle approaching and stopping on the gravelled space at the front of the house caused Darcy's head to turn from mirror to window. *Brant.* A glance at the still light sky, then at her wristwatch told her he was earlier than expected. That meant they could relax and wind down together this evening and enjoy a full day together tomorrow before he left again for London. He had managed to wangle at least one day at home despite the urgent and secret mission that had taken him away prematurely. She had already decided not to tell him about the hypnotherapy incident; he was almost certain to disapprove. She was still trying to decide whether or not to say anything about the most significant events of that day when he walked into the room.

"Hi sweetheart." He crossed the room in a couple of strides and pulled her into his arms. "God but it's good to be home," he murmured into her hair.

"Missed you too," she whispered.

A few minutes later he released her from his embrace and stared at the medallion hanging between her breasts. He reached out and cradled it in his hand. "Where did you get this?" Then when she failed to reply added lightly "got a secret admirer have you?"

"Don't be silly." Flushing, she looked away and laughed.

"Teasing. But why the secrecy, love?"

The moment of decision; whatever she said or didn't say now would have to be followed through. It was already too late, she had hesitated too long.

"Darcy," he said sternly so that she had to turn her head and look into his eyes. They mirrored his disquiet and she flushed on account of being on the brink of telling him yet another lie. This had to stop.

"I went into Lancaster with Caro. Walking back to the car there was this old man. In the precinct you know," she began hesitantly.

He nodded and gestured for her to continue and haltingly Darcy related the tale.

"Okay, so why the need to hide it from me?" he demanded when she had finished.

"Guess I felt stupid." She looked down at the carpet, tracing with one foot a scroll of the traditional gold on blue pattern.

He took her chin in his hand and forced her to look at him again.

"And afraid I would feel all this was getting too wacky, or is sinister the right word? – and withdraw my approval?"

For answer she shrugged and looked away again, then feeling the tug at her neck gave him a startled look. The medallion was still cradled in his hand and he was tracing the figures and symbols with the other, an odd expression on his face as he did so.

"What is it?" she asked sharply.

"A reminder."

She stared at him, tried not to acknowledge the cold finger of panic touching the length of her spine. It had been said with such heart-stopping surety yet in a robotic sort of voice.

"Of what?" she managed to whisper.

"To let you know *Dea Mater – The Great Mother –* still lives. To remind you that nothing ever really dies."

"How do you know this Brant?" she said grabbing his arm, but he seemed not to hear and his eyes held a faraway look. Her fear crystallised as he turned the pendant over and studied the obverse surface. She was afraid to ask the question yet must, knowing he would answer.

"What does it mean Brant?"

"*Indomita.*" He intoned in that same techno-voice that incongruously brought to mind Stephen Hawkin.

"What does that mean?" she repeated.

"She who is wild and untamed."

"Why? Why would it be engraved there?" But even as she spoke Brant let the medallion drop from his fingers and she felt the weight and coolness of it once more between her breasts.

"Fancy a drink before I cook dinner? My treat" he said in a normal voice, smiling and with the faraway look banished from his eyes.

"Fine, yes," she stammered, forcing an answering smile.

It was a perfect evening spent drinking wine and listening to music before the sitting room fire, and despite her preoccupation with his bizarre response to the medallion, she felt much closer to him than of late. He had prepared that delicious pasta meal, been charming and attentive in every way and the old spark rekindled.

"Early night?" she whispered in his ear, snuggling closer to him on the settee.

"So what's wrong with here?"

"Nothing at all."

His lips found hers as he pulled her close and his hand explored her body. He touched the pendant suspended between her breasts and as the kiss ended she wondered at the strange expression that flitted across his face. His hand returned to cup her breast, his fingers teasing the nipple that perked at his touch revealing her own mounting desire. He undressed her slowly and sensuously, dropping first her skirt then her underwear onto the floor whilst whispering endearments. A log shifted in the grate and dropped a fraction causing a spurt of flame and he stopped abruptly, causing her to draw a sharp breath at the sudden cessation of intimate contact.

"What's this?" he demanded, touching the reddened areas along her forearm so that she could not avoid wincing with pain.

"There's nothing there; come on darling," she whispered, attempting to distract him by drawing his head down to her exposed breasts but he resisted and pulled back. He sat upright, looking down at her body. The firelight flickered across the flesh betraying her secret; the bruises and burn marks, previously hidden by carefully chosen sleeves, had faded but far from disappeared.

He frowned, took hold of both arms and peered more closely.

"What has caused this Darcy? The skin looks reddened and sore."

"It's just the glow from the fire," she said, attempting to draw away but his grip tightened.

"You're lying Darcy. Now tell me the truth."

She held her silence but his expression told her she had better come clean.

"Okay, I went to this hypnotherapist," she began, and stammered her way through the story.

As she finished he was still grasping her arm.

"Brant, let go," she commanded, suddenly frightened. The strangeness had crept between them again; his eyes had that faraway look and distorted by the flickering firelight, the face above her was not that of Brant. The redness from the glow in the fireplace spread outwards engulfing them both and a strange humming sound filled the air. The body was leaner and harder than she remembered, the muscles appearing to ripple in the light from the flames. *The body of a warrior befitting any age.* That thought came free of conscious bidding. As he stood over her she shrank in fear, not of Brant but of what might be happening here. The walls of the room were retreating to reveal an open space, and the air was redolent with damp earth, mosses and foliage, creating the secret and slightly mysterious ambience of a sun-dappled glade in the forest.

"Brant, you're scaring me!"

"I told you not to go there."

"What the hell do you think you are doing?" she cried, struggling furiously to extricate herself from his grip.

"Contemplating teaching a disobedient child a lesson!"

It was said humorously but with an edge she didn't like.

"Stop this, *now!*" she snapped, renewing her struggles as his grip tightened.

"If I cut myself a switch it may curb your insolence my girl!"

Again, it was said conversationally and without menace, but the uncharacteristic strangeness of words and atmosphere chilled her to the bone.

Suddenly the light of insight exploded in her brain. Of course she was not getting through; if she had it right, at this moment he could not possibly relate to either name or situation. The damp mossiness of the air still clung in her nostrils and its coolness moistened her bare skin so that she shivered slightly. That was it: in some situation beyond her knowledge she was not supposed to be here in this glade.

"I am sorry; I shall not go through the woods again," she said quickly, and ceasing her struggles remained quiet and unresisting to emphasise her words. She tensed in readiness but nothing happened. Then his grip on her arm was released and she felt his fingers run lightly along her spine. His other hand cupped her breast and he kissed her forehead. The red glow around him dissipated, the humming ceased and the walls settled back again to enclose her own space.

Abruptly and without a word he turned and left the room.

That night she slept, albeit fitfully, on the sofa. Mainly, she told herself, to make a point because whatever the trigger she could not be seen to condone such behaviour, but in truth because of her own conflicting emotions and a need for solitude to work them through. There had been something ancient and incredibly sensual about that figure standing there in the firelight; a compelling power and eroticism that disturbed her more than she cared to admit. And she did not know how to treat Brant: she supposed she should be angry and confront him, but if what she suspected was true then he was an innocent party. More than this though, she stayed away to avoid further possible phenomena. Because that was what it had been, she acknowledged. Brant was not responsible; somehow he had been used as a channel. Such behaviour was out of character – and hardly politically correct in this day and age, *but accepted as normal perhaps in another.*

Or had she been mistaken about the whole thing? As dawn tinged the blackness with grey Darcy passed a hand wearily over her eyes. Had it merely been an unexpected sex-game on Brant's part? Had she, in a state of heightened emotion, imagined the strangeness, unfamiliar surroundings and red vapour? But Brant would have been under no illusion about the nature and reality of her protests and therefore would not have persisted in playing the dominant male. Giving up the struggle she drifted towards uneasy sleep.

It was then, during that floaty, in-between sleeping and waking stage that it happened. She had been lying facing the fire, watching the last of the flames and then the remaining glow. The redness was imprinted behind her eyelids as they lowered in readiness for sleep. She could still see it, but instead of the logs in the fireplace it was radiating from within the huge entrance of Mediobogdum. She was back outside the porta praetoris, the main gateway with its huge timbers, metal bosses and flanking towers. A stiff breeze was fanning the flames into an inferno. A standard crowned by a gold eagle rose proudly from the top of the gatehouse. There was a legend painted or embroidered on the material part of the standard beneath the eagle: an emblem and one or more words. She screwed up her eyes against the glare and the heat that seared her face and tried to decipher it, but the fabric part was rippling from the combined force of wind and heat and was partially obscured by smoke.

As she watched the flames rose higher. The metal of the eagle atop the standard began to slump and the features became distorted in a scene from a tragi-comedy. The power of the outspread pinions dripped into helplessness and obscurity; the ferocious hooked beak elongated and drooped in humiliation onto the proud chest, and the eyes closed and first one then the other slid downwards into oblivion as the metal melted in the inferno. As she watched the death of the eagle Darcy was overwhelmed with sadness.

TWENTY-FIVE

~

She awoke around seven o'clock to the rattle of cups on saucers and an enticing aroma of ground coffee. The vision of the previous night still clung to her mind, the images and emotions lingering like tendrils of mist wreathing the fells of an autumn morning. It had seemed so real. It was then that she recalled Dr Reynolds' warning about the possibility of flashbacks. Probably that was the answer. Being unsure of how to react she pretended to still be asleep when Brant entered from the kitchen.

"Coffee Darcy?" He placed a cup and saucer on the occasional table and waited as she shifted into a sitting position.

"Lovely – thank you." She deliberately spoke normally and took a sip of the scalding coffee whilst he hovered, watching her with an anxious and slightly sheepish expression. It seemed maybe he did remember the strange events of the night before. She took another sip of coffee to avoid having to be first to speak.

"Darcy, Have I upset you in some way?" he asked, frowning.

"No, not really." She stared down into her cup to avoid looking at him.

"There's obviously something wrong, and what do you mean by 'not really'?" he insisted.

She was perplexed; Brant seemed to have no idea what she was talking about.

"The dominance game."

"It must be me." Brant shook his head and ran fingers through his already tousled hair. "I think I'll go back to bed and try getting up again."

Darcy chewed her lip. By now the answer was clear; he definitely remembered nothing. End of sex-game theory and that left only creepy alternatives.

"No worries, it's not you Brant." She reached out and touched his hand, then flushed slightly at the unintentional aptness of her words. "Just a dream I had."

"Why didn't you come up to bed?"

"Too much wine, couldn't be bothered moving and woke up here this morning," she said smoothly.

He gave her a piercing look, as though recalling perhaps the way she once couldn't wait to get into bed, to snuggle against him and nestle beneath the shelter of his arm, but he let the subject drop. Her heart ached and she wanted to reassure him that her feelings had not changed and that this was something beyond her control, but could find no suitable words. It would take too long, too much energy and most of it lay beyond her own understanding.

Harmony was restored and an hour or so later Brant left for London again. I need to get away for a spell, be alone to sort this thing out, she realised whilst packing a bag in preparation for her return to Manchester, and that meant remaining in the area of the fort if resolution was to be achieved. With this in mind she packed mainly casual gear; there were suits, shirts and shoes at the flat if in the end she had to stay there. Maybe Mistletoe Cottage was going empty. It was unlikely though, the cottage given to her by her parents and where she was staying when she met Brant, had been more or less solidly booked since deciding to let it out after her marriage. As she could not bring herself to sell it it had seemed the sensible alternative; now the loss of her bolt-hole was keenly felt. She would check the bookings on going downstairs. One thing was becoming clear, whilst she stayed around Brant, there was every likelihood of bizarre and maybe destructive events taking place. She would leave him a letter explaining that she had to stay away for a while in order to sort things out and get herself together. This decided she zipped up her bag and went downstairs. Upon checking she found as expected that visitors were booked into Mistletoe Cottage until the end of the year and beyond .

As luck had it Frank was away from the office on a three day conference in London so she set out to clear her desk of 'urgents' and plan her work schedule without interruption. There were two features to be drafted: the first entitled 'Looting or Survival?' in which she intended to explore the phenomenon of pillaging following natural disasters like the flooding of urban homes and commercial premises, and where state response is seen to be slow or inadequate, and compare it with the seemingly opportunist and mindless crime-waves following a riot or terrorist attack. The second piece was an investigation into possible regional differences in available resources for dealing with an outbreak of bird flu. The research and interviews had largely been done and Frank had okayed the ideas so no problem there, the actual writing of the articles could be done away from the office.

Agenda sorted it was time to contact Caro. There had been nothing from her, no call, note or email since the Setter episode. The first time she dialled Caro's number at the university there was no response, so Darcy delved into her pocket book and tried an old mobile number but this proved to be defunct. When they did make contact she must rectify this oversight and ask Caro for her current one. Several attempts on the land line later Darcy began to feel paranoid; maybe Caro was avoiding her after what happened the other day. When she tried again a coffee and trip to the loo later Caro's voice sounded at the end of the line.

"Darcy. Oh, hi."

"What is it Caro?"

There was a moment of awkward silence then "I don't know what you mean?"

"Not hearing from you for a start then, well – you sounded 'off' just now when you answered and found it was me."

"I've just been busy that's all, and my head was elsewhere when you rang – you know what it's like when you're into writing a paper."

"Yeah, yeah I know, but hey come on, this is me – Darcy. Now are you going to come clean Caro or do I have to come there and drag it out of you!"

There was another long silence followed by a long sigh.

"I'm sorry Darcy."

Silence again, but Darcy managed to contain her impatience to give her friend time.

"There's no excuse," Caro said finally. "I'm a miserable coward and you've every right to be angry."

"I'm not angry Caro, just concerned."

" That thing with the dog and the old guy. It threw me; scared me actually if you want to know."

"Hey, same here Caro! And I guessed it was that."

"I mean, come on Darcy it was freaky. I come back from something as normal as buying a packet of tea bags to find you surrounded by a crowd and kneeling at the feet of the scruffiest guy in Christendom whilst he hangs a medal around your neck!"

"It just happened."

"Okay, and we go back a long way Darcy, and have shared some pretty bizarre situations, but this was like mega-weird, even for you!"

"I know. I can't blame you for wanting out Caro," Darcy murmured, not managing to keep the misery out of her voice.

"Don't be daft! I've thrown my little wobbler, so forgive me for the Victoria Falls act and for God's sake let's get this thing sorted!"

"Victoria Falls?"

"Wet!"

"Ah! Or as H.M. once famously said on a state visit: 'A trifle damp, don't you think?'" Darcy said with a laugh, partly out of relief that their friendship was still alive and partly from amusement at one of Frank's favourite quotes from the royal archives. It was good to hear Caro laughing too; it would have been awful to lose her friendship over this.

"I mean what sort of a friend would I be to pull out now?" Caro added as though she had read Darcy's thoughts. "Besides, you ain't safe to let out alone!"

"Gee thanks!"

"No problem. So what's the latest crack?"

"You don't want to go there."

"Probably not, but tell me anyway."

Intimacy restored Darcy related Brant's strange reaction to the medallion, managing to convey his aberrant behaviour without disclosing the intimate details. "I need to get away for a time Caro. If I stay around Brant this thing, whatever it is, will get worse, but Mistletoe Cottage is fully booked."

"Could you not stay at the flat, tell Brant you need solitude to write up a piece for Frank?" Caro suggested.

"The answer is here not Manchester."

"I see where you are coming from and wish I could help, Darcy. If I think of anything…"

"Sure."

"Darcy,"

"Yes?"

"Don't let this come between you and Brant. What you have with him is real, try to hang on to that."

"So is this Caro; you know that for yourself now."

"I don't doubt you, how could I after the other day? But it is a *different* reality and doesn't belong in this one. Think Wittgenstein Darcy; we have to live in the World and make sense of it."

"Yeah, well I am trying. Stay in touch and take care."

As she replaced the receiver, loneliness wrapped itself around Darcy excluding her from that normal world. The house felt empty. Life felt empty, except for that other reality, that other persona that somehow was linked to her own. A major admission and one she had not thought to make. She was isolated from ordinary things, the end of that conversation with Caro had proved it. It was impossible to convey the depth of emotion, the vibrancy of that different reality that Caro had spoken of but could never understand. Frank, Caro and yes to an extent even Brant, were becoming more and more remote whilst Antonius and his reality were drawing ever closer and looming larger, dwarfing the things of everyday life and diminishing their significance.

Given the situation with Mistletoe Cottage she ought to set off for Manchester but there was little inclination to do so. Maybe if she worked here today on one of her two projects she would be more resolved by morning as to her best course of action. Once this was decided upon she was able to go to her study, switch on the lap top and start work on the 'Looting' feature. Albeit her hands hovered above the key board with unwarranted frequency, her gaze becoming fixed at some point beyond the window whilst her mind trawled through recent events and searched for possible answers, but by early afternoon she had a creditable first draft. For the rest of that afternoon she roved the cliff top with Mab and Brock as she would have to take them to Mrs Jenkins the following morning on her way back to Manchester.

"I suppose I shall have to go babes," she said aloud to the two spaniels who broke off from sniffing a fox or badger trail to give her a brief look. Their tails drooped – new law apart, Brant was dead against docking – as they picked up on her melancholy but then returned to their own business of running nose to ground along the cliff top.

"Come on you guys, time for home," she called as the pale sun hovered above the horizon, a huge pearl in an autumnal gauze of aqua, mauve and rose.

On the way back she turned several times to peer over her shoulder. She could not shake off the feeling of being followed. On a peaceful evening like this it was hard to remember that Ted Tulley was still on the run, and she cursed herself for staying out too long.

"Mab, Brock!" she called sharply as they lingered on the far side of the little bridge that crossed the stream at an intersection of paths. As it began sinking below the horizon the sun turned a dull red, staining the purple and gossamer greys with streaks of crimson. Dusk would fall early tonight and they were still a fair stride from home. Red sun, red-stained haze, not a good time to be out alone. Her gaze darted from side to side of the path. She turned frequently now to look over her shoulder and occasionally, heart thumping, stopped to stare as shadows lurking behind rock and scrub appeared to shift and change shape. She waited for the strangeness to come creeping in but the red sun sank out of sight as the farmhouse came into view. A false alarm this time.

"Chill, Darcy," she muttered aloud and smiling with relief ran for the door with the dogs bounding at her heels.

She stumbled through the front door and into the hall with the dogs jostling and pushing against her in their efforts to get there first.

"Not exactly good training but great fun eh, babes?" she said laughing, but the words echoed hollowly and the smile died on her lips. Something was not right. Mab and Brock sensed it too; they ran back to her and cowered behind her legs. That chill in the air for a start. For sure the temperature outside was dropping, in fact there could easily be a frost later, but it was not that cold yet. Besides the central heating should still be on. That was it, she thought with a sigh of relief; there must be a fault on the boiler, or more likely Brant had messed up the timer setting when the clocks were put back the previous week. It often amused her: Brant may be a brainy astro-physicist but when it came to everyday gadgets in the home he was worse than useless. Yes, that must be it. Making her way to the light switch she reached out to flick it on.

'Shit!' she exclaimed under her breath as nothing happened. Another power cut. At least that explained why there was no central heating. The observatory and its priceless equipment was protected under special arrangements made by the Government, but evidently the ministers concerned had not considered the occupants of the house to be worthy of similar consideration. There was a portable generator and since that last emergency – and she shuddered now to think of the darkened and evil smelling hall – Brant had brought it

208

from the barn into the house for her convenience should the power go off during his absence. He had also exchanged the massive old pull-string one that she had no hope of starting for a compact modern one with a starter button. It was seated in the kitchen near the Aga and she made her way there now.

Mab and Brock hung back at her heels rather than scampering ahead as usual anxious after their walk to claim prime place in front of the Aga.

"Come on guys, not afraid of the dark are we?" Darcy joked, as much to comfort herself by breaking the eerie silence as to reassure them. Damn. She had forgotten to renew the battery in the torch on her key ring. Feeling her way with one hand along the ice-cold wall she eventually arrived at the kitchen door. As she pushed it open the blast of heat to her face was instantaneous causing her to recoil. She stood there uncomprehending; the contrast was utterly confusing after the icy hall. Seconds later the stench registered and caused her to gag. The reek of rotting flesh was worse than anything she had ever encountered. The nearest she could get to describing it was the stink from a butcher's shop shut up for weeks in the midst of a heat wave. A reddish glow at the far end of the kitchen pulsed with energy. Instantly she was transported back to the *porta praetoris* and that pitiful standard, then just as swiftly back again. Obviously flashbacks were going to be a problem. Out of combined force of habit and shock she reached for the light switch. Something cold and slimy moved beneath her fingers.

TWENTY-SIX

~

She screamed again and hurriedly withdrew her hand. The sound of terror reverberated around the room, bouncing off a row of copper saucepans glowing on their shelf. Filled with dread now for what she might have inadvertently touched she scrubbed her palm against her jeans. Mab and Brock slunk into the room and as her eyes became accustomed to the red glow she realised its source, and that of the intense heat. Somehow the Aga had overheated, an unprecedented event given it ran on Calor gas and had a built-in thermostat. The whole of the metal casing throbbed with radiant energy. Thank God she had left no towels draped over the rail to air; the place would have gone up in flames. Again that flashback to a different fire, on a different scale and in a different time. She blinked and forced her mind to focus on the present.

"Here Mab, Brock!" she yelled as they made for the glowing stove. She was aware of an unpleasant metallic taste in the mouth as she opened her mouth "Come here!" she yelled again, terrified they would be burned. Instinctively she ran after them, slipped on something soft beneath her feet and sprawled full length on the floor.

"No! Oh no!" she moaned, recalling the previous time in the hall and filled now with loathing and fear at what she might find. She scrambled to her feet whilst gagging from the stench and also the knowledge that her hands and clothes were sticky with slime. Terror of the unknown gripped her, rendering her helpless and devoid of will. She was jerked out of the stupor by a sudden yelp and the added smell of singed hair.

"Come away Brock!" she yelled, as he continued to hover by the Aga seemingly as fazed as she was by events and just visible in the crimson radiance. The stove, usually the heart of their home, now seemed to throb with a hostile energy, irresistibly calling to mind the malignant juggernaut of 'Duel'.

Candles, she must reach the cupboard for matches and candles. Never mind what lies on the floor, you are already filthy so nothing more to lose. Just get some light and you can sort it all, she told herself sternly. Swallowing the vomit that rose in her throat but gagging all the way she took a step forward, then another, her feet slipping and sliding with each footfall. The heat was sending her dizzy and making it almost impossible to breathe. Beads of perspiration blinded her and she brushed them away with the back of one hand. Just when she thought it impossible to go on, there was a fizzing and spluttering sound and a flickering of light from the bulb in the central lamp that made her raw nerves scream. It fizzed and glowed redly for a moment then blazed as power was restored.

She almost fainted at the scene before her eyes. Holding her hand over her nose and mouth against the stench she picked her way through the maze of red earth writhing with white worms and some fat glistening creatures that looked like a cross between an overgrown maggot and a slug. Instantly struck by a horrible notion she turned to face the door leading into the hall. Sure enough more of these creatures clustered the wall. Hence the cold sliminess beneath her hand on feeling for the light switch. The realisation made her retch and she was immobilised by horror. Don't think about that now; get the dogs out of this foetid furnace before they are not only covered in slime but suffering heat exhaustion or worse. She flung open the back door and grabbing the collars of a dazed Mab and Brock hauled them through into the yard and slammed it shut. Next she opened the window with a violence that sent it banging against the outside wall, cracking a pane in the process. Despite this action she heaved for breath and sweat coursed down her face leaving white rivulets in the grime.

Air, she had to have some fresh air. On reaching the door she turned and shook her fist in the air.

"Bastard! You filthy bastard!" she yelled, "why do this to *me*?" Even as she shouted the words she knew he was trying to drive her away, out of this house and her cosiness to that bleak place on the fell.

"What is it you want so much?" she shouted then, her voice breaking on a sob. The bizarre glow from the Aga intensified and her head throbbed, her eyelids drooped and she almost sank to the floor; only the knowledge of what unutterable things waited there kept her upright. The flashback again, and this time the rippling heat and smoke that gave the eagle a semblance of flight dissolved and receded to fully reveal the standard. The legend was clear to see. *LEGIO IX.* She started as Mab and Brock set up whining and scrabbling at the door to be let back in and the image disappeared. She grabbed a torch from the shelf and spent several minutes outside, reassuring Mab and Brock until they were relatively calm and her own head and lungs cleared sufficiently for her to think with a degree of clarity.

"Okay, now you guys have to stay here just till I get the worst of that mess off the floor," she soothed striving to keep her voice steady. Slipping a leash over each head she led them to the small out-building next to the barn with the intention of shutting them inside whilst she turned off the gas supply to the Aga and began mopping up operations But a flicker of light behind one of the outhouse windows brought her to an abrupt halt. It might have been the reflection of her own torch, but then it might not, and she could not face another trauma.

Turning abruptly she dragged the dogs back to the house and opening the door led them inside. The first thing she noticed was a complete lack of searing heat. Secondly the Aga no longer glowed with that malevolent energy but appeared cosy and normal. Under ordinary circumstances that simply could not happen; it would take several hours minimum to cool even if she had already turned off the gas. However nothing about this situation was normal; the rules of logic were dormant. These were answers looking for questions and she didn't know which ones to ask. Keeping Mab and Brock on the shortest lead possible she led them through the kitchen, avoiding as best she could those loathsome heaving piles on the floor. Shutting the dogs in the sitting room she made her way back to the kitchen and set to work first with a shovel, scooping up and tipping the wriggling piles into a bucket before taking them across the yard for tipping into the bushes.

Her breath smoked as she worked. The temperature was dropping to minus and with a bit of luck the frost should deal with the slimy creatures. She cast many a wary look the way of the outhouse but the window panes stared blankly out, shiny black and impassive the only light being that reflected upon them from the moon. Several trips later the last bucket was emptied of its foul contents and with a sigh of relief she hurried back inside and bolted the door.

At last the place was redolent of disinfectant, detergent and essential oil of lavender. She was able to shut the windows against frost and dark and any would be intruder. The Aga was performing normally and Mab and Brock had been fed and were settled in their basket. She had bathed and scrubbed herself until pink and her soiled clothes were rotating in the washing machine. She should have been far too traumatised and nervous to dare go upstairs to bed but exhaustion dictated otherwise. A mug of hot milk laced with brandy and a lavender filled sac heated in the Aga helped her relax and her eyelids began to droop. Her biggest fear now was what might be encountered during sleep. Worms and slugs she could deal with, just – but flashbacks and nightmares were beyond her control and therefore a dreaded threat.

However she slept undisturbed and awoke to crisp sunlight filtering through a gap in the curtains. On drawing them back she looked out on a world of white filigree branches, sparkling shrubs and beyond these a backdrop of tall grasses, gorse and heather silvered by frost and sun. It was almost, she could not help thinking, as though he has driven the message home and no longer needed to traumatise her into action. Her mood of optimism was short lived. On leaving the house to take a subdued Mab and Brock to Mrs

Jenkins in the village – they always seemed to sense when it was time for her to depart again – she was brought up short by yet another nasty shock.

OUT OF TIME IX

~

The visit to Glannaventa coupled with his unease over the man Lupinus was giving Antonius much to think and worry about. On impulse during a routine ride he decided to call in at Rowana's settlement and judge for himself the mood of the inhabitants, and to subtly alert Myrddin to the possible danger of Rome's change of policy. And if Rowana happened to be there at the time, well so much the better, he thought with a smile tethering Gaudita along with the mounts of Justinus and their escort of half a dozen cavalry soldiers.

"Best stay with the draco," Antonius said with a wry smile to the signifier, "Else they will think us a war party come to raid them! Besides, it won't do to let them see our secret close-up!"

"Aye sir," the draconarius said with an answering grin, ramming the metal-tipped shaft of the dragon effigy into the ground. With movement the wind would fill the wind sock giving the dragon a terrifying semblance of life, and a weird unnerving shriek would be emitted due to the whistles lodged inside. An effective curb on enemy zeal when carried full tilt into battle. "And I'll mind the horses, legatus. We don't want to find any missing as we leave!"

Antonius nodded. He had opted for an approach on foot so as not to appear hostile or cause resentment by riding in as the conquering hoard.

They entered the compound by a gate set into the timber palisade. Antonius absorbed the scene without turning his head thus appearing cool and unconcerned, but the fact that the entrance was left open and without a guard had aroused his suspicions. He checked but as no-one appeared to challenge them he waved his men on towards the sizeable community of round houses, barns and, judging by the chinks and hammerings that issued forth, the settlement's forge. As they advanced men and women going about their daily business froze and watched with furrowed brows and eyes that were narrowed in suspicion. A woman drawing water at the well let the rope slip through her fingers so that the bucket hit the water with a dull splash. Scooping up her child who was drawing in the dust with a stick she scuttled into a nearby doorway. Antonius, sensing something amiss, stiffened. He heard the faint swish through the air and cursed as the spear thudded into the earth at his feet.

In the span of seconds a shock of impressions: broad shoulders draped in animal skins and muscled legs splayed in challenge; a shield bearing the effigy of a boar's head with flashing eyes and a conical helmet giving a gleam of copper in the rays of the sun; and flowing from beneath it a mane of hair, bleached and stiffened with lime water to frame an imperious head. A giant warrior dressed for battle, the gold torque of leadership clasped around a bull neck.

Instantly Antonius' hand found his own weapon as he rapped out orders:

"Draw swords, battle formation. Raise shields and wait for the order."

Mentally he sized up the opposition. Men had appeared as though by magic in the gaps between the thatched dwellings. Like their leader they were wearing skins and furs and each warrior clutched a massive shield and long-sword. Antonius heard his men moving into position and Justinus' breath hiss between his teeth. His own mouth went dry and he felt the tingle peculiar to battle creep up his spine.

Then unbelievably the warrior was laughing and striding towards them, teeth gleaming white in his painted face and the eyes of the boar on his rectangular shield – pieces of coloured glass Antonius now realised – winking in the sunlight.

"Sheep-shit and wolf-slit!" Antonius swore under his breath.

"The man is a cock-brained lunatic!" Justinus exclaimed aloud as the Briton advanced. Antonius however turned and frowned at the tribune, signalling him to be silent.

"A dangerous game to play friend," he said shaking his head and forcing himself to speak politely to the man who now stood before him. The warrior shrugged broad shoulders draped with wolf pelt.

"A little welcoming ceremony, that is all. Our sentries saw your arrival and we decided on a little show."

Of your tribe's power more like. With an effort of will Antonius swallowed his pride and anger; they were too few against this painted horde. There was naught to gain and much to lose from forfeiting their lives, a certain result should he allow himself to be provoked into unprepared action.

"But had it gone wrong you and your men would be dead."

"Or you – and yours." The man fearlessly held his gaze.

Peaceful resolve wavering, Antonius bit his lip and humiliation gnawed at his belly on seeing the half-smile of derision on the other man's lips. But Hadrian's initial directive – to offer no provocation and encourage confidences via overtones of friendship – in the absence of further direct orders still stood; he had no wish to advance the inevitable consequence of that order by instigating rebellion. He was saved from having to say more by a voice dry as leaves in autumn yet somehow carrying the power of a gale force wind crackled across the compound.

"Cadoc! What are you about, frightening away our visitors?"

"A little sport Myrddin, no more," the warrior replied with a shrug of those wolf-clad shoulders. He stared defiantly at the owner of the voice who stood at the entrance of the largest and only rectangular dwelling in the compound, the lines that furrowed his face deepening into a smile. Antonius noted with satisfaction that the man called Cadoc was first to look away.

"I'll leave you to play host then," he said sourly to Myrddin, then turned back to stare insolently at Antonius. "I hope I didn't give you too much of a scare, Roman!" Moving forward a few paces he yanked the spear out of the ground and backed away.

"Hardly. I am still here, am I not?" Antonius replied with affected politeness.

"I'm sure we shall meet again," Cadoc said silkily.

Signalling to his men he disappeared between the huts.

"Greetings Myrddin. A routine visit in passing, that's all," Antonius said, turning to the old man whose white robe billowed in the breeze revealing the winter-stick ankles. The whiteness of linen accentuated feet as tanned as the lattice of thongs that bound them.

"Of course it is. Greetings – commander." The slight pause and the way Myrddin inclined his head combined with the hint of irony in his tone made a mockery of his obeisance. "Do step inside," he added gesturing at the open door of the dwelling.

"Sir!" Justinus' voice was heavy with warning as he stepped forward a pace.

"Your legatus will be quite safe with me, young sir." Myrddin wagged a forefinger much to Justinus' chagrin and Antonius' amusement. "I assure you there is nobody within except perhaps my ward."

Justinus flushed with annoyance and would have followed but Antonius held up a hand.

"Wait there, tribune. With the fort a mere crow's flight away, I'm sure Myrddin realises the health of this village depends upon my safe return."

He smiled at Myrddin to soften the sting behind his words.

"Indeed. But then whoever heard of sparrows attacking the eagle? Especially one with a loud voice and so many fledglings," he added artfully. Antonius gave him a sharp look but with a shrug of the shoulders followed him through the doorway, down a short passage and through an inner door.

Antonius blinked, adjusting to the dimness after the brightness outside. As his eyes became adjusted to the change he saw that the walls were of wattle and daub freshly white-washed. Smoke from a fire in the open hearth at the centre of the floor belched at intervals filling the room with a pungent herby cloud before the up-draught caught it, sucked it into a spiral and drew it up through the aperture in the roof. His eyes smarted and his nostrils were filled with the tang of the forest mingled with applewood, and an odour he could not put a name to.

"Do be seated."

Myrddin was indicating one of the wooden seats placed at a table that, like the timber roof supports, was heavily carved.

"First, some refreshment for my men – bread, ale, whatever you have and can spare," Antonius said curtly, faintly rankled by Myrddin's composure.

"They are already being served by the women of the village," Myrddin answered mildly.

"Thank you, that will be appreciated I'm sure."

Antonius stepped over rugs of dyed wool woven in a pattern of scrolls and whorls as he walked to the table. He sat down, wondering why he felt ill at ease.

"So where do you hail from Myrddin?" he asked, aware that the ancient's dialect did not match that of Rowana and her people.

"Mona." It was said without hesitation.

"I see." Antonius frowned; that peninsular off the coast of Cambria had been the stronghold of the Druidae until Seutonius Paulinus led the attack that wiped out the sect. It is well-known by Rome that those who survived had gone underground to practice their craft. Was Myrddin then one of them? he wondered not for the first time.

"If I was, would I have volunteered Mona as my birthplace?"

That disconcerting trick again. Antonius coughed and looked away.

A rustling from a corner of the room made him start. Peering into the shadows a shiver ran down his spine. A white-owl stirred on its perch, the heart-shaped face ghostly in the gloom. With a flurry of feathers it settled again, one talon tucked beneath its snowy breast. The yellow lamps of its eyes were briefly scaled as it blinked.

Blodeuwedd

For an instant he was back in the wood listening to her song.
He was returned to his present surroundings by Myrddin's voice.
"I found her frozen by the roadside last winter; she chose to stay."
"When did you come North then?"
"When did the mountains first appear? The eagle learn to fly?"
"A long time ago I take it," Antonius said dryly. "And what is your standing here in the civitas?"
"Oh, an old man must be prepared to sit rather than stand."
"Look, can we drop the riddles for once!" Antonius sighed with exasperation, "I'm being patient but…" The rebuke was interrupted by a female voice from the doorway.
"The food is waiting, Father Myrddin. Shall I bring it in?"

His heart leapt in his breast. Antonius stared at Rowana and just in time bit back a greeting. She was obviously aware of the need to suppress any familiarity for she studiously ignored him and leaned against the timber support with characteristic haughtiness and what came close to insolence.

"Ah Rowana, yes, serve us now please, our guest must be famished," Myrddin said turning to face his ward.

Hard as he tried Antonius could not draw his eyes away. Here, in this dim and charged atmosphere there was something different about her, something nagging at the back of his mind. A fleeting glimpse, a brief feather-light touch, or merely the sensation of somebody sharing his space – her presence brought to mind the strangeness of those experiences back at Mediobogdum, and later at Glannaventa. Was Rowana also the presence that haunted him or was that something different and unknown? Yet it was rather like entering a strange country only to dimly recognise that hill, or that tree forked by lightning. He blinked and turned away as the owl suddenly shifted on its perch, talons rasping against the wood and wings briefly rustling as they were stretched and folded again. When he looked again, Rowana had gone.

He became aware of Myrddin watching him with eyes bright and sharp as those of a bird. This guardian of Rowana suspected something more than mere acquaintance between them, of this Antonius was sure. However he was unsure as to whether or not Myrddin had guessed they were now lovers. He duly affected the air of polite boredom that might be ascribed to a sophisticated officer of Rome on a routine obligatory visit.

"The man Cadoc, who is he?" he inquired, as much to break the unnerving silence as to satisfy his curiosity.

"He is chieftain of his tribe."

"Yet a word from you and he backs off."

"I have what he wants."

"Which is?"

"Rowana."

"I see." Antonius carefully guarded his expression; so the information brought back by his spies about their betrothal could be true. Abruptly he changed the subject. "But I suspect he also knows you also hold power, does he not?"

"The power if any lies in my potions not my person." Myrddin replied with a casual shrug of his sharply angled shoulders.

"The inhabitants consult you?"

"Sometimes, when they are sick. Then there is the spate of fever that strikes each year."

"Fever?" Antonius looked alarmed.

"Aye, when 'horn' means more than antlers and the tup clambers the ewe. Mind, those struck by Cupid's arrow don't seek a cure, only the power to infect!" Myrddin's shoulders shook with mirth as he tapped the table with a gnarled finger.

"Very droll, Myrddin." Antonius' smile was as sour as the lemons from Hispania. Cupid was the Roman god of Love so what was he implying? Was this a covert reference to himself and his passion for Rowana?

As though picking up on the thought Rowana reappeared carrying two bowls of broth, the steam rising from them redolent with sage and rosemary. She placed them on the table without looking at him and withdrew, then returned with a large trencher holding a basket of bread still warm and fragrant from the oven, and a platter laden with cheese, apples, pears, a bowl of blackberries and a jug brimming with cream the yellow of coltsfoot and as thick as the honey in the earthenware jar. He willed her to look his way but she resisted, her brusque movements and stony expression conveying the dignity of a queen condescending to serve a slave. She walked across the room to a set of shelves. As she reached for a flask and two goblets stored on the uppermost one, the tilt of her breast beneath the robe of fine white linen was a delight. Antonius coughed and looked away, aware of Myrddin's renewed scrutiny.

"This broth is good, so is the bread," he said to cover his confusion as she set the flask and goblets on the table.

"Then enjoy your meal," she said coolly, and ignoring his tacit invitation to converse she left the room.

"Rowana has a light hand with the dough." Myrddin smiled and nodded.

"She doesn't mind acting as servant then?" Antonius broke off a piece of bread and soaked up the last of the broth. It seemed so out of character for the haughty wise-woman and warrior maid he had come to recognise and revere.

"Hostess, never a servant!" Myrddin reproved.

"She is not wed?" he asked

"Not yet." Myrddin replied stressing the final word and smiling irritatingly.

Antonius recalled his host's disclosure about Cadoc and his lust for Rowana. Coupled with her declaration that he would kill them should she openly wear his pendant, this must mean they were betrothed or at least expecting to be.

Aware that he was being baited by that seemingly innocuous remark, Antonius decided to steer away from this dangerous topic. Business must take precedence of the day. This man was less of a fool and more of a threat than that swollen tit of a warrior outside, albeit the one with the temerity to mock the authority of Rome. He watched thoughtfully as Myrddin tipped his bowl, drank the dregs and wiped the rim of broth from his cotton-grass whiskers with a scrap of linen extracted from his voluminous sleeve.

Antonius reached for the platter and selected a pear. "Myrddin, contrary to how things may appear, I wish you and your people no harm," he said carefully, picking up a knife to peel the pear so as not to meet Myrddin's gaze.

"What one wishes and what may take place are not necessarily the same."

Antonius did not at first respond but continued peeling the pear until the skin dropped to his platter in a coil. Myrddin was uncomfortably close to the truth and obviously aware of the implicit warning.

"You are a wise man, Myrddin."

"My wisdom is merely an illusion seen by those with a simple need."

"Oh, and what is that?"

"Why, everyone needs to hear there own wisdom from the mouth of somebody else! I simply tell them what they already know."

Suddenly an uneasy silence filled the room.

Antonius shivered as Myrddin's eyes locked with his across the table.

He tried to look away but could not. Something was passing between them, a flow of energy that made his flesh crawl. A change was taking place in Myrddin: he sat tall and straight emanating power and his eyes burned with a light that commanded respect. The flames in the hearth flared turning the grey of his hair and beard to silver.

"Do I know you old man?" Antonius whispered.

Myrddin did not answer but within his eyes Antonius glimpsed an image: an ancient at the forum, and a red ball held out to the boy who runs to his mother. *Calpurnia. And a reminder of her barbarian lineage – and through her, his own. And through him the means of destruction and death.* Myrddin's eyes became clouded then focused between his own. He felt a pulling sensation, a drawing-out that bordered on pain. His eyelids drooped because they were so heavy.

"And now Antonius, what would you have me tell you?"

Myrddin's voice reached him from the end of a long tunnel, a voice from his youth and the familiarity of address brought no sense of surprise or affront.

"What must I do to avert this tragedy?" he said with unaccustomed humility.

"You will be spared from having to live with it. But this you already know. "

Antonius shuddered as the Death Crone flexed her wings and prepared to fly, casting her shadow over the battlefield.

"To be the instrument of catastrophe is not the same as being worthy of blame," Myrddin continued. Now, is there anything else?" he added, his voice echoing from far away.

"Who is she, the girl you call Rowana?"

"Ask yourself instead 'who is she not'? and this too you already know," Myrddin intoned.

Antonius blinked. The room was once more normal and Myrddin simply a wizened and elderly man watching him from across the table. Just what, Antonius wondered, did he burn on that damned fire? It was known that smoke from the bark or roots of certain trees and shrubs could induce hallucinations, or maybe there was something in the wine. He rubbed his smarting eyes and struggled with a wave of panic; he may have been drugged to render him helpless. When he opened his eyes again Rowana was standing in the doorway.

"Just smoke from an unseasoned log or two that have found their way into the basket. Open the door, Rowana – I think our guest will then feel more comfortable!" Myrddin said slyly.

Humiliated, Antonius scowled, fully aware that Myrddin knew of his fears. Rowana walked across the room lithe and silent as a cat and through the short passage to the stout timber door which she unlatched and pulled open to create a cross draft with the roof aperture and allow the smoke to escape.

"Time to leave. Thank you for your hospitality," Antonius said abruptly, taking advantage of the opportunity to depart.

He paused at the door. As he moved to go through Rowana brushed against him so briefly that it could have been an accident yet he knew was not. She looked him directly in the eye before moving silently away and disappearing into the nether room. A promise of a 'fortuitous' and more intimate meeting perhaps, he thought stepping outside. In view of the risk she was taking, despite their new intimacy he must leave the running to Rowana.

"Sir!" Justinus, waiting with obvious anxiety stepped forward as Antonius emerged followed by Myrddin.

"As I said before, Myrddin, I wish you no harm. The omens predict a season of draught for this region. Maybe it would be wise to think about moving your people on to a, shall we say, an area with a more agreeable climate." he finished, fully aware of the absurdity of predicting draught in this land of lakes, becks and water-logged gullies and knowing Myrddin would also be aware of this.

"I take your meaning, legatus. But this land has fed and watered us for generations; I doubt it will fail us now in a time of, shall we say, harshness," Myrddin said formally whilst holding his gaze.

He knows Rome has turned, Antonius thought with a flush of guilt, and that is the harshness of which he speaks.

"Think hard on my words, Myrddin – they are well meant," he said quietly so none other could hear. "Come Justinus, time we were away," he added, nodding briefly to Myrddin and turning to leave the clearing. He had dealt with the business that brought him here and there was nothing more to say.

That night he tossed and turned on his bed haunted by thoughts and images of Rowana and what might happen to her should Rome order him to implement the campaign of subjugation. Whatever happened he would see that she was safe. As to the rest, would Myrddin heed his words and move his people out to a safe place somewhere in the mountains? He doubted it; he was stubborn as a mule that old man. But he was more than an ancient, wasn't he? On recalling it he felt again the feeling of unreality and disorientation, and how many times had that same old man pre-empted him and filled the gaps in what he was about to say? It was no use; sleep had deserted him. Maybe a breath of cold air and a little exercise might coax it back again. He rose and wrapping his heavy winter cloak around him moved to the door. In any case, no harm to be had in checking the granary and the weapon store, he thought pausing to buckle on his sword belt.

Once outside he drew breath sharply as the sudden blast of icy air hit nostrils and throat. The moon was at the gibbous waxing stage and by the fullness of its light the bulk of the stone-built granary and tiled roof stood out in sharp relief, the buttresses casting deep wedge-shaped shadows onto the walls. He looked up with something akin to wonder. At intervals pale clouds drifted across the moon goddess' face dimming her light and softening shade. At times rogue cumuli stalked and briefly swallowed her whole, only for her to slip out again within minutes to glide forth with untroubled beauty. But enough of mysticism and down to the business of surveillance. The sentries on the ramparts cast long shadows; he had taken care to alert the officer in charge of the night watch of his intent and so moved about unchallenged. Satisfying himself that all was well at the granary he walked over to the weapons store, placing his sandaled feet with care so as not to alert any intruder. All was still and in darkness within, the outer walls faintly lit by a half-veiled moon. He was just about to turn and head back to his quarters when he was stopped in his tracks.

He whipped round and a runnel of shock ran down his spine as a hob nail rasped against stone. His hand automatically moved to his side. The moon chose that moment to hide behind cloud dipping the scene in darkness. He peered into the shadows, sword already in hand.

"Halt and show yourself!" he commanded, scanning the gloom for sight of the prowler. From the sound of that boot on stone and the lack of any other he guessed there was only one intruder; no need yet to call the guard and risk whoever it was getting away in the interim.

"Come forth or I shout the guards!" he threatened. Looking from left to right and listening for sounds of flight but hearing none, he waited. The moon slipped out from her hiding place flooding the area with icy, bluish light. He watched in silence as the figure emerged from around the shadowed corner.

"It's me, Lupinus. I'm sorry I startled you, sir." Lupinus stepped forward into a pool of moonlight apparently unperturbed at being discovered.

"What in hell's name are you doing here, soldier?"

Antonius turned his head slightly as a voice hailed from the rampart.

"Is all well below?"

"Aye, all's well. Return to your watch, soldier," Antonius answered before turning back to Lupinus.

"One more time soldier before I have you taken inside for interrogation. What were you doing here?"

"Just checking, sir." Lupinus eyed him boldly through slanted eyes that did indeed give him a wolfish look. "I woke up needing a piss and thought I heard something so I came to investigate."

"H'mm." Antonius eyed him suspiciously, sword still at the ready. "I'll be watching you soldier, see you keep your nose clean. And next time you hear anything out of the way, alert the sentry."

"Yes sir."

"Now back to barracks and stay there."

"Thank you, sir."

Lupinus saluted, turned on his heel and disappeared into the darkness.

Suspicious, but no obvious transgression to pin on the man. As he listened to the retreating footsteps, Antonius resolved to alert Justinus and Rufinus to keep an eye on him, and this time to trust Marcellus too. He would wager a year's pay that the prefect had no part in whatever treachery the man Lupinus was plotting. But that Lupinus was planning treason he had little doubt. Nothing to go on other than an uneasy feeling in his gut on sighting him – but that uneasiness had always served him well in the past. Pausing to reassure the guards he made his way back to his quarters. Once there he stood, deep in thought, looking out of the darkened window whilst mulling over the piecemeal elements that were pointing to betrayal.

TWENTY-SEVEN

~

It took a moment for it to sink in as Darcy peered through the bedroom window. The odd tilt of the vehicle drew her attention to the slashed tyres. Both the front ones had been viciously sliced with a knife or similar implement and were completely flat. For a moment Darcy stood and stared, unable to make sense of the situation. Given the paranormal events of the night before, her immediate reaction was to view this latest event as yet another manifestation. A few minutes reflection however made her see the absurdity of this: slashed tyres were a particularly modern and human method of exacting revenge. She nodded grimly, this had to be the work of Ted Tulley. The light in the barn the previous night suddenly made sinister sense.

"Mab, Brock!" she called sharply. Screwing up her eyes against the glare of sun on frost she turned slowly on the spot, surveying bushes and outbuildings but nothing and nobody caught her attention. Well that was the end of her plans for an early start. Fortunately the tiny garage down in the village usually kept a spare set of tyres in for herself and Brant given their regular custom and remote situation. So with a bit of luck they could be fitted later and she would still get away today. No way was she spending another night alone in this house.

The dogs came running and she was about to take them back inside when the thought struck that she had better check for other damage. Moving slowly around the vehicle checking paintwork, mirrors and windows she worked her way round to the front. There was no further damage, but something worse. As her gaze rose from checking out the bonnet for scratching or gouging she froze with shock. Across the windscreen several words had been scrawled with a finger on the frosted glass: *NEXT TIME IT WILL BE YOU!*

Sick with anger and fear she opened the car door and rummaged frantically in the glove compartment for the ice scraper. It was no use the frost was too hard. No matter how she scrubbed and scraped at the ominous message it refused to be budged. Using the heater would take far too long, she needed to rid herself immediately of this obscene threat. Beyond thinking clearly now she ran for the standpipe outside the barn and grabbing a bucket shoved it beneath the tap and turned it full on. It wheezed and coughed a little but nothing came out. She thumped the frozen pipe and swore with frustration then ran towards the house, dogs yapping at her heels. She returned with the bucket full of warm water and with unnecessary violence flung it across the windscreen and gained satisfaction from watching frost and words being swept away. She paused for a moment to look at the gleaming glass darkly reflecting trees and outbuildings and to take pleasure in relief and in a sense retaliation.

It was only after speaking to the mechanic at the garage that she realised it had been wrong to swill those hateful words from the windscreen. Without that proof of sinister intent the police would treat the slashed tyres as petty crime. It would be put down to local envy or someone protesting against Brant's work in the area. The local media had followed MOD directives and reported his activities as 'climate monitoring', but many believed they were connected to the nuclear plant further down the coast. In that event there was no point in involving them at all. At best they would be an inconvenience and at worst provide Brant with reason to come on heavy about abandoning her investigation. But what to tell the mechanic? So far she had simply said she needed two new tyres fitting, but the minute they saw the vehicle the reason would be transparent. And they might mention it as some stage to Brant. There was nothing for it but to cook up some story to account for the damage. Some crackpot demonstrators against nuclear power, perhaps – and not to mention it to Brant as it would worry him unnecessarily, her being here alone. Oh what webs we weave, she thought staring out of the window at a landscape glowing with autumnal colours now that the sun had melted the frost. Despite her promises to Brant, here she was plotting yet another deception

Around mid morning the telephone rang. It was Caro with a surprise piece of news: she had thought of the dilapidated building where the team had hung out during excavations at the fort as a possible solution to Darcy's problem. She had made a couple of telephone calls and was able to confirm that it was standing empty and that Darcy was welcome to use it during her 'investigations of the remains in preparation for writing a feature.' This was the official version and the one Darcy was to give if anyone queried her presence there, though given it was situated within a mile or so of Mediobogdum and therefore equally isolated, this was highly unlikely.

"I don't know what condition it is in nowadays," Caro warned.

"No worries. Whatever, it'll do fine for camping out," Darcy reassured her.

She then related to Caro the events of the previous evening and her need to abandon the house before nightfall; and also the morning's drama, playing down the latter to avoid worrying her overmuch, going so far as to repeat the theory about protesters against Brant's work that she had offered to the mechanic when he arrived to fit the new tyres.

"It seems your team were right about the Ninth Legion," she interrupted swiftly as Caro began to voice concern about Darcy's safety at the camp billet given that she would be there alone. "And so was Dr Reynolds when he said there may be flashbacks".

"Oh? Tell!" Caro demanded, her attention diverted as intended.

Darcy related the dream and the spontaneous images showing the standard of the Ninth.

"That also confirms the team's theory about the firing of Mediobogdum," Caro said excitedly, "and your experiences seem to suggest it wasn't a routine destruction of the fort prior to an orderly departure but the result of an attack. Although you did already know about those findings so we have to be cautious here: it could just be your subconscious supplying info to fill the gaps."

"Which is why I need to stay in the area and clear this thing up once and for all," Darcy said neatly.

"I can see it's useless to argue but for God's sake take care Darcy and get in touch whenever you have signal. By the way, you ran off some shots of the fort didn't you? Have you had them back yet?"

"Oh damn, with all that's been going on I forgot to hand them in at 'Graphics' for computer transfer and printing. No worries, I'll drop off the cassette at Ambleside or somewhere for processing. And don't worry, I shall take the dogs with me when I go."

Caro's fears at least in part allayed, Darcy set about loading her vehicle with food and equipment including bowls, food and beds for Mab and Brock; a duvet, a couple of pans, matches, oil lamps and torches and a selection of basic provisions. A short note was left for Brant telling him that Caro was arranging a place for her to work in solitude on the Mediobogdum piece but she did not yet know its exact location, which was not a lie she consoled herself. After a loving closure note she added a P.S. to the effect that she would contact him a.s.a.p. but that there may be no signal for her mobile so he was not to worry if he heard nothing from her for a while. No doubt he would be far from pleased, she thought toting her bags to the car whilst trying not to step on or fall over an excited duo of dogs, but this it could not be helped and he would get over it once she was safely home. Far better to remove herself given the two sources of danger that now threatened: Ted Tulley and the unpredictable inhabitant of Mediobogdum who nowadays seemed to have taken to visiting and causing chaos at her home.

The latter, she realised as the dogs jumped into the rear of the car and she shut the tailgate, was the biggest obstacle to solving the mystery. The fact that his presence was at times amorous and at others downright threatening made it impossible to deduce his motivation or goal. And without this knowledge, she conceded, there was no hope of laying whatever it was to rest. It also, she mused starting up the engine, prevented her from divining her own emotional response. Love? Desire?

Compassion? Or maybe hatred and fear. Which of them should predominate? At present it seemed she felt a blend of all these. There would be some answers soon, she vowed, pulling away from the house.

Over the Wrynose Pass, and the mountains seemed higher, bleaker and more barren than remembered. Their summits were wreathed in cloud on this grey day, and they overshadowed the deep-cut valley and far from giving a feeling of protection their guardianship instilled a sense of dominance and claustrophobia. The blocking of radio waves and the constant buzz-crackle-hiss that was the result reinforced this impression. The stunted rowan and blackthorn that dotted the floor of the gorge and clung precariously to the lower crags shivered in a brisk wind, whilst the pewter surface of Blea Tarn trembled with each cold breath. The solitary one-storey building that was her destination cowered beneath a mountain scowling its lofty disapproval. Overwhelmingly grand but not exactly a heart-warming prospect, was Darcy's verdict of the terrain as she pulled off the single track that ran with comparative ease along the valley bottom before it eventually struggled over the formidable Hardknott Pass.

Still, the ominous landscape did befit the mission, she thought parking up on a stony plateau flanking the river that sliced the valley in two. White-water crested, it was fed by the countless becks that spouted and foamed down rock and gully in their obsessive rush to the sea.

"Out you guys, come and get acquainted with your new pad!" she joked releasing the dogs. Her words seemed to affront the silence so she said no more and peered over her shoulder with a distinct sense of unease. Feeling compelled to look up, her eyes were drawn to the western end of the valley where the track clambered up and over and around bare rock, wending its way to the summit of the pass. A shock of recognition electrified her nerves: on the other side lay the rocky plateau and Mediobogdum. She had not realised it would be so close. Instinctively she took out her mobile phone; the screen showed 'no network'. How would it feel to be lying in bed alone, with no means of communication and less than a mile from that dread fortress?

"We won't think about that now," she said aloud, defying the ponderous silence. Mab and Brock scampered about sniffing, trailing and generally showing an air of unconcern and in that at least she found comfort.

The accommodation offered by the granite building was basic but adequate and surprisingly spacious. From the outer door she entered a corridor that ran the length of the building providing access to the various rooms. She wrinkled her nose in distaste: the aura of damp and mustiness spoke of years of emptiness and neglect.

"Come on you two," she said aloud to test the acoustics. Her voice echoed due to the sparseness of furnishings and the dogs' claws clicked along the bare boards as they cautiously followed. Whilst not displaying the alarm they had obviously felt at the fort, they were not entirely at ease in here and stayed close to her heels. She opened the door almost opposite the entrance and found herself in a large rectangular room with a trestle table and chairs dominating the centre and reminiscent of the schoolroom. So strong was this feeling that she glanced round the walls, almost expecting to find a blackboard fixed there.

As in all the rooms she would find, the interior of the walls were panelled with wood and had at some stage been painted a uniform cream, but the paint had now yellowed and was cracked and peeling in places. A pot bellied stove with a black pipe that disappeared through the roof sat against one wall and a wicker basket by the stone plinth on which it was standing still contained a couple of logs and remnants of kindling and bark.

"At least we shan't be cold tonight," she said with false cheeriness as the dogs stood behind her with bowed heads and drooping tails. "Come on, let's go fix you some chow!" she chivvied. "Then we'll go gather some wood," she added, aware of an air of oppression that she put down to nerves about staying here alone but which made her able to empathise with the dogs, sensitive as they were to atmosphere and those things of which humans may not be aware. At least there was no reaction similar to that at the fort or during the phenomena at the

233

farmhouse. In fact given the mildness of their unease it was probably due on this occasion to merely being in a strange and unlived in space

The kitchen at the end of the corridor was square and slightly smaller than the first room and contained another stove, this time with a couple of hobs on which to cook or boil water for tea. There were several large buckets and a chipped pot butler sink in one corner but no running water. There must be a pump or well somewhere outside; she would take a look once the car was unloaded. A shelf had several tin plates and bowls stacked upon it and some white mugs, the enamel chipped in places, hung from a row of hooks. Another smaller trestle table held three metal jugs of diminishing sizes and there were folding chairs stacked against one wall. As in all the other rooms the floorboards were bare and the windows devoid of curtains, but apart from a light film of dust and the occasional cobweb, the place was liveable-clean.

The room at the other end of the corridor was the largest, running as it did across the width of the building. Obviously this had served as a dormitory for the duration of the dig, and whoever had used the place prior to the Hilldean archaeology team. A row of iron beds with rolled-up mattresses were ranged the length of the room, and a bank of metal lockers of a dark regulation green stood against the wall.

"Stand by your beds!" Darcy murmured, not for the first time getting more than a whiff of the schoolroom or rather, as her tour progressed, the military. The latter was obviously down to her current obsession and her reason for being there, although the wisdom of this was becoming more uncertain by the minute. She chose a bed by the window, and sitting on it bounced up down to test springs that protested with a succession of loud creaks and groans. The mattress looked and smelt suspect too. Rising she stood by window looking out on bleak fells, the harsh stone-chocked river and a deserted valley bottom where stunted rowans could be counted on one hand and even the sheep were in short supply. Suddenly the significance of what she was doing hit home. To be staying here alone after the experiences of the past weeks was sheer lunacy. As the isolation and austerity of her surroundings began to make itself felt Darcy felt panic rising.

Anyway, you aren't really alone; there is always 'sir' up at the camp for company, she told herself grinning, but then it wasn't amusing really and the smile quickly died. Better to stick with the dogs! Keep busy; that had always been her maxim at times of stress and she called upon it now.

This is more like, she decided looking around. Her gear was unpacked and a blanket hung at each of the bedroom windows. Naked panes in kitchen, refectory and elsewhere she could handle; but even the thought of someone or something peering in at her as she slept made her flesh crawl. The only other exception was the tiny 'bathroom' with its tin bath hung on one wall. A white jug and bowl with more chips than enamel stood on a rickety table, and in the corner stood a camping toilet with a half-full container of chemical left on the shelf. Primitive but adequate, she decided. A tea towel hung at the tiny window ensured her privacy here. The bed it turned out was acceptable once the flock mattress had been unrolled, taken outside, shaken well and left to air for an hour or two before being lugged inside again and covered with a blanket topped by the duvet. A couple of cushions brought from the car would serve as a pillow.

The kitchen stove presented rather more of a challenge. Eventually she had it raked out and re-laid using kindling and logs from the wood store discovered outside at the end of the building. A half box of matches later the wood caught and as the flue warmed a red glow and leaping flames cheered the kitchen. She decided not to bother with the one in the room she had come to think of as the refectory as there was no possibility of her sitting in their alone after eating. Now to find some water and get a kettle on to boil. Opposite the back door she found what might be a well. On removing the solid wooden cover by tugging and heaving for several minutes, the intense cold, damp and mossiness hit her face with a rush. The black circle of water far below winked and blinked in the sudden light and reflected the greeny mauve of the twilit sky after maybe years of absolute darkness. Looped over a bracket fixed near the top of the stone shaft was a length of rope with a hook at one end. She brought several buckets from the kitchen and lowered each in turn down the dark, stone-lined well until they hit the water with an echoing *plash,* then heaved on the rope and hauled them up again full of crystal clear water that on tasting proved delicious but with a coldness so intense that it caused her to gasp for breath and brought an ache to the back of her nose.

Soon a kettle of water was on the boil to make a comforting pot of tea. Packets of cereal, pasta, mash and dried vegetables; cans of tomatoes, peas and beans and jars of pesto sauce were stacked on the shelf along with tea, coffee, tinned and dried milk, biscuits, bread, and crackers for when the former ran out; a bottle of olive oil and a carton of spread, and a box containing a dozen eggs. Candles, matches and a torch were placed in both bedroom and kitchen for handiness and several bottles of wine sat on the shelf with the food. After all, she told herself, there was no telling how long she would be here and any unused and non-perishable food and drink could be left for the next inhabitant, maybe hikers in need of a night's shelter or those caught out in a storm. A sack of dried dog food and some tins were stored in the pantry off the corridor, along with various treats and chews stored in one of the jugs from the kitchen and then she was done.

Dusk was gathering now at the windows and stove and oil lamps gave off a welcome glow. The mustiness and dampness of misuse had been largely put to flight by the scent of wood smoke and earlier on, fresh air admitted by opening every available window and door. Now they were closed to the night and the bolts on the latter tugged across for security after greasing the rusted shafts with olive oil. She had cooked and eaten a simple meal of pasta tossed in basil sauce and topped with a boiled egg and now sat in the kitchen nursing a mug of tea and a feeling of contentment. The basket had been replenished with logs from the store, Mab and Brock had been fed and were settled on their beds next to the stove. She switched on an ancient portable radio she had brought given the absence of telephone lines for high tech modems, but reception was blocked by the mountains. A series of whines and crackles and at best a faint smattering of Manx Radio was all that could be coaxed out of it. She gave it up and read for a while until her eyelids began to droop. It took some nerve however to take herself along the corridor to the dormitory and that uninviting bed.

Contrary to expectations though the night passed quietly enough and the following morning she looped back the blanket at the window to find the room filled with golden light. The fells were almost smiling as their cladding of frost-burnt bracken was kindled into an orange glow by the rays of the sun. The sky was blue and her mood swung to one of optimism. She dressed and on impulse took the pendant out of the secure pocket of her overnight bag and placed it around her neck. The morning was spent working up the first draft of a piece on 'looting –social depravation or greed?' and by lunchtime it was finished, aided in part by the need for precision and concentrated effort in order to get it done before battery power on her lap top ran out. She managed it with eight minutes to spare and as a ready charged battery was stored in the case there was every chance of getting the second project finished the following day. That afternoon, given the lack of internet access, she drove to the lakeside town of Ambleside in order to drop off the cassette that held the photographs of the fort and then send the article to Frank by special delivery.

I ought to call him, she thought guiltily as she emerged from the post office and for once her mobile registered a strong signal. At first she declined, anticipating one of Frank's famous 'verbals' but then reasoned that he might just be appeased by her call, and if not there was always the 'losing signal now Frank' excuse to fall back on.

"You've got balls, I'll tell you that girl!" was his initial response.

"That's a contradiction in terms Frank!"

"Maybe, but true. Where the hell are you?"

"Up North," she said, deliberately vague.

"Skiving at home you mean!"

"Absolutely not. I'm in the field on this Ted Tulley case; I gotta lead."

Which was true, she told herself recalling those slashed tyres.

"Don't know why yet Frank but he seems to be homing in on me."

"Christ Darcy, get to the police!"

"Negative. The 'News' can wrap this one up – think of the kudos Frank!"

"Ain't no joy in a dead reporter!"

"No worries. I've got balls – you just told me so!"

"Sure did. But I'm not confident of squaring this one with Max Dearden. You'll have to come up with some actual-,"

"Just posted the 'Looting' piece to you Frank," she interrupted, not entirely clear about which was causing Frank most concern, her safety or his job.

"Great!" She heard the sigh of relief and realised with gratitude that he had been covering for her absence. "But it's still mega risky," he added, the concern back in his voice. "This Tulley guy has killed remember. Betta get back here like now."

"Frank, I do believe you are missing me!"

"Your brass cheek maybe."

"Seriously, I'll be fine. As soon as I suss out where he is holed up I'll go to the cops, okay?"

"Make sure you do then; and I want you back in the office next week – *whatever*, got me?"

"Sure have – and thanks."

There followed a moment of silence and Darcy was about to switch off thinking he had gone when he spoke again.

"How's the rest of it going then?".

"What do you mean Frank?" She pretended not to know he was referring to Mediobogdum and her obsession with its past inhabitants.

"Are you hanging on in there Darcy?"

She thought of the heaving worms and Brant's weird behaviour and said with feeling "Just about."

"Plenty in it then?"

"Yeah. Plenty scary."

"There was another silence. She could sense the conflict that raged between an editor tempted by a sensational story, and the boss with an obligation to protect his staff. "Darcy remember, *nolis nothis permittere te terer!*"

She almost dropped the mobile at this sudden foray into Latin. "What does it mean Frank?"

"As a rough translation, don't let the bastards get you down!"

The line went dead. Good old Frank. She was smiling as she made her way back to the car.

On the way back to camp as Darcy had begun to think of it, she collected the empty cassette for her camera and an envelope of prints that she put into a pocket of the dashboard to be viewed later, judging this to be prudent as there was no telling what phenomena those images might evoke, then decided upon a detour to Tarn Howes. Half term, when the place would be thronged with visitors, was well past and this being mid-week the car park was deserted. Mab and Brock ran on ahead, made skittish by a gusting wind and enjoying their freedom after being confined in the car. The tarn, actually three made into one and surrounded by wooded foothills and bare fells beyond, sparkled in mellow sunlight. Silver birch, oak, beech and rowan blazed their autumnal splendour and were perfectly mirrored on the surface of the lake; a strange upside-down world and she stopped for a moment on the perimeter path as it triggered odd associations. Golden daggers of light rushing towards the bank on the crest of each ripple drew her gaze, held it and lulled her into an almost hypnotic state.

Suddenly she was struck by a flash of insight. Maybe that was how it was for Antonius and herself: different dimensions that sometimes overlapped, each mirroring people and events from the other. That would explain Brant's uncharacteristic behaviour at times, and maybe that of Ted Tulley too. Perhaps they, like herself, were being infected by fragments of disjointed events so that they reflected somebody else's actions and emotions that because they overlapped became intensified. Suddenly Brant's theory of that night in the observatory shifted into sharper focus and made greater sense.

She walked on along the water's edge, dazzled by the intensity of the sun gilding a diminishing path along the surface, her mind racing on from that initial insight. Was she being confused with somebody else? If these episodes that were the result of a distortion in Time caused emotional disorientation in herself and Brant, then surely it must be the same for Antonius? Her foolishness suddenly became clear: she had expected a coherent story with feelings and events following a logical sequence, a history that made sense. If she had it right now it would explain why he appeared as the suppliant for relief from a terrible need; whilst at others she seemed to be the butt of his anger and at still others the target of an overwhelming passion. She shied away from the word love.

The most sensible explanation – if such a word could be used in this context – would be that she was right in surmising there was something he desperately needed to have resolved, and that any visitor to the fort who was remotely sensitive to such things could be targeted as a possible means of achieving this aim. This would account for the frustration and aggression when she failed to satisfy that need. It would also justify her belief that she was being forced out of the farmhouse and back to the scene of whatever tragedy drove him. Neat: but just to complicate things there could be aggression towards someone else mixed in there, along with a whole corollary of emotions displaced in Space and Time. Such as –yes, love. It would be denied no longer. Love for some woman who shared his own reality, who had through some tragedy or betrayal had left him with a sense of devastation and loss. She walked on, surprised by her own feeling of bereavement. She railed against herself for being mawkish and stupid, for reacting like a heroine in a second-rate romantic novel and struggled instead to be objective, the investigative reporter simply going about her job. It could have been anyone; right time, right place that's all. But disappointment clung like a cobweb round her heart. These feelings are dangerous, she thought eyeing the redness of the dying sun spilling like blood across the water prior to setting.

Calling the dogs she veered away from the tarn and its potentially dangerous light to climb Tom Heights on a track littered with sycamore wings, pine cones and all the debris of Autumn. They walked the ridge, Mab and Brock exploring the miniature cols and gullies as they went and Darcy pausing to admire the view: at her back the shining expanse of Coniston Water and the Old Man of Coniston looming against the skyline. Across the valley the bulk of Wetherlam rose and the unmistakable cluster of the Langdale Pikes. To the north Helvellyn hunched its broad back beneath a greenish violet sky; but over to the north west the volcanic giants brooded. *His place.* She suppressed a shiver and walked on. That is where you should be, she told herself, not pottering about these foothills like any carefree tourist. A feeling of guilt crept in as the truth of this struck home. The sole reason for staying over was to confront whatever was there and if possible find some sort of resolution. The sun bled into the sky and sank towards the horizon and the water glimpsed below through a gap in the trees blazed crimson. The air began to buzz. Contact had been made. The pull towards those far fells stretched reason to unbearable thinness. She resisted the guilt, the insane desire to apologise for her absence. Then she laughed aloud and the sudden sound cut the current. She was alone again. Not today, this is not your territory, she thought with a rush of defiance. The buzzing inside her head ceased and she strode out with confidence for the next cairn along the ridge.

Time to return, in fact she had stayed too late. The temperature had dramatically fallen and twilight was settling over the fells. She glanced at her watch and her stomach flipped. It had stopped, never a good sign. No problem, the path would come into view beyond this outcrop. A sea of dried bracken and heather swished around her calves impeding progress and there was still no sign of the path.

"Mab! Brock!" she shouted, realising they were nowhere to be seen. Precious minutes were spent in searching. Eventually she found them in a large basin-shaped hollow, evidently as stressed and disoriented as herself because they barked and growled at her sudden appearance then on recognising her rushed forward to greet her with obvious relief.

"Stay at heel," she commanded, stroking their heads with a hand that shook. Her breath came faster as disorientation tightened its grip

241

and she tried to ignore the strangeness of her surroundings. That gleam dissolving with distance should be Coniston Water but then that made the mountains all wrong. They were the wrong shape, in the wrong places. Gone were the low fells of Ambleside, so too was the broad back of Helvellyn. She rummaged in the pockets of her jacket, the one she habitually wore when out walking, and her fingers what they sought. She gasped as the needle of the compass swung wildly to and fro. In every aspect the landscape had undergone change: the volcanic peaks of the West glowed with an ominous red light and hemmed her in on all sides.

Somehow he had drawn her into his Time and Place.

TWENTY-EIGHT

~

"Come on, let's get off here like *now!*" she cried aloud to the dogs, her feet stumbling over turf and bracken and slipping on slopes of scree. She halted breathless and close to tears. Judging by the twilight she had dragged them around for about half an hour in search of the track. The cold penetrated her gloves numbing her fingers and pricking her skin with minute barbs. Her light walking shoes were drenched with dew as the temperature plummeted towards freezing and her feet ached with cold.

"You can feel it too, can't you?" she whispered to the dogs cowering at her heels, referring not to the intense chill but the sinister atmosphere that saturated the heights. As she watched a red-tinged mist crept up from the valley and ghosted towards her across the ridge. A harsh croaking made her look up: a couple of ravens glided above the sheets of vapour and their presence filled her with dread. Birds of ill-omen that know-all and see-all.

He is everywhere, she thought backing away. His presence dominates the heights and his power permeates the mist. She tried telling herself that so far Antonius had done her no actual harm. It was no use. She knew nightmares were harmless yet that did nothing to allay the terror they caused, the blind unreasoning terror such as she was feeling right now. He was angry, the woods and slopes resounded with his anger. She was not in the place he thought she should be.

Indomita Indomita

243

That word again: *She who is wild and untamed.* Instinctively her hand went to the pendant around her neck. The whisper came again, seemed real rather than inside her head. It echoed through the trees, gathering force and returning even louder. Her mouth gaped but the scream would not come. The ground underfoot became steeper and stonier and progress all the harder. She strained to catch a sudden sound. The dogs whined and pawed frantically at her legs. There it was again: a distant and impossible sound. The thud of hoof beats on ground made hollow by a nexus of burrowing roots. Impossible because that very ground with its crags, hollows and tangle of undergrowth was impossible terrain for any horse. At least, she amended with a stab of fear, any normal, physical horse.

She paused again to listen. No drum of hooves this time but someone was crashing through the bracken. The violet of deepening twilight deceived her as she moved on so that she started at every bush swearing it had moved. Despite the creeping cold her clothes were now drenched in sweat. Dying must be like this, she thought, this terrible sense of isolation, of being the only person on Earth. Chill out, she told herself sternly; that sound was real and external which means that someone else must be on the heights. *Ted Tulley?* Her legs began to tremble uncontrollably as she recalled his aggression and threatening behaviour at the time of that encounter on the cliff road. Now she was on foot and alone on an isolated ridge at nightfall and nobody knew she was there. How stupid she had been. It had never crossed her mind that he may follow her vehicle. There was no reason why Ted Tulley should not have a car, either one from the farm or one stolen whilst on the run, so it was possible he had discovered her presence in the valley and followed her through to Ambleside. It seemed unlikely given the crowded streets and his fugitive status, but he was deranged so who could predict what he might do? The redness of sky and mist coupled with the aura of strangeness had indicated something else; but that natural red glow from the dying sun may have coloured her perception causing her to feel what she expected to feel. At that moment she could not decide which of the two was preferable: Ted Tulley or the long-dead inhabitant of Mediobogdum.

Reaching into her pocket she took out her mobile but the signal was blocked by the mountains.

One thing was sure, whoever was stalking these heights there was no mistaking the sense of threat. She began to run, Mab and Brock scrambling around her feet, their eyes showing the whites in their fear. Her foot caught in a bramble pitching her forward. She lay where she fell, her will to survive sapped by a terrible apathy. The sound of footfalls and dry twigs snapping underfoot drew closer. Mab and Brock barked at her head and scrabbled at her clothes with frantic paws. Ashamed of her weakness she pulled herself upright, she had to get them away from the unknown stalker and off this ridge before nightfall.

Commanding the dogs to stay at heel she stumbled forward again as fast as she dared. The light was fading fast, the mist growing thicker and denser with every step. It was tempting to give up on finding the track and simply head downhill – anything to get off this damned ridge – but the slopes were steep and cloaked in a tangle of bramble, bracken and shrub. Soon it would be totally dark and then it would be all too easy to trip in the blackness and hurtle down to the bottom and end up perhaps with a broken leg. Nobody would hear her cries for help or the barking of the dogs. She paused to listen for sounds of pursuit. The silence was reassuring and she heaved a sigh of relief. The path should be just around this outcrop; she remembered the twisted hawthorn tree and the rowan next to it which meant they had walked in a circle, but never mind it was all right now. She pulled aside the prickly branches in order to pass and a scream was torn from her throat. A face leered at her in the half light. The features were distorted by some violent emotion, the eyes wild with a fixed stare like those of a wolf confronting its prey. Even so she recognised Ted Tulley.

"Gotcha this time," he leered grabbing her arm as he emerged from his lair in the hollow where he had lain in wait. The voice grated along her nerves, coarseness and cruelty in every nuance. Whatever the greed or entity driving Ted Tulley it had taken over, transforming the kind, hard working Jekyll into obnoxious Hyde. She screamed again then gagged and retched as a hand that stank of tobacco smothered her mouth. The two spaniels barked and growled furiously and Mab dived for his ankle. Darcy shook her head in distress as the bitch yelped and howled and was bowled over by a savage kick. Darcy's struggles earned her a blow to the head that had he not had hold of her would have sent her spinning. As it was she slumped, overcome by dizziness and nausea and he let her sink to her knees. As the offensive hand was removed from her face she gulped at the cold clear air.

"Not so cocky now miss, are we?" he taunted, brandishing something close to her face. The gleam of red light on metal told her he was holding a knife. As he loomed over her taunting her with the blade she thought *I am going to die.*

She screamed then in earnest. No-one would hear but it was an instinctive reaction. Mab and Brock barked frantically and she screamed again as the blade flashed. This time Brock was the one to squeal in pain. Even in the half-light she could see the red gash opening across Brock's shoulder as undeterred, he rushed in to her aid again.

"Oh, no! No!" She sobbed fearing that he would be killed, and fought like a wild thing. Momentarily distracted by the need to defend his legs from the teeth of the dog, Tulley released his hold.

"Back Brock! Back!" she yelled, as Tulley raised his knife for a second slash.

At the same time she rammed her fingers into his face and brought up her knee with a force intensified by fear and fury. With a grunt Ted Tulley sank to the ground like a wounded bull. He shook his head to and fro, one hand covering his gouged eyes and the other nursing his crotch. Thank God Brant had insisted on giving her elementary defence training sessions. Shouting to the dogs to follow she ran past Ted Tulley who was still on his knees and with a sob of relief found herself back on the path.

The light was fading fast and it was darker still in the wood. They

246

had entered a world of mist, silence and a peculiar half-light that distorted shapes and shadows. Undergrowth tangled about her knees as the path seemed to disappear only to re-emerge again a few yards further down the incline. Her breath was torn from her lungs in painful rasps and the cold sweat of fear ran down her spine. Several times she cast a glance over her shoulder as the fear of being followed grew. A cry of pain escaped as she missed her footing, and shortly afterwards hit her head on a branch in the darkness. A twig snapped, an owl screeched and somewhere deep in the wood a roebuck at the rut roared. Then silence. She pressed on, checking only to see that Meg and Brock were following, not daring to take the time to inspect their wounds. First the crack of a dry twig snapping underfoot, then the scrape of boots sliding on scree confirmed her worst nightmare. She had almost reached the bottom when a hand grabbed her by the shoulder and spun her round.

She found herself staring into the livid face of Ted Tulley.

"Bitch! Bloody bitch!" He seemed wilder and more deranged than ever. Even here in the murk of the wood the wildness of his expression could be seen. Runnels of white streaked the dirty cheeks, testament to the way her fingers had stabbed at his eyes. He raised his arm and she sensed the knife in his hand. She screamed as his other hand shot out and grabbed a handful of her hair, forcing her head back so that her throat was exposed. Mab and Brock set up a frenzied barking. His arm hovered, his teeth were bared in a grimace as he drew breath and prepared for the slicing action across her throat. It was then that she heard it again; the thudding of hooves approaching over hollow ground and this time no mistaking the sound. Louder and louder as they came closer until she feared they would both be ridden down. Ted Tulley paused, hand raised and knife blade ready to end her life. He stared wild-eyed into the trees, head to one side as he listened. Obviously he could hear it too. Mab and Brock fell silent and cowered close to the ground.

The thudding ceased and she peered through the twilit haze: the silhouette of a horse was partially visible through the red mist, forefeet

247

flailing the air and nostrils flaring. Tulley gave a loud cry and released his grip on her hair. The wind that previously wafted along the ridge suddenly blustered and raged so that the mist began shifting and drifting to reveal and conceal in turn. The shape of the rider appeared and disappeared then reformed again so that she could not be sure of having seen it. Instinctively her hand went to the pendant around her neck. Time seemed to stand still and the dogs fell silent. The wind howled and whined and tore at her clothes and hair with manic fingers. The *crack* of splintering wood echoed through the trees. Ted Tulley let out a terrible cry and fell to the ground like a stone. Nothing then, except what could have been the flick of a cloak or the wing of a bat before mist and darkness closed in again. The *thud thud thud* of retreating hooves faded and died away. Ted Tulley lay inert on his back, his face covered in blood, the splintered bough of oak resting across his body. Shivering and shaking with trauma she backed away and called to the trembling dogs. The mini whirlwind dropped as quickly as it had come. But where in God's name was the tarn? Brock was showing signs of weakness and lagging behind; the knife wound must still be bleeding. The hairs at the nape of her neck rose and prickled. He, Antonius, was near. On horseback, on foot or whatever his presence was all around. Her skin recoiled from the tiny reverberations of energy.

"You have to let me go," she moaned, realising that somehow he had trapped them between dimensions, in a surreal world that was neither wholly his nor entirely hers and therefore not navigable.

"Please," she pleaded in a whisper, pausing for a second or two to cradle the pendant before staggering on through a wood of deepening shadows.

Indomita

She whirled round as the whisper came from first her right, then her left then from behind.

Veni, Indomita, veni!

Although the words were alien the emotional content was clear.

"Soon, I'll come soon," she promised, stumbling over roots, stones and dying bracken.

She felt a breath on her cheek that may have been just the wind and a caress that could have been the touch of a cobweb. Then she was out of the woods and on the level and the tarn lay before her, a mirror of polished pewter reflecting a crescent moon and the final streaks of crimson cast by the setting sun. Horizontal ribbons of cloud and lengthening tree shadows staining the grass added to an aura of calm and blessed normality. More reassuring than anything else, the air was clear of mist. A swift examination of Brock's shoulder reassured her that clots had formed and the bleeding had stopped and although Mab was limping she showed no signs of serious injury. She stood on a grassed knoll close to the car park, pendant in hand and sent out thoughts of gratitude for her life. The realisation that she could have been lying up there with her throat cut sent her hurrying for the car.

She pulled in on reaching the Ambleside by-pass and after ensuring the 'number protected' function was activated, checked for signal, dialled 999 and requested Police. Swiftly she informed the person who answered that she had seen Ted Tulley whilst out walking and that he was lying injured on Tom Heights. When asked for her name and details she pressed the 'end call' button and switched off.

Despite the sense of isolation the primitive dwelling in the valley felt like a luxurious haven as she took the torch from the shelf, ushered the dogs indoors and drew the bolts across. She advanced warily however wondering what might be lying in wait. The beam of the torch swept floor and wall of each room but revealed nothing sinister. No writhing piles of worms or slimy slugs lay in wait for a careless footstep.

"Thank God." She breathed normally again and lit the oil lamps and candles and placed a lighted match to the paper and kindling laid ready in the stove.

"Brock, here boy, let's take a look at that shoulder," she said taking down the first aid box from the shelf. "The bastard," she muttered under her breath as she bathed the encrusted blood from the cut then applied antiseptic cream and a dressing. Hopefully the police would have located Tulley by now and have him in custody; the need for security rather than pity had motivated that call.

"You're tuckered out lad, aren't you," she said softly, fondling Brock's ears as he lay at her feet unresisting. "You too, Mab," she added, stroking the bitch's head and at the same time checking her over for damage caused by that vicious kick. She winced and whined a little when Darcy touched the place but fortunately seemed to have escaped with nothing worse than bruising. Both dogs were stressed and Brock's breathing was shallow and irregular. Measuring drops from a bottle of calming herbal infusion into some tepid water and adding a spoonful of honey, she filled the dropper and administered half to each.

"There, that will make you feel better." She put a kettle on to boil whilst preparing a light meal for them of bread and butter soaked in warm egg and milk. Soon they were settled on their beds by the stove and Brock's chest rose and fell with a normal and regular rhythm.

Unable to eat much after her ordeal, Darcy opened the door of the stove and soaked up the warmth whilst eating from a packet of digestive biscuits. A mug of tea sweetened with honey and laced with brandy from a miniature brought along for medicinal purposes was the best she had ever tasted. She watched the flames subside as the logs began to glow and give off real heat and let her mind range over her situation. Logically she should pack her things and be off home that night but weariness ached in her body and dulled her mind. Besides who knew what might be waiting for her at the farmhouse. An involuntary shudder ran through her at the thought of those slimy manifestations. Added to that possibility there was the problem of Brant's reaction. She counted off the days on her fingers: Friday tomorrow and Brant could well be home the following day if he managed to get leave from his mission, and how would she explain Brock's injured shoulder? The whole thing would have to come out and there would be one hell of a row. Brant would go ballistic about her putting herself and the dogs in such danger. Not a good idea to set off in the morning then either. Besides, she had done the sensible thing and made that anonymous call to the police, so she was no longer in danger from Ted Tulley as he was either dead or should either be in hospital under guard or banged up by now, and if not soon would be. As for the rest, well it may be psychologically disturbing but thus far it was scarcely a threat to life, and indeed seemed to have saved her from that maniac's knife back there on Tom Heights.

So no sense in stressing over what happened, she told herself firmly. After all the whole point of this mission was to confront the situation and try to unravel the mystery. It was the only way in fact, she thought soberly, otherwise she could be haunted by this for the rest of her life. Her lifespan was as nothing when compared with the couple of thousand years or so this thing had remained unresolved. Of one thing she was now sure: Ted Tulley was a significant player in that mystery. Leaning forward she picked up a handful of kindling and tossed it into the glowing heart of the fire, then added a log from the basket. Sitting back she idly watched the sparks flying and flames creeping up from under the log. So was she right in her theory about his involvement?

'E's not bin the same sin' he found them...' Darcy shook off drowsiness as she heard Jane Tulley's voice in her head. She was sure now that her assumption that Ted had accidentally found something of great value on his land was correct, but was she right in her guess at the nature of his find? Maybe not – it could be a store of weapons, buried to prevent them being used by the native Brigante troops at the time of the assault on Mediobogdum? She quickly dismissed the idea. Ted Tulley's farm was too far from the fort to make such an excursion feasible whilst already under attack, and from what Caro had said the strength of the native tribes lay in guerrilla fighting and the element of surprise, so there would have been little or no advance warning. All this apart, a down-to-earth man like Ted Tulley would probably not be over-impressed, even if he recognised what they were, by archaeological remains of metal disintegrated and corroded by time.

Suddenly she sat upright again as a devastating thought struck. What if the eagle standard had been buried to prevent it falling into

251

the hands of the enemy? The Ninth being a prestigious legion the eagle may have been made of gold which would survive the ravages of time and climate. But Jane Tulley had said '…sin' he found *them'* and presumably any other sacred regalia buried with it would, like the hypothetical weapons, not have survived intact. No, her initial hunch that he had found a cache of Roman coins was undoubtedly correct.

But why should it be hidden there? If on account of an assault then the same objection applied: no time to bury the coins once the attack was under way. Her frown cleared as inspiration struck. What if the wealth had been hidden not to safeguard it from the Britons but simply to have it away from the fort? Someone with access, an officer say, could have been pilfering money or simply making something on the side by selling weapons, goodies and booze to the locals or the lads of the cohort. Over weeks or months they would amass a small fortune. Or maybe there had been a traitor up at that fort and the coins were intended to fuel an uprising of the local tribes. Unlike weapons, presumably the hoard would have been buried in a protective covering, maybe a lead-lined box or something to keep the contents safe until the opportunity came to retrieve them. Either that or they were fashioned from gold. Whatever the reason, if in his deranged mind Ted Tulley thought she knew about it and was plotting to take the hoard from him he would certainly want her out of the way and sufficient reason too for shooting the man from Defra. He was probably looking around on a routine but unannounced visit and accidentally came across Ted with his find. Ted Tulley's comment that night on the cliff came to mind: "You knew about it. Came lookin', *just like 'e did"* and Darcy knew she was right. Stephen Pettigrew was now dead due to Tulley's paranoid delusions and for the first time, the closeness of her escape truly registered.

There was still the question of his obvious mental breakdown. Although her life had been disrupted and her nerves shredded by seemingly inexplicable events, she had not succumbed to madness and murder. He must have become secretive, she decided, tormented by the thought of losing his hoard and in this disturbed frame of mind become sensitive to red-shifted events. Maybe guilt and greed had then warped perception and made him susceptible to the darker side of whisperings and visions. Whatever, enough theorising for tonight. Exhausted she made her way to bed.

Some time later whilst still half asleep she fumbled for the torch. The loud *clunk* of it hitting bare boards then rolling to somewhere out of reach brought her fully awake. She pushed back the duvet and felt her way round the bed to the far side, the iron rail of the bed-end cold beneath her hand. Her breathing quickened and was expelled in minute currents of white vapour. The wind chimes in the rowan tree tinkled briefly as though to direct her attention. Pulling aside the blanket hung at the window with a hand that slightly shook, she gazed out on the moonlit night. Her sudden intake of breath sounded loud in the deafening silence. He was still there.

TWENTY-NINE

~

The uniform brought to mind old newsreels and sepia photographs of the First World War. He stood by the stunted rowan and hawthorn that flanked the dirt path leading from the valley track to the main door of the building, his face pale as death in the moon-glow. He was standing perfectly motionless, looking back at the window as though aware of her vigil. He is so young, she could not help thinking. A surge of anger caught her by surprise, at middle aged officers playing with models in war rooms, despatching droves of adolescents to enact their fatal manoeuvres. As he continued to stare in her direction she was moved to silent tears. There was such a sadness and loneliness about him, that unmistakable yearning for a loved one missed or permanently lost; the pathos of a soldier far from home. He seemed to be pleading for her to somehow ease his pain.

Antonius

Unbidden and seemingly inappropriate the name escaped her lips.

Mab and Brock must have heard; a crescendo of barking shattered the silence. Shivering in the bitter cold she turned at the sound to peer into the moon-shot dark. The final shreds of sleep splintered and fell tinkling into the depths of inner space. Previously it had failed to register but now the incongruousness of the scene outside struck, along with the realisation that there were no trees – rowan or otherwise – flanking the path, let alone wind chimes. The barking ceased, but when she looked out of the window again the soldier had vanished. Awash with cold silver light the valley appeared chill and desolate, inhabited only by wind-bent trees and dry stone walls, the latter snaking like slow-worms across the valley bottom. Moving to the bed she searched for the torch by moonlight and finding it returned to the window to adjust the blanket. Beyond the window the scene ached with loneliness. The blanket falling back into place blotted it out.

What did it all mean? As the greyness of dawn filtered into the kitchen she sat with a mug of coffee mulling over the strange events of the previous night. She was reluctant to think of it as the *dream* of the night before because although that was how it had started, she had obviously been awake upon leaving the bed and standing at the window and the unknown soldier had still been there. Suddenly something inside clicked. The Unknown Soldier: was that what it was all about? Was something or someone trying to close the time and culture gap, show her by that poignant icon that some things are unchanging and universal and just as relevant today? The scene was still there behind her eyes, etched on her mind with crystal clarity. More disturbing than this was the emotional residue; the sadness and yearning still clung to her like a second skin. It all seemed so real, yet common sense told her that this soldier in his vintage uniform could not really have been out there in the middle of the night in this desolate valley. The whole thing, she thought in a flash of insight, was like wearing a faulty contact lens that appeared to fit but which actually distorted reality.

Moving on in her thinking she decided it was imperative to discover the latest on the circumstances and whereabouts of Ted Tulley. Not only for her own peace of mind but because Frank should be alerted to a scoop she thought guiltily, glancing at her watch. When tested again the radio crackled with the same infuriating intensity, and as the daily drama of Manx life was of less than minimal interest right now she gave the whole thing up. It would have to be Ambleside. Yet it made little sense; her car may have been spotted in the vicinity of Tarn Howes. In fact it was more than likely that as the news about Ted Tulley's capture broke, someone would recall seeing that 'flash red job' as Brant described it. But there was no alternative. If she failed to get the 'inside angle' over to Frank before the Nationals chewed up the story, he would never forgive her and Max Dearden would probably fire her on the spot. Sitting down with a mug of strong coffee she entered the bones of her encounter with Ted Tulley into her mobile and stored it in 'drafts'. She would e-mail it to Frank on reaching civilisation and that would secure an eye-witness first for the Paper. On her return she would flesh out that initial report to a mind-blowing feature about her near-fatal ordeal at the hands of Ted Tulley. Frank would forgive anything then and she would be restored to 'favourite' status! Around fifteen minutes later she was ushering Mab and Brock into the car.

With the mountains at her back now she switched on the radio and experienced a surge of comfort at the sound of another human voice. It was just gone seven thirty and initially the only other road users she came across were farmers driving Land Rover, sheep truck or tractor. However on nearing the turn-off for Hawkshead she spotted several police cars patrolling the area but this, she told herself, was only to be expected. So intent was she upon the need for caution on driving into Ambleside that it was only as she was parking up in a deserted alley that Darcy realised there had been no mention of Ted Tulley on the News. Strange, especially as it was an item of national but also peculiarly local interest, but perhaps the police had trouble locating the spot and had only just picked him up. After all she had been vague and in the dark with only 'somewhere on Tom Heights' to go on the search could have taken all night.

At least her mobile had signal here. Despite it being a little after 7.45a.m. Frank immediately answered the call to his direct line.

"Frank, I tipped off the police to go pick up Ted Tulley and can give you the full on-the-spot story!" She gabbled excitedly before he could speak.

"What the hell is going on girl! Have you lost it entirely?" he barked.

"You don't understand, I've got the full bit for you Frank – he tried to kill me and I was responsible for his recapture – it's a fab first, a scoop for you and the News!"

"Negative."

"It's true I tell you, I left him there bleeding from his head."

"No recapture."

"What!" Following Frank's laconic disclosure Darcy felt the blood drain from her face. "But he was unconscious! I left him there I tell you and called the police."

"Yeah, the police received an anonymous call – only they're treating it as a sick hoax!"

"But I don't-,"

"They found nothing and nobody," Frank grated before she could finish.

"Oh my God!" The exclamation was more related to fears for her safety as the potential embarrassment of the 'News'.

"But I left him there unconscious with his head bleeding Frank," she reiterated, feeling as though she was lost in some labyrinthine nightmare.

"That's as maybe, but they found nowt! Now get you're a'sse back here like yesterday."

"So why no mention of this 'hoax call' on the news?"

"Nothing to gain."

"Then how come you know about it?"

"I'll pretend you didn't ask that."

It was rather stupid she acknowledged, Frank had privileged access to the network and never revealed his source.

"An unsuccessful murder hunt along the Heights at a popular beauty spot?" he was saying sarcastically, "Wouldn't do much for tourism would it!"

It's true, Darcy thought striving for control in this nightmare scenario. Tarn Howes in its autumn splendour drew weekend visitors in droves. They flocked into the needy shops and hotels of Hawkshead and Ambleside and helped keep them alive.

"Besides, they're keeping low profile over this one – just in case it wasn't a hoax."

257

"Of course it wasn't!"

"They don't know that do they!"

"Suppose not."

"You've got some explaining to do to the authorities – so get back here now!"

"I can't do that Frank."

"It'll be your job this time girl."

Suddenly swamped by weariness and unable to cope, Darcy switched off from Frank and his dire warnings.

She sat for a time wondering what to do then as a delivery van turned into the alley and the town generally began to stir, she backed out and headed back to Langdale. Once clear of civilisation and potential discovery she pulled into a passing place and called Caro.

"Darcy! I've been so worried."

"I'm okay."

"You don't sound it."

"No, actually." Not wanting to alarm her further yet needing to talk to someone about it, Darcy gave Caro a boiled down version of her escape from Tom Heights and the conversation with Frank.

"Frank's right this time Darcy. You have to come back – it's not safe for you to stay there alone."

"Yeah, yeah. Okay." Darcy spoke mechanically, deciding on the line of least resistance rather than trying to explain and convince. "But moving on a tad Caro, I had this strange dream last night," and she went on to tell her about the soldier and her theory about the significance for today.

There was a moment or two of silence before Caro spoke again.

"Did I not tell you Darcy? That place was used during the last war. The rest of the buildings are long gone but the University applied to the M.O.D for permission to make it more substantial and use it as a field base."

"What was it actually used for during the war?" Darcy asked in a tight voice.

"An army billet and a camp for detainees".

"Detainees?"

"Persons seen to be of dubious background. "

"Such as?" Darcy waited with a knot of coldness in her stomach.

"German, or-," the pause was slight but long enough to tell Darcy that the significance had dawned on Caro too. "Italian POW's." There was a mutual silence then Caro added "How very strange."

"Do you reckon something was being said to me, like 'Roman or Italian' – 'things aren't that different and this, whatever it is I'm mixed up in, still matters?"

"I reckon you need to get out of there fast." There was an edge of panic to Caro's voice now.

"Okay, I've already *said,"* Darcy reassured her impatiently, "And I've not lost my marbles – yet! But there is something important being pointed up and I'd like to know more about it before I leave. Any suggestions?"

"Well," Caro sounded dubious, yet evidently decided it was better to compromise than champion a lost cause as she continued "there used to be an old guy, up on the fell in a crumbling hunting lodge. An academic, bit of a boffin on Romano-Celtic history and also the two World Wars. An eccentric though – odd as a four-sided triangle. Now what the hell was his name? I know," she said triumphantly, "Nemo, – or something like it. Don't know if he's still around – you could ask at the village post office and store over the pass, then if he is still alive go investigate once Tulley's caught."

"Caro, you're a star!"

"But you must promise to leave for home now, not go wandering up there alone with that maniac still on the loose. I mean it Darcy!"

"Don't worry. Thanks Caro – I'll be in touch." Darcy ended the call before Caro could press for a promise she was unable to keep.

THIRTY

~

Caro's suggestion of asking at the tiny post office over the pass paid off. Darcy bought some mint cake and extra hiking socks then via the near-truth that she was trekking the moor to do some research for a book, she asked her questions. As far as the current postmistress knew Ambrose Nemo was still alive though nobody saw him these days and there was never any mail to deliver which, given the climb and legwork involved the only access being via the Corpse Road which was no road at all, was just as well, the obliging postmistress provided.

"Corpse Road?" Darcy had asked, intrigued.

"That's right. Got its name from the days when coffins had to be carried over the fell from the next valley to be buried here in Eskdale. No church in Wasdale in those days you ken. Anyway, if you're thinking of looking in on old Ambrose's place-, "

"How will I recognise it?" Darcy asked stemming the flow.

"Easy – 'tis the only one up there."

Perhaps in the hope of a mention in this hypothetical book, the postmistress offered to 'keep an eye ' on Darcy's car whilst she was away.

Her belongings had been hastily packed and loaded into the car before setting off that morning. So here she was, trekking over the fell with Mab and Brock careering around like mad things as though

260

they were merely on a day's outing. However Darcy frequently turned to look over her shoulder, never for a moment forgetting that Ted Tulley could be stalking her even now. With this in mind she had a small but sharp paring knife tucked into her inside pocket – just in case. Unlawful maybe but survival now was the game. Besides up to now the law had not done overmuch to protect her, she told herself in justification. *No other house up there* the postmistress had said, but that had not prepared her for this lofty hanging moor with its windswept grasses and vast empty sky. She cursed as her ankle turned in a deep rut and icy water surged over the top of her boot. This Old Corpse Road was more of a beck in places she thought, limping painfully on.

Yet it had a beauty that took away her breath. A wintry sun had broken through and cloud shadows laid ever-changing patterns over moor and mountain as white cumuli bellied up and over a background of fells clad in ochre and russet. The track running through a treeless sea of grass and bracken seemed endless. There was something odd about this moor too; from the beginning she was aware of a background buzz of energy, rather like that given off by a true charismatic. Once she had been lucky enough to attend a press conference in the presence of Mother Theresa, and that never-to-be-forgotten sensation was similar to what she was feeling now. As she moved deeper into the territory it became an audible low-level hum.

An hour or so later she stood on the crest of a mound admiring the sapphire tarn spread below. It was surrounded by a breath-taking panorama of peaks: Scafell, Kirk Fell and Lingmell with Great Gable poking over its shoulder. To her left the long summit of Illgill shadowed the surface of the water. Two chimneys, one of which was lazily trailing smoke, poked up from beneath the knoll. The background hum of energy was most noticeable here, thrumming in her ears and tingling along her skin.

Descending to the hunting lodge which she now saw was L-shaped, built of stone and standing on a mound by the shore, she crossed a compound bounded by a dry stone wall. This presumably was meant to protect the vegetables growing within from being sampled or trampled by sheep and cattle grazing the moor. She turned as a tinkling sound chimed in her ear and looked around for the source. As in her dream, a set of wind chimes had been tied to the branch of a slender rowan tree bearing blood red berries. A shiver rippled along her spine.

The house, topped by a roof of Westmorland slate speckled with yellow stonecrop, crouched on its mound with an air of defiant decay. Somehow despite the crumbling walls, peeling paint, windows stained by weather and bird droppings, in its utter isolation it still cocked a snook at the world. A hoarse croaking cry sounded from overhead and two dark shapes shadowed the roof for an instant then were gone. This house, or rather its situation, also evoked fear. There is a darkness here she decided wandering round to the rear, though not perhaps the darkness of evil. Rather it suggested something so old that it had passed from memory and the light of understanding. It was as though an ancient power had seeped into rock, peat and lake-bed to make its home and repel newcomers. Mounting the stone steps to the front door she raised a doorknocker pitted with rust cast as the head of a wolf.

"Don't do campers!"

Taken aback, Darcy stared into a face of parchment crumpled by sun and wind. "It isn't my fault if your tent is washed out!" the man snapped before she had chance to respond. His voice surprised her: it had the strength and dryness of the wind that swept the moor and betrayed none of the reediness of old age, nor the expected local dialect but rather the dated BBC accent of a traditional Cambridge don.

"Mr Nemo! Please wait, Mr Nemo!"

She placed the palm of her hand against the door to halt its imminent closure.

"I'm not a camper!"

"Eh?" He watched her, head to one side, with all the attentiveness of a gull doing sentry-duty on a seaside breakwater. The door opened a fraction wider.

262

"The postmistress said-,"

The lines on the parchment face deepened and multiplied as he smiled.

"Then you had better step inside young lady."

"What about my dogs?"

"Are they well behaved?"

"Oh very," Darcy pledged with absolute gravity, suppressing the urge to cross her fingers behind her back whilst fervently hoping the old man did not keep a cat or other chaseable animal. The thought of leaving them loose on the moor, or indeed of entering this man's house without them was out of the question.

He glanced sharply down at Mab and Brock waiting with unaccustomed docility at her heels, then nodded and beckoned.

Two rooms led off from the hall, one that was obviously the kitchen because through the half-open door she could see the an old-fashioned range with a fire blazing in the grate, and the smell of baking bread wafted through to make her feel suddenly hungry. Her host was holding open the second door and she entered a square room with a view that caught at her breath: Scafell and solitude were mirrored in the tarn with Lingmell and Kirk Fell tilting the sky beyond. The room was redolent of dust, old leather and the indefinable aura of learning.

"Do sit down," Mr Nemo said scooping a pile of books off the seat of an armchair sprouting tufts of white stuffing from slits in the worn upholstery. Nevertheless Darcy upon sinking into its depths had to admit to its superior comfort.

"You shall lie here," he said fixing Mab and Brock with a stare and pointing to the rug before the fire. Darcy watched in amazement as the two spaniels, usually taken to sniffing and an enthusiastic exploration of any new person or environment, meekly lay down as directed. "And I shall sit here where I may see you." He chose a leather armchair whose seat and arms were polished from years of use and which stood opposite Darcy's at the side of a hearth in which peat blocks glowed.

"Am I disturbing you sir?" she inquired politely.

"No." The reply was short to the point of rudeness:

Delving into the prolapsed pocket of a worn green cardigan he produced a pipe and proceeded to fill it from a battered leather pouch.

Watching him as she waited for him to finish puffing at his pipe to ignite the peculiar but also sweet-smelling mixture, Darcy noted the threadbare knees and frayed turn-ups of his brown corduroy trousers. Only to be expected from an elderly man living alone in the middle of nowhere, she told herself; yet that aroma of home-made bread was scarcely compatible with the notion of self-neglect. Neither she thought trying to hide a smile, was the perky red bow tie. It sat in perfect incongruity above the shabby cardigan and its badge of egg yolk enamelled by time. Mr Nemo is an enigma, she decided looking around her as head bent he continued to labour at his pipe. The room was dominated by books: they spilled from shelves and cupboards into precarious piles on the faded carpet and littered every available chair and table as well as the top of an upright piano. She returned to watching Mr Nemo as he tamped the smoking mix down into the bowl of the pipe with one long index finger. She decided he had the hands of a pianist.

"I do play," he confirmed, exhaling a cloud of blue smoke rich with the fragrance of herbs and hay blossom.

"Er, you do?" Darcy stammered, taken aback. How on earth had he pulled a trick like that; perhaps he had seen her glance at the piano.

"Now tell me about yourself Darcy." Mr Nemo exhaled more smoke.

This was less easy to shrug off. She cast her mind back to their conversation since he opened the door but could not recall having given her name.

Darcy watched Mab and Brock anxiously as a black cat with clear green eyes and a ragged ear slithered sinuously through the gap in the doorway and joined their party. Far from being phased by the presence of two strange dogs on its territory this feline simply gave them a disdainful glare and stalked past them.

"Up here Tabitha," Mr Nemo said smiling, and Tabitha duly settled on her master's knee. Even more surprising was the way Mab and Brock started and half rose ready to chase but with one look from Mr Nemo lay down quietly again.

"So what do you do in life Darcy?"

"I'm an investigative reporter with a city newspaper."

"Ah, you tell stories," he said with a nod of satisfaction.

"Well," she was about to attempt a correction of this gross simplification then decided it was not worth the effort. "Something like that," she said smiling.

"Do not underestimate the power of story-telling," he said severely, "Think of the Mabidogian, or Morte D'Arthur or even the Bible – they are all stories expressing a truth, and with the power to change people's lives."

"I never thought of it that way," she admitted humbly.

"But now you will. You see, one has to be very careful about what one writes because words are powerful and one day somebody may believe and act upon them."

Darcy nodded and Mr Nemo looked even more satisfied.

Darcy glanced at the onyx clock on the mantel that serenely ticked away the minutes despite a missing hour hand, then at her wristwatch. She realised with a shock that she must have been sitting here drinking tea and talking to this elderly man for more than an hour yet it felt like minutes.

"You have been getting to know me – and I, you," Mr Nemo said with a mischievous smile whilst stroking the ecstatically purring Tabitha.

There he goes again, she thought uneasily, almost as though he can read my thoughts.

"More tea?" His smile mocked her fear.

Feeling that she now knew exactly how Alice must have felt at the Mad Hatter's tea party, she held out the china cup with faded blue flowers and an incomplete line of gold leaf round its rim. Mr Nemo stretched for the silver teapot that hid its value behind a mask of tarnish. Tabitha jumped from his knee, arched her back then gave one forepaw a couple of disdainful licks before perching on a precarious looking pile of books to oversee the proceedings. The warmth from the peat glow, the light in all its blueness and that electric quality so characteristic of the moor, and the mini-clouds from Mr Nemo's aromatic smoking herbs were hypnotic. Her eyelids began to droop. She was jerked back to wakefulness by a sudden awareness that Mr Nemo was staring at her chest. Despite this stranger's advanced years she felt distinctly uncomfortable, until she realised that rather than eyeing her breasts he was looking at the medallion.

"So, you have taken up the challenge." He watched her face and stroked the grizzled beard.

At his words drowsiness fled and she sat upright on the chair to stare intently into his face. *Was* he a stranger? For an instant she was watching an old man with his dog walk down the sun-slatted precinct. Take away the beard and put him in a shabby mac and it was just possible. His eyes were gimlets of blue, skewering her gaze so that it was impossible to look away.

"That's how it feels," she said softly.

"That's how it is."

"Yes."

"Good."

Mr Nemo leisurely drew on his pipe. Instinctively Darcy knew the matter was not to be pursued, that a decision had somehow been made and that something inestimable would be lost if questions were asked and perhaps answered.

"It is decided then," he said blowing out smoke, "you will stay as long as you need."

"Is it?"

"Oh, yes," he assured her nodding his head.

"But I can't just-,"

"Do you want?"

"Yes."

"Then you can."

"Yes," she agreed but not without a sigh of exasperation. Mab rolled in her sleep and Brock heaved a sigh of obvious contentment before resting his head on his sister's belly. It was almost as though they approved of the plan to stay. No wonder Mr Nemo's trousers are worn, she thought observing the habit he had of crossing and uncrossing his knees with an almost child-like excitement whenever he got his own way.

"But," she added firmly, "I insist on paying for my stay."

Mr Nemo's eyes gleamed as though in anticipation of a fresh clash of wills.

"Very well. The price is an hour per day of your time to take tea with me."

Darcy laughed at this clever move. As it turned out she was not carrying much cash and a cheque, she guessed, would be left on table or mantel to yellow with age.

"I'd be delighted – but shall we say ten pounds per day as well?"

"My offer or nothing," Mr Nemo said firmly, shaking his head.

Her company, she realised, would be of far more value to him than money he could not spend.

"Done, but I refuse to be rushed through my tea in an hour!"

"Done!" he echoed with a delighted smile.

Teacups were raised in a silent toast.

Some half an hour later he led her up the dark narrow staircase to show her the room that was to be hers during her stay. Mab and Brock had been fed on slices of Mr Nemo's freshly baked bread spread with butter and soaked in a lentil broth and were now comfortably installed in a small utility room off the kitchen with a thick blanket folded to make a bed.

"Where do you get your supplies?" she had asked, consumed by curiosity given the isolation of the house.

"They are happy enough there," he replied, totally ignoring her question. He paused now as they reached the landing and turned to face her.

"I'll take the car into town tomorrow and stock up the larder."

"No, once you leave my dear, there can be no return."

"Why is that?" she asked, puzzled.

"It is the way of things."

"But we cannot take your food," she persisted, preferring to stick with the practicalities rather than invite further butterfly ideas that fluttered out of reach as soon as she attempted to grasp them.

"Mother Nature provides." This enigmatic answer and the accompanying sternness of expression told her this also was not to be pursued.

"Have you always lived on the moor," she asked instead.

"I remember no other life," he said with a laugh as though at some private joke and the sound ruffled her nerves.

"It must be a lonely one."

"Oh, there's Tabitha, and I have lots of visitors. There's owl, curlew and in summer the skylark. They all come to be fed."

Darcy thought that he did not look unlike a bird himself with his bright round eyes and nodding head.

"Then there are the ravens: devils in fable but gods in flight. They treat me to wonderful aerial displays, especially the courting dance. And robin of course. Down from the fort on the fell I shouldn't wonder." He smiled and gave her a sly look so that she felt embarrassed and wondered if her secret was still safe. "Yes, straight from the legions and no mistake: all efficiency, stabs and pecks is Roman Robin!" He cackled with laughter and shook his head in mirth. "Then there's the sheep of course," he continued, leaning against the dusty banister rail as he warmed to his theme, "They huddle beneath the front wall when snow drifts above the window sills. Heroes they are, dangling gobbets of ice from their fleece for medals. Come the spring thaw I usually find one poor victim. Clever devils though. Know how most survive?"

"No," she confessed shaking her head, "what is their secret?"

"Eat one another's wool."

"Whatever for?" Darcy exclaimed, wondering whether she was supposed to laugh.

"The lanolin. Fat keeps them alive."

"Not so daft as folk make out then?" she said smiling. *And neither are you, Mr Nemo!*

268

"Certainly not. Every creature has its own special gift. No, I'm not lonely," he muttered sinking into a secret world from which she was excluded.

"Why, only last spring She-wolf brought her cubs so I could tell her how clever she was to-,"

"Wolf?" Darcy interrupted, her eyes widening with shock. She felt a sudden chill creep up the stairs and the gloom on the landing seemed darker and deeper.

Mr Nemo's eyes flickered electric and lost their expression of Far-away. "I meant vixen of course, silly of me, yes vixen," he added swiftly but then stroked his forehead in a gesture of confusion. "The memory you know. Plays tricks All so long ago." and his voice trailed off into indecision.

"No wolves in your life-time though?" Darcy persisted.

"This is your room."

He opened a green painted door and a disquieted Darcy followed him inside.

Upon entering she felt a rush of delight and something bordering on recognition, which probably rose from it exactly matching her idea of the perfect bedroom had she the choice. The Victorian wrought iron bed to her surprise was ready made up with spotless linen, an eiderdown and a patchwork quilt covered with roses. Almost, she could not help thinking, as though her arrival had been expected. The dressing table and wardrobe, unlike anything else in the house, were free of dust and painted a soft duck egg colour. The fact that the surface was scuffed and chipped in places only added to the charm. Shabby chic for real, she thought, reaching out to stroke the scarred top of the dressing table. A Persian carpet had lost most of its fringe to moths and mice and the net that filtered the light at the window beneath the eaves was yellowed with age. Plaster had perished and smartness had died but elegance held its own and the view from the cobwebbed panes ached with life. A sea of parched grasses and bracken flamed in the dying sun whilst the tarn sang the blues and captured Scafell in its mirror. A solitary rowan at the end of the compound fluttered a last pennant of russet, its silver bark and bare branches turned pink by the light of the dying sun.

"It's perfect," she breathed.

"Welcome Darcy."

She stared at his palm. Mr Nemo was offering her a key.

OUT OF TIME X

~

It was their second confrontation. Cadoc, menacing warrior and determined claimant of Rowana, stepped forward and grabbed Gaudita's bridle as she came to a halt at the centre of the compound.

"Take your hand from my horse," Antonius said quietly, determined not to be provoked into hostile action.

"At least I only handle your horse." The words were spoken in an undertone so that neither Cadoc's men nor the Roman soldiers could hear.

"Hey you, back off!" a voice rapped out from Antonius' rear.

"Call off your watchdogs." Cadoc jerked his head at the guard who had spoken. "This is a private matter between two men."

"There is nothing between us and therefore nothing to discuss. Last warning: let go." Antonius turned and nodded and two of the guards stepped forward menacingly. There was a tense silence then Cadoc let his hand fall from the bridle and stepped back.

Justinus studied the face of his commander and the anxiety in his eyes was plain to see.

"Stop fussing like a nurse-maid Justinus, I am well out of my swaddling clothes!" Antonius snapped, his irritation largely due to his secret misgivings about this mission, and also the knowledge that though his love for Rowana was mutual and too powerful to deny, he was not blameless in this conflict with Cadoc. However if there no formal understanding – and surely if there was either Myrddin or

Rowana would have said so –then this warrior's proprietary air was self-styled and unfounded. Furthermore, he thought recalling her confessed fear for her life at his hands, Cadoc was bent on threatening and bullying her into an alliance. The truth of this alleviated his guilt. But Justinus was also right; in all probability his agreeing to this mission was ill-advised and rash.

However it had been made difficult for him to refuse. Myrddin had something to show him, or he had said upon a 'chance' meeting at the roadside the previous day; though any event involving Myrddin was unlikely to be down to chance. Then when Myrddin made it clear that they were to travel alone together, Antonius had refused out of natural caution, but had risen to the scorn and challenge in those gimlet blue eyes and the thinly veiled insinuations disguised as humour. Against his better judgement he had at last agreed to accompany him alone. Now he wondered uneasily if that meeting had actually been contrived given Myrddin's uncanny powers.

"Just take care sir." Gaeus, a veteran who should be home tending his vegetable garden but who refused to believe it, lent his support to the tribune. "There are places made for assassination – natural traps of forest and rock that this lot know like the backs of their hands."

"The legatus is afraid of an old man? Or does he think himself so powerful that it would take a hoard of warriors waiting in ambush to despatch him?" Cadoc sneered.

"Enough! Keep your opinion until I ask for it!" Antonius ground out, goaded beyond endurance by both this arrogant warrior and the fact that his men were aware that he had been over-hasty in agreeing to this dubious mission. Cadoc faced him, legs astride and challenging.

"You would not dare ask for it though, would you? Especially in front of Myrddin and your own men. Things may come out that you would prefer to stay hidden."

"You try my patience Cadoc. Do not presume to threaten me." Antonius hissed.

"And you take care not to cross me, Roman. I could be waiting in some gulley or behind a rock."

"Very well, if I am not back by nightfall, raze the village to the ground and execute the inhabitants," Antonius snapped, but instantly shamed, he turned away from the expression of horror on Gaeus' face. This elderly man worshipped the ground he trod and his censure was indeed hard to take. Justinus' expression conveyed his distress also, but he kept his silence. Already the outburst was bitterly regretted, but Antonius heard the long hiss of breath leaving Cadoc' lungs and knew it was too late to retract. To back down now would be taken as weak and give Cadoc and his warriors the confidence to stage a rebellion and possible assassination of his self.

"You cannot do this! Such a decree is illegal. We are not officially at war with Rome," Cadoc snarled.

"It is a pity then that you and your people did not realise it earlier instead of waging useless resistance against Rome," Antonius snapped, turning on his heel to escape the shocked and accusing expressions of his own men. His pride made excuses to lessen the secret shame: better they think their commander brutal than weak.

As he followed Myrddin to the perimeter wall and gate, Antonius stared ahead, ignoring the sullen-faced Britons lining the route. Their hatred rose in a miasma and caught at the back of his throat. Once outside the gate Myrddin confronted him.

"That was not well done of you sir."

Without another word he turned his back and strode out onto the fell. Cloaking shame in anger Antonius followed.

Over an hour had now passed. He paused to survey the bleakness of this moor that seemed to go on forever. From all around came the incessant whispering of grasses, sighing of wind and the gurgle of water over stones. Occasionally the haunting cry of a curlew bubbled up and spilled into the wide heavens. Even so, he thought uneasily, the silence seems intact. They had been walking some time now and despite Myrddin's shuffling gait at the compound he still managed to surge ahead, white hair streaming in the wind and cloak flapping like the wings of some giant bird of prey.

Antonius sighed deeply and unconsciously quickened his pace.

273

The distance between them was not only physical, it symbolised the old man's rejection because of that hasty threat to the village. Maybe Myrddin knew that he and Rowana had crossed the Rubicon, that he had at last tasted her sweet white flesh and that she had enfolded and welcomed his manhood. Her guardian may have intimated as much to Cadoc and this might be some elaborate scheme for revenge. Hence the decree. A routine Roman threat meant in this case solely as a deterrent, but he had not realised this journey would take so long and now it was bitterly regretted. The unimaginable had become distinctly possible and the burden crushed his conscience.

At length he crested a hill to stand at Myrddin's side. He drew breath sharply as the monotony of the terrain was dramatically broken. Below them the track meandered over the moor drawing the eye to a range of volcanic peaks capped with snow. Immediately beneath them a tarn shivered in the wind, its surface fractured into planes that reflected fragments of grey sky. Myrddin raised a skinny arm and pointed his staff at the distant peaks.

"Over there lies the place."

Antonius followed him down to the gravel flats that edged the tarn. It seemed the old man's thoughts came clearly to him: *time to eat and rest.*

He shrugged off the uncanny feeling and took a flask and some flat bread and dried meat from the pouch at his belt.

"My thoughts exactly," Myrddin murmured joining Antonius as he sat on a flat rock, the nearest thing to shelter the moor had to offer. Antonius, secretly gratified by this lessening of hostility, half-smiled and nodded.

Myrddin accepted the bread that was broken and offered but refused the meat.

"You eat no flesh?" Antonius remarked, chewing on a piece of dried pork.

"I have no fancy for cannibalism."

"They are just animals."

"And my friends and kin," Myrddin retorted, nibbling a handful of nuts and berries from the pouch at his waist. "And no creature is *just* anything!" he added severely. "Each has its own talent. Can a man weave an intricate nest with his nose? Or a web from silk within his belly in order to catch his food?" he demanded, raising one bushy white eyebrow.

"I take your point Myrddin!" Antonius said laughing, deliberately quashing the thought that reverence for animals was attributed to Druids. "But it's a damned cold day to tramp this bloody moor so here, have some wine then we must be on our way."

Unthinking he held out the leather flask. Myrddin met his gaze, accepted and drank before handing it back.

"Thank you – *Antonius.*"

Antonius's hand engaged in replacing the stopper froze in mid-action. His eyes flew to Myrddin's and there was a pause before he nodded acknowledgement. Here there could be no distinction between conqueror and vanquished. They were simply two travellers crossing a terrain that measured centuries as seconds. In fact if anything, he thought uneasily, the balance of power had shifted in Myrddin's favour. This was his land and he knew every path and nuance of mood.

"I love her even in her capriciousness!" Myrddin confirmed with a smile, embracing the tumult of mountain and sky with a sweep of his winter-stick arms. Antonius gave him a sharp look then studied the huge black cumuli billowing in from the western coast.

"We must delay no longer," he said and there was fear in his voice.

Myrddin's eyes clouded with sadness. Then his mood underwent a lightning change.

"Indeed, it would not do for us still to be on the moor at nightfall, would it?" he snapped, digging his staff into the ground with open aggression as he made his way back to the track.

"Up there," he said shortly, pointing with his staff at a high ridge to their left.

The ascent was accomplished in driving rain, numbing cold and a wind that tore at their clothes like the Furies. Myrddin stood on the summit, cloak flapping and cracking like the wings of some enormous bat defying the elements. Antonius, bending his head to the icy blast, pushed the last few yards to stand at his side. The sky began to tilt, the mountains topple as he stared down into hell. They were standing on the brink of a sheer escarpment where tongues of ice choked the gulleys that bit deep into the flank below the rim. A fragmented rock face dropped away at a vertiginous angle into the sinister waters of a great lake, a cesspit of the primordial. Myrddin pointed with his staff. Antonius looked: far below and to the right the dalehead skulked within the walls of volcanic rock, a triad of craggy mountains smoking in the swirling mist. Rain scourged his body and chips of ice stung his face. Waves of shock, terror and helplessness rose from the dalehead to engulf him, the grey-faced fear that rippled through the ranks of an army trapped in the forest and facing certain death. *A natural trap of forest and rock.* Justinus' words returned to haunt him. Almost he could hear the tramp of marching feet then the sudden screams. Had some major tragedy happened here then? Maybe it was just the wind screeching around those hell's-teeth gullies. A numbness suffused him as though the mist that swirled across this ancient landscape had also seeped into his mind.

"Antonius."

He whipped round. Myrddin was offering something in his outstretched hand.

"This is for you, the colour of Mars, blood and berries."

Suddenly filled with dread Antonius stared at the red ball nestling in Myrddin's hand. Those words again, spoken long ago to the boy and now again to the man, yet it was impossible for Myrddin to know them. And was he hinting at *Rowan* berries meaning Rowana?

"Take it," Myrddin urged.

And think sometimes of an old man. The words whispered through Antonius' head and he was back in that dusty corner of the forum watching an old man juggle brightly coloured balls. His fate it seemed had been sealed even then.

"Enough chicanery!" The rawness of his nerves caused him to explode in anger. "What part are you playing now Myrddin?"

"The Fool like as not."

276

"Why have you brought me to this godforsaken place?"

"That is for you to determine. Perhaps to remind you that it is not too late to change the direction of the spear before the point becomes bloodied."

"Always you talk in riddles! Say what you mean Myrddin or be damned!"

"I rather think it is you who will be – should you not swerve from the intended path."

"Clearly you have brought me to this place because something dark and sinister took place here."

"Or is about to," Myrddin interrupted him quietly. "Past or present – or never. It is for you to choose. It is your hand that stays or throws the spear."

He stretched out his hand and his eyes urged Antonius to accept the ball.

"You are straining my patience old man!"

"Just an apple – see. Accept it with good spirit."

Antonius blinked and a chill ran along his spine; the ball he had thought to have seen was indeed now an apple. He grabbed it and sent it arcing out over the waters of the lake.

"So be it." This time there was no mistaking the sadness lurking in Myrddin's eyes.

The wind had abated and the rain dwindled to a persistent drizzle but despite the improvement in the weather the light was fading rapidly. Myrddin strode out along the summit of the ridge. Antonius caught him up and grabbed his arm.

"The path lies down there." Face dark with suspicion he pointed to the track far below that wormed its way across the moor.

"This land, sir," Myrddin's voice was heavy with scorn, "hosts our highest mountain, deepest lake and bloodiest earth. Would you make it bloodier still? I think not," he added before Antonius could speak, "So stop wasting my time! We must follow the crow not the snake."

Antonius hesitated a second then removed his hand from Myrddin's shoulder and with every step he took, rued his threat to the life of the village.

He stumbled along the ridge, following the grey shape of Myrddin's cloak just visible through the mist that swirled and shifted but revealed no comforting huddle of huts, only another gully, another fell to wearily climb beneath the darkening sky. At length he halted in despair but Myrddin pushed him on, down into the belly of the gorge and across the beck that grumbled and splashed in anger. *This gully has swallowed me whole* he could not help thinking, staring wildly up at the mountains that surrounded and condemned him as fatigue and fear gnawed at logic. What if they were too late? Even if by a miracle, or Justinus' insight, Rowana was spared the slaughter, she would hate him through eternity for what he had done. How hastily had he spoken, but with a lifetime left to regret.

The flanks of the gully were drawing in. Already it seemed he could hear the screams of women and children, smell the bitter-sweet odour of charred flesh. He heard his father's voice whispering in his ear: *Pull yourself together boy, or must I have you beaten?* Antonius cringed: father, Saturninus – that paragon of the Roman Ideal. The shade of Saturninus moved in and whispered again: *Do not shirk your duty son, what are the lives of a few peasants to Rome? Rome is above condemnation.* For a moment he was tempted to grasp at the comfort of letting Rome take responsibility for his actions. But then Calpurnia whispered in his other ear, *'you would do this to my people, son? Destroy your own roots?* Somewhere on the moor a wolf howled and the mournful cry pierced his heart. Myrddin stood by, a silent witness to his torment.

"I do not want this to happen old man. I do not wish them to die." Antonius whispered.

Coward! Weakling! Object of shame! The shade of Saturninus whirled away into shadow. A gnarled hand patted his shoulder.

"Then come, for there is light in truth," Myrddin said gruffly.

Antonius followed as Myrddin bent his back to the ascent.

The trick, Antonius found, lay in keeping his gaze on the ground thus confining his panic within the measure of his tread. As they climbed he was troubled by boyhood memories of his father's harsh treatment. It is not only the future that is lost when people become

278

estranged, he reflected sadly, the past is a casualty too; the good times are distorted by hurt and anger and only the destructive things are recalled. In the end his father was merely a product of his time and the established Roman values of stoicism and discipline. But there were more crucial issues to worry about; the light in the sky to the west had all but faded.

At last they emerged from the abyss onto a vast dark plateau. The first of several stone circles rose before them dwarfing its smaller sisters. Antonius stared at them in wonderment and fear.

"See." Myrddin pointed his staff at the largest pair of stones topped by a horizontal slab. A single shaft of daylight pierced the opening and streamed into the circle. "The light of your truth."

Suddenly Antonius knew he had been granted a second chance. They would be back at the settlement before his terrible order could be carried out. He sank down on one knee at Myrddin's feet, head bowed in humility.

"Forgive me old father for what I almost did."

Myrddin touched his shoulder and led the way across the plateau and down to the village.

During a brief visit to inform Myrddin to expect a gift of olive oil, wine, fruits and cheeses for the village as a token of appeasement, Antonius managed a short and secret word with Rowana to demand a meeting. For a moment she looked at him without speaking, then sensing his coolness and seeing the sternness and determination in his eyes and line of mouth, offered no argument and merely nodded in agreement.

Watching her approach across the high-grassed moor to the peat hut after midday he struggled with his emotions. He was angry and needed to know the truth. The man Cadoc must feel he had legitimate claim on Rowana to confront him like that. In fairness to them all she must make the situation clear. Yet as she entered the hut where he waited his heart leapt, but he was determined on the truth.

"What is it, Antonius? What has happened?" she demanded without

279

preamble, brushing shrivelled leaves from her cloak and pushing back from her face strands of hair dishevelled by her trek across the windswept moor. Her eyes and expression betrayed her anxiety.

"I am hoping you will tell me, Rowana," he replied, suppressing the urge to take her into his arms and smooth away her disquiet.

"I don't understand – what is it you wish to know?"

"The truth about you and Cadoc."

"There is no 'me and Cadoc'!" she said with sudden asperity.

"He obviously thinks different."

"He is confusing wishful thinking with reality!"

"Slightly more than that to confront me in public as he did!" Antonius moved a step closer and grasped her arm. "This is not the time for games Rowana! Now the truth –how does it stand between you?"

The mutinous look and proud tilt of head that he knew so well told him she was not about to capitulate. Still holding her arm he shook her slightly and saw the instantaneous look of mingled fear and outrage flash into her eyes. For that second he saw himself as she must, as an officer of Rome still, regardless of their intimacy.

"What are you hiding Rowana?" he pressed, fighting an urge to hold her close. He must not weaken; the safety of all concerned demanded an end to duplicity and evasion.

"Nothing." She looked away and pulled her cloak closer about her body.

"I don't believe that. I shall ask you once more and if you fail to answer, leave here for the last time. I shall not be able to help you or the people of your village," he said evenly Releasing his hold on her arm he stood back and regarded her gravely.

She stood watching him for a moment, deliberating before finally speaking.

"First you must promise not to take action against Cadoc." Then seeing he was about to protest she continued, "If you do so, it will confirm his suspicions about us and he will turn on the village instead of protecting it."

"I cannot promise that without knowing the facts. But I do promise to seriously take into consideration what you have disclosed."

Still she hesitated, then obviously decided that this would have to do.

"Very well. Any 'understanding' is solely on Cadoc's side not mine;" she began, "I have agreed to nothing. However," and here she dropped her gaze to the leaf mould, herb and heather-strewn floor, "I had to play for time and so told him I had no wish to be married as yet, and so he became more persistent thinking he had a chance."

"Why the need for time?" Antonius, seeing how difficult it was for her to make these disclosures moderated his tone.

"Ever since the invasion we have been under the threat of Rome," she said raising her head to meet his gaze. "Cadoc is a powerful warrior and his men are well-trained in rural combat and will follow him anywhere. Our people need his protection." She paused and scanned his face anxiously as though fearing his condemnation.

"I understand, Rowana," he reassured her, "But why are you afraid of him?"

"I fear what he might do," she corrected, her head coming up sharply as she regained her pride. "He became impatient and when I refused his demand for a betrothal he threatened first to leave the village to its fate, and more recently to take action against it if I continued to deny him what he wanted."

"But why would he threaten his own village?"

"It is not his birthplace. Originally he is from the Votadini in the North East.

He came here with his band of warriors and vowed to protect us in return for being instated as leader of the tribe. Passion apart, a handfast between us would strengthen his position. My non-compliance frustrates his plans. "

"Has he threatened you?" Antonius asked evenly, placing his hand beneath her chin and so forcing her to look him in the eye. "Recently I noted a fading bruise on your arm, and before that one on your face which you explained away as due to an accident whilst gathering apples."

"The price of his protection is my compliance," she said moving back a step thus avoiding both his gaze and a direct answer to his question.

"At *any* price, apparently." Antonius turned from her and paced the floor of the hut in an attempt to contain his anger.

"His pride is outraged to think I prefer a Roman to himself. But he also sees me as a traitor," she said bitterly. "But I would never betray my people."

"This I know, Rowana. But he cannot be allowed to abuse you like this." Ceasing his pacing he stood before her, his expression stern and unyielding.

"No – you must do nothing, my Antonius!" She grabbed his hands and held them to her breast. "Since the day you travelled the moor with Myrddin he has not pestered me, I think he has other plans. Do not stir up the bees' hive or we may all be stung!"

"Now you are sounding like Myrddin!" he said with a reluctant half-smile.

"If you hear a little of his wisdom in my words, then heed them and for now do nothing," she said pleading with her eyes.

He hesitated, searching her eyes for truth and finding love for him there too.

"For you, Rowana, and for now," he added warningly as her face lit up with relief, "but what you have told me sounds the alarm call. This tale of ruthless ambition stinks like rotting fish on the wharf. Should he threaten you again or overstep the boundary between sullen non-compliance and rebellion, then he will pay the price."

"I understand," she said gravely.

He drew her to him then and with her head on his shoulder, spoke in her ear whilst stroking her hair.

"Let us not waste this opportunity my love; it may be the last," he whispered on a sudden premonition, and he shuddered involuntarily as though a shadow had passed over them both. His lips found hers and his hands caressed her gently. Beneath her robe his fingers touched the hardness of metal and smoothness of precious stone and he knew she was wearing his pendant. Pushing dark thoughts of treachery aside he laid her gently on the soft and aromatic floor.

Later, as he reluctantly left her to return to the fort, he sensed Myrddin's gaze boring into his back, yet on turning saw only an empty expanse of weather-bleached grasses and burnt bracken and beyond it desolate grey peaks marching across the horizon. As he moved his clothes and person released her scent. It seemed the heady fragrance of heather, rosemary and wild thyme would stay with him for ever.

THIRTY-ONE

~

This old man is turning my life upside down, Darcy thought dryly, standing by the window to gaze out over the moonlit moor. The oil lamps had been extinguished, Mr Nemo had gone to bed, Mab and Brock were snoring on their blanket and the house slumbered peacefully, creaking now and then as old timbers shifted with the change of temperature. Beyond the window the frosted fells brooded in silence and the moon-washed moor sparked ice-fire . As Darcy watched a rangy, hound-like shape slipped through the shadows. The flame of the candle she was holding wavered and spluttered as she snatched at her breath, then her taut muscles relaxed again as the brindle fox emerged into a patch of moonlight and stood on an outcrop of rock above the tarn. It raised its head, apparently looking up at the window as though aware of her presence. It loomed large and seemingly ominous for a fox, and for an instant there she could have sworn it was a wolf. Mr Nemo's story about the She-wolf bringing her cubs must have made an impact, she decided. Nothing here was as it seemed. Still worth a striking moonlit picture though. As she reached towards her bag for the camera the fox turned and disappeared over the top of the outcrop.

She let the curtain fall back into place and was about to get into bed and extinguish the candle when she remembered the photographs retrieved from the car and transferred to a pocket of her jacket. Taking them out she sat on the bed and shuffled through them: shots of the bath house and the main gate; then some of the granaries, Headquarters building and Commander's quarters. It took her on a pictorial journey through that first visit, evoking clear images and strong emotions as the memories flooded back. Then some breathtaking views of the valley and sea beyond taken from the rear of the fort – and then the shuffling abruptly stopped.

"It can't be, I'm seeing things!" she whispered, poring over the photograph whilst holding it closer to the flickering candle. It was shadowy and indistinct but there could be no mistake. A figure was standing on the outcrop of rock above the precipice, the folds of the cloak blending with the purple shadows cast by rampart and gate towers.

The photograph fell from her fingers as a sibilant sigh drifted around the room, the sound of a warm wind breathing life into the moor following the pseudo-death of an ice-bound winter.

Existo Existo

She leapt up as the whisper sighed around the room and echoed in empty spaces that were not really voids but cells of vibrating energy. The sound ceased and the stillness and solemnity of the moor crept into Darcy's heart.

"Yes, I believe you do," she whispered, retrieving the photograph and holding it to her breast.

Suddenly Brant and her life at the farmhouse seemed very far away.

The following morning she took the photograph from beneath her pillow where she had slipped it before finally falling asleep and took it over to the window to examine it in the clear light that washed the moor and banished shadows. Half afraid it would not be there and half afraid it would be she stared at the shadowy image and closed her eyes in relief. She had not lost her marbles. Somehow he had found a way to convince her of his existence.

"Antonius," she whispered staring out over the fell garden and across the moor to the mountains beyond where Mediobogdum sprawled over the spur of rock above the bend in the river for which it was named.

285

"Now show me what you need," she whispered, replacing the photograph beneath her pillow whilst willing the ether to carry her thoughts to the man.

She exercised Mab and Brock on a moor sparkling with frost and realised with a shock that Autumn had faded into winter without her really noticing. After eating a breakfast of porridge with cream from the cows that roamed the compound and toast spread with bramble and rosehip jelly, she joined Mr Nemo in the sitting room. He seated himself at the table and set to work on a partially completed carving whilst Darcy explored the piles of books at his invitation. The image in the photograph, along with a secret sense of elation that bubbled up inside and was difficult to conceal, still occupied her mind. Hang on Darcy, she told herself severely as she leafed through an ancient leather-bound book, jotted down a reference then replaced it on the shelf; this is the guy who terrified you half to death and contaminated your space with piles of slugs and worms then almost burnt down the farmhouse. Yet deep inside she knew those things had been done not out of a malignant desire to harm but desperation to get her attention. The reign of terror had ended with her decision to go off for as long as it took to seriously take this thing on board and investigate . In fact whatever phenomena was at work here seemed now to be protective, she thought recalling Ted Tulley and the nightmare on Tom Heights. *Because it needs you* she reminded herself, deliberately depersonalising the energy in her thoughts. He is becoming too real, too close she told herself, picking up the volume she sought.

"Ah, you have found what you were looking for," Mr Nemo commented with a smile, glancing up from his woodwork.

"I'm writing a piece on Roman History in the area," she replied, colouring slightly even though this was not exactly a lie but merely an economy of truth. "I saw a reference to a report on the fort over there," she continued, crossing to the window and indicating with a gesture the general direction of Mediobogdum.

"And is it of interest?" he inquired still smiling.

"I'll tell you when I've read it!"

"Yes, do that."

Resting the bound editions of the Transactions of the Cumberland and Westmorland Archaeological Society on the table she sat down and on finding the article she sought began to read. Several minutes later she suppressed a cry and her hand flew to her mouth.

"Is there something wrong?" Mr Nemo asked politely, peering at her over the top of a pair of gold-rimmed spectacles with a crack in one eye glass.

"No, er that is, no – it's fine." Darcy stammered, turning back to her reading. The words seemed to burn the page:

'*No burial ground has been found at Mediobogdum, but given evidence unearthed at the recent dig indicating the possible visit of a legionary commander a cairn close to the stream by the road is enough to excite suspicion*'

Struggling for self control Darcy closed the book and returned it to the shelf.

"I'm taking the dogs for their walk Mr Nemo, I'll see you at tea-time," she managed to say in a fairly normal voice.

"Where do you think you will go?"

She glanced at his face, suspicion aroused by the casualness of manner but saw nothing there beyond polite inquiry.

"Maybe over to the fort to confirm some research," she said, feeling it was useless to lie; if he chose to watch from an upstairs window he could easily track her progress across the moor.

"It's a fair stride just to check a pile of ancient stones."

Darcy's eyes widened in disbelief: was he referring to the fort itself – or could he have somehow picked up on the burial cairn?

"What are you carving?" she asked swiftly to change the subject. Crossing to the table she stood by his side. "Oh, it's an eagle!"

Her voice defied her attempts to keep it steady as she gazed at the majestic bird in miniature, wings outspread ready for flight.

"It's exquisite," she breathed, taking in the fine detail of hooked beak, plumage and powerful talons. "Have you done it from a photograph or book illustration?"

"No, memory." Mr Nemo continued carving.

"You have seen one? I didn't know there were any here on the moor."

Mr Nemo serenely worked on smoothing a tail feather before looking up at her over his glasses.

"The eagle hides at Wasdale," he said evenly, gazing directly into her eyes so that she found it difficult to look away.

Darcy cleared her throat and ran a finger around the neck of her sweater as the air in the room became suddenly thick and oppressive making it difficult to breathe.

"I must walk over there before I leave; I should love to see one!"

The minute rasp of sand paper on wood began to fret her nerves in the sudden silence that befell them. Tabitha sat on a corner of the table watching her with unblinking stare.

"Leave?" Mr Nemo paused in his carving and eyed her over his spectacles.

"I cannot stay more than a day or two Mr Nemo – I shall have no job to go back to!"

"Ah, your stories." Mr Nemo nodded slowly and raised his eyes to study her face.

"In that case we must hasten the conclusion."

"Conclusion?" Darcy swallowed hard.

"Of the carving," he said smoothly with the suggestion of a twinkle in the faded blue eyes.

Darcy blinked several times as light streaming in through the window behind Mr Nemo reflected the glow of sun-blazed and wind-burnt bracken, flushing the room with a rosy radiance. By now she was so accustomed to the low-level hum of the moor that for most of the time she was unaware of it, but now it became very noticeable. The grey hair was transmuted to silver and his features became indistinct, except for the eyes which had lost the vagueness of old age and were now as sharp as those of the real-life model for the eagle he was carving. He held out a gnarled hand. The redness deepened and seeped into her brain smothering rational thought. A low-pitched humming buzzed within her head and her breathing became more laboured, her vision blurred. She stared at the red ball nestling within his palm.

"This is for you."

The words seemed to come from afar, echoing as though they bounced off solid rock then returned to haunt the listener.

She swayed on her feet and it took a massive effort of will to remain upright. Suddenly Tabitha yawned and stretched, her claws rasping minutely on the surface of the table as she emitted a yowl of contentment. The sound broke the membrane of silence and pierced the glamour that held her in thrall. She stared bemusedly at the carved eagle in Mr Nemo's hand.

"But I saw..." she stammered, brushing a hand across her eyes.

"When it is finished of course," he said equably, replacing the effigy on the table.

Darcy mumbled some word of gratitude, then excusing herself on grounds of needing to check the dogs, hurriedly left the room and donned her walking gear.

Autumn was giving way to winter and the stunted rowans and blackthorns had mostly relinquished their leaves to frost and marauding winds from the north. The moor looked bleaker than ever yet the land had lost none of its beauty in revealing its bare bones. Darcy strode out towards the distant dalehead and triad of mountains that marked Wasdale Head in the hope of spotting at least one of the pair of eagles that Mr Nemo claimed nested there. Mab and Brock, being tired out from their walk earlier in the day, had been left behind to snooze with Mr Nemo in front of the kitchen stove as their madcap presence, Darcy reasoned, was scarcely conducive to eagle watching. Had she brought them, it would maybe have given some sense of security so that she would not have to pause every so often to turn and look over her shoulder due to a feeling of being followed. The dogs of course would have alerted her immediately to the presence of another human being on the moor, and she put her nervousness down to the fact that she had to rely for once on her own comparatively inadequate senses.

She made her way across gravel flats threaded with rivulets fed by Whillan Beck and picked up the path for Wasdale Head. The Screes. On reaching the summit she stared down a chimney of death, a gully with fangs of ice that bit the face of the sheer escarpment and was glad she had left Mab and Brock behind. This, she thought sombrely, at a depth of two hundred and sixty feet is England's deepest lake and is both sinister and awesome. The crags of shattered stone plummeted into the primordial waters, over two thousand unforgiving feet from summit to lake bottom. Darcy shuddered and turning her mind from dark thoughts provoked by the scene before her, such as the feeling that still lingered of not being alone, scanned the skies for a glimpse of Mr Nemo's professed eagles. Turning her face to Scafell, snow-capped and retreating into silence, she made her way slowly and carefully along the summit ridge but saw nothing larger than a pair of ravens. She watched them for a time revel in flight as only ravens can. They rose, dived and rode the thermals and she stood entranced by the impromptu display. However she glanced uneasily at the bank of storm clouds rolling in from the coast, conquering galleons impatient to discharge their arsenal in a volley of booms and flashes. Shivering slightly she made her way down to the path that sidled over the folds and furrows of the moor.

After walking for about fifteen minutes she stopped to get her bearings, and decided she must have taken the wrong fork at the wooden bridge on Whillan Beck. Anxiously she looked at a sky that was heavy and already purpling to dusk. The air was oppressive yet she shivered; the temperature had sunk like a stone dropped into the lake. Following the path that was little more than a sheep track now she came to a wide flat plateau marked out with several stone circles. Pressed into the earth by Time they punctuated the silver-strip horizon. *Full stops. No need to go further for here you will find yourself – your true and ancient self.* Resolutely she ignored the whispering inside her head and pressed on.

The deserted plateau teemed with surreal life: shadows flitted through the twilight beckoning her on and the air hummed with an accretion of power. At times her heart missed a beat as it seemed she detected something more substantial than shades, but the moment she focused upon the space where the movement had been there was nothing to be seen. There came an immediate flash of fear upon stepping into the largest circle, especially given the sunken but unmistakable mound of the barrow at its centre. Who lay within? She found herself thinking – man, woman or child and had they died a violent or natural death? A sacrifice maybe to the long-ago deities to whom these circles were doubtless dedicated.

Then came a sense of recognition, of a thing ancient in its power with an echo within her self. Instinctively she followed the inner promptings and ritually paced the circumference, anti-clockwise – *widdershins, and where did that come from?* – counting out the paces and powerless to resist the strange compulsion. Now start again, once, twice and thrice and revel in the wind that seemed to blow up from nowhere that tugs at clothes and hair and blows away the dross of civilisation. Now move slowly to the centre and stand arms outstretched to embrace the horns of the sickle moon riding the violet that prowls above Scafell. *Lady Moon. Lady Goddess and Great Mother.* As she stood thus it dawned upon her that the grass inside the circle was fresh and green, whilst all around was parched and bleached to the colour of ripe wheat.

So lost was she in this reverie that night had advanced unnoticed and the shadows within the circle had deepened. The air had become oppressive and the sky rested its leaden weight upon her head. A low rumble from the west and its echo from the surrounding fells added to the ominous atmosphere, as did the battalion of nimbus marshalling forces overhead. The prospect of being caught in a storm on this exposed fellside made Darcy's heart quail and she cursed her stupidity for not heeding the signs at Illgill Head. A movement on the periphery caught her eye and the resulting jolt in her stomach brought her attention sharply back to the present.

She blinked, screwed up her eyes and stared fixedly at the stones, especially the largest one that dominated the others by something other than mere size, but the purpling half-light was deceptive. No, no mistake; her eye picked up another movement behind the silhouette of its bulk. Her scalp crawled and despite the creeping chill sweat beaded her upper lip and forehead. Not bringing the dogs now seemed less of a good idea. Looking wildly about her she became frighteningly aware of her vulnerability and a growing conviction. As the first spots the size of ten pence pieces splattered her face and clothes that conviction grew. This circle was now inhabited by something other than shadows.

THIRTY-TWO

~

It came at her on a rush. Paralysed by fear she stood for a moment staring at the figure as it advanced, much like a rabbit or deer paralysed by the headlamps of an onrushing car. In the semi-darkness she could not make out who or what it was and that in itself created more fear. Her mind raced: there were no humans for miles around, so was this part of Antonius and his past or something far older and darker still from the depths beneath that burial cairn?

"Help me Great Mother, help me for I am your child," she whispered without knowing why. Then survival instinct kicked in and she turned and fled the circle. Whatever had emerged from the shadows and rushed her was now in pursuit. Stumbling over bracken and heather she searched frantically for the path that would take her back to the bridge at Whillan Beck. Her heart thumped and the blood thrummed in her ears as the sounds of pursuit grew louder. She gasped and risked a glance over her shoulder The drops of rain had now turned into a downpour and the grass became slippery underfoot. Sobbing with terror she threshed about as her clothes became enmeshed in the spiteful barbs of a clump of gorse. Her attempts to pull free were hampered by the wind that buffeted her back and hampered her efforts to disengage the spiny arms.

Never had she felt so alone. If only Mab and Brock were here – but better that they were home and safe. I might never see them again, or Brant, she thought panic-stricken as the true peril of her situation dawned. A surge of fear-driven adrenalin gave her the strength to wrench free of the gorse and she felt warm blood trickle down one icy cheek. The rustling and thudding sounds drew closer at her back. She screamed from sheer terror and the need to be heard by someone or something but the downpour was now a deluge and the rumble of thunder and hiss and splatter of rain drowned the cry. Fingers grasped and clutched at her clothes so that she slipped on the wet grass and bracken and almost fell. A second scream was torn from her throat to be snatched away on a howl of the wind. A hand grabbed her neck from behind and instinctively she spun round arm raised to strike her attacker. A blow to the side of her head shocked her into immobility. She reeled as the streaks of pain registered and a tide of blackness threatened. Cruel fingers anchored in her hair. Her limbs threshed the air and more screams were borne away by the wind as she was dragged stumbling and crawling back to the circle.

Fear and shock brought her to the brink of oblivion, but the icy slash of a wind-driven torrent across her face brought back consciousness in a rush. Although sunken and partially overgrown the stones of the burial cairn dug into her back and grazed her skull as she struggled to rise.

"You!" The words came out as a strangled cry as her assailant loomed over her and recognition dawned. The face of Ted Tulley was contorted with rage and madness, his eyes wild and the whites oddly luminous in the dying light. Runnels of dried blood still streaked his cheeks and forehead from the injury on Tom Heights. The tip of the knife pricked her throat as he leered into her face.

"Gotcha for real this time bitch!" he snarled then threw back his head and laughed so that the rain washed the dried blood and his face took on the bizarre look of a performer whose make-up had streaked and run. The manic sound of that laughter turned Darcy's blood to ice.

"No escape this time bitch!"

"They know where I am – are searching even now," she dared, her teeth chattering in her head and her body wracked by shivers from combined effects of exposure and shock. He sobered suddenly, his lip curling back to show stained and yellowed teeth and his breath stank in her face.

"Lying cow! There is no 'they' – only that feeble old fool you're shacked up with! And what's he gonna do, eh?"

Paralysed by terror she stared into that evil face and remained silent. Her head came up from the ground with shock as a clap of thunder sounded almost overhead and she gasped as the rain lashed her face with renewed venom. Ted Tulley seemed to be unaware of, or at least unaffected by, the viciousness of the weather. Water streamed from his face and clothing and despite the tearing of the wind, plastered what hair he had to his bony skull giving him now the appearance of a Dickensian villain.

"I know all about your find Ted," she bluffed, playing for her life, "and left a letter with my solicitor telling him to go to the police if I don't return."

The knife point ceased to prick her flesh as he straightened his spine slightly to study her face with the exaggerated concentration of madness.

"So what? They're after me anyway!" he cackled, but his laughter this time held the hollow ring of desperation.

"But the letter tells them where it is. They will go and dig it up. Then you will face a murder rap and nothing to show for it."

"Let you go and I'll have nowt!" His head swayed to and fro like a bull wounded in the ring as he strove to make sense of her words within his distorted world.

"Not true, let me go and I'll withdraw the letter unopened and you will at least have the treasure and the same chance as before to escape," she bluffed, desperately hoping her guess as to the nature of his secret was correct. His silence dared her to hope. But then his eyes narrowed with spite and menace and with a chill in her heart she knew she had lost and her attempt at bargaining had only made him more angry.

"Nah!" He rose to his feet as another crash of thunder sounded directly overhead and the wind drove the rain in horizontal sheets. "Interfering bitch, you don't know where it is. Nobody knows except ol'e Ted."

"Your wife told me," she threw at him, playing her ace. "you put it back again and covered it over – in the bottom meadow."

He stared at her manically for a moment deliberating.

"You're lying – there's no bloody letter! You want it for yourself. *My* hoard – nobody else's," he barked into the wind. "On yer feet!"

He yanked her up by the arm so that she cried out in pain from an injury to her shoulder sustained when he dragged her into the circle. She swayed on her feet, buffeted by the wind and lashed by rain.

"Shift the stones!" he ordered, raising his voice almost to the note of hysteria in order to make himself heard. She stared at him stupidly, not understanding. When he made a series of gestures and realisation set in, she stared at him in horrified silence.

"Move!"

She screamed as the knife-slash penetrated her sleeve and seared the flesh of her arm.

"Go on, move 'em!"

At this point Darcy's mind blanked out and she moved through a nightmare or the script of some improbable horror movie. This is not real, she told herself as she began scrabbling at the stones of the burial cairn with bare hands to loosen the earth's grip upon them.

"You can do better than that!" he taunted cruelly as the pile of stones at her side slowly grew. She cried out as the point of the knife dug into her back and then enraged by pain she let fly:

"You filthy mad old bastard!" she screamed into the wind and rain and paid dearly for her outburst. A blow across the face sent her staggering and the world spun crazily round.

"Get on with it bitch!" he snarled.

Defeated now she tore up turf and dug for more stones with broken nails and hands that bled from her efforts.

"That's enough."

She dropped the stone she was holding onto the pile, and face streaked with earth and hair plastered to head turned from the hollow she had created to face her tormentor.

"You're going to kill me and put me in there." It was not a

question; the horror of his intention was only too clear. As the rain snatched the words from her mouth and tossed them away she thought he had not heard, but he leered and pushed his face closer.

"Not until after the ritual my sweet," he said with a wolfish grin. "Human sacrifice and all that, that's what they did here, isn't it?"

Darcy's heart stood still.

"Come on now, be a good girl and take off all your clothes and be ready to please the gods."

"You really are mad – totally crazy," she whispered. Was this then to be her end? Raped, murdered and left to rot in a shallow grave on this lonely moor a thousand feet up from civilisation? The only comfort lay in the fact that Mr Nemo knew she was out here somewhere and her body eventually would be found and taken home. But to whom and how would he report her missing?

"Help me, Great Mother, help me in my hour of need", she murmured as even the hope of this last comfort died.

"Shut up and strip!" He moved in closer and gestured with the knife.

Fingers numbed by cold and those cruel stones she fumbled with the zip of her jacket playing for time. Not this, anything but this, she thought in an agony of distress.

"Come on, come on," he shouted, rubbing himself in anticipation and stabbing the air around her with the knife in a fever of impatience. He gestured at her combats with the knife and the vomit scalded Darcy's throat. Yes, anything – even death – was preferable to what he planned so what was she waiting for? She would die anyway, so at least go fighting and without submitting to his insane and depraved lust. Whirling round with her last ounce of strength she picked up a rock from the pile.

As her arm came back to hurl it a tremendous crack split open the heavens and lightning zig-zagged across the fell illuminating the nightmare below. Unaware of the pain in her injured shoulder she balanced the rock held ready for launching but was helpless to move in this freeze-scene. It appeared that Ted Tulley was also held in thrall for he made no move of retaliation. In that eerie blue effervescence she could have sworn that a figure appeared atop the knoll that overlooked the circle. Silver hair streaming, white robe flapping and cloak streaming out in the wind it appeared to conduct the storm as it pointed a staff at the heavens. Then it was gone with the lightning and darkness fell once more. She jumped and cried out as seconds later a cannonade of thunder echoed around the fells.

When she stared again at the knoll the rock was empty except for a whorl of leaves and dead bracken spun by the eddying wind. A second strobe of lightning streaked across the sky and the circle vibrated with cobalt light. As he lunged forward with knife raised she mustered all that remained of her strength and hurled the missile. It hit him centre-forehead. He let out an animal howl and dropped to his knees like a bull felled by the hammer. A cannonade of thunder hurtled around the fells and shook the moor.

"Wolfshag!"

Darcy stared, stunned by the ancient nuance of the word that was spit into her face. He staggered to his feet with blood oozing from his head She waited helpless as he drew back his arm for the fatal thrust. From across the moor came another howl, this time unmistakably non-human and the expletive took on a deeper significance. A second primordial howl rose above the wind, this time closer at hand. She tensed, paralysed with fear, too focused on staring death in the face to challenge the irrationality of the sound. Ted Tulley's arm hovered and an evil grin split his face. In a matter of seconds the knife would descend, enter her body and rob it of life. She determined not to plead; at least he would be robbed of that satisfaction. Another strobe of lightning shuddered across the sky this time emitting a blood red glow. *Red is for you, the colour of Mars, blood and berries.* The whisper echoed in her ears and the redness seeped into mind and pore.

The rain was turning to drizzle and a red mist was creeping across the moor and seeping into the confines of the circle. Her mouth opened to scream but no sound escaped as the grey shape appeared, poised on the knoll where the figure in white had once been. Yellow eyes narrowed to slits, the ears became flattened as the head went back in slow motion, the skull becoming compressed and broadened over the cranium, thus taking on the triangular shape of an arrowhead. Her mind was filled with the image of red jaws, bared teeth and her ears hurt as the bloodcurdling howl was released. Ted Tulley yelped with fear and turned to run then froze, enveloped in red mist and the paralysis of his own fear.

It was over in seconds yet seemed like a lifetime. The beast leapt effortlessly from the summit to lope through the long grass. *Pad pant, pad pant,* it went, breath steaming and yellow eyes focused unblinkingly on its prey. *Greedy meat, easy meat* it seemed to say over and over in Darcy's brain. Ted Tulley screamed as the beast leapt. *Greedy meat, easy meat.* Threshing and thrashing he fell flat on his back with a force that made the earth tremble and caused the knife to be flung from his hand. The air was filled with snarls and screams and the odour of blood and fresh meat. Darcy backed away sobbing hysterically yet unable to avert her eyes. The dreadful sounds of slobbering, sucking and slavering assaulted her ears as the feast was consumed. Then silence, and Ted Tulley was still, a gaping cavity now in the place where throat and heart had once been. A split second of something like recognition as the yellow eyes met her own and held the gaze. A swift passing of tongue over blood soaked muzzle, an elegant turn and a swing of heavy tail followed by the soft *pad pant, pad pant* of departure, and the grey was swallowed up by swirls of crimson mist.

THIRTY-THREE

~

Bleeding, soaked to the skin and in shock she somehow made it back to the hunting lodge and banged on the door before slipping into a dead faint. The next thing she knew she was coughing and spluttering and starting up with a cry, only to sink back into softness and comfort as Mr Nemo's welcome voice penetrated the fog of fear.

"You are home now and safe my dear."

She was lying on the sofa in front of the sitting room fire with her nostrils stinging but her head now clear. Mr Nemo was standing over her holding a wad of cotton wool and a dark green bottle that looked as though it belonged on the shelf of an apothecary. Tabitha watched wide-eyed from her perch on the padded arm and now and then kneaded the cloth with her claws.

"Good." Mr Nemo put down the pad and placed a glass stopper into the neck of the bottle, then shook his head and held out his hand in a negative gesture as she would have struggled to rise. "Be still my child," he counselled, "give yourself time to recover."

"What on earth was in that?" she murmured, wrinkling her nose and pulling a face as she leaned back against the cushions; in truth she was glad to do so: her head ached abominably and her sleeve she noticed was soaked with blood.

"Burnt feathers, cow dung and fox pee," Mr Nemo promptly answered.

"It smelt like it."

"Good, you are feeling better already," he said with the gleam of mischief in his eye. "Now," He turned to the hearth where a peat fire glowed and a poker had been thrust deep into its heart. Wrapping a cloth round the end he withdrew it so that the hearth was showered with sparks of red and gold. He plunged the glowing poker into a pewter jug with a hissing of steam that gave off a pungent aroma and poured a draught into a small green glass. "Drink this infusion of wine and herbs and I promise you will feel quite the thing again."

"Wine? Out here?" Darcy queried, her shocked mind going no further than Shiraz, Pinotage or Pino Noir and a Sainsbury's supermarket.

"Blackberry, rose hip and elderberry. Though of course it is unwise to pick blackberries after Michlemas."

"Why is that?"

"During that time the Devil spits or pees on them. But don't worry," he added with a mischievous smile at her expression of disgust, "These were collected in September. Now drink, then you shall bathe away all that mud so that I can tend your wounds and then you shall tell me all that happened."

Not quite all, she reflected an hour or so later as she sat in an armchair by the fire after bathing in a tin tub filled via bowls of hot water that whooshed directly from the tap in the utility room in an ecstasy of steam. She had found this convenience surprising and later discovered from Mr Nemo that rain water, collected in a huge tank at the gable end, found its way along an ancient and melodious system of pipes to the boiler behind the kitchen stove and from there to the pot sink. Mab and Brock dozed at her feet; they had been admitted by Mr Nemo and allowed to express a tumultuous welcome before being ordered to settle by the fire which to her astonishment they did. The gash to her arm was cleansed then spread with rose, thyme and lavender ointment and dressed with a strip of clean linen; and the side of her face where Tulley had punched her bathed with witch hazel to soothe and take down the swelling. It would also, Mr Nemo reassured her, prevent a black eye that might suggest she had gone several rounds with Sugar Ray Robinson. At this she had to suppress a bubble of laughter that had she released it might have proved to be the onset of hysteria; obviously Mr Nemo was stuck in a time trap in which not even Mohamed Ali figured, let alone Chris Ewbank and his many successors – and she was right in there with him.

However her wounds were soothed and the trauma of that nightmare in the circle now felt less acute as Mr Nemo's infusion began to take effect. Soon mind and body were suffused with a delicious languor and whilst she was still aware of what happened it troubled her less. In fact she was able to focus more on the positive element: she was now free of the threat of attack from a man who had twice attempted to kill her and almost succeeded and who had obviously dogged her every move from the outset. Upon being prompted, she related with relative calmness an expurgated account of events, merely saying a man who appeared mentally disturbed had attacked her on the moor and forced her to prepare what was intended to be her own grave. As to how he had met his end, this had required rather more ingenuity. That he had been struck down by lightning was her final choice. Mr Nemo, she reasoned, was weird enough without involving him in something even weirder. Even the thought of explaining made her feel exhausted. If he had doubts about the likelihood of this explanation he forbore to express them.

Later after eating a supper of bread soaked in warm ewes milk with a large spoonful of clover honey stirred in, and fortified with a medicine glass brimming with sloe gin she became not only relaxed but careless.

"It's horrible really, what greed can do to an ordinary hardworking person," she commented forgetting she had not told Mr Nemo of Ted Tulley's involvement in the strange events surrounding Mediobogdum.

"Greed – and ancient influence," he commented, looking her in the eye and somehow making it impossible for her to look away.

"Indeed," she mumbled at last, deeming it best to say as little as possible whilst avoiding telling more lies. Yet this was too good an opportunity to miss. "Talking of ancient," she began hesitantly, then continued encouraged by his nod and attentive attitude, "The day I arrived here you mentioned a She-wolf and her cubs."

"Did I?"

"Yes, Mr Nemo, you did," she persevered, mildly irritated by his constant answering of questions with yet another question.

"The vixen I meant, but this I explained at the time."

"But did not tell the truth!" she dared to challenge.

"For you to know that, you in turn have not told the truth about your attacker's demise."

She stared at him nonplussed. *He knew.* Impossible and illogical though it was, he knew.

"But how could that be? There are no wolves any more," she whispered, running a hand through her already tousled hair. "unless, as was suggested for the Highlands, a controlled pair have been experimentally introduced to-,"

"No."

Mr Nemo's monosyllabic interruption, and also his hand that was held palm outward in the classical 'no-go' gesture, stopped her short.

"Mysteries are for the celebrating not explaining," he intoned. Suddenly afraid she looked away, but felt him willing her to meet his gaze again and like ocean to moon she obeyed the pull. Instantly she was reminded of an imposing white-robed figure standing on an outcrop with cloak flapping in the wind as he raised his staff to the heavens. A prompting of inner wisdom ensured her silence. She did however venture to broach the subject of the eagles.

"I climbed to the top of Illgill," she began.

"And did you see the Unicorn or Tyrannosaurus Rex?"

"No, but I know what you mean," she said with a smile. "That is one scary place. I didn't see any eagles either; you did say I would find them at Wasdale?"

As he shook his head the firelight played on Mr Nemo's hair transmuting the grey to silver. "I said *the* eagle *hides* at Wasdale," he said with careful emphasis. "Think about it. You went to University; what is the touchstone of logic?"

She could not recall having mentioned her days as an undergrad at Hilldean, but let it pass. "What must I do about Tul-, the man lying dead in the circle?" she asked instead, biting her lip at this near-betrayal of the fact that she knew the identity of her attacker. Her voice was hesitant, her expression troubled, testament to her inner distress despite attempts to not dwell on the horror.

"Nothing."

"But-," she began to protest, frowning.

"Will anything you do bring him back to this life?"

"No."

"Would you even want it to do so?"

She shuddered and briefly closed her eyes.

"No, if I am honest."

"Then why cause yourself more distress? Give secret thanks for the powers that intervened," he said wisely.

She thought of the snarling grey form, the bloodletting and that mournful howl haunting the moor.

"What will happen?" she asked simply, placing a child-like trust in this elderly eccentric without knowing exactly why.

"He will be found, eventually. A fugitive hiding out on the moor that has died of exposure and provided carrion for a rogue farm dog. They have been known, you know, to roam the moor after turning bad with the lambs."

A fugitive? Ted Tulley had been on the run from the police; how much did this strange old man know?

"To act as he did, he was probably wanted and hiding out anyway," Mr Nemo said with a little smile as her startled gaze flew to his face.

"Why am I here?" she asked abruptly, holding his gaze.

"To find the truth."

"I don't know how to do that."

"Yes you do; follow the path to which you have been led. Or as you young people say – go with the flow," he said with a smile.

"I might not be able to do it."

"If that was the case you would not now be on it."

" But I'm frightened."

"And so you should be. The path becomes narrow, stony and sheer – but tread it with courage and there you shall find your truth. But enough of this dismal talk! I shall play for you now."

Rising from the armchair he crossed to the piano, flexed his long fingers and seated himself on the stool.

Mr Nemo's fingers made that old piano sing, and the poignancy of that haunting music soothed her fears and anxiety. But it was the words he uttered that were to echo through her mind, repeated over and over as she lay in bed that night. Not, strangely, those connected with the major trauma arising from her knowledge of Ted Tulley's death and location of his remains, but that reference to *the* Eagle – like with a capital 'E' – and the 'touchstone of logic'. Whatever he meant it was significant, this she intuitively knew.

Giving in to its insistence she put sleep on hold and lit the oil lamp and browsed through the Pocket Thesaurus (kept in her organiser bag to aid the compiling of reports in the field where there was no signal) and allowed her mind to free-wheel. Touchstone; criterion; benchmark – each one looked up in turn. And suddenly there it was in the list – *standard*. Surely it could not be that simple? The idea once sown germinated and blossomed. Going back over all the clues she could see the pointers had been set from the very beginning: the dream of the fire at Mediobogum; the 'eagle that is hidden at Wasdale'; the legend of the 'unlucky' Ninth. The mega problem of what to do about it still remained, but maybe now at least, she thought blowing out the candle, she knew 'why' and 'what' and it only remained to discover 'how'.

During the dark secret hours of the night she received confirmation.

Indomita Indomita

She was back on the lofty summit of Illgill in the fading light of day and she reached out to him with her mind, to the unseen presence that called and sought her – and he came. He was standing motionless some little way off along the ridge. His head was bare and the rays of the setting sun fired autumn sparks in the wintered, bracken-bronzed hair. The sternness of expression was softened as she felt his gladness streaming towards her, but there was anguish too, and conflict. She stood there, helpless in the face of his pain then tried to communicate through her mind, sending out the feelings much as she imagined radio waves transmitted sounds. *What is it Antonius? How can I help you?*

For what seemed an age he stood as though carved from the very rock upon which he stood, silent and apparently uncomprehending. She mentally traced each line of his face, the colour of the eyes that changed with each nuance of light from the slate-green of a limpid pool to the sun-flecked shade of woods in summer. Then the answer came: not verbally at first but in waves of feeling that flowed through her being, filtering nuances, nurturing a different knowledge so that words sprang up in her mind like green shoots piercing the earth in spring.

Mea culpa Mea culpa

She sighs and sends out her compassion and understanding. *For what are you to blame?* The red orb of the sun sinks beneath the mountains. Stunted trees sigh in a bleak wind as the valley below subsides into darkness. He is barely visible now, a dark shadow blending into the gloom. Her mind, having somehow forged a link with his, conjures strange pictures: bare trees and ice-chocked rivers; a horde of warriors streaming through the night in an unstoppable tide bringing swords and axes, blood and death. A great fortress looms on the horizon spewing flames and billows of black smoke that blot out the stars.

The images fade and she is back on Illgill head with the vast stretch of water below, black and shiny as pitch. At the dale head a triad of mountains surrounds a dense dark forest. An army is caught in its snare. Helpless and terrified soldiers break rank and run in all directions, seeking an escape but losing all sense of direction. Men open their mouths to scream as the long-swords come from the darkness to slash and hack them to pieces. Then the forest is silent. All the soldiers lie dead or dying. A horde of warriors woad-daubed and clad in skins sets about the gruesome task of ritual defacement. Armour is stripped from broken bodies leaving them exposed to shame. The warriors defile the naked corpses with streams of spittle and urine. Roman heads are lopped and tied to bridles as trophies and captive spirits. An eagle-topped banner bearing the numeral IX lies on the blood-soaked earth. An eagle soars above the scene of carnage, over water stained red by a dying winter sun. Then as Antonius watches in anguish it drops, hit by a stone released from the war-lord's sling. Down, down it plunges towards the waiting earth. Pinions flutter and ruffle in disorder, helpless against the on-rush of wind. Body spinning and out of control it hurtles towards its doom. She screams at the moment of impact as flesh, bone and plumage collide with the surface of the hostile lake to plunge into its depths.

"Antonius, Antonius!"

She weeps in the darkness. But then the crimson water parts and the eagle hovers amid a plume of water; a phoenix rising from the ashes, though not within the flames but from the ice-fire depths. Droplets cling to wing and tail feathers, hover for breathless seconds and finally fall, sparkling like chips of ice caught by the light as the icicle shatters. A great wind whips the surface of the lake, howls around the rocks and bends the treetops until they must surely snap. A shaft of moonlight slices the pewter surface turning the spumes of grey to silver as the waters part and the eagle surges upwards in slow motion, head angled to a spear point, wings pinioned to resemble the flight of some gigantic arrow. It drips crystals from hooked beak and yellow eyes glint in a triumph of rebirth.

She awoke with a suddenness that left her feeling disoriented and unreal . Her fingers shook and her movements were clumsy as she fumbled for candle and matches. She paused, listening, afraid she may have awakened her elderly host. No sound in the old house except for the occasional creaking of timbers or the scratch and scuttle of tiny feet on wood as mice and bats went about their nocturnal business. Outside an owl screeched and a silhouette flitted past the drawn curtains. Briefly she wondered at the apparent lightness outside that permitted the image, then was lost to mundane things as the residue of the dream enmeshed her once more in tormented threads. So much now made sense; Mr Nemo's cryptic remarks about the Wasdale eagle and the dream about Mediobogdum being on fire. And given the content of the dream it seemed she had guessed correctly Mr Nemo's 'touchstone of logic'. Touchstone was amongst other things another word for *standard*. By applying its military rather than general meaning the answer becomes clear, and it had been hidden all along in that one clever phrase. That realisation gave birth to another: she had interpreted the standard purely as a device to convey the identity of the legion in the earlier dream about Mediobogdum but had failed to see its loss as the answer to two vital questions. Constantly she had asked herself *why is this happening?* and *what does he want?* Rightly or wrongly Antonius had blamed himself for the loss of the standard – or rather what that stood for: the massacre and subsequent shame of the Ninth. Here was unfinished business that spanned the centuries, preventing him from resting in peace. But why had she 'seen' the massive fortress under siege and engulfed in smoke and flames? Where was it, and what was the link with the standard of the Ninth?

She sat up in bed watching shadows chase one another along the walls and ceiling as the candle flame danced and dipped in the draught that whistled through the window frame with each gust of wind; over the seasons birds seeking linseed oil had pecked away at the putty thus breaking the seal. Suddenly a light bulb flashed on inside her brain. That email attachment of Caro's, the one received the day she left the farmhouse for the field camp now held deeper significance. The extract from the excavation report prepared by the Archaeology Department at Hilldean University had ended in speculation about the fate of the 'unlucky' Ninth Legion – and the probability of a large detachment being annihilated in a surprise attack on Mediobogdum. It had also stated that the Legionary Headquarters in the North were at York – or Eboracum.

Was this what she had seen in the dream? Excitement rose as the strands began weaving into a significant whole. The massacre at Wasdale; an attack on the Legion's H.Q. at Eboracum; and a shock attack on Mediobogdum. What if they had been carried out *simultaneously?* Was that the answer: a concerted effort to rid Northern Britain of the hated Roman occupation? A three-pronged attack involving not only the local Brigantes but troops of warriors throughout the North. And was this the solution to the mystery of the disappearance of the Ninth? From what Caro had said it had always been argued that the Barbarian tribes were too wild and unruly to organise themselves into a cohesive army to wage a concerted attack – which is what would be needed to wipe out a legionary force that at full strength comprised a thousand men. Even allowing for a full sick leave roster the numbers would still be formidable. The wintertime would be chosen with just this in mind, of course, when soldiers originating from warmer climes would likely fall sick in a frost and snow-bound Britain.

Even so an attack on the formidable and heavily-manned military H.Q. would have been a disaster – unless a large detachment was sent up north to Wasdale in response to rumours of a dangerous uprising there. It would have been easy enough to fuel the flames, given the Roman habit of trading and whoring with the inhabitants of the settlement that grew up around any major fortress. Such rumours would then inevitably reach the ears of those in command – *like Antonius?* – and they would be forced to act by sending troops to quell the rebellion. Had Antonius received orders from Rome to head the detachment sent to the North, or had he made that fateful decision himself? And what single event had motivated those disparate tribes to unite in an organized campaign? In all probability the answer to these questions would never be known, she concluded.

So what about the final part of that dream? It was fairly simple, she reckoned. If Antonius was to rest in peace, the legion regain its honour and her life return to normal, somehow she had to retrieve the standard. "Is that it Antonius? Do I have it right at last?" she whispered after blowing out the candle and settling back on the pillows. A warmth surrounded and caressed her, and it seemed, a flush of approval. Not for now the worry of how she was to accomplish this impossible task. For tonight this is enough, she told herself succumbing to weariness and the need for sleep. Guiltily she found herself wondering if it would be all that desirable to have her life returned to normal. Her last thought before slipping into oblivion.

OUT OF TIME XI

~

He stands on the rear rampart looking out over mountains flushed by the rays of the setting sun. It seems her face is etched on their elephantine flanks, then above them she lies supine, her naked body moulded by clouds of pink and pearly grey that follow the undulating line of the summit ridges. In the tumbling becks he saw her tears, in the sunrise her hopes and in the blood of the dying sun, the light of Rome's edict, her possible death. Not by his hand or order, even if that meant falling upon his sword to avoid a terrible traitor's death. He stares down at the precipitous drop to the valley floor and winding ribbon of water. She, the confusion over her identity and the dilemma of Rome, are driving him insane. He sees her everywhere. She *is* his landscape.

He shook his head and breathed deeply to focus on the business at hand. Slowly he turned and scanned the western stretch of valley but nothing unusual caught his attention. No swarming hordes or stealthy approach. No warning flashes from the fort at Glannaventa ruddied by the setting sun hitting the sheet of polished metal used for signalling the alert. Yet something had prompted him to check the precipice and deep-cut valley for anything out of the ordinary. Descending to the via decumana he passed the barrack blocks to either side and stopped outside the principia. Marcellus was waiting at the courtyard entrance and saluted then stepped forward.

"Nothing doing, sir. Yet there's," Marcellus shook his head and shrugged his broad leather-clad shoulders. "Oh, I don't know," he finished lamely.

"Something in the air?"

"You feel it too."

"Almost like the old days, eh Marcellus?"

"Aye, on the Rhenus."

"Night before battle sort of feeling."

"That's the one," Marcellus agreed, nodding emphatically.

"Well that's unlikely here."

"Sometimes wish we did have some action, just to break the monotony," Marcellus said gloomily, dislodging with the toe of his boot a weed that had dared to squeeze between the flags. They both briefly looked up at the sounds of stamping feet and curt orders which signalled the end of the watch and the beginning of the next.

"What you need nights is that wife of yours in your bed," Antonius said grinning.

"Oh sir!" Marcellus grimaced.

"Now come on, you know you need taking in hand, as you might say!"

"She'll never come out here," Marcellus said smugly.

"She will if I request it!"

"Then I'd best make the most of my freedom!" Marcellus laughed then picked his tooth with a sliver of wood.

"Well come spring the extra wing will be finished and I shall be gone.

"I'll be sorry at that, sir." Marcellus shuffled his feet and looked embarrassed. "So will Rufinus. We've, well, we've sort of got used to having you about the place, if you know what I mean."

"I knew you would turn out well, Marcellus." Antonius clasped his arm in friendship. "I'm glad I didn't turn you into raven-fodder!"

"Bless you, sir – I'd have given them indigestion from one full moon to the next!"

"That's why I spared them!" Antonius said laughing. "Now finish your rounds, man."

"Aye sir." Marcellus grinned and blew on his hands. "There'll be

312

snow tonight," he predicted over his shoulder as he went on his way. After a last look round Antonius followed.

He paused at the stable and listened at the door. Gaudita's gentle whinny told him she had sensed his presence.

"Good night girl," he whispered, and smiled at the answering snicker. Then he frowned because it was followed by snorting, rustling of hay and rasp of hooves on stone. By the sound of it the entire inmates of the stable were as wide awake as youngsters at an illicit midnight feast. Such restlessness was unusual at this time of day. On impulse he retraced his earlier footsteps but before mounting the steps to the rampart paused at the porta decumana.

"Halt! Name and rank?" the order was rapped out by one of the two sentries on gate duty.

"Antonius – Legatus"

"Watchword?" The sentry who had issued the challenge stepped forward two paces, leaving his companion on guard at one side of the gate, which unlike the others was single rather than double portal. Antonius approached and spoke softly so that if unauthorised ears were listening they would not overhear.

"Mithras."

"Pass, sir."

"Is all quiet?"

"Aye sir."

"Carry on soldier."

Antonius mounted the steps to the rampart for one last check.

The sentry on duty there saluted and stood to attention. A different man since the change of the watch. Antonius searched his memory. There was a tension and familiar slyness about this man.

"Step forward soldier."

The sentry advanced a couple of paces and stood at attention.

Ah, now I have it. Even in the ruddy glow of a sun sinking below the horizon, the eyes were pale, the eyes of a wolf. Lupinus.

"Anything to report?" Antonius demanded curtly.

313

"All's quiet, sir."

Antonius frowned. The reply had been made with a note of servility rather than that more usual sullenness that bordered on insolence. And there was about him an air of something unusual – suppressed impatience or urgency perhaps? Or just nervousness maybe at sensing his commander's dislike and mistrust. Or nervousness at something being discovered? Something illicit, traitorous even? But he had no grounds to suppose so, except for that aura of malevolence about the man.

So why did he feel no great sense of security in knowing the safety of the fort was dependent on the watchfulness of those particular eyes? Any attack, he reasoned, must of necessity come from the rear. An approach along the road from east or west would be instantly detected and therefore impossible to pull off, and the south was cut off by a solid wall of mountain. He supposed the precipice could be scaled by desperate and determined men, but it was highly unlikely and its steepness should provide a formidable enough deterrent. But it was not impossible. Should this man be playing accomplice to some treachery, all it would take was a quick thrust to his comrade's back, a slipping of bolts and the enemy would be inside. Coincidence too that he was on rear gate duty tonight? Maybe, but easy enough to swap places on the roster with a mate keen to avoid the night shift.

But he was probably being paranoid, Antonius acknowledged, rattled by the situation with Rome and fears for Rowana. Dislike of the man was not grounds for calling him traitor. Lupinus waited at attention.

"Carry on," he said curtly, "And be sure to report any anomaly to me. I am holding you personally responsible for the safety of this area."

"Yes, sir." Lupinus saluted.

Antonius turned away and descended the steps. As he did so he heard Lupinus noisily clear his throat and spit.

He made his way slowly back to his quarters, unwilling to be alone with his thoughts. Such stillness; such silence. And an impression of waiting – for what? Like his nerves, the night vibrated with unease. A flurry of snowflakes drifted down and melted on contact with the stone around his feet. Marcellus was right about the weather. He stood for a moment looking up at the stars above the ridge of the mountain guarding the south. How large, how close they seemed tonight, almost he could reach up and touch them. They and the mountains never seemed to change, he thought, and that brings a measure of security in this mutable world.

Suddenly he was overcome by a great wash of longing.

"Come to me Indomita, come to me," he whispered, not entirely sure to whom he was speaking.

THIRTY-FOUR

Veni, Indomita, Veni

She breathes him into her being through the wind. He is on the wind; his scent, his essence, his love and his hate. She inhales deeply so that he fills her nostrils, her lungs and the corpuscles of her blood which carry his essence to every cell of her body. He *is* the wind.

Antonius

She reaches out to him, to the invisible presence that calls her with such urgency.

She awoke from a fitful sleep and the remnants of a dream that clung to her heart like the gossamer strands of a cobweb. She breakfasted with Mr Nemo who watched her with an eye not too far removed from the eagle of that traumatic dream of destruction and renewal, but who refrained from making comment about her scanty conversation and lack of appetite.

Beyond the windows of the lodge, moor and mountains were white with frost providing the answer to why she had been able to see the shadow of the owl on the drawn curtains the previous night. Muffled against the bitter cold she walked the dogs across the moor to Wasdale, taking care to avoid by a very wide margin the path that led back to the stone circles. She shuddered and turned to look over her shoulder at a harsh croaking and two black specks hovering over the distant site. Ravens: those Masters of the Scavengers Guild. If someone did not discover him soon there would be little chance of recognising Ted Tulley. As she watched the spiralling and dipping specks anxiety churned in her belly. The sky was low, oppressive and ominous-looking and she feared a return of the previous evening's storm. Her breath smoked in the brittle air but the sense of urgency in the dream made her hurry on. This time instead of trailing to the top of Illgill Head she called the dogs in and followed the path from lodge and tarn that eventually dropped down into Wasdale.

Down-in-the-Dale, and the storm of the previous night had taken its toll: branches and even whole trees were down, at times blocking the path so that she had to clamber over whilst Mab and Brock bellied their way beneath commando style. Upon reaching the dalehead the sense of oppression that had grown steadily stronger with her approach pressed down upon her head and crushed her spirit. That nightmare vision had seemed so real that she had almost expected to see a forest and scenes of carnage with bodies and weapons strewn around, rather than the whitewashed (and today apparently deserted) inn further up the dalehead, and tiny stone church and graveyard where many unfortunate climbers ended their days surrounded by sentinel yews. The heaviness of atmosphere increased and calling to the dogs she turned her back on that 'natural trap of forest and rock' (whispered words orbiting her mind but no idea where they had come from) and wandered down to the shore.

Wastwater stretched into the distance, the coldness and colour of pewter and with no living soul to break the bleakness and isolation. A bitter north-easterly ruffled the surface whipping up peaks and troughs with each gust. To her left rose The Screes: dark, stark and forbidding, a sheer escarpment of two thousand feet to the top of Illgill Head and plunging down with a vengeance to the bottom of England's deepest lake. They were, she knew, covered in loose boulders and treacherous gravel pounded from rock by Time and exposure to wind-driven rain, blizzards and rock-splitting frost. These elements, along with glacial and volcanic movement, had gouged the dark and satanic chimneys that split the upper face of the ridge for the whole of its length. Standing on the shore below gave a different

317

but just as awe-inspiring perspective as when she had stared down one of the crevices from the summit of Illgill Head. Worryingly the gullies were still chocked with ice that hung from the ledges in dinosaur fangs. Only now did she appreciate in full Mr Nemo's dry comment about Tyrannosaurus Rex.

She stood still for a time wondering what to do. Why had she come here today? What could she seriously hope to achieve? Even if her interpretation of events was correct, given the vastness of area and time scale involved it was madness to think the standard could be found. Overwhelmed by feelings of foolishness and inadequacy she looked about her in an agony of indecision. The very air of this place sapped hope and vitality. Then, whilst at lowest ebb, the image at the end of the dream came to mind. Once again she watched the eagle standard rise, forced to the surface by water swollen and agitated by the storm. The symbolism was clear enough. The storm may have thrown it up from the primordial depths, or maybe from a ledge of rock where it had lodged many feet below the surface. But *where?* she thought, distress unrelieved; given the circumference of this massive lake, it would take a miracle to find it.

The dogs had been snuffling around in the undergrowth but as a sudden clap of thunder boomed around the surrounding rock Mab gave a startled yelp and bolted towards the Screes.

"Mab, here girl! Mab!" Darcy shouted, trying to keep the panic out of her voice so as not to further spook the terrified dog. Ignoring her commands to return Brock raced ahead in pursuit.

With an anxious glance at the lowering sky Darcy pounded after the dogs, calling to them as she ran so that soon her breath was coming in painful gasps and all thought of the standard was pushed aside. By now Mab was out of sight but Brock was still visible, his sturdy body weaving through the undergrowth as he left the path in pursuit of his sister. Lightning streaked a zigzag of electric blue across the sky and Darcy cursed, knowing this would freak Mab out even further. She never used to be fazed by storms, Darcy reflected, stumbling now along a path that was ever-rising and bringing the Screes unnervingly close. Her present fear had to be down to the storm during that first visit to Mediobogdum. She shouted in vain for Mab and Brock to return but by now both dogs were out of sight. A second growl of thunder rumbled along the tops and she glanced anxiously at the sky, noting the brownish tinge to the pall of cloud that shrouded the valley. With a bit of luck these grumbles were the residue of the previous storm rather than a resurgence, she thought, clambering over fallen branches and driftwood thrown up from the lake by the unprecedented violence of the squall.

That hope proved well-founded as the rumbles died away but a second menace threatened. The wind was gathering force and that sepia sky should have acted as a warning. The first flakes of snow stung her face as she reached the base of the Screes.

"Mab! Brock! she called, her voice cracking on a note of panic as there was still no sign of the two spaniels. Then a bundle of fur and flying feet burst into view.

"There you are!" This time relief sharpened her voice as Brock came running towards her. "But where's Mab? Show me Brock, take me to her."

Brock turned and to Darcy's dismay scampered off along the path that ran along the base of the Screes, the very last place she wanted to go.

To call it a path would be a gross case of misguided optimism. It was less than a sheep track, an intermittent scar tracing an impossible line along the sheer mountain face. Not for the first time since this whole thing began Darcy cursed her foolhardiness in setting out without making proper provision by way of map, compass, torch – the basics essential to survival . But then she had not intended crawling along this perilous route in pursuit of a distressed dog. The flakes were falling faster now, swirling and eddying in the rising wind and making it difficult to see more than a yard or two ahead. Constantly calling Mab's name as she went, she edged her way round boulders that over time had careered down from the shattered summit to block what remained of the track. Her best hope lay in Mab having made it across the Screes to the far end at Nether Wasdale; her second best that she was stuck on a ledge somewhere, though hopefully not with an injured leg or paw because that would present an insurmountable problem in terms of getting her back. The worst scenario involved Meg falling into the icy water – but Darcy determined she was not even going there, that she would get both dogs off this hell-scape alive and in one piece.

Despite wearing gloves her fingers were numbed by cold as they probed for a handhold in the rock, and her feet skidded on stone marbles. Her ankles ached unbearably due to the unnatural angle of her feet given the steepness of incline. The only sound now was the constant *lap-suck-lap* of the water against the flank of the Screes some thirty feet below, a sound that frayed the nerves and gave the impression of a bottomless lake awaiting a false move. A stifled cry escaped as one foot skated from under her and she slid on her side towards the swirling water. Desperately she dug in with her other foot and grabbed at an outcrop to halt the slide. A breathtaking jerk then pain raced along her spine with the suddenness of the stop. The gunmetal water was now but a foot or so away. She stared through the whorls and whirlpools of snow at waves whipped up by the wind and crested with white. It was wild and grim and primordial and her courage caved in. This was the end; a blackness washed over her and hope was sucked beneath the heaving dark waters.

A sharp bark jerked her out of the mire of despair. *Mab!* Pulling herself inch by inch back up to the track she called the spaniel's name to give reassurance. Brock too gave an answering bark and paused, turning his head to make sure Darcy was following his precarious lead.

"Go on, Brock," Darcy encouraged. Mab was still alive; there could be no giving up now. Snow whirled in her face and she screwed up her eyes and peered ahead, keeping a desperate eye on Brock's white rump and hoping for a glimpse of Mab. Her stomach was churning, heart thumping and blood pounding remorselessly in her ears but there could be no thought now of turning back.

Mab was crouched on an overhang, snow caking her coat, claws bleeding from scraping and gripping bare rock and eyes rolling in her head with terror. "Thank God!" Instinctively Darcy grabbed an excited Brock's collar and restrained him, swaying with the movement so that one foot slipped off the track. Her heart leapt into her mouth as a shower of pebbles rolled and splashed seconds later into the waiting water. She steadied herself by clinging to a boulder before giving the order:

"Brock – back!" The tone of voice and the gesture to get behind her were enough to convince him this was serious business and he edged past to cower at her heels.

"It's okay babe," she crooned, inching towards the shelf, terrified lest Mab make a sudden move out of excitement or panic and end up in that heaving, sucking water from hell. A few minutes in that freezing lake be all it would take. "I'm here now. We'll soon have you off'a there babe." Her voice was strangely muffled by the whirlwind of white that obscured not only the far shore now but the whole of the lake. Visibility either way on that horrific path was down to around three or four metres but she calculated they now stood roughly half way along the Screes. She continued to edge towards the outcrop. Mab it seems was too terrified to move either way and lay, belly to rock, watching her approach but making no effort to run to her side.

The reason for this soon became apparent. As she advanced Darcy became aware of a thickening of the oppressive atmosphere. At her heels Brock began to whine in a quiet subdued sort of way. Darcy felt the hairs at the back of her neck prickle and dark fear cloaked her mind. It was difficult now to breathe normally so clammy was the air, and almost impossible to push a way forward due to an increase in density. She inched forward in silence; the calling of reassurances to Mab expended too much energy. The track on this stretch ran downwards with the result that each step took her closer to the eagerly lapping water.

This also meant that it was littered with debris thrown up from the depths by the previous evening's storm, thus making her passage even more difficult as she was forced to clamber over rotting logs, branches and a mass of unidentifiable organic matter. Not long ago a body had been found she recalled, on a narrow ledge beneath the surface where it had lain for years. If she remembered it right, the wife of a Cheshire doctor murdered by her husband and dumped in the lake. The thought of what may have been thrown up by the storm brought forth a shudder of fear and revulsion and she took extra care over placing her feet and not just from fear of falling.

The darkness enfolding her mind thickened into despair causing her to falter. *I can't do this; I cannot go on.* Far easier to sink down here on this snow-bound hell-side and let the elements have their way. *But those 'elements' are not just related to weather, are they not? After all you have endured are you about to let them steal the prize?*

Darcy forced open eyes that were almost closed as Mr Nemo's voice seemed to take her to task.

"Them?" she whispered through lips that were numbed by cold. Suddenly an image from that fateful dream arose in her mind of the slashing, stabbing painted hoard and the massacre at the dalehead and the endangered standard. No, she was not about to be cheated of her prize. Given the fierceness of opposition her goal must be close, but her determination was equally fierce. Only here on this prehistoric mountain in the midst of a blizzard could such thoughts hold any credence. She pressed forward and felt the increased resistance of the force field surrounding Mab.

Hopelessness flooded her mind and sapped the new resolve. She faltered and almost fell as a dark hostility ranged itself against her and seemed to physically resist her efforts to advance. Waves of fury and hatred battered her mind so that she cried aloud as though from a physical blow and Brock howled at her back in abject fear. With each step now she stumbled. In addition to the stone marbles rolling beneath her feet, snow had settled along the scar of the track obscuring it in places and making it even more treacherous. Something was forcing her inexorably closer to the water that surged and sucked a mere foot or so now from her ankles. One more push and she would be lost, swallowed up by that black, heaving, primordial soup. Dark thoughts of what might lurk there threw up images that made her cringe: phosphorescent creatures swimming at unfathomable depths where daylight never penetrated; black and slimy eels with a body the thickness of a man's arm and a serpent mouth with protruding fangs; a legendary pike the size of a shark with cold black eye and jaws and teeth waiting to devour. Weakness and fear threatened to overcome her as she crawled on all fours resisting the magnetic pull of the water.

It was no good; the blackness cloaked the reason for being here on this perilous ledge; the standard and even Mab were forgotten in her despair. Then Mr Nemo's words seemed to echo inside her head: *The path becomes narrow, stony and steep – but tread it with courage and there you shall find your truth.* Well it could not get narrower or steeper than this so she must be on the right track! Marshalling her last ounce of strength she ranged herself against the hostile force that barred the way to Mab and God alone knew what else. Dimly, through the fug that poisoned her mind there shone the light of reason. Could Mab have been used in the same way as Brant and herself, and to an extent Ted Tulley too, to further a bigger cause? One last mental and physical push, then a breath-stopping moment when unseen hands seemed to pluck at her body and an unearthly howling sounded in her ears, then she was through the malignant barrier to the outcrop.

It was obvious then why Mab had not moved in response to Darcy's call and presence. The outcrop overhung the track then sloped down almost to the surface of the lake. Her hind leg was enmeshed in a length of twine embroiled in the tangled mass of debris deposited there from the lake-bed by the storm. Her struggles had only made the tangle worse. Calming an excited Brock with a command she set about freeing Mab whilst talking gently to soothe her fear and distress. Disconcerted, she frowned as she worked with fingers stiffened by intense cold and shaking with trauma: there was still no response from the normally intensely friendly and exuberant bitch. Indeed her eyes held the blankness of a robot. Once free she would have to walk, Darcy worried, noting how the dog's coat was clotted with heavy gobbets of snow; she would scarcely be able to lift let alone carry her back to safety.

"Almost there babe." Darcy moaned and tried to shift her weight as sharp stones cut into her knees. The twine was looped around something heavy caught up in the mound of snow-covered debris. Brushing snow first from her eyebrows and lashes, then scraping it from the jumble of branches, weed and many unidentifiable objects before dropping them back into the lake, she worked through Nature's scrap pile.

"Got it!" The object tugged forth was encrusted with algae, mud and weed and resembled an intricate piece of driftwood, yet given its weight and feel it had to be made of metal.

"It's okay girl, we're there," she soothed, casting worried looks at Mab who was whining and trembling like a leaf in a storm and pressing her belly flat to the rock. Darcy unravelled the end of the twine severing the object from Mab and the whining abruptly stopped. She was about to drop the thing back into the water when something about the shape arrested her attention.

THIRTY-FIVE

~

Later she would realise that she knew even before taking a sharp piece of rock and scraping away a section of the organic mantle. The metal beneath gleamed dully in the half-light and she gasped in disbelief. To have survived submerged on a ledge for God knows how long without corrosion and decomposition, she reasoned, it had to be made of gold. Pulling away strands of weed and slime that clung to the extrusions she hauled it onto the sloping part of the ledge just below where Mab was now sitting quietly watching. It must be hollow, she guessed, cast in gold; had it been solid there was no way she could have moved it, despite it being a little smaller than expected. She recalled from her research that the reason for this was that it could be snatched from its shaft and hidden at times of grave danger. There could now be no mistaking the eagle shape.

Yet such was the significance of the find that at first she could not take in the fact that she was holding a momentous piece of history. For around two thousand years this standard, or what now remained of it as the short and hollow shaft of metal that once housed the stave was intact, but the wooden staff with its metal point had probably been discarded on the site of battle and in any case would be long gone, had been the object of endless searching and speculation. She could not even begin to think about the effect it might have on the man she had come to know as Antonius. From her research she knew that the loss of a legion's standard was considered a major catastrophe

325

and the ultimate disgrace, undermining as it did the legion's status and honour. Its recovery would surely generate an equivalent tide of jubilation.

All this aside their immediate predicament was more pressing. It was still snowing and blizzard conditions now prevailed. She still had to get herself, two traumatised dogs and a heavy metallic emblem off the Screes before dark if they were not to succumb to hypothermia; no way was she leaving the latter now that finally it was in her possession. Thankfully Darcy noted the blankness had faded from Mab's eyes to be replaced by the spark of life. No wonder the poor dog had been severely traumatised, she thought, given the object to which she had been tethered – and the fact that she had been at the epicentre of a malevolent force bent on thwarting its removal.

"Come on, girl we're going home," Darcy said gently, looping a slip lead over the spaniel's head.

Darcy would never quite know how the journey back along that narrow and treacherous scar, in blizzard conditions, trailing two stressed-out dogs and toting a bulky and weighty object was accomplished. But it was, and in relative safety give or take the odd slip or two. There was one heart in mouth moment whilst edging round a monster of a boulder, when Darcy's foot slid from beneath her on the loose shale and the loop of Mab's lead slipped off her wrist where she had placed it in order to have both hands free to carry the eagle. She hugged it to her chest with one arm and with the other clutched at an overhang in order to save both eagle and herself from the brooding water. The fear was that Mab would panic and bolt but she waited at the far side of the rock, body pressed to her brother's flank.

That trek held hazards apart from physical danger. As they progressed at snail's pace along the base of the ridge doubt began to assail Darcy about the nature of the object she carried. It could not possibly be the Eagle of the Ninth, the voice in her head whispered; it was wishful thinking on her part; it was a piece of driftwood that with a little imagination could be seen as the shape of an eagle with wings outstretched ready for flight. No, not driftwood; it is made of metal, she argued silently back. Okay, the voice in her head went, some sort of ancient tack, or harness or farm implement. Whenever she came up with a contra-argument the whisperer cast still more doubts.

As belief was eroded so the thing she carried became heavier and more unwieldy, giving rise to the temptation to let it drop back into the water. *Yes, let it go back to whence it came. This worthless object is holding you back from safety* the whisperer urged. Fears about the weather on the return trip across the moor added to her dark mood. The closer she drew to the dalehead end of the path the more insistent the whispering became. So much so that she faltered in her step, felt stupid and naive for believing and doubtful even of her sanity. She was about to drop it back into the inky depths, walk away and forget the whole wretched business but before she could do so a different voice spoke clearly in her ear.

Indomita Indomita Non me falle

Do not fail me: the urgency of that sibilant voice carried the meaning and rang true. She staggered on still bearing her burden.

Almost an hour later she felt the urge to laugh and cry simultaneously as she ushered the dogs off the Screes and the ground no longer sloped at a vertiginous angle. The blizzard for the time being had blown itself out, and although the snowfall had been heavy the air was clear and cold and visibility back to normal, so her worries about the return trek to the Lodge began to subside. Mab trotted quietly at her side, subdued but apparently unharmed by her escapade, whilst Brock ran ahead but Darcy noted how every now and then he turned to look back and wait for his sister. Obviously they were not unaffected by what had happened, she thought sombrely, stooping to pat the top of Mab's snow-impacted head. Relief was tempered by exhaustion but adrenalin kept her going. She had done it; achieved the impossible. Unless she was seriously wrong. The doubts began to set in again eroding mood and motivation.

Something prompted her to pause and look back at the Screes and her heart turned over. A dark silhouette was perched on a large rock about half-way up the shattered flank. As she watched, it spread its wings and posed as though to emphasise a shape that exactly mirrored the object she carried. Then slowly, slowly the pinions flapped: once, twice, thrice and into lift-off. The great bird rose to the air in stately flight, tail feathers fanned, wing-tips feathering the currents and each beat of those massive wings bringing it closer and closer still. Darcy stood mesmerised by the sight, a tingle of emotion running the length of her spine. It seemed to move in majestic slow motion but at last was overhead. There it hovered for a full minute or more as though in acknowledgement before turning and soaring out of sight over the top of the Screes.

It was hard going on the climb out of Wasdale up to the moor, but once there progress became easier. Apart from an occasional flurry the snow had finally stopped. The moor lay still and silent beneath a white mantle, the snow crisp and crusty as fresh baked meringue beneath Darcy's feet. At last they were on the moor and back on the track that would take them to the Lodge. On arriving there on impulse and for some reason she was only partly aware of, Darcy laid her burden down in an outhouse and covered it with an old sack before proceeding to the house. Vaguely it had something to do with the fact that the time to quit the lodge was approaching, and Mr Nemo might try and prevent her from taking it with her when she left.

He was seated at the sitting room table sanding the carved eagle. She glanced suspiciously at him as he worked, an enigmatic smile upon his face.

"Does it do justice do you think?" he asked, holding it up for her inspection.

"That I couldn't say," she fenced.

"No, silly of me; you haven't seen it yet, have you?"

His eyes bore into her soul, or so it seemed, willing her to confide.

"I'm going to my room to change and rest for a while, may I take a book?" she said instead, and as he waved assent turned to the pile on the table to avoid that gimlet gaze.

"Yes you do rather look like a snowman, or can one not say that these days?"

"Snow-person," she corrected gravely, trying not to smile but failing miserably.

"And now you are teasing me dreadful child! But tell me, how far did you walk? I was quite concerned when the blizzard got up."

"Oh across the moor and back," she said with deliberate vagueness. "I've rubbed down Mab and Brock and left them on their bed in the utility room."

"In a moment I shall take them a bowl of warm bread and milk each," he said nodding.

"Thank you, they will enjoy that; you are very kind." And she meant it; in fact a lump rose to her throat at the realisation that she would soon be gone and in all probability would never see this eccentric and learned old gentleman ever again. Afraid of giving herself away she made her escape.

Once in her room she dropped the book on the bed, changed her wet clothes for dry ones and put her boots to dry. Yet she began to shiver despite the ornate and ancient paraffin heater placed there by Mr Nemo. Shudders wracked her from head to toe and she paced the room, unable to settle. A feeling that she should be somewhere else troubled her mind. It seemed a voice whispered from the corner: *Indomita, Indomita! veni, veni!*

She was crushed by a sense of impending doom. The normal background hum of the house became a whine, then a roar and floor and ceiling began to spin. Her hands gripped the edge of the table for support until the dizzy spell passed.

Veni

Instinctively she knew he was pleading with her to come to the fort.

It would be madness to go out again, she thought shaking her head; there would be deep drifts and the sky was heavy with more snow. On impulse she slipped her hand beneath the pillow and drew out the photograph. She cried out and her free hand went to her mouth. A dark stain was seeping down from the shadowy figure on the precipice. She touched it with her forefinger and crossed to the window. Against the glare of the snow the tip was clearly stained red.

Darcy reached for boots and car keys.

House and tarn now lay behind. She had managed to creep down the stairs and out of the back door without being challenged by Mr Nemo. Mab and Brock were sound asleep, exhausted by the trauma on the Screes and the trek back to the house and made no sound as she left. She had not intended taking the eagle, had tried to hurry past the outhouse afraid of his eyes at the window, but it had drawn her with palpable magnetism. Without understanding why she knew it had to be taken back to Mediobogdum so it was now crammed into her backpack, albeit with one wing tip protruding at the top. At least this time she was prepared: the pockets held map, compass, torch and spare batteries, mint cake, survival sack, twine and a penknife. The moor was covered in dazzling damask, the patterns changing with each play of light and reflecting the rays of the sun. It had a compelling beauty yet Darcy knew, was not to be trusted. She gave a cry of alarm as the snow underfoot gave way yet again and she sank to the thigh; drifts were everywhere, cloaking the gullies and becks and the weight on her back did not help.

A hush had laid itself over the moor, or maybe the low-level hum was muted and smothered by the blanket of snow that tucked itself into every fat-cushion fold and crevice. Yet the snow had not blotted out other sounds: every now and then the mournful bleating of sheep could be heard and the croaking of the ravens. A shaggy Herdwick ewe, gobbets of ice dangling from its fleece, watched her progress from an outcrop but made no move. Something is wrong, she thought, risking an increase in pace yet already feeling the drag on calves and thighs as she plunged through yet another drift whilst searching for the path. The weight on her back seemed to increase with every step, as did the sense of urgency. Since crossing the moor on her search for Mr Nemo a lifetime ago, she had forgotten how far the lodge was from the village.

At last she was on first a cobbled drovers track, then through a gate and onto the road serving the village which led to the main thoroughfare, albeit a narrow, twisting one. Any ideas she may have had about starting the car fled on seeing the snow-covered mound still parked outside the post office. She carried on walking through the village to the road that led to the pass. This was well churned and the banks stained an ugly brown where tractors had flicked up a tide of slush. However as it began its vertiginous climb the snow was still virginal, unmarked by tyre or foot. The drama of white crags, filigree trees and frozen falls for once left her unmoved.

Veni Indomita, veni!

That urgent whisper again.

"I am coming Antonius, I am coming," she panted, feeling the pull of the climb. Progress was necessarily slow, given the weight on her back but she made her way up the treacherous road to the fort.

OUT OF TIME XII

~

Antonius grunted; the voice persisted.

"Indomita?" he murmured, his voice thick with sleep and confusion. At times it seemed there were two of her; Rowana and a side of her that was a stranger but despite this he was consumed by love for them both.

"Sir, wake up!"

He awoke with a start to find Gaeus shaking him roughly by the shoulder. The old man's eyes in the light of the lamp he carried were wide and staring. Antonius swung his legs out of bed and ground his knuckles into his eyes.

"What is it Gaeus?" Yet even as he awaited the answer he was pulling on boots and armour as the acrid smell of burning wood and pitch filled his nostrils.

"We're under attack sir!"

The voice was firm but Antonius noted with a stab of compassion the trembling of the old man's hand as he held up the lamp. The door burst open admitting the screams, the crackle of burning timbers and all the cacophony of nightmare that had been held at bay by the thick stone walls. Justinus, dishevelled and sword in hand, stood on the threshold.

"Who? How many? And where's Marcellus?" Antonius snapped buckling on his sword belt.

"Circa three hundred at a guess; Brigantes – climbed up from the valley and in at the rear gate; that traitorous dog Lupinus had lifted the bar and loosened the bolts but not enough to be noted. I wondered why he was so eager to volunteer for last watch when the rear duty sentry took ill – no doubt Lupinus slipped something into his food."

"So the bastard was supplying the Brigantes with weapons – I thought as much. Where is he now?" Antonius snapped, ramming his helmet onto his head.

"Leaching his life blood onto the cobbles!" Justinus answered laconically and with obvious satisfaction. "I left Marcellus holding the principia – but not for long I fear," Justinus shouted in order to be heard over the din.

There was no time to say more. They burst in, two warriors brandishing long-swords, faces painted with blue woad. Rallying from the shock, Antonius took the first and Justinus' sword, after a brief struggle, finished his companion. But it was too late for Gaeus. The blow from the massive sword had all but severed the old man's head.

"Ah no!" Antonius made to go to his body but Justinus, face smoke-grimed and gaunt, dragged at his arm

"You cannot help him now. Your place is out there."

Antonius, at once the professional, nodded.

"Stay close Justinus," he shouted as they rushed outside into hell.

Britons, yelling ear-splitting war cries and daubed with woad, swarmed over Mediobogdum: a plague of locusts intent on stripping it bare. The air was thick with the acrid smell of burning and stench of blood. Antonius blinked hard. His eyes, inflamed by the smoke, were streaming.

"Organisation – it's our only chance. We must find Marcellus then split up three ways and each command a section," he bawled over the sounds of the fray. Justinus nodded but Antonius saw the hopelessness in his eyes. "Justinus – be with me if you can."

Justinus bit his lip and nodded; his eyes brimmed with emotion.

"I promise."

Antonius was satisfied that this tribune who was more like a son understood his meaning and would, if humanly possible, keep his word. Time to move.

He stabbed and parried with his sword, using his shield to ram a way through the confusion of bodies. He checked as a huge Briton with a patch over one eye blocked his path, axe raised ready for the death blow. He drew back his sword arm then saw the warrior's eyes glaze as death came from behind. Antonius' eyes met those of the young guard as he withdrew his blade from the dead man's back.

"You saved my life soldier," Antonius said, clasping his forearm, knowing full well he could have dealt with the situation himself; but if the lad was to die, well then it was little enough to give – a word of gratitude from his commander. He pushed past, choked by the radiance of pride on the lad's dirt-streaked face.

He halted at the rear section of the fort. A slash from a Brigante sword had opened his left shoulder and chest, but he was oblivious to the pain and flow of life-blood. He needed to breathe and order his mind and to this end climbed over bodies and up the steps to the rampart and tower where all the guards lay dead. The sky in the far distant east glowed red, as though by some impossible quirk the sun had set in the opposite quarter. He puzzled over this for a moment then smothered a cry as realisation dawned: *Eboracum!* The military H.Q. was also under attack. The orders from Rome had been the undoing of them all, as he knew they would. With so many on sick leave it was madness to send him here with a detachment of two hundred men plus reinforcements, and only this week another of similar size to encamp in a valley north of this one in response to rumours of an uprising there. Rumours, he now had no doubt, that were unfounded and put about deliberately in order to divide and weaken. It had left H.Q. manned at less than half-strength. But there was nothing he could have done in face of those edicts issued by Senate.

Or was there? Would this disaster have been averted had he spoken up and stood his ground? He would never know. Until now the tribes of the North had not shown themselves capable of uniting and organising a concerted attack, so who was behind this and what had motivated them? He blenched beneath the grime and blood that streaked his face as Rowana's words came back to him: Cadoc was originally of the Votadini. The answers were now clear: firstly Cadoc, ambition – and passion. And he, Antonius, must take at least some of the blame for the latter, despite the Rowana's avowal that she had never agreed to his demands for a union.

Secondly Lupinus, nursing some grievance real or imagined or simply consumed by greed, had turned traitor, working undercover with Cadoc. Antonius sighed deeply, his leniency with Lupinus and love for Rowana had proved fatal for them all. But there was no time now for guilt and remorse. Smoke belched and flames leapt to the sky; at least two of the barrack blocks were already ablaze. *The stables are at the rear!*

"Gaudita!" His anguish and love for the mare were carried on that cry. The screams of terrified horses rose above those of dying men. He threw himself down the steps, slipping on blood and men's guts to battle forward, stabbing at Britons and pushing men aside regardless of their allegiance. Images blazed across his mind: Gaudita trapped by the flames, eyes rolling back in her head, hooves helplessly flailing the air. He stopped and listened, then his knees almost buckled with relief as the drumming of stampeding hooves thudded past with all the joy of a victory hymn. Someone had thought to open the stable doors.

Slashing and hacking a way through, he made his way back to the Headquarters building. Marcellus lay sprawled on his back in the gateway, spilling his guts on the ground from a gaping wound in his belly.

"May your gods, whoever they are, be kind my friend." For in the past few months that was what Marcellus the engaging rogue had turned out to be, Antonius reflected. In the early days, after confessing his pilfering of provisions and dereliction of duty. Marcellus had justified the clemency given in consideration of the harshness and isolation of the prefect's lengthy posting into consideration. Pay chests were often delayed, requests for leave and a relief posting were either ignored or denied. Antonius had little sympathy for a Rome that failed to look after the guardians of its far-flung provinces. In recent months Marcellus had proved an exemplary prefect. In this wild and isolated place where infantry, cavalry and officers were all forced into close proximity for weeks and months on end the fabric of formality frayed at the edges. In fact of late they had shared many a cup of wine together. Now Marcellus was dead.

He advanced into the deserted courtyard. It would not remain so for long. Soon they would be here searching for the pay chest and valuable insignia, once the killing was over and looting began. And Justinus, what of him? Was he not to be spared long enough to prevent that rat Cadoc from taking the terrible trophy? Were they not then to die together side by side? Somehow that would have made the inevitable easier to accept. His shoulder and chest were throbbing now, the blood loss sapping his strength. As easy to lie down here and die. And what about that stinkhound Cadoc? Was he to get away with this slaughter? His mind ran on, grabbing at anger to give him a handhold on Life. *Dea Mater!* He would die yes, but avenge the deaths of Gaeus, Justinus, and all his brothers-in-arms by killing Cadoc first and cheating him of the dreaded prize! A vow that sent life-force pumping through his limbs.
"Cadoc, wolf-spunk, where are you?" he roared. He turned slowly on the spot as his voice echoed round the courtyard and beyond. He was smiling now. That proud braggart could not resist such a challenge. He shouted again, his voice rising above the background din.
"Cadoc – are you a stinking coward as well as a self-styled cuckold?" And that should do it. He would come; it was only a question of time. Pain raged in his shoulder and constricted his chest as the minutes passed like hours.

"I am here, Roman pig!"
Antonius swung round on his heel and a cry of pure agony was

torn from his throat. By the light of the leaping flames billowing from the principia, he saw Cadoc standing beneath the arched gateway, Rowana at his side. She was dressed in the golden breastplate and blue cloak of their first meeting, but in place of the studded battle skirt of hide she wore a simple white robe, now torn and splattered with blood. Her face was blackened, and not only by smoke given the swellings and contusions. Nevertheless her beauty still broke his heart.

"You bastard Cadoc! Let her go. Come, fight a man for a change!"

Bloodstained hunting knife in hand, Cadoc advanced into the courtyard dragging Rowana by the arm so that she stumbled and almost fell.

"You dare speak to me of bastards, Roman?" he snarled, his lip curling back to reveal teeth that gleamed white in the grime of his face. Antonius frowned, then gave an involuntary start and the blood drained from his cheeks. He had not guessed; she had said nothing.

"Yes, that's right," the other man taunted. Rowana screamed as he released her arm to grab a handful of her unbound hair. He wound it around his fist and she cried out again as her head was yanked back and her body arched. Antonius watched helplessly; the point of the dagger was resting against Rowana's white throat. He could do nothing but watch as the nightmare unfolded.

"This is for your bastard, Roman."

"No!" Antonius's cry echoed Rowana's scream as Cadoc drew back his arm and plunged the knife deep into her unprotected belly.

"Antonius, my love." The whispered words were her last. She sank to the ground in a pool of blood.

A terrible cry escaped Antonius, the howl of a wounded beast in its last throes. He took a step towards the inert form then realised the futility of the move. Runnels of white on the grimed cheeks marked the progress of his grief but the tears dried in the heat of the flames and his unquenchable anger. A red mist fell over his vision and his voice when he spoke would cause the bravest of men to quake.

"Babe-killer; woman-slayer, I am going to take your head," he snarled.

He had the satisfaction of seeing the warrior before him involuntarily flinch. In the Celtic world this was the worst possible threat; to take a man's head was to hold his spirit captive, hence his plea to Justinus to stay by him and if possible prevent the heinous act. But time had run out and he must act now. If he were to fail that would be his own fate: his head would dangle from Cadoc's bridle. Unspeakable torment if he were to die thus and in full knowledge of the blow that would sever. Cadoc would make sure he knew.

He must not fail.

THIRTY-SIX
Synchronicity

Darcy stands at the main entrance, overcome by a feeling of dread and with tension knotting her stomach. On the moor the air has a crispness and coldness but here at Mediobogdum it is heavy and turgid with moisture. Anxiously she watches the slow seepage of mist as it rolls down the flanks of the high fells and across the crest of the pass enclosing her in a secret world. In the western sky a huge red sun is sinking turning the Scafell range a rosy pink. It is only when it has sunk below the horizon and she stands watching the progress of the mist does she realise something is wrong. Normally white mist should pass without notice over snow; instead it swarms down in a red tide. What she has taken to be reflection from the setting sun is obviously something more sinister.

The clouds roll in and a premature twilight falls. She shivers and glances at her watch: it has stopped. She attempts to move forward but fear forms a barrier across the main gate. Her feet are rooted, limbs feel as heavy as the eagle on her back.

Indomita! Veni, Indomita!

The emotion carried on that silent cry impels her through.

Great Mother help me to help him, she prays without realising it. Because something here is dreadfully wrong.

The principia lies straight ahead: snow has drifted against the walls. It is impossible: there are no walls, she tells herself in panic. Yet there they are, looming through the crimson mist that now covers the spur on which Mediobogdum stands. Such stillness and silence. A pain jabs and stabs with urgency inside her head. Shadows steal through the four gates, gathering at the Headquarters building. The snow crunches like crushed ice beneath her feet and she wants to place a finger against her lips with every footfall. She halts before the principia gate: it is arched and the coping stones that top the walls are visible through the shifting, curling red vapour. The courtyard within swirls with mist that is changing to thick black smoke. She struggles to label the odour in her nostrils. Smoke yes, but something else too, a stench that nauseates and taints the very air. She stops for a moment, trying to place it. That is it: the butcher's shop smell that has haunted her dreams. Her legs begin to tremble. *Am I awake, or is this one of those curious dreams where I am watching myself?* she wonders. She puts her head to one side, listening. There it goes again: the sound of metal studs scraping cobblestones, and with a stealth that fills her with dread.

They circle one another, a pair of cautious cats each awaiting a move from the other. The only sound is the scrape of metal stud on stone.

"You are finished, Roman"

Antonius makes no reply, concentrates instead on deflecting the Briton's blade as it comes slashing down.

"Where is your legion now then?" Cadoc taunts.

Antonius' eyes never leave his opponent's blade.

"I'll tell you then. Nourishing our earth with their blood. Dead or dying – every last one of them! And not just here but at the dalehead shown to you by Myrddin, that 'natural trap of forest and rock' remember? The fate of your reinforcements! And have you seen the sky to the east? Proof that your Headquarters has fallen! The supposed might of Rome is no match for the Brigantes and Votadini alliance. You hadn't reckoned on that, eh Roman?"

With each taunt the warrior's slashes grow wilder. *Discipline and control* Antonius reminds himself over and over. *Let the braggart strut and crow then catch him off guard.*

340

"You disappoint me Roman. I had hoped for better sport."

Good. See how he now grows careless. Antonius waits, eyes narrowed. Now!

He lunges beneath Cadoc' guard.

The Briton bellows with pain and fury. The clink of metal on metal, then as he withdraws his sword Antonius senses metal grating on bone as the blade grazes his opponent's rib. A stain spreads across the warrior's tunic, but the huge bronze disc he wears on his chest prevents the thrust from proving fatal. Antonius dodges the double-handed blows that rain down in retaliation. Exertion further opens the wound to his chest and shoulder and his hand is sticky with blood. He thrusts, and again, but both blows glance harmlessly off the coloured glass bosses on Cadoc's shield. By the light shed from burning buildings he notices irrelevantly how the man's horned helmet gives his shadow the appearance of a demon dancing on the opposite wall.

Breath comes now in painful gasps. The cobbles are slippery with blood. Cadoc notes his weakened state and raising his sword high opens his throat, releasing his war cry. The blade descends; Antonius side-steps and his sword bites deep into the wrist of Cadoc' sword arm. He roars with pain. Antonius smiles; he has waited a long time for this.

"Strike Roman, you may as well, but your whore and your bastard have gone before me."

Antonius sees again that scene in slow motion, the thrust, Rowana sinking to the ground, her lifeless body. His heart is ice. He draws back his arm for the death thrust.

Antonius!

He whirls round at that silent cry.

Darcy gasps with horror as two shapes materialise from the swirls of mist and smoke. Two men circle one another and one of them is:

"Antonius!" she screams.

She strains forward to reach him but cannot push the invisible barrier aside. Her legs are leaden, her feet fast to the ground. Tears of helplessness and frustration course down her face. She watches fresh blood spurt from the wound in his shoulder, sees he is weakening fast.

"Antonius!" she screams again.

Was it Rowana calling to him from Beyond? He turns to listen. Cadoc' hand comes up. Antonius turns again in time to see the flash of the knife. Too late. The steel feels cold in his belly.

"No! Oh God please, no!" Darcy sobs, straining impotently at the invisible barrier. A gyration, incredibly slow and full of bitter grace as he sinks to the ground. Tears streak her smoke-begrimed cheeks with runnels of white that match the ones on his face. Tears of bitterness and grief.

"Antonius, Antonius," she keens aloud.

He cries out to her. A long drawn-out cry he feels sure, yet all he hears is a whimper. The principia wall feels cold and hard to the back. Cadoc' face swims before him, alternately waxing and waning as though in a nightmare. *Have pity, do not bring me back.* He fights hard to remain in the womb of darkness. In the well of darkness where Rowana waits – or is it Indomita? He cannot remember; as in life, the two are confused. A voice loud and rough draws him back to pain and awareness.

"I want his head. Do it."

Cadoc is about to claim his trophy. How terrible to die in that knowledge. Would his spirit really be captive? A greater fear this than any dread of simple dying.

It is of little consolation that the dog cannot manage the deed himself due to his half severed hand. He has brought a henchman to do it; long sword at the ready. Antonius' helmet clatters against the cobbles and he feels a blast of cold air to the head. He watches Cadoc' uninjured hand reach out, feels his fingers grasp his hair .

Darcy is drowning in grief. It all flashes before her, a kaleidoscope of poignant images: Mediobogdum in sun-haze, glimpsed from the crest of the pass; emerald eyes dark with anger, now light with humour but always intense with longing. Sunlight and storm clouds, love and hate but no more doubt; mountains in mist, the lines of his face, that frown; the incredible spiral of intimacy, the name Indomita – and her own lack of courage, a failure to commit.

"Antonius, what can I do?" she pleads.

She tastes blood as she chews her lower lip. His hand is reaching out to her, the seal ring plain to see. He is imploring her to help.

"What can I do my love, what can I do?" she cries again. Her hands claw the invisible wall but it holds, driving her mad with anguish and frustration.

"Let me through! I want to be with you, to die with you if I must!"

She wonders if he can hear her words.

The ultimate sacrifice has been offered; the barrier splinters.

"Leave him alone, wolf-shit!"

Antonius' head jerks forward as the cry rings out and Cadoc' hand releases its hold on his hair. *Justinus.* He sees him through mists of pain. Justinus, soaked with blood, mortally wounded and barely standing but come to fulfil his promise. He is taking on the would-be executioner and surely no man can withstand such righteous fury. *Oh, good man!* The Briton falls to the blood-swilled cobbles, adding his guts to the mess.

"At your back Justinus!"

Somehow the strength is dredged from the pit of his being to croak a warning to this tribune and son he never had. But the brave tribune is weakened by pain and loss of blood and does not hear. *Ah, how I hate to see you fall to that bastard Cadoc. He still has the strength to wield the knife with his other hand. But we'll take him with us Justinus!* One last super-human effort, fingers crawling to reach and curl around the hilt of his sword, unnoticed because he is thought to be beyond action. What little strength remains is gathered with a momentum born of selflessness and righteous rage against the slayer of Rowana and their innocent babe. Nemesis sanctions the cause and hovers on wings of retribution. *Now!* His fingers tighten around the hilt of the gladius; the short stabbing sword is perfect for the task. Beads of sweat run down his face with the effort of shifting his body into a crouch. Cadoc's arm is drawn back for the thrust as Justinus turns his head, somehow aware of his commander's intent. With all remaining strength Antonius lunges forward onto left knee and right foot – an upward surge and all remaining strength focused on the sword arm and the blade cleanly enters Cadoc' belly. A bellow of surprise and rage as realisation dawns and Cadoc drops to the cobbles, blood bubbling through his lips and eyes glazed in death.

Antonius sinks down against the wall as Justinus half raises an arm in thanks then falls to the ground, bleeding profusely following his battle with the would-be executioner. His face is bloodless now and his eyes close. As the final breath leaves his body on a sigh Antonius whispers:

"Farewell for now brave friend, I am soon to join you."

It is hard, yes, but easier to bear than watching him fall to Cadoc.

I wish Death would take me now but Mors seems to be in no great hurry. How much blood can a man cough up and still live? I can bear the pain, now that you have seen to it that I keep my head, Justinus. Without his leadership, Cadoc's clan is no army – just a tribe of undisciplined rebels interested only in finding weapons and gold; they are ready to flee already now he is dead. I can hear them shouting and clattering round the courtyard; the clamour recedes as they head back to the principia, the strong room, and the lusted-after gold. Of course they will find none. Prior to his death that treacherous wolf Lupinus would already have had it away and buried for digging up later once the carnage was over. Satisfaction indeed that he didn't live to enjoy his double treachery.

A leaderless rabble has no interest in trophies that cannot be spent and will soon flee with their loot of weapons, wine and oil. But the standard has gone further north with the detachment on active duty. May *Dea Mater* forgive me if that dog Cadoc spoke true and they have been massacred too. If the standard is taken and lost forever then we shall bear the eternal shame. A whole legion lost if Eboracum has fallen to a combined Votadini and Brigante force. Rome is unforgiving of defeat.

The barrier splinters and Darcy pitches forward into the courtyard. The weight on her back has become unbearable. In her torment she has forgotten the eagle. Now it seems to be crushing her, using its weight as a reminder and urging her to action. Shrugging the rucksack off her shoulders she follows the inner promptings and unfastens the straps with hands that shake and are numb with cold. The eagle, encrusted and filthy yet still emitting its ancient power, is held aloft. He must be here somewhere, but the courtyard is shrouded in shadows and writhing red mist. She calls out hoping he will hear.

"See Antonius, I have it! The standard is in safekeeping. There is no shame! I shall make known what happened here today. You and your legion shall be exonerated."

"Indomita!"

Or is it Rowana, hair lifting in the breeze and the smile is one of pure impudence. Good: the blood grime and horror seem not to have touched her. Strange, but along with the blood, pain is now spilling into the earth. There is no shame. The how's and why's of it are unclear but that doesn't matter. It seems the Eagle of the Ninth has not fallen into enemy hands. *Now I can let go.*

Spinning: spinning along a long dark tunnel that hums with increasing loudness towards a circle of light. Closer it looms, and the brilliance blinds. Light. Lighter. My body feels lighter. No more pain, just pressure. A slight jolt, a shock like diving into an icy pool on a hot day

And

Out!

Into warmth and freedom. Into a sunlit woodland glade. There is birdsong, and the sound of human singing:

> *For your shadow is tied to the moon, to the moon,*
> *Yes your shadow is tied to the moon.*

"Indomita!"

Darcy flings out her hand to reach him and lurches forward into stillness and silence. A cathedral-quiet, the type one is nervous of breaking. No more choking black smoke, just swirls of white mist around a deserted ruin. Somewhere above a raven harshly croaks and the ink stain of its shadow glides over the snow. Then that too disappears as somebody throws the switch and the light goes out on her world.

She came to again, afraid, stiff with cold, and heart-sore. Yet there was peace in the stillness and silence, and a tremendous weight had been lifted from her shoulders; not simply the physical weight of the eagle but the burden that had been lodged there so long that she had of late become accustomed to its presence; paradoxically only by its absence did she become fully aware of its toll. Yet she felt bereft, desolate even; this man Antonius had become so much a part of her life and now he was gone. Guiltily she realised she had scarcely thought of Brant since leaving the farmhouse, let alone attempted to make contact. It had not been possible, she justified, as for not thinking about him she had just been too busy trying to stay alive. Whatever, grief must take its toll and would not be denied. Replacing the eagle in her backpack and stowing the compass in a handy pocket, Darcy took her torch and picked her way over the uneven, overgrown ground to the main gateway and down the approach road.

The circular bath house stood stark in the moonlight, a solid reminder of that first visit and sadness flooded her being. On impulse she turned to face the porta praetoris and solemnly gave the Roman salute. At the roadside she paused again, recalling the burial cairn reported by the Cumberland and Westmorland Archaeology Society. Strangely, despite surrounding drifts the stones when she found it were free of snow as though protected by some inner warmth. She reached up to a branch of the rowan tree growing nearby and plucked a bunch of the berries which she placed on top of the cairn. She had now done all that she could.

Darkness had fallen, yet the light from the galaxy of stars and a full moon on this crisp cold night was reflected by the vast expanse of snow cloaking mountain and valley. A full moon, symbolising a time of completion, she recalled from her research into Celtic beliefs. She stood looking about her indecisively. As weariness both physical and emotional set in, it crossed her mind to return to the village, pick up the car and spend the night in the field hut. The idea was quickly discounted. She must get back to Mab and Brock tonight. Granted Mr Nemo would see to their needs but they may be fretting, and he may be worrying given the snow. It seemed irresponsible to stay away when there was no means of sending a message. Compressing her lips and putting back her shoulders she walked away from Mediobogdum for the last time.

Once you leave my dear, there can be no return
As she climbed the path up to the moor Mr Nemo's words returned to haunt and disturb. It was, she decided, a spin-off from a day crammed with traumatic events: from the ordeal on the Screes and finding of the eagle to that horrific scene at Mediobogdum and culminating in this awful sense of emptiness and loss. The moon-washed and bone white moor deepened the mood, and a palpable death-hush reduced her to tears.

"Antonius, Antonius," she whispered, "Where are you?"

The hairs on the back of her neck rose. From somewhere across the moor there drifted the mournful ululation of a wolf-howl.

At last she stood at the top of the rise above the hunting lodge, aching with weariness and instead of the anticipated relief, filled with apprehension. The house stood defiant as ever, the snow-clad roof stark in the moonlight but somehow dark as ever. She shook off a sense of misgiving. A glass of Mr Nemo's herbal infusion would soon put her to rights; if she knew him at all he would have some already heating on the hob. Thoughts of warmth, food and Mr Nemo's welcome drove her forward again, down through the drifts, through the gap in the wall and across the compound to the back door. As she pushed it open the sudden sound of barking made her start, then once more silence draped itself over the house. She stepped within and flashed her torch beam around the kitchen in search of oil lamp and matches. Her hand froze and she stood there unmoving, rooted to the floor with shock.

THIRTY-SEVEN

~

Table and dresser wore the bloom of neglect, the wood-burning stove was cold, and instead of the warm aroma of baking bread the place reeked of damp and mould. The oil lamp sat in its usual place on the table, but the matches were damp and refused to ignite when struck. Instead she used the old flint lighter kept by Mr Nemo for lighting his pipe, and as the yellow glow from the lamp revealed more dust and cobwebs, stood looking about her in dismay. For a moment – given stress and exhaustion, the moonlit night and the snow that hid and distorted the landscape, she wondered if she had entered the wrong house. Maybe it had been someone else's dog barking. *There's no other house up there* – the postmistress's words returned to mock her. Disoriented and heart pounding she hesitated, then moved to the utility room and opened the door. A sigh of relief escaped her as Mab and Brock blinked in the sudden light and looked up at her sleepily from their bed. She was in the right place and definitely was not losing her marbles; two bowls had been placed by the dogs' bed.

"He promised to bring you a bowl of bread and milk each," she said sadly, picking up the now empty dishes to place them on the dusty kitchen table. Mab and Brock seemed strangely unfazed by events and she found herself wondering what herbal mixture had found its way into that milk. Indeed their eyes were closing even before she pulled the door to.

Lighting a candle in a brass holder from the oil lamp she began to search for Mr Nemo. She called him once, but the sound of her voice and his name echoing through the old house, rippling the silence but obtaining no answer, was too disturbing to be repeated. The books in the sitting room lay beneath a layer of dust and loneliness and the grate held only peat ash and cinders. The bed in the room that had been Mr Nemo's was empty and had the air of one that had not been slept in for a long time. Her own room was much as she left it, except it looked tired and dusty and the lace at the window was yellowed and moth-eaten in places resembling the cobwebs that draped the corners of wall and ceiling. Propped up on the dressing table was a cream envelope addressed to herself in a dated but elegant hand using sepia ink and, she would guess, a dip-in pen with a proper nib.

With hands that shook she put down the candle and picked up the letter, holding it closer to the flame in order to examine it more closely and postpone the breaking of the seal. Finally she found the courage to open it, take out the single watermarked sheet and begin to read:

My dear Child

> *Try not to be too sad. I know how you must be feeling but you are not yet seeing the whole picture. You are weeping because he is dead, are you not? But was he not dead before – and by some two thousand years? So what is different tonight except you have witnessed the manner of his dying? I can feel your indignation Darcy, you want to accuse me of callousness, and of disbelieving you, of saying he does not exist. But maybe you are saying that?'*

"No!" she exclaimed aloud, shaking her head vehemently so that the candle flame dipped and rose in the draught, "I could never say that," then was disconcerted on starting to read again for it was as though this wise old man had heard her exclamation.

> *Are you saying then, do you think, that Death as you understand it does not exist? And that Time as you know it has no relevance?*

349

Good. I think you are beginning to take the point!

All will be well dear child; you know what has to be done. With restoration comes healing.

Finally, I deeply regret the manner and suddenness of my leaving. Tonight of all nights you should not be coming back to a cold and empty house. I did warn you that once you leave you cannot return. You had no choice in this; neither did I. Even so, I wish I could have been here to welcome you in person and ease your sorrow, but be sure that all is well with me and as it should be, and my thoughts are with you. Sleep sound for you shall be held safe.

Wear the pendant from time to time and think kindly of an old man.

You have done well and undergone much. It will not be forgotten: you shall reap your reward for helping to right a great wrong.

Nemo

Now she understood that strange comment about not being able to return. He had not meant to the house itself, but to that particular status quo in which she found it. The candle guttered in a sudden draught from the window and she leaned closer to read again the last paragraph. She shivered in the cold stream of air then exclaimed aloud as the flame flared and curved towards her, seeming almost to leap across the intervening space to the sheet of paper. It licked at the top right corner then fanned by the air current greedily devoured, licked and bronzed the tinder dry document until she was forced to drop it onto a china tray on the dressing table. A sudden blaze, then all that remained was a curl of black ash. The flame of the candle settled and burned steadily again as though it had done its work. Darcy sighed and tears of loneliness, exhaustion and self-pity coursed down her cheeks. A night of loss indeed. Now she had nothing.

You have the eagle, child; and there is work yet to be done.

She whirled round at the sound of the sibilant voice that seemed to come from the threshold. The door moved to and fro slightly in the draught. Nobody is there, she realised sadly. Seconds passed then she exclaimed aloud; she had read often about the 'aha! principle' describing how scientists make their greatest discoveries; that seminal moment that had nothing to do with theories and logic and workings out and everything to do with a burst of intuitive knowing that made them exclaim aloud – as she had just done. She hurried across to the bedside cabinet, took out the Pocket Gem of Latin Words and Phrases that she had taken to keeping with her of late and rushed back to the candle.

Feverishly she leafed through with fingers still numbed and tingling with cold. She peered closely at the small print, struggling to decipher it in the light from the solitary candle. it was there. In fact it had been staring her in the face all along ever since coming to this house: *Nemo* and the meaning: *Nobody*

No *body.* There was a sound suspiciously like Mr Nemo's laughter, but it may have been merely the wind chimes in the rowan tree stirring in the night breeze. She shivered again at the touch of cool air that caressed her skin like the soft winds up there at Mediobogdum. Suddenly weariness overcame her and unable to think any longer she lay down on the bed and slept.

She does receive her reward. Around 2 am and something – a sense of weightlessness maybe causes Darcy to open her eyes. It is difficult to keep them open; sleep whirls in lazy coils filling her head and a sensation of warmth and lightness brings a buzz, a high. At first the location seems alien, suffused with an aura of strangeness, but there is the cracked oval mirror on the dressing table, pale as a nun's face in the moonlight. There is something odd: the bed is below and the ceiling close enough to reach up and touch. It doesn't make sense to float around naked in winter, yet there is no sensation of cold and it all seems perfectly natural. Yet the weightlessness, the feeling of being out of her body is at odds with the sensations. How can one tingle with arousal without a body to be aroused? Then comes realisation: she is not alone and their essence is now the same.

351

His warmth seeps into every pore. He is there, visible on that screen at the back of the mind, hair the deep bronze of dying bracken and eyes the green of a mountain pool. He too is naked, stripped of Roman finery, body lean, hard and firm. He is insistent in his advances yet is still holding back.

Me invoce Indomita Me invoce!

Obediently she calls his name once, twice and thrice, understanding that he is not allowed now to invade but must be invited.

And now he, Antonius, no longer holds back. He is no longer on the screen at the back of her mind, but clasping her to him, to his body of pulsing light.

It is frightening to be swept along on a flood of absolute intimacy. What is it like? She tries to describe the experience. A hurricane of emotion that turns the body electric blue; a furnace of feeling that melts flesh and bone leaving the spirit exposed and open to ultimate joy; an end to loneliness and separateness so there is nothing left in the Universe to fear. Yes, that is what it is like.

Dimitte! Dimitte!

But she is too frightened to let go. Strangely she understands despite not knowing the language. There is a shared knowing that has nothing to do with words. *Hold back, hold or he will devour your soul! Close your mind and shut him out before it is too late.* It is already too late: too late to resist this whirlwind of love that sucks everything down to its centre. All within is flux. Sparks of red and gold are flying, a firmament of stars that are reeling, wheeling and dying as the universe implodes. Too strong to resist; there is nothing for it but to let go.

There follows a lull, a moment of detachment in which to think how odd, no weight pressing down, no sighs or trickles of sweat or odour of love, only this essence of masculinity, the imperiousness of the commander and the tenderness of the man. The stillness passes and she moans, dying a little with each invisible thrust. She places her hand on her belly and feels the surge, the bulk of his invisible phallus beneath the flesh.

352

He is within and without and in total possession. The struggle is over, the clash of wills resolved. Stroke for stroke they are matched as souls unite. Now there is no more holding back, only a letting go to oblivion – and possible death.

She doesn't die. She awakes and lies drowsing and replete in the rays of sunlight that slant across the bed.

"Antonius" she whispers, and a smile lights her face as she hugs her secret. Nobody should know of what happened last night, not Brant, not Caro or anyone else. It was for her alone to know, and in any case she would not be believed. He is no longer in pain and torment but free, she thinks with gratitude, and a weight lifts from her heart as the shadow of his shame melts away in the sunlight.

But there is still work to be done. Swinging her legs off the bed Darcy crossed to the window and looked out on a cerulean sky and sunlit moor. Snow drips and slides from the rowan tree branches and falls to the earth with an audible *plop* revealing the blood red berries. The chimes sway and tinkle in a light breeze. Whilst gathering and packing her things a thought struck: the eagle Mr Nemo was carving – he had said it would be hers once it was finished. She carried her bag downstairs intending to look for it but then suddenly stopped as his exact words came to mind: *This is for you*, he had said holding out the carving, then *When it is finished of course*. She knew then there would be no carved eagle for her to find. It was one of Mr Nemo's enigmatic riddles. The 'it' to be finished referred to the trauma of the past twenty four hours. Her 'gift' was to be the recovery of the real eagle, the one being fashioned from wood being merely a symbol. She smiled and hurried down the last few steps into the hall and made her way to the utility room to rouse Mab and Brock ready for the journey.

She set off immediately, munching on a piece of mint cake to sustain her for the trek. Mab and Brock raced around in the Mr Whippy snow, apparently none the worse for their experience. She paused at the top of the rise, had promised herself she would not look back but was unable to resist the temptation. The house stood with its back to the sun, face shrouded in shadow and chimneys rearing against the heavens, bold and dark and rejecting pity. The windows were shuttered against the sunlight, the chimneys blocked; smoke from the peat fire would no longer rise above the mottled slate roof. Yet it stood proud in its background of loneliness, sadness and hope – a Wuthering Heights of a house waiting for smouldering Heathcliff to bring back his Cathy.

"Farewell Mr Nemo, and thank you," she said softly, cradling the pendant that hung from the chain around her neck.

About an hour and half later she drew up outside the farmhouse on the cliffs. Despite the constant warmth of the Aga there was an air of absence and neglect about the house. At first she felt apprehensive about entering but her fears proved unfounded: no slime or mounds of writhing worms awaited and she had to remind herself all that was in the past. That realisation brought mixed feelings: relief of course, but also an emptiness that brought a lump to her throat. It also engendered a feeling of insecurity: now she had to function again in a world that was hard-edged and unfamiliar. There was heartfelt relief however from the knowledge that Ted Tulley was no longer a problem.

Mab and Brock were tired from their trek across the moor and after wolfing down a meal they settled in their basket. Darcy wandered aimlessly round the house for a while, noting with some concern that Brant had not been home since she last saw him. The absence of socks on the bathroom floor, or a whisky tumbler on the coffee table, tea stains on the drainer and all the other little things that normally irritated were now sadly missed. She decided it was time to pull herself and her life together, starting with Brant. Moving to the telephone she picked up the receiver and prepared to dial his mobile number, but the message tone sounded and she decided to check it out first. She froze and closed her eyes in dismay. Here was the telephone call she had always dreaded.

354

THIRTY-EIGHT

~

It was a spokesman for Brant's Department, saying they had tried several times to contact her and needed to speak urgently. She pressed the pad to return the call but there was no response. Obviously this was a top security matter and she would have to key in her special coded number. She dialled, listening to the thump-thud of her heart beat along with the ringing out tone.

"Mrs Kennedy", a voice said at last.

"Yes. Is Brant all right?"

"We have been trying to contact you but-,"

"Just tell me – yes or no will do," she said tersely, gripping the pendant fiercely with her free hand and whispering *'please God, please God,'* over and over.

"Yes, we think so."

"Thank God!"

"Bear in mind Mrs Kennedy as yet we have no official confirmation."

"I understand. What has happened?"

"A terrorist attack. Your husband was on the Underground; they have taken a group of passengers hostage. We have reason to believe he is amongst them."

"Was any one killed?" she asked breathlessly as her chest constricted.

There was a brief silence then the voice answered.

"Yes, but I'm sure you appreciate that I am unable to discuss the details."

"How do you know he was not one of them?"

"We have reason to believe-,"

"For God's sake!" she exploded.

"I cannot discuss the details, Mrs Kennedy," the voice intoned again, "But please believe that we have every reason to think he is alive and well."

"What happens now; what shall I do?" she asked crumpling as the reality of the situation registered.

"Nothing. We wait – and let us know immediately if anyone makes contact."

"And you will…"

"Of course. Try not to worry Mrs Kennedy."

The line went dead.

Feeling as though she moved through a nightmare Darcy ran through her other messages. Caro! She pressed 'return call' and waited, praying that she would answer.

The sound of her friend's voice brought forth a heartfelt sigh of relief.

"Caro?"

"Thank God! I've been worried sick, what with Ted Tulley's body being found and knowing you were up there alone. And now this." Caro's voice was unnaturally high with stress. "How did you-,"

"Just got back – on my messages. They think Brant is one of the hostages."

"I kept waiting to hear from you."

"There was no signal."

"At least you are safe. Stay cool, Darcy, Brant will be okay."

"Oh God, Caro – he has to be!"

"It will be fine, honey – trust me. Look, what are you going to do?"

"I'm off to Manchester right now."

"What if the Department rings again?"

"I can divert my calls and messages to the flat and they have my mobile number for when I'm travelling."

"I'll meet you there in a couple of hours."

"Thanks Caro. I need you."

"And I'll be there. Drive carefully – we want you in one piece to welcome Brant home!"

Not for the first time Darcy wondered as she put down the receiver what on earth she would do without Caro.

Mab and Brock were deposited with Mrs Jenkins in the village and Darcy drove on to Manchester. A maelstrom of emotions whirled her from guilt, to love, to fear and regret, hope to despair and back again. Already wearied by the physical exertion of the previous day and depleted by the emotional strain involved, by the time she arrived outside the flat nothing made much sense. She let herself in, busied herself with routine things like boiling a kettle for tea as an immediate comfort and preparing for Caro's arrival by raiding the freezer for food and the cabinet for wine. Only then did she reach for the remote, turn on the set and after taking a deep breath scroll down to the News Channel.

No change, was the bottom line. The initial stand-off had been defused and the kidnappers had made their demands, the basic ones of which like food and communication equipment had been met. As to their more serious demands, the authorities were in discussion. Thank God for that at least, Darcy thought, angry kidnappers were bad news for hostages. She forced back the tears whilst viewing scenes of police officers patrolling the area to keep it clear of the public, knowing that Brant was inside there and possibly hurt or worse. The phone shrilled and she jumped violently then leapt off the settee. Call divert was redundant.

"Just to let you know things are under control Mrs Kennedy, and that we know where you are should you be needed."

"Thank you." No point in asking how they knew; the Department knew everything but said nothing.

"No news is good news Mrs Kennedy."

"I hope you are right."

"Don't worry, we are."

"Are the authorities negotiating?" *Just give them whatever they want*, her heart cried, even though her head told her this would be wrong and endanger future lives. But love focuses the emotions; paradoxically makes us selfish on behalf of the beloved; how else could it move mountains? All she wanted was Brant away from there and safe in her arms.

"I'll call with any news Mrs Kennedy."

She sighed with frustration and replaced the receiver. All she could do now was wait.

She felt better the minute Caro walked through the door. Solid and dependable yet witty and stylish she exuded calm and common sense. After enfolding Darcy in a bear hug she poured two glasses of wine, made Darcy prepare the salad ingredients she had brought telling her it was best to keep busy.

"Put that frozen stuff in the fridge for you and Brant later," she said with positive emphasis on his name. Taking charge, she bustled about. Fishing a pack of fresh pasta and tub of tomato and basil sauce from out of her bag she set about cooking the meal.

"Quick and simple tonight," she said, tossing the pasta in the heated sauce and piling it into two dishes.

"Sorry Caro, I can't eat tonight," Darcy said putting down her spoon and fork.

"Yes you can," Caro said firmly, "You only think you shouldn't!"

Darcy had to secretly admit there was something in this but still did not start to eat.

"Come on Darcy buck up! Brant is being strong you can bet your life on that, so keep up your strength for his sake. They may need you to communicate with them, you know, make an appeal. If so you need your wits about you."

"You think that might happen?"

"It could. I don't mind betting the other hostages are ordinary citizens; the Secret Services will use everything they have, including their agent's wife."

"You're right, they will use anything and anyone." Darcy's voice held a hint of bitterness but under Caro's watchful eye she did pick up her knife and fork. She had to admit once she started to eat that given the meagre diet and exertions of the previous day she was actually very hungry and feeling decidedly weak.

Later they sat with their glasses of wine and the T.V. on mute but with subtitles so they could talk without missing any developments. "The Department will let you know first anyway," Caro reassured her.

"We won't get to know anything by watching this," Darcy disclosed. "If the S.S. are sent in to negotiate or storm the place it will be top security and absolute secrecy – no-one will know about it until it is all over."

"So do you want to tell me what happened at the field camp? To take your mind off things whilst we are waiting."

"There's plenty to tell," Darcy admitted, nodding. A meal and fortifying glass of wine had restored her strength and also faith in Brant's ability to survive, and whilst feeling no less worried she felt more able to cope with the trauma. "I did go out to Ambrose Nemo's place; in fact I stayed there for a while."

"What are you like? You do take some risks Darcy."

"Yes I did actually, but not concerning Mr Nemo."

"Ted Tulley? Then as Darcy nodded Caro added "Tell me."

Darcy related the story, her expression and flat tone of voice reflecting her distress at the memory.

"Good riddance to him Darcy! Waste no sympathy there," Caro declared brusquely as she finished. "Thank God though you weren't involved directly in his death. It's very strange how that mad farm dog attacked him but not you, but let's just say thank God for that too!"

A little smile hovered around Darcy's mouth and she turned her head and coughed in order to conceal it. Caro was sticking to the reported version of Tulley's death, but obviously that was her coping strategy and it was not for anyone else to challenge.

"In fairness Caro, he had been got at by the same force that drew me in. "

359

"Greed and paranoia you mean, once he found that hoard of Roman coins on his land!"

"The police found the hoard then?"

"Oh, fancy forgetting to tell you about that! But a hundred or so silver denarii were completely nothing compared with fears for your safety! Yes, his wife spilled the beans once she knew he was dead. The coins were wrapped in oiled cloths and then in a bitumen-coated box and were perfectly preserved and therefore very valuable."

"I already knew – but not the details." Darcy nodded; there was satisfaction in having her deductions confirmed.

"Anyway, you went through a terrible time but it didn't turn you into a double murderer. And it didn't put the rapist tendencies in him either; they must have been there and dormant Darcy, so don't be naïve."

"He lost his mind at the end, and I can't help feeling for Jane Tulley." Darcy shook her head sadly.

"There is probably an element of relief for her that the nightmare is over. My guess is he terrorised her into silence. But what about the man from Defra's widow? Her husband's chest blown out just for doing his job! No Darcy. If you are ever tempted to feel sorry for him, just stop and think – it was very nearly a triple! It would have been the discovery of *your* body I was reading about in the papers and hearing on the news!"

"I guess you're right."

"I am!

"Now, back to Mr Nemo," Caro said, assuming her no-nonsense lecturer's tone normally reserved for recalcitrant students and designed to discourage further discussion on a particular topic. "Has he held on to his marbles? He must be getting on by now."

"A little eccentric I suppose," Darcy said carefully, "but fully *compos mentis*." She paused and winced at this involuntary use of the Latin and the memories it conjured, then noticed Caro looking at her with suspicion so carried on speaking.

"He was charming and very learned and cultured actually." Which was absolutely true and no need to disclose more, even if she knew how to put his powers and the nature of his existence into words, which she did not, though she did add: "and far more complex than he at first seemed.

"So what happened?"

"It would take all night; I think it would be easier to show you something first!" So far she had made no mention of her momentous find. Darcy rose and went into to the hall and returned carrying the rucksack.

On first seeing the contents Caro exhaled the air from her lungs in a long drawn out hiss. Then whilst Darcy made coffee, she worked in silence and with great intensity using a minute set of pocket tools to scrape away the debris from a very small area. This done to her satisfaction she stood back and surveyed the whole, then took measurements and recorded all her findings in a notebook from her bag.

"Do you know what you have here?" she asked in awed tones, clasping her hands together to still their trembling as she struggled to suppress her excitement.

"I think so. But you tell me."

"Well without doing the appropriate research and tests, I can't say conclusively – but for Chris'sakes Darcy, I'm something like 99 per cent certain this is an eagle cast in gold from the top of a Roman standard, and look," she gestured excitedly for Darcy to approach the table. "See this." She pointed to the area she had been working on at the base of the emblem. "Look what is inscribed there!"

Darcy stared at the small cleaned area in the encrusted gold plaque and the legend she had dreamed of: *Legio IX*

It made all the difference, seeing it spelled out.

"But how did you know to clean it off just there?" she asked impressed.

"Well forgive the pun, but the design is 'standard'," she said with a smile.

"Caro!"

"I know, awful wasn't it," Caro said mischievously, her laughter sharp-edged with near-hysteria. She quickly sobered as though feeling levity was inappropriate at such a time, so that Darcy wanted to reassure her and tell her it was okay – that a bit of lightness and normality helped rather than offended.

"Are you going to let me take it back to the Archaeology Department at Hilldean for testing and verification?" Caro asked, patently trying not to appear pushy or insensitive.

"Where else?"

Darcy raised a wan smile at Caro's expression of sheer delight and excitement.

"Oh Darcy that's wonderful! It will put us on the map!"

"You deserve it Caro. But there is one condition."

"Oh?" Some of Caro's euphoria evaporated.

"No worries. But you must help me do things right. For starters, no way is it getting carted off to London! And I'll need your help setting up the rest but first off we contact the York museum."

Darcy outlined her plan, pausing now and then as fear for Brant intruded and she almost broke down, then pulling herself together by concentrating on staying strong for his sake.

Somehow she got through that night. Just before midnight the telephone shrilled and Darcy rushed to answer, her face suddenly chalk white. Her hand shook as she lifted the receiver. At first there was no response then a series of clicks that filled her with alarm. She was about to replace it when the man spoke.

"Mrs Kennedy, it's me again. I'm calling you on the secure line with an up-date. We have it on good authority that your husband and all the hostages are alive and being treated well. And some good news; we hope to effect release tonight."

"Will it endanger his life?"

"Aim to stay positive Mrs Kennedy. Please, try to get some sleep now."

Before she could ask further questions the line went dead.

At 1.30a.m. Caro insisted Darcy went to bed. She did so, but rose several times, left the bedroom so as not to disturb Caro and paced the living room floor. She felt as though she would go mad from helplessness and frustration. She wanted to do something, anything, to help Brant but could only stay by the telephone and wait. She started as the door was pushed open but it was only Caro.

"Can't sleep?"

Darcy shook her head.

"Okay, here's what we do: I'll make a pot of tea and as I still don't know the full script you can tell me the rest of the story," Caro said making her way to the kitchen. Darcy nodded and sat down to wait. The finding of the eagle had grabbed the limelight, then the 'phone call from The Ministry had ousted everything but talk of Brant.

"Do you really think he'll be all right Caro, or are you just saying it to make me feel better?"

Caro nursed her mug of tea and looked Darcy in the eye.

"I believe it in here." She tapped her ample chest and nodded to emphasise the gesture. "Look sweetheart, you know better than I that Brant is trained in conflict resolution and hostage management."

"He will know what to do, will help the others stay calm," Darcy agreed, nodding. "He always says it is the sudden flashpoint action or word that triggers tragedy."

"There you go then."

It was true about the training and Darcy gleaned some comfort from the thought. Although Brant's field was astro-physics, because he was attached to the M.O.D. and his work often took him into designated high-risk zones, training in dealing with such situations as this had been mandatory. "It's just that if after denying him a baby the worst happens-," she broke down and was unable to continue.

"I guessed you might be thinking along those lines. But you can't start a family Darcy on a worst scenario basis! It has to be something you both want at the time, *all* the time."

"Well, put like that-,"

"Truth can sound brutal at times, but that's where it is at."

"Yes mother!" Darcy smiled through her tears and reaching across touched Caro's hand in gratitude.

"So, what did you get up to at Mister Nemo's?" Caro asked in a factual manner. "Apart that is from finding the most sought-after Roman relic in the world!"

Darcy related a brief and emotionally-cleansed version of the scene she had witnessed at Mediobogdum, then her return to the house only to find it empty and ended on the burning of Mr Nemo's letter.

"You were not meant to bring it back into this reality," Caro said promptly.

"I did wonder about that," Darcy said thoughtfully, unconsciously fingering the pendant. "it wouldn't do to have that sort of proof, would it?"

"No. Yet you still have that!" Caro pointed to the pendant on its chain around Darcy's neck. "You know, I'm still not comfortable with that incident. Was there do you think some connection?"

"Let's just say it's a good job you didn't come on this field trip with me and leave it at that," Darcy said, attempting a smile. It was odd, the way Caro appeared to accept certain aspects of the 'unknown', yet rejected others almost to the point of sprinkling holy water! But then, she supposed, most people were like that. All of it was exciting to whisper and speculate about, but not so when things actually started happening to yourself, or under your nose to someone you know. Expertly she geared the talk round to a safer topic.

"So how do you rate my theory about a three-pronged attack that wiped out most of the Ninth?" she challenged.

Caro sat up on her seat, her interest immediately engaged.

"It works. There have been all sorts of theories of course from historians, archaeologists and even the military but they all leaked water in places. Your version best fits known events and answers the main question of how a whole legion trained in Roman precision, obedience and tactics, stationed in a top security fortress, could either just 'disappear' or be defeated by an undisciplined hoard. If you are right, Rome would instantly put into action a major cover-up and damage limitation exercise. It would be seen as a major cock-up and wouldn't be tolerated; it would undermine the army's morale and give out wrong signals to Rome's enemies. Any survivors would be immediately whipped off to somewhere like the Lower Rhine out of the way, which explains the stamped tiles belonging to the Ninth found in Holland. Later they were probably offered a handsome exit package in exchange for their silence – backed up of course by death threats to ensure they kept it!"

"Will the 'experts' buy it?"

"If not, they would have to disprove it."

"And I'll challenge them!" Darcy declared, her eyes briefly shining as she mentally picked up the standard for Antonius. "The truth about what happened must be told."

"He really got to you, didn't he?" Caro said softly.

"Why the hell do you think I'm feeling so guilty about Brant now?"

Darcy's eyes filled with tears; it was the first time Caro had referred to him as a person.

As though to assuage some of that guilt she turned to the television and clicked on the remote to restore the sound.

"Oh my God! Something is happening!" she cried, standing up in her agitation. The outside broadcast showed people thronging outside the Underground entrance being held in check by uniformed divisions. A couple of helicopters droned and hovered like giant dragonflies above the water of the Thames and several ambulances, blue lights flashing, waited on the ground. "Oh God Caro, what's going on? Why haven't they told me anything?"

"Stay cool Darcy, it will be okay," Caro soothed, rising to place an arm around her friend's shoulders but Darcy could see the anxiety in her eyes.

"What in hell's name are they doing?" Darcy cried. "They'll push them into violence with all this activity. They've got communications systems down there remember, they'll know what is going on."

"We have to just wait Darcy."

"Wait be damned! I'm going to call the Ministry."

She dialled the coded number with fingers that fumbled so that she had to start over again. There was no connection.

The telephone call came at 5.16a.m.

Caro, who was slumped on the sofa dozing, stirred and blinked as though trying to make sense of her surroundings. Darcy was already picking up the receiver.

"Yes?" she said tersely.

Caro hauled herself upright and grabbed Darcy's hand as she cried out.

"Oh Darcy, love," Caro whispered in a broken voice. Fearing the worst she held tighter to her friend's hand.

"Brant! Oh, Brant!" Darcy cried out again, and weeping she slumped against the back of the settee.

THIRTY-NINE

~

"Brant is it really you?" Darcy sobbed, relief kicking in to unravel her previous stoicism. "Where are you?"

"I'm leaving right now for the flat."

"Oh thank God, Brant. I thought-,"

"I know; but I'm fine Darcy. Go get some sleep now. I'll be with you in about four hours."

"Will they let you?" Darcy said suddenly afraid her brief joy would be snatched away by the Department.

"I've had a mini-debrief and a couple of hours sleep. They are letting me home to you now but then I go to Manchester H.Q. for debriefing proper."

"So what time did they get you out?" she said indignantly. "Nobody called-,"

"I'll explain later. I'm on my way darling."

The line went dead and Darcy grabbed Caro and squeezed her tight.

"He's safe, Caro, he's safe!" she chanted over and over again.

Given the evidence of the clock on the bedside table she must have dozed for an hour or so but had no recollection of falling asleep. She opened her eyes at the sound of Caro's voice drifting through from the living room.

"Go on in; I'll wait here."

It must be a dream. Her eyelids drooped again, then seconds later she opened them as a voice whispered in her ear.

"Hello sleepyhead."

"Brant!"

He was standing by the bed looking down at her, weariness etched onto his features, his clothes crumpled and chin shadowed, but with a smile upon his lips.

"Sorry I didn't have time to wash and dress for the occasion!"

"Brant!" She was up and out of the bed and into his arms before he could speak again.

Five minutes later he gently disentangled himself from her arms saying

"I could use a shower and change of clothes my love, and er Caro is out there," he added in an embarrassed whisper, jerking his head at the door, "So I guess we have to put this on hold till later, but don't you go anywhere!"

"It's a date!" Darcy said, her eyes shining with joy as she watched him walk to the bathroom.

Late afternoon and Caro had gone, bearing a huge bouquet from Brant and a suspiciously bulky backpack that fortunately Brant did not seem to find unusual. She hugged Darcy and gave her a knowing look, saying she would be in touch during the next day or two.

Darcy and Brant sat down together with a coffee and it seemed neither could tear their gaze from the other. Apart from a few terse inquiries from Darcy about the other hostages and equally brief answers from Brant, they talked about Caro, what to do for dinner that evening and all the normal things that couples usually talk about. It seemed neither of them wanted to depart from this semblance of normality that felt so safe and secure.

"I have to go to the office Brant," Darcy said reluctantly after a while, then when Brant groaned she added wryly "to see if I still have a job! So why don't you have a nice relaxing bath then get your head down for a couple of hours? We have a lot of catching up to do later and right now you must be shattered."

"Okay. I am rather tired. But don't let Frank send you off on some wild assignment – I mean it Darcy," he warned sternly, taking hold of her wrist as though he would not let her leave. "I want you back here again a.s.a.p. You've been through a helluva lot too you know – that apart, I've hardly seen you in weeks and we need some time together."

"I promise."

"Besides," he brushed back his hair from his forehead in a self-conscious gesture and looked away, " I've missed you like hell," he added gruffly.

"Don't worry darling, I'm almost back already!" she said stroking his hair before grabbing her bag and heading for the door.

Frank Kelly peered at her over the top of his gold-rimmed spectacles when she appeared in the doorway of his office. Which was not a particularly auspicious sign, she reflected, as he had taken to wearing contact lens but on difficult days found they made his eyes sore and inflamed. Specs meant a stressed-out Frank – and that was not good.

"Good afternoon madam; can I help you?" he inquired with exaggerated politeness.

"Okay Frank. I'm sorry."

"Should I know you madam?"

Grinning despite her trepidation at this reception Darcy held up her hands in a gesture of surrender.

"Come on Frank, you've had your little joke." And indeed he had: she had been treated like a visitor and an unwelcome one at that. He had kept her in the waiting room for fifteen minutes before telling an embarrassed and apologetic receptionist to 'send Miss West up'.

"This had better be good," he growled, ramming his cigar into the right hand corner of his mouth, then manoeuvring it to the left via contortions of lips and tongue as he waved her to the opposite seat.

"Oh it is Frank, but I'm not about to offer excuses."

"No?" He assumed an expression of exaggerated surprise so that once again she felt a nervous desire to giggle but suppressed it in time.

"Look," he continued, sighing "I know about Brant of course – must have been hell for you – but that was during the past twenty four hours and we are talking of almost two week's absence here, and no word!"

Darcy stared at him in confusion: was it really only that long? It felt as though she had been away for half a lifetime.

"I had to go; I was stranded; there was no signal – and I almost got myself murdered!"

"Pity."

"You mean pity they didn't succeed?" she said eyeing him with suspicion.

"Darcy would I say or even think a thing like that?" He twirled the cigar between thumb and forefinger and to her relief she saw the gleam of amusement in his eye.

"Whatever," she said shrugging dismissively as though to say 'let's get down to business here please', "I have not one but *two* scoops for you Frank!"

"Oh yeah?"

"You're being hard work boss."

"Good – you gave me much grief buggering off like that, time you had some back."

"Look, I didn't go off on some relaxing jaunt you know! Besides you knew where I was from my phone call. I took a lot of risks and had a lot of hurt – and all in the course of my job."

"Job my fanny! You were off chasing some imaginary guy in skirt and sandals.

At this Darcy did laugh aloud. "Don't let him hear you Frank! Serious now, I've got a couple of brilliant inside stories that will have the Nationals slavering."

"Oh yeah, well the hostage's wife angle is always worth something," he admitted, puffing on his cigar and squinting at her through a haze of blue smoke.

"No – although come to think of it that makes it the hat trick! But think *big* Frank – then bigger again!" she said, leaning forward, eyes shining with excitement.

"Okay, shoot."

"How about these for headlines: 'A narrow escape: I was almost Ted Tulley's last victim' and 'Eagle and Honour Restored: My quest for the Lost Ninth Legion'."

"Are you kidding me Darcy to get your own back?"

"No way. Ted Tulley stalked and assaulted me remember?" She paused as he nodded, the cigar bobbing up and down as he did so, "well he followed me to this place I stayed and twice tried to stab me to death. The second time-, well it was the last."

"Christ! You were there when he was killed?"

"I sure was. But I don't want to put that about; you see I didn't go to the police. I've already roughed something out to cover it – I simply end by saying I heard a terrible growling sound followed by a scream, and ran into the night, that sort of thing."

"They'll want to question you though." Frank was moving to and fro on his chair now, eyes almost closed whilst chewing on his cigar, a sure sign of his excitement. "But the coroner has returned a 'misadventure' verdict. I guess you'd get away with it," he muttered as though to himself.

"Bloody hell Darcy," he boomed, stroking his forehead. "I'm scared to ask about the second one!"

"You'll love it: I found the Eagle of the Lost Ninth."

"Now you *are* joking."

She shook her head whilst holding his gaze. "Caro Stevens is 99% certain already but It's gone to Hilldean University Archaeology Department for testing and official verification."

"My God, Manchester is going to be on the map – and the epicentre will be the News, these blessed offices!"

"That's right chief."

"Well, I have to take it all back Darcy – you've done a magnificent job. I just wish you'd go about it in a slightly more conventional way!"

"You sound like Chief Superintendent Strange sounding off at Morse."

"Well now I know how he feels. Hey hang on a minute, I ain't got Strange's corporation yet!" he exclaimed in mock indignation whilst slapping his ample belly. Suddenly his eyes narrowed.

"Okay, what's the price?"

"They're both of them long and thrilling stories and will have to be serialised." She stated, not bothering to pretend ignorance of his meaning.

"You have a column remember? You ain't got a page yet never mind a bloody supplement!"

"So give me one."

The cigar moved rapidly from one side of his mouth to the other and back again. "Okay, you got your page."

"Double of course," she said innocently.

"What! Never!"

"And centre spread, full colour and with a Leader from yourself of course – oh, and trails for the next five days to allow me time to write the first couple of instalments."

"Are sure you that will be all?" he asked silkily.

"Well you can throw in promotion too if you like."

"Out!"

She rose laughing and crossed to the door.

"Go show that guy of yours how glad you are to have him home," he said quietly.

She didn't miss the note of sadness and guessed what he was thinking.

"I shall."

"I don't know how the poor devil puts up with you mind!"

"See you tomorrow Frank."

"Well done girl! "Oh, and Darcy-," he added as she reached the door.

"Yes?"

"I'd have personally shot that bastard had you come to any harm."

"I know it Frank."

She smiled and closed the door.

After an early dinner Darcy and Brant sat down together sipping coffee and brandy and talking through all that had happened. By now

Darcy had heard on the News that seven people had lost their lives and twenty were injured in the explosion. Of the hostages taken all were alive and well on release. Now Brant proceeded to fill in the gaps, of how negotiations broke down over the kidnappers' demand for the release of 'political prisoners' – in actuality convicted terrorists. An S.S. squad stormed the Underground via the network of sewers and the kidnappers were shot dead, he concluded in a matter of fact voice.

"I was so scared Brant," Darcy whispered.

"Me too!" Brant smiled in an attempt to make light of it.

"You could have been killed."

"All part of the job."

"It made me think, the fact you might not come back. About you wanting a baby I mean."

"I thought about that too; you know when I'd done what I could and there was nothing left but to wait."

"What I'm saying is, if you-,"

"No, don't say anything yet Darcy. You see it made me realise how much I love you, and how lucky I am – and yes, how stupid I've been of late, resorting to emotional blackmail and piling on the pressure. No," he said holding up a hand when she began to protest, "It's true. Believe me, there's nothing like the possibility of imminent death to focus your attention!"

"Yes. I know."

There must have been something about her tone and expression because he gave her a long hard look before continuing:

"It also made me realise what a sexist a'ss hole I've been: Darcy your job is every bit as important as mine and as dangerous. You and people like you are the guardians of Democracy."

"That's pompous bullshit Brant!" Darcy exclaimed laughing.

"I mean it. You speak to and for the people, and against injustice – and risk your damn life doing it! Anyway, what I'm trying to say is – you are more than enough for me, okay? If you decide later on that you want to start a family – fine, and I promise we'll adapt our life accordingly and I'll do my fair share of parenting. If that time doesn't come, then that's okay too. Right now I don't want to share you with *anyone*. No more pressure."

"Thanks, I appreciate that Brant. I feel the same about you."

"Good.

"Now", he said brusquely, "tell about your Close Encounter."

"Excuse me?"

"With Death. I need to know what has been happening to you Darcy, in order to understand."

"How did-,? Understand what Brant?" she amended quickly

"To answer the first," he said wryly, "by your expression a few minutes ago. As to the second – your going off like that without a word. Did you think I wouldn't worry, not hearing from you, and unable to contact you because I didn't know where you were or why you left?"

"It wasn't anything about us Brant," she reassured him quickly, flushing as she met his steady gaze. "And I couldn't tell you for the simple reason you would have tried to stop me – and I had to go."

"Where – and why?"

She took a large sip of brandy and a deep breath; anticipation of this moment had been a source of anxiety since leaving Mediobogdum for the last time. She told him about the field camp and that wasn't too bad. Then haltingly, about Ted Tulley attacking her on Tom Heights, and in a low voice and with eyes cast down, his last attempt on her life at the circle on the moor. It was harder even than anticipated; speaking of it – and to Brant of all people – brought back the horror and emotions experienced at the time. Brant, frowning and obviously containing strong emotions with difficulty, poured a stiff measure of cognac into her empty glass with an order for her to 'knock it back'.

"For Chris'sakes Darcy," he exclaimed watching her and slowly shaking his head " – and you were worried about *me*?"

She coughed after downing the brandy and smiled mischievously through her tears. "All part of the job."

"Darcy!" he warned, but he too was grinning. "Touché, I guess! But you seriously frighten me. I'm not going to let you out of my sight after this!" He leaned forward suddenly grave again and shot the question at her: "Did you have a hand in his death?"

"No."

"Thank God for that!" He heaved a massive sigh and leaned back against the cushions of the settee. "I wouldn't blame you, in fact the opposite, but it might have been a tad difficult to get past the Department! So tell me about this wild dog that is supposed to have attacked him."

For a long moment she looked at him in silence, not knowing what to say.

"I need to know all of it Darcy."

"All? Are you sure?"

"Absolutely."

"You won't believe it."

"Maybe not, but try me," he said firmly.

So now he knew how Ted Tulley really died, and her theory that he dug up a Roman hoard that was somehow cursed by treachery, and the darkness entered his mind and soul and fed upon his greed and hatred of the authorities. She disclosed the desperate walk along the Screes and the finding of the eagle, and how Caro had taken it back for tests at Hilldean. With regard to the massacre at Mediobogdum, Darcy gave him the 'facts only' version offered to Caro, and omitting the subsequent dream sequence or whatever it might have been, as this was an intensely private experience and not one to be shared – especially not with Brant. She did give him a truthful account of her return to the hunting lodge only to find Mr Nemo gone, but played down the layer of dust and neglect and the impression of the place having been empty over a long period of time.

"Well?" she said as he tale drew to a conclusion. "Are you ready to have me sectioned?"

"Oh, I reckon I'd have trouble getting two doctors out at this time of night! My God, but you don't do things by halves, do you Darcy?"

"Do you believe me?" she asked directly, anxiously scanning his face.

"It's a lot to take in all in one go," he said cautiously whilst watching her thoughtfully before continuing: "but I will say I believe something strange was going on and I have implicit trust in your integrity Darcy. Even if these events did not actually happen in the way you think, you were made to *believe* they did."

"But how could that be?"

"By synchronous but non-interactive Time-events."

"Excuse me?" she said pulling a face.

"Okay, put simply you may well have witnessed certain things and been influenced by them, but not been actually involved in them except emotionally. We're back to red shift."

"But Mr Nemo wasn't just light-waves," she protested, "I shared his house for over a week!"

"An eccentric old hermit, one taken to periodic wanderings over the moor perhaps which would explain his disappearance on your return?"

> But not the fact that the house had obviously not been lived in for a considerable length of time!
> Of course you don't know that, and I think it is a step too far for you Brant, so we'll move on.

"And the wolf? What was left of Ted Tulley was well dead!"

"Given your extreme distress at the time, lightning flashes in the dark and the spooky location, I guess a farm dog turned feral could easily be mistaken for one."

"Farm dogs, even ones gone wild, don't usually rip out a man's throat Brant!"

"A storm can instigate abnormal behaviour patterns in animals."

"So you don't believe me," Darcy said resignedly. "I know it all defies logic but,"

"I didn't say that." Interrupting her, Brant put down his glass on the table and leaning over gave her a hug of reassurance. "I think you have been through a trauma much greater than mine my love, and I also happen to think you have shown great courage in seeing it through on your own. I've only advanced a couple of ideas – I cannot explain even half of what you have told me. But you are right, I shouldn't be trying to rationalise your very real experience. When it comes down to it the particle physicist has only experience to go on and experience is our basic means of making sense of our world. There are other aspects of quantum theory besides red shift that might be helpful."

"Like?"

"The Many Realities Theory for one."

"Isn't that where I could be performing an action like running upstairs in this reality, but be running down them say, in a parallel one," Darcy said looking thoughtful, "but in this reality I am unaware of myself in the other one. You told me something about it way back."

"That's right," he said nodding, "in the particles from the meteorite caper. According to the theory consciousness is confined within each separate reality. So it's possible there was more than one phenomenon going on at once. Maybe your Roman's great need and your empathy with it allowed you to briefly cross the barrier and, uniquely, retain a conscious memory of it. I don't know darling; I can only guess."

"But going back to what I was saying about experience, and your comment that none of this is logical, it is accepted amongst physicists that the rules of classical logic cannot correspond with experience. The real world follows different rules than the world of symbols. Physicists call the rules of experience Quantum Logic."

"That's really interesting," Darcy said, her face brightening. "It makes me feel a whole lot better to know there is an accepted system of logic that relates to my experiences rather than invalidating them. They were real enough Brant, not delusions brought on by wishful thinking or stress."

"I know, and it was cowardly of me to try and explain them away. It's scary stuff Darcy! It's acceptable at a distance in the world of particle physics, but very disturbing when it impinges on everyday life! Whatever, you are safe and that's all that matters now."

He released his hold on her and leaned back slightly so as to have a clear view of her face. He studied her expression, and his own was troubled.

"You must have loved him."

"I don't know what it was I felt; I can't answer that." She only knew she could not deny him by saying she did not, but also could not hurt Brant whom she also deeply loved.

"To endure so much on his behalf; to have shared such a mind-blowing and unique experience," He left it unfinished and Darcy could sense the hurt and sadness behind the words. She chose her own with care.

"But you are real."

"That must mean he is a fantasy, your ideal." Given his tone he might as well have added 'and that's worse'. She knew where he was coming from: a human rival could be challenged and vanquished, but one cannot fight a phantom. As her ideal he would be forever there beyond reach. Not exactly a level playing field.

She regarded him in silence for a moment, at a loss to understand this show of insecurity in a man usually so sure of himself and in command. But not in the realm of emotions, she recalled. Ever since his first wife had left him for another man and a life of City glamour, he had been wary of commitment and reluctant to admit his feelings. For Brant's sake she wanted to say 'he is *not* real' but could not bring herself to do so. Even the thought brought ripples of knowing and a crushing sense of reproach. Instead she said quietly:

"No, he is not a fantasy, an ideal – far from it; at times he was very frightening," and was aware of a ridiculous sense of approval, of having said the right thing – and from Brant's expression it seemed he thought so too. It was true, she thought, recalling the obnoxious worms and ordeal by fire. That was not to say he was always so, nor that fear was the only emotion he evoked. The thin wire trembled as she balanced precariously between reassuring Brant without denying Antonius. She passed a hand wearily over her eyes. "I can't label it Brant, test and analyse it as though I was in your laboratory."

"Of course not. Stupid of me. Forget I spoke," he said with forced lightness but his stance stiff with embarrassment. "Now, let's go to bed."

"It was the standard that really mattered," she said looking down so that he might not see the hurt mirrored in her eyes. "He used me to get it that's all."

"I think not."

Startled by the severity of tone her gaze flew to his face. For a split second she saw eyes that were green, hair bronzed and expression grave. But that could not be, could it? Because now he was laid to rest.

"I love you," she said pausing by the door. "Don't ever doubt that, not even for a minute." For one brief moment she wondered if she was speaking to one man or two, but then let the thought go. It skittered away, a small bronzed leaf sent whirling by a whimsical gust over the edge of the precipice, to be borne aloft on a sigh that was not of the wind.

"Let's go to bed," Brant said kissing her forehead. "I believe we have a date to keep."

FORTY

~

Darcy stood alone in a special room at the museum. A lump came to her throat as she looked at the standard in pride of place at the centre of the display. It was stunning: the eagle – free of the silt and debris accumulated over two thousand years – now gleamed, the gold carefully burnished as it must have been prior to parade or battle. The shaft and banner of the standard had been faithfully recreated and the panel hand embroidered with the legend: *LEGIO IX*

It stood proud and erect now, bringing to mind a sentence from Mr Nemo's parting letter: *with restitution will come healing.* Aided by Caro she had fought fiercely to bring the standard home to York – *Eboracum* – the military H.Q. where the Ninth Legion for around half a century was stationed. and for the right to be involved in the design and content of the permanent exhibition. Tomorrow the opening ceremony would take place for an invited audience of celebrated historians, academics and members of the media. Thenceforth the doors would be open to the general public and the true story of the 'Lost Ninth' would be known at last.

Stepping forward she pressed the button to start the sound track. As she listened to the voice-over she nodded from time to time and smiled with satisfaction. Then, after an explanation of the virtually simultaneous attacks on the triple targets of Eboracum, the Dalehead and Mediobogdum came her favourite bit:

'Rome's dubious decision unquestionably lay behind the annihilation of the Ninth. Recent evidence suggests that Tacitus Sextus Antonius – a commanding officer of the Ninth directing operations from Mediobogdum following reports of a planned major uprising by a coalition of the native northern tribes – had previously warned the Senate about the possible danger of leaving Eboracum inadequately protected. However it seems that the Emperor Hadrian's lust for conquest and glory over-rode humanitarian concerns for one of his most loyal fighting forces and its noble commander. Despite valiant efforts a massacre was the result. An unfinished new wing to the Commandant's quarters is a poignant detail. Rome put into operation a massive cover-up and the legion was removed from the military record.

The eagle standard was considered to represent the spirit and soul of the legion and its loss was considered the utmost disgrace and also an omen of ill fortune. However contrary to belief, the standard of the Ninth Legion did not fall into enemy hands to be paraded, defiled and destroyed. It was found at the base of the Screes, dislodged from its ledge many feet below the surface of Wast Water, England's deepest lake, by an unusually violent storm. Experts agree that its position is unlikely to have been random, but points to a deliberate action by the Aquilifer, the eagle-bearer, or in the event of him falling in the battle, by an intrepid brother-in-arms to prevent the standard from being taken by the enemy.

Given Rome's incompetence and the fact that the standard did not after all fall into enemy hands, and given the return of the eagle, the honour of this legendary legion is unreservedly restored.'

Darcy smiled and nodded as the voice-over came to an end. Okay, so maybe that last bit was stretching it a bit, but who could say? How did it then get there? The Brigante would scarcely pitch it into the lake; rather it would be carried back in triumph to the settlement as a trophy. She preferred to believe that the Aquilifer escaped with his precious burden and crept along that same path above the water line at the Screes, then lowered it into the lake for safe keeping. One thing was sure, from what she had witnessed there could be no doubt about the courage of those men of the Ninth. Romans may well have been brutal and corrupt, but that was not her remit and in any case did not excuse such a massive injustice. Nor, she thought with a secret smile, did that fit her personal experience of a Roman. *Antonius.* His name arose unbidden to her mind.

She switched off the soundtrack and stood before the standard in all its glory. Closing her fist and raising her arm slowly she gave the Roman salute, then turned and walked away.

Something within had been healed during this private viewing and ritual of closure, but she also felt emotionally drained. There was an acute sense of loss, an emptiness where this other reality had been. Life suddenly felt normal and – flat. Halfway to the door she turned and paused as shock waves buzzed along her nerves and her attention was caught by a flicker of movement to her right. For a split second she could have sworn that a figure was standing there in a shaft of sunlight: the flick of a cloak and then it was gone leaving only dust motes dancing in the sunbeam. The whisper though was certainly not a figment of her imagination. Not *Indomita* this time, but *Cara,* whispered several times in her ear.

Then *Amatrix, mea amatrix.*

She smiled. The tone in which it was uttered left her in no doubt about the sentiment being expressed. The passionate love that consumed him in life lived on, and somehow she was now a part of it.

Dear Reader, thank you for taking the time to read. If you enjoyed this book (and I hope you did!) please be kind enough to leave me a review on Amazon.

Thank you and Best Wishes,

BIBLIOGRAPHY

Ancient History

A Companion to Roman Britain, Peter Clayton; pub. Phaidon Press, 1980.

Ancient England, Nigel Blundell & Kate Farrington; pub. Promotional Reprint Co. Ltd., 1996 ed.

Celtic Britain, Lloyd Laing; pub. Granada Publishing Ltd., 1981.

Life in Celtic Britain, Anthony Birley; pub. Batsford Academic & Educational, 1981.

Hardknott Roman Fort, Cumbria, Paul Bidwell, Margaret Snape and Alexandra Groom; pub. The Cumberland and Westmorland Antiquarian and Archaeological Society, 1999.

Hardknott Roman Fort, Tom Garlick; fourth impression, 1984.

Roman Forts, Roger Wilson; pub. Bergstrom & Boyle Books Ltd., 1980.

Roman Lancashire, Tom Garlick; 1977.

The Annals of Imperial Rome: Tacitus, translated by Michael Grant; Penguin Books Ltd., 1961 edition.

The Celts, T.G.E. Powell; pub. Thames and Hudson, 1980.

The Golden Eagle, Michael Everett; pub. William Blackwood, 1977.

Quantum Physics

A Brief History of Time, Stephen Hawking; Bantam Books, 1997 ed.

Black Holes and Baby Universes, Stephen Hawking; Bantam Books, 1994 ed.

The Dancing Wu Li Masters – An Overview of the New Physics, Gary Zukav; pub. Fontana Paperbacks 1984

* * * *   *   * * * *

More Mystery Books by Nina Green in Pendragon: Paperback and Kindle

DARK STAR

*A novel of dark and chilling prophecy: the dark star
of the North brings Retribution, Silence and Death.*

The first Darcy West novel. A strange meteor is found on a lonely
Lakeland mountain. It falls into the hands of an unscrupulous
physicist with terrifying consequences. Darcy must do battle with
greed, corruption and the dark powers.

ISBN 0-9530538-0-6 £6.99 + pp – paperback edition
available from **www.amazon.co.uk**
or email: **books@pendragon-press-ltd.co.uk**
and **now available on Kindle**

A GRAVE AFFAIR

Brutal murder and a fatal passion: medieval lovers reach across the centuries in search of justice and revenge.

Following a broken love affair, writer Jo Cavanagh sets off for a remote cottage in the heart of Lakeland. A new grave is being dug at the tiny local church. *But is it new?* The terror begins as long buried passions are released.

ISBN 0-9530538-1-4 £6.99 + pp paperback edition
available from **www.amazon.co.uk**
or email: **books@pendragon-press-ltd.co.uk**
and now **available on Kindle**

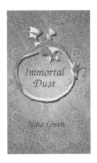

IMMORTAL DUST

*The remains of a medieval knight are unearthed on the wild
Cumbrian coast after being buried for 700 years: bizarre
burial rituals have kept the body preserved.*

The second Darcy West book and Darcy is obsessed with the quest
for this man's identity. Astronomy and alchemy, ritual and mysticism
lead her into a maze where past and present entwine. With Brant
Kennedy she finds passionate love but betrayal lurks in the shadows.

ISBN 0-9530538-2-2 £7.99 + pp. Paperback edition
available from **www.amazon.co.uk**
or email: **books@pendragon-press-ltd.co.uk**
and now **available on Kindle**

The Moon Map Chronicles
Also by Nina Green

A unique series of uplifting books giving amazing insight into the
compelling exploits and spiritual life of the author's family of English
Setters, told by the Setters themselves and illustrated with full-colour
photographs

The First Moon Map Chronicle:
Memories of a Moon Map: The Extraordinary
Adventures of an English Setter Pack
*A thrilling and moving book based on true events
in the life of the author's pack of Setters.*

(229 pages with full colour illustrations)
Told by the Setters themselves, and beautifully illustrated with their
colour photographs. Ben, the pack's late patriarch, is the chief narrator
from beyond Rainbow Bridge. This is the first in a series of books
giving amazing insight into the social and spiritual life of dogs. Often
funny, ever touching and at times chilling these books are
unforgettable and will change the way you think about dogs – and
life. Unique and mould-busting a **must-read** for dog lovers of all ages.

Ben *"Although I passed over the Rainbow Bridge some years ago, because
of a love stronger than death I'm allowed to tell my story... my time span*

now is different to yours; I can travel to and fro through the years and talk with those who died before I was born and those who followed on."

ISBN 978 0 9530538 3 4 **£7.99 + pp. Paperback edition**
available from **www.amazon.co.uk**
or email: **books@pendragon-press-ltd.co.uk**
and **also available for download on Kindle**

The Second Moon Map Chronicle:
D'Arcy Wolf-Shadow: More Magical Adventures
of an English Setter Pack
The second in the unique series of enthralling books chronicling the adventures of the Setters in their remote Lakeland home.

(192pages with full colour illustrations)
Top Dog D'Arcy must undertake the quest of Grey Pelt, the Spirit of the Last Wolf of Lakeland, and in so doing risks his life. Desolate and alone, His gifted sister and pack bard Destiny works to hold a splintered pack together during his absence. The members have their adventures too, and she encourages them to share experiences past and present, and voice their feelings to strengthen the bond. Between times she is secretly supporting D'Arcy though he is unaware of her efforts on his behalf.

D'Arcy is befriended by a beautiful young she-wolf, and events reach a thrilling and mystical crisis at the time of the Winter Solstice.

Sensitive, insightful and action-packed, this is another **must-read** un-put-downable book for dog lovers of all ages.

ISBN 978 0 9530538 4 1 **£7.99 + pp. Paperback edition**
available from **www.amazon.co.uk**
or email: **books@pendragon-press-ltd.co.uk**
and **also available for download on Kindle price £1.99**

**The Third Moon Map Chronicle:
Mysteries and Miracles: More Magical Adventures
of an English Setter Pack**
The third in the series: two books in one and the most enthralling of all.

(640 pages with full colour illustrations)
In Part One the Setters share their stories and adventures and a newcomer joins the pack, but then in Part Two they are devastated by an unexpected and shattering event. To say too much here would be to give too much away! Suffice it to say that this is the true and heart-warming story of a little miracle!

This book will challenge your preconceptions and beliefs. Not to be missed.

ISBN 978-1-5272-0901-5 **£8 + pp. Paperback edition**
available from **www.amazon.co.uk**
or email: **books@pendragon-press-ltd.co.uk**
and **also available for download on Kindle price £2.99**